Permanently
Etched

*To my sister/bff who believed in me when I
didn't believe in myself
To every single reader who decides to give my
book a chance* ☺

CHAPTER 1: RYDELL

Breathe. Jesus Rydell get your shit together and take a deep breath. What would mom say if she saw you right now? Probably something like, "I don't know where this is coming from, there's nothing to be anxious about". And maybe she's right about that, but sometimes I can't help it.

Nope that didn't help. Actually, I'm pretty sure it makes it a whole hell of a lot worse. What would Andromeda say? Most likely she'd shove some lavender in my face and tell me that it will help me relax. My little sister is obsessed with essential oils and thinks it's the solution to every problem. And sometimes it's a solution to this problem, but I've deeply inhaled half the fumes from my lavender oil and I'm still hyperventilating like I'll never be able to catch a goddamn breath.

Ah panic attacks. My favorite way to start off a probably already shitty day. That was sarcasm if you didn't catch it. You see, ever since I switched schools in 3rd grade, something in my brain clicked on to instant panic mode, and I've been dealing with panic and anxiety attacks ever since.

And I know what you're thinking, "That's such a stupid reason to get panic attacks", or

"You're probably faking it, if that's the worst thing that you've gone through." I've heard it all before and I wish I could say I was faking it because, at the moment, I feel like I'm on the verge of passing out. But alas, I am not. And trust me, I'm aware that my problems aren't nearly as big as others. And I know that I probably have no reason to feel anxious all the time, but there's just something fucked with my brain, and I really don't know what started it. Actually, I have an idea of what might have started it, but that's something that I haven't opened up to anyone about. Not my parents, not Andy, not Sam, not a single soul, and probably never will. Because my grandpa touched me in inappropriate places when I was 8 fucking years old, and when I told my grandma about it, the look on her face was so horrific that I said I was probably dreaming and left it at that.

I wasn't dreaming, but I couldn't bear to look at my grandma's face that instantly paled because I hate seeing people upset. And now I'm a 21-year-old senior in college and if I said anything now, no one would believe me. And I mean it only happened like 3 times when I was 8, so it's not that big of a deal, right? Right, because other people are dealing with shit so much worse than mine and I refuse to put that type of burden on anyone else. I can deal with it myself; I always do. Plus, I've lasted this long without going completely insane, so what's the rest of my life doing just that?

"Hey Del, are you up yet?"

Oh shit, I thought Sam already left for class.

"I've decided to make the executive decision to skip sociology this morning because I don't need Professor Douchebag's toxicity today. Mental health

4

days are important, am I right?"

I can't physically answer her because I'm currently sitting on the ground trying to take a simple breath and apparently that's too hard. And I don't want her to come into my room because then she'll just worry about me like she always does.

But life hates me because about 5 seconds later I hear my door open and the concerned voice of my lovely roommate, "Fuck Del, you should have come got me as soon as this shit started."

I give her a little wave of the hand as if to say, "Please, this small thing? It's nothing."

Sam crouches down to my level. Takes my hands off my ears and puts my fingers on the pulse on my wrist.

Sam knows the drill by now. When I have panic attacks, I like to feel my heartbeat. I don't know how I picked that up, but after about a year of getting panic attacks, I wrapped my fingers around my wrist and the feeling on my pulse somehow calmed me down a bit. I think it reminds me that I'm alive. Gives me a reality check if you will. And when I start to count my heartbeats; it gives me a distraction from my mess of a mind.

Sam has been my roommate since my freshman year here at Daxton University, and we instantly clicked. I remember it like it was yesterday. I walked into the dorm, super nervous to start my first year of college, and there was Sam. In all her 5'2 glory. Mouth of a sailor, medium length black hair, olive skin, and hazel eyes that are so big I swear she looks like an animated character. She was hanging up a *Goonies* poster and I knew we'd be instant friends. Not gonna lie, she did give me quiet the scare at first. Because when I walked in and said,

"Hello, you must be Samantha, I'm Rydell." She looked me dead in the eyes and said," Call me Samantha one more time and I'll rip your vocal cords out and shove them down your throat." Then she proceeded to laugh until she turned blue and told me that my face was priceless and to just call her Sam.

Sam is the type of person that doesn't give two shits about what anyone thinks of her. She's got confidence the size of a skyscraper, and even though she's short, she's intimidating as hell. But that's just all the more reason to love her. And I think the fact that we are essentially polar opposites is why we get along so well. She gets me out of my comfort zone, and I am her voice of reason that keeps her out of serious trouble.

"Are you counting your fucking heartbeats, or do you need to count my fingers?" Sam asked, pulling me out of my thoughts.

Honestly, just having another person I trust with me helps the situation a little. Because now I'm counting the beats and my lungs are starting to feel the air come in.

"Good," I push out.

"Ok, say that again, and this time make it more convincing," Sam replies.

That gets a breathy laugh out of me and now I can feel myself getting over it.

"Good," I say about a minute later now that my breathing is almost all the way back in rhythm.

Without another word Sam leaves my room. You might be thinking that was a bitch move, but I bet you anything in about 1 minute she'll come back into the room with a cup of ice water for me.

And a minute later she does indeed come in

carrying a glass of ice water.

Sam is used to my craziness after 3 and ½ years of knowing me. Panic attacks are usually a weekly occurrence for me. If I'm lucky, they'll only happen about 2 times a month, but the first time Sam witnessed one she lost her shit, which didn't help the situation. I swear, she thought I was dying. She was so scared that she almost called the ambulance. But after I pried her phone from her hands and threw it across the room, she figured that it was unnecessary. Because let's be real, no matter how much pain I'm in, I will never call the ambulance. That shit would drain me about $1,000 that I don't have in my bank account.

Seriously, I could get my arm chopped off and I'd rather drive myself to a hospital than call an ambulance. Plus, ambulance drivers are always so attractive, I would want to save myself the embarrassment of bleeding out in front of them.

After completely breaking down in front of Sam the first time, she had me write down a detailed list of things that she could do to help me when I get them. Said list is currently taped onto our fridge, even though she already has it memorized. What's on this magical list? Glad you asked:

1. Put her hands-on wrist or neck pulse
2. Make sure she's counting heartbeats
3. If she can't concentrate on heartbeats, start having her count your fingers until she gets to ten
4. If she still isn't getting over it, put on her Spotify playlist called "songs to play when people ask me what my favorite type of music is" and have her try to sing the lyrics

5. Sit with her until it's over
6. Get her water when she catches her breath so she isn't sporting a massive headache for the rest of the day

Sam hands me the water and I gulp down as much as I can, spilling half of it down my chin and onto my shirt in the process. Great, now I'll have to change.

"You should really start seeing someone," Sam says, with that little crease between her eyebrows that she gets when she's worried.

"I'm fine. I told you, I went to therapy, it doesn't help. It just sucks $30 out of my wallet a session and I'd rather spend that on something more useful."

"Del books are not more useful than therapy," Sam rebuttals.

"Actually, reading is a coping mechanism. I learned about it in psych 1. And also, retail therapy is a coping mechanism. Therefore, buying and reading books is two ways to deal with my problems, and therapy is only one. So, ha."

"No, reading and buying books is a way to escape your problems, not deal with them. You're deluding yourself Rydell," she tries. Even though she knows I've already made up my mind about therapy and knows I'll never go back, we have this conversation after every panic attack.

"Oh no, you called me Rydell, you're getting serious," I try to joke.

"I am getting serious Del, I hate seeing you like this." I know she's worried about me, but I have everything under control.

"Sammy, I have them, they go away, and I keep living my life. I've taken enough psych classes,

I'm practically my own therapist by now," I try to convince her. "Now can we please drop it. You're not going to soc, come grab a smoothie with me before my 10 o'clock. I'll drive and then you can just wait on campus until your 11:30 class. I'll buy," I say, changing the subject.

"Dammit Del, you know I can't resist free food."

I do indeed know that she can't resist free food. And that's how I get her to drop the therapy talk every time. By bringing up the subject to grabbing something to eat and telling her that I'll pay. Works like a charm.

"Let me get changed and then we can head out," I tell her as I walk into my closet. I strip off the white knit sweater that I spilt water on and replace it with a white cropped t-shirt to go with my high-waisted, plaid green pants. Then I slip on my black high-top converse and walk into our living room. I go straight to the whiteboard and whip out my phone, clicking on my National Holidays app. Friday, September 28th is National Drink a Beer Day according to my app, so I write it down on the whiteboard, drawing a little beer glass next to it. I make a mental note to ask Sam if she wants to go to the bar tonight to celebrate.

Sam stands up from the couch and grabs her keys and purse as she walks to the door. I grab my jean jacket off the coat rack, because September in Massachusetts is cold (for a girl who was born and raised in California) and I'm now in a t-shirt instead of my thick sweater.

Sam and I are currently living in a two-room condo that's about a 5-minute drive from campus. We moved in at the beginning of our sophomore year and have been here ever since.

If our schedules allow for it, we usually carpool to campus, and just wait in the library or link up with classmates while we wait for the other. I'm majoring in computer science and minoring in psychology. Sam is majoring in graphic design and also minoring in psychology, so are schedules aren't too far apart.

That's another reason why Sam and I get along so well. We are currently designing a video game designated to help control aggressive behavior in kids who are in the important developmental ages.

Sam actually started off as a psychology major and I've wanted to create video games for as long as I can remember. I don't even remember how exactly we came up with the idea for our game, but one-night freshman year, we were drunk, the idea sprung out of nowhere, and ever since then we've been working on it. Sam and I get educational when we're drunk.

Anyways, once we started seriously working on our project, we realized that we needed someone to create the graphics for it. I knew that Sam liked art because her AP Art projects from high school were hanging around our dorm, and when she's not working or in class, she's doodling on her iPad so I suggested she come up with a couple of sketches.

And those sketches were fan-fucking-tastic. About a week later, Sam changed her major to graphic design, we both picked up psychology minors, and the rest is history.

We pull into one of the campus parking lots and head to Smoothie Palace, which is conveniently located in the Hub of Daxton U.

Smoothie Palace is probably the best thing about this school. They not only have great smoothies, but they also have great smoothies that are only $2 for students. That's why we are now currently waiting in about a huge ass line; it's almost always packed here.

After waiting to get our smoothies, about 25 minutes later (totally worth it), Sam and I go our separate ways. My 10 o'clock Spanish 4 class is my absolute least favorite class in the entire world. Everyone at Daxton has to take at least up to level four of a language course, and I pushed mine off for as long as possible. We can test out of them completely or test into a higher course to save ourselves the trouble of taking all of them if we wish to do so. And even though I took and passed the AP Spanish test with a 4 in high school, I still have to take the stupid class. I tested into Spanish 4 at the beginning of my junior year thanks to my high school courses of Spanish and am finally getting it over with so that I can graduate.

Don't get me wrong, the Spanish language is great. But half of our grade in this class consists of oral presentations and I hate public speaking.

I approach the lecture hall, smoothie in hand, and open the doors to hell.

CHAPTER 2: SCOTT

Shit, I'm late. All day yesterday I was thinking that it was Friday, even though it was Thursday, so when my teammates asked if I wanted to go to the bar for a drink after practice, I said, "Hell ya".

Now I'm waking up with a blonde head on my chest, looking at my phone that says it's 9:47 am, Friday, realizing that yesterday was not Friday, and I'm about to be late for my 10 o'clock class. My 10 o'clock class that I absolutely cannot miss.

I failed Spanish 4 my junior year, so now I have to take it again as a senior and it fucking sucks. Literally the worst class because my white ass can't seem to get pronunciations right and gets marked down for it every single fucking time. That and I don't give a shit about my grades, so studying isn't really one of my priorities.

But if I don't pass this class, then I don't get to play hockey. And if I don't get to play hockey my life is over. I'm currently the captain of Daxton U's hockey team and this year is the year I go pro. The Massachusetts Bruins are going to pick me up for the team this year, I'm manifesting it. My older sister is into manifestation, astrology, and what not and told me if I say it out loud or repeat it to myself enough times it will happen. I told Penelope that she was full of shit when she said that, but I'm not taking any risks.

Anyways, after last year's grade slips, coach said that not passing Spanish 4 in the fall semester would get me a spot warming the benches for the rest of my senior year and that would be a real shame considering how close I am to making it to the league.

And attendance is about 10% of our grade in that class, so I'm determined to go to all of them.

Bolting out of bed, the blonde head falls off my chest and I grab the first pair of boxers I see, shoving my legs in them and tripping to the ground in the process.

With the sudden bolt and loud thud of me falling the blonde rises clutching my sheets to her chest. "Come back to bed," she pouts.

"Sorry Lauren…"

"Laura," she cuts me off.

"Right, Laura. I'm late for class."

"Skip it," she pleads.

"Can't, sorry. You go back to sleep though and let yourself out when you're ready," I reply.

She's looking at me with eyes that tells me exactly what she's about to say before she says it, so I'm not surprised when she asks, "How about you give me your number and we can meet up some other time."

Happens every time. Before any hookup, I let the girl know that it's just that, a hookup. Nothing more, nothing less. We have some fun with no strings attached and then go our separate ways. And I clearly lay it all out for them before we hop into bed. No phone numbers exchanged, no breakfast and cuddles in the morning. Just sex.

But each morning I wake up, they ask for my number, I say no, and then they say I'm a dick.

"Sorry Lauren."

"-Laura."

"Laura, but I don't do numbers, I told you that last night".

"Yeah, but I thought-," she tries.

I cut her off, "Well you thought wrong." Yes, I know, I'm an asshole. But I don't have time for a relationship with hockey and a man has his needs.

"You're such a dick," there it is.

I don't acknowledge her any further as I pull my black pants up and slip on a white t-shirt with some random logo on it. Then I jog downstairs and into the living room, roll the bottom of my pants up, put on my black vans, and adjust a Daxton U beanie onto my head.

"I'm surprised you're up this early after last night," I hear Max say from the kitchen.

"Can't talk, I'm late for Spanish," I reply as I grab an apple off the kitchen counter and make my way out.

The senior hockey house, my current place of residence, is exactly the type of house you're probably imagining. Basically, a frat house for the senior hockey players. We are required to live together with the teammates from our year. Our places tend to have slightly unhygienic bathrooms from the parties we throw, 5 or 6 bedrooms depending on your year, and are almost always loud.

The senior house has 5 bedrooms, but there's only four seniors this year, including myself, so we all have our own room. As for the other guys living here it goes as follows:

1. Max Rudderord (AKA Ruddy): resident dad of the group and the team's goalie.
2. Asher Webb (AKA Webbs): the jokester of the group and starting left defenseman.
3. Oliver Davidson (AKA Davies): the nerd of the group and starting right defenseman.

Then, or course, there's me. Prescott Bridges (AKA Scott/Scotty), captain and center for Daxton Universities hockey team.

I know, I know Prescott is such a pretentious name, I get made fun of it all the time. And yes, it is a pretentious name, but I'm also pretentious as fuck. You see, my family comes from old money. My great-great-great something grandpa brought over PVC pipes to America from Europe and that apparently sky rocked and left our family set for life. The Bridges family owns the most popular PVC pipe company in the States. When my Grandpa wanted to retire, my Dad took over the company, and since I'm the oldest son, I'm expected to do so next.

That's why I have to finish college before I can go pro. I need my business degree if I'm expected to run the family company. My parent's fingers are crossed that I don't make it to the league so I can start working for them right away. But fuck that shit. I will go pro and only when *I* decide to retire from hockey, will I go into the business.

You see, my whole life has always been planned out for me. Everything has been picked to a tee. Go to a college that fits my parent's standards, graduate, work for the family, get married to a girl from a respectable family, and have kids to continue the family blood line. That's another reason why I stick solely to hookups, my marriage is probably already planned for me. My parents, grandparents, aunts and uncles were all pushed into loveless marriages to keep our family rich. Because money is everything right?

Hockey is the only thing that wasn't picked for me. My parents needed me to have an after-school activity so that they didn't have to deal with me, so when I came home from school with a permission slip to play, they didn't take a second to think about it. And ever since then, I can't remember many days when I wasn't on the ice.

What they didn't know was that I'd fall so in love with it that I'd become determined to be the best.

And I am one of the best. Not to sound cocky or anything, but right out of high school I was offered a spot on a couple of different pro teams. And I would have taken them without a second thought if not for my parents.

I enter the lecture hall, four minutes late, letting out a breath when I see that the attendance sheet is still being passed around.

"Bridges," I look over to my left to see Jake McCombs, a junior on the team, waving me over to an empty seat next to him in the back row. "Late night?" he asks.

Jake transferred to Daxton this year and he lowkey annoys the shit out of me. But being captain, I feel like I have to give everyone a fair chance and suck it up if I don't like them, and that's why I fake out a laugh and sit down next to him with a, "Yeah."

As he opens his mouth to say something else the professor speaks up, "Okay, as the attendance sheet is being passed around let's go over some housekeeping," and praise the lord for it because the last thing I wanted was to have a conversation with McCombs.

"As you all are hopefully aware, half of your grade in this course consists of an oral presentation," she begins. "If this is a surprise to you, then you clearly haven't looked at the syllabus."

I already know everything about this class, I took it last year, so I know exactly what project she's about to assign.

"Well, your oral presentation will be a month from today," with that half the class groans.

"Ya, ya, I know, no one likes public speaking but it's a requirement that I am not allowed to get rid of. And trust me, I would if I could because listening to some of you try to speak Spanish is like nails to a chalk board," this lightens the mood.

"For the oral presentation in this class you are allowed to work with one other person, or you can choose to work solo." Bingo.

Last year, I made the mistake of partnering with one of my buddies from the baseball team, and let's just say that the studying was neither of our strong suits.

As the professor continues to drain on about the details of the presentation my eyes wonder off and land on a brunette with glasses and a jean jacket. Rydell Rivens.

You see, this year I have everything planned out. Coming into the class, I already knew all the projects we'd have. I also knew that for our oral presentation, we would have the option to partner up. And that's exactly why I've been scooping out the class for the perfect partner since the first day of the semester.

And on the first day, it wasn't hard to pick out who might be a smartie that could present me with the opportunity to breeze through the class.

I spotted her right away that first day. I mean it wasn't hard because as soon as she walked into the lecture hall, she tripped on her own feet and nearly face planted. She was wearing overalls and a Star Wars shirt. I mean come on, that was the first clue. When she pulled out her book and started reading as soon as she found her seat, that was almost the sinker.

She took a seat in a middle row which means that she wants to pay attention to the class but doesn't need to feel validated by sitting in the front. That tells me that she's confident in her grades.

Trust me, I've done all the research on these types of things because, again, I cannot fail this class.

Now, I had my eyes on a couple of other people, but on that first day we had to take a test to prove that we were fit for the class. Little Ms. Smartie turned her test in first and when we came back for our next class it was handed back to her with a 100% on it.

And there I had my girl.

"Why are looking at glasses like you're a predator, she your next victim?" Jake asks in a low whisper.

"She's definitely not my type," I mumble, "she's gonna be my partner for this project. She's smart, and my ticket to an A in this class."

"Well, she has to say yes first," he laughs.

"Oh, she'll say yes. The ladies can't resist my charm."

"Yeah, and then you'll have another girl desperate to have you as their boyfriend," god he's so annoying.

"I'm not going to sleep with her. I'm just going to get her to be my friend and then when I get an A, it'll be the end of it. Simple," I say, hopefully shutting him up.

"Well good luck with that. Glasses is gonna be all over you." Jesus his voice makes me want to punch something.

Class comes to an end and I rush out of my seat and set a path in Rydell's direction.

As I near her I call out, "Hey." She looks up at me for a second, glasses edging down the bridge of her nose, then goes back to packing her bag.

Ok. Rude. "Hey, Rydell, right?" I try again.

She looks at me and circles her head to her the left and right, as if looking for someone else I could be talking to, then points at herself. "Hey? Hey me? Are you heying me?" she responds, hazel eyes the size of saucers.

"Yep, unless there's another 5'6 brunette who goes by Rydell around here," I joke.

"Well, I'm 5'7 so it can't be me then," she

deadpans. A couple second later letting out a small laugh. Cute. "So why are you heying me? And how do you know my name?" she integrates.

Shit I haven't thought ahead this far and now I look like a complete stalker.

"Well, I make it a habit to know the names of all the pretty girls in class. And I'm heying you to ask you to be my partner for the oral presentation." There's absolutely no way she'll say no.

"No- "

"Great how about I get your number- wait- no?" what the fuck.

"Sorry, that was rude. What I meant to say was that I'm going solo on this one. My schedule is way too packed to try to coordinate with," she explains, "but I'm sure lots of people in here would love to be your partner."

She turns on her on the heels of her feet and makes her way to the door, leaving me frozen in place.

No? She said no. What the hell has my life come to? I mean I know I didn't have time to brush my teeth this morning, but I sprayed some cologne, so I probably smell fine.

By the time I recover from the utter shock of it all, I rush out of the lecture hall, but I guess I was standing there for longer than I thought because she's nowhere to be found.

Well, we still have 2 weeks until we have to present so that gives me a couple days to convince her. I'll put on all my charm and make myself so irresistible that she'll be begging *me* to be *her* partner. Because there is no way I'm

letting that easy A slip through my fingers.
  I just need to find her first.

CHAPTER 3: *RYDELL*

The bar is packed. But that doesn't entirely surprise me considering it's a Friday night. And who knows, maybe people got the memo that it was National Drink a Beer Day.

But as I take a look around, I mainly see girls in miniskirts taking shots with frat boys who probably go by the name Kyle or Jason. So, I'm guessing Sam and I are some of the only ones in this place to know that today is indeed National Drink a Beer Day.

I look down at my outfit, which is the same from earlier, kinda wishing that I dressed up just a little more. But I figured I'd only be here for one or two drinks max because I have an early morning tomorrow.

"Did you tell the 106ers we'd be here tonight?" I question Sam.

The 106ers, Abby and Liliana, were our neighbors freshman year, and basically my only other friends besides Sam. Their room number was 106, hence the nickname.

"Ya but Lils refuses to come back to Boots because she's scared that Ryan will be here."

Ah Ryan, the resident baseball douchbag.

Him and Lils dated for about 7 months before she found out he was cheating on her for the entirety of their relationship.

"Don't the baseball boys prefer The Nest?" The Nest and Boots are the two popular bars amongst Daxton students. I prefer Boots because every now and then, someone will drink out of a disgusting, 100-year-old looking boot and the place goes nuts. Seriously, something about this magical boot instantly makes people happy, and seeing people happy makes me happy.

That's how Boots got the name. They have this one special boot that brave souls will drink out of to get a free drink. They only offer it about twice a month because people will do anything for a free drink, but it's always a good time.

"Ya but the breakups still fresh and she's scared that she'll either take him back or kick him in the balls if she runs into him," Sam explains.

That instantly makes me feel bad. Here I am celebrating National Drink a Beer Day while my friend is grieving over her shitty ex.

"After this drink we should pick up a 6-pack and head over to their place," I suggest.

"Ok but can we get like Mike's Hard or something, beer taste like piss," she grumbles as she looks down into her drink.

"The whole point of today is to celebrate drinking beer not hard lemonade, plus that stuff always gives me the worst headaches."

"Fine you grab beer and I'll get my own pack," stubborn woman. "Oh fuck yes, the hockey boys are here."

I look to the door to see about 8, tall as trees, guys walk in towards one of the booths in the back that is notoriously known as the hockey team's table.

Sam loves hockey. She grew up in Massachutes watching it. Plus, she claims that hockey boys are the most attractive species of men.

I, on the other hand, know absolutely nothing about hockey. That probably has to do with my SoCal roots. "Yippee," I deadpan.

Not that I have anything against hockey players, but I've seen the way most of them treat girls, so I make sure to stay far away.

"Why is Bridges staring at you like you're his next meal?" she questions.

I look up from my drink, instantly making eye contact with Prescott Bridges. He's not hard to spot considering he's about 6'5 and towers over everyone. I instantly bring my gaze back down to my drink like it's the most interesting thing in the world.

I shrug, "He wanted me to be his partner for a Spanish project and I said no."

Sam chokes on her beer, "Please tell me you're joking, why the hell would you do that?"

"Afraid not. I don't have time to coordinate working on a project with anyone, all my free time is spent at the orphanage."

Whenever we can pick up hours, Sam and I work part time at an orphanage not far from campus. It was the orphanage Sam was at before she was adopted.

Sam's been working there since she turned 16, and when we became friends, she took me along one day because they needed extra hands for a field trip. Going into college, I knew I would need a job to help for tuition. Lucky for me, I fell in love with it instantly and have worked there ever since.

"Ya but if you said yes, then you could have introduced me to all of his hot hockey friends," she whines, "plus, who wouldn't want to work with that? I mean look at him."

I glance back to Scott to find him still looking at me with a smirk plastered on his face. He gives me a little wave, which I pretend to not see as I look back at Sam.

"Please, if I said yes, one," I held up one finger, "I would probably end up doing all the work. Two," I hold up a second finger, "he'd flirt with me, making it seems like he likes me only to stop talking to me the second the project was over. And three," I hold up a final finger, "I've seen better looking."

Sam laughs, "Better looking? I'm starting to think that I should sign you into a hospital for the crazies. God took his time sculpting Prescott Bridges."

And she was so extremely right about that. Prescott Bridges is painstakingly gorgeous. Like, I wouldn't be surprised if a person used a picture of him as reference for plastic surgery. With his dark brown hair, pretty green eyes, and body of a God, it hurt thinking that people could look so perfect.

"I'm sorry, but are you forgetting about Dylan O'Brien, he is not on that level."

"Well, I guess we'll just have to agree to disagree on this one then," she replies plugging her nose and chugging the rest of her beer, "Holy shit he's walking this way."

My head snaps up so fast I swear I almost

got whiplash, and sure enough Prescott Bridges is headed our way looking like he's on a mission.

And even though Boots is jammed packed to capacity, I swear people are parting for him like the fucking Red Sea.

Not wanting to deal with another conversation with him, I jump up from my seat saying a quick, "Bathroom," to Sam and speed walk to the restrooms like a Grandma running late to bingo night.

I walk up to the sink and wash my hands hoping that the cool water will make me feel less nervous.

Good lord, why am I even getting worked up over this? It's only a boy wanting to be your Spanish partner, he's not asking for your hand in marriage. I look at myself in the mirror, patting down the baby hairs, "Get yourself together Rydell."

I take a deep breath and exit the bathroom hoping that Bridges lost interest and went to find a conquest for the night.

Scanning the bar, I smile to myself when I don't see him anywhere in sight. Aha, I lost him, that's right I'm like a freaking ninja.

"You know Books, a guy might think you're avoiding him with all the running around you're doing," a deep voice says from behind me making me jump.

Dammit. "Oh, hey you. We have Spanish, together right? And Books?" I play oblivious.

He chuckles deeply, "Playing it dumb. Cute. And Books because every time I see you, you have a book in your hands," he flicks the book that I am indeed holding. I can't help it, I always have to be prepared. "You know, if we were Spanish partners, you wouldn't need to bring a book with you, I'm great company."

"I'm sure you are but, like I told you early, I'm just too busy to coordinate with another person's schedule. I'm really sorry, but I have a friend in the class who needs a partner, I can give you their number," I say as nicely as possible.

I wouldn't call Jenna a friend per say, but I always ask at least one person for their number in any class just in case. And Jenna also asked to be my partner, but like Scott, I politely declined. And I know for a fact that Jenna would love to work with him. I hear on the daily how cute she thinks he is.

"What if I said that you're the only person I wanted to be partners with." He takes a step closer to me and I take a step back.

"Then I would be slightly confused, but my answer would unfortunately still be no." He looks like he's never been rejected before and it's making me feel bad for saying no, but I have to keep my priorities straight. "Really though Jenna's super smart too." I have no idea how smart Jenna is, but he keeps stepping closer to me and it's making me nervous.

"I doubt she's as smart as you." I'm now up against a wall and he lifts his hand up to my cheek brushing a stray piece of hair behind my ear.

"So, the reason you want to be partners with me is because you know I'm smart?"

His hand rest on the nape of my neck, "I've

done my research."

Great. Another person who wants to use me and then leave me when they get what they want. That's it, no more mister nice gal. "Well listen here mister," I remove his hand and shove my pointer finger on his chest. Oh my gosh his chest is rock hard. Seriously how do people like him exist? Focus Rydell you're putting down your foot on this one. I duck around him, and he turns on his heels to face me again. This time I make sure there's an arm's length of space between us. "Even if I didn't have a busy schedule, I wouldn't be partners with you just for me to do all the work and you get a good grade because of it."

As he opens his mouth as blonde who looks like she walked here straight from the runway wedges her way in between us and glides her hands up his chest.

Yes, escape, escape. I walk so fast I'm practically jogging as I make my way back to the table. I chug the rest of my beer so fast you'd think I'd not had any liquid in a month. Then I grab Sam's arm and drag her out of the bar.

~

The next morning, it was hard to get out of bed. After the little bump in with Scott, Sam and I went over the 106ers bearing alcohol and I ended up drinking one of those damn hard lemonades, even though I know they give me headaches.

Now I'm curled on the ground shielding my face with my hands as 3 girls the size of leprechauns whack me with pillows.

When I take morning shifts at the

orphanage, I roll in at about 6:30 and help wake and dress the younger kids for their day.

This morning I was ambushed.

"Stop, stop, I surrender," I exclaim as I get tackled by Sophie.

She wraps her little arms around my torso as I lift to sit criss cross on the floor, plopping down on my lap.

"Why can't we just wear are pjs all day," she whines.

"Yaaaaa," Rosie and Tessa agree. Soph, Rosie, and Tessa are the elementary aged girls here, and the ones I'm in charge of for the day.

"Because today is recycling and movie day." The orphanage has an agreement with the city committee and some of the local businesses that allows us to collect their recyclable bottles to use for funding. Every weekend we pick up the recycling and then use the money for an activity that the girls vote on. This week they wanted to see the new Disney movie that came out.

"How about we skip the recycling part and just go to the movies," I look up to see Kendall leaning against the door frame. Kendall is one of the high school aged girls here, and right now she's going through the whole 'I hate everyone and everything phase'. "We aren't the cities little slaves just because we have no family."

"Hey," I warn, at the same time, I look down at Sophie to see her bottom lip trembling. Sophie is 5 and has been at the orphanage for a little over a year now. Her drug addicted mom waltzed through our doors and into the backyard, where we were having doing our daily outside activities with the girls, and basically dropped her off saying, and I quote, "I don't want her anymore." It broke my heart. And Sophie was at an age where she didn't fully understand the situation, but she could understand that her mom was leaving her for good. "You have a family here Kenny. Right Soph?"

"Right," she smiles, heading to her bed and grabbing her clothes that I laid out, then walking out of the room to get changed. I sigh, glad that no tears were shed.

"Really Ken. You know how sensitive Soph is about that stuff."

"It's not like I said anything that wasn't true," she huffs, leaving the door.

As I wait for Soph, Tessa, and Rosie to finish getting changed Sam pokes her head in the door, "I saw Ken leave from this direction. How's the little ray of sunshine this morning?"

"Not great, but that's not really a surprise, is it?" Even though Kendall can be a pain in the ass, I feel for the girl. It's not likely for girls as old as her to get adopted and she's been in the orphanage for about 8 years.

"Ya, I'll talk to her," Sam pads away in Ken's direction.

~

"Anymore word from the hottie with a body," Sam asks as we wait in the concession line at the movies.

"Hottie with a body?"

"You know the God of a hockey player that was practically drooling over you last night."

I roll my eyes. "Not since last night thankfully." Replaying our bump in and remembering how he smelt like chocolate and beer. After I staged my escape Sam asked me for all the details saying that my life is "straight out of a romance book". But if my life is a romance book, I will bury my own grave before Prescott Bridges becomes my main love interest. Not that he's bad looking, because holy hell that man is gorgeous. But I know guys like him. Heck, I've dated a guy like him, only instead of being the star of hockey, he was the star of the high school surf team. And trust me, guys like them don't settle for girls like me.

I swear I'm not a pick-me girl. Guys like him don't settle for any girl; they keep their options open. And I sure as hell and not the type of girl to be a booty call waiting around for a guy to be with my monogamously.

"Maybe I should transfer into your Spanish class and then I can be his partner."

"If we weren't too far into the semester, I'd say go for it. I told you you'd regret taking French." Freshman year Sam decided she was going to take French for her foreign language solely because she thought that French accents were hot. I told her that was stupid, and that Spanish was a much more practical language.

"Ya, ya," she waves me off.

~

After the movie and our shift at the orphanage was finished Sam and I headed back home. I dropped Sam off and then drove to the campus library to get some coding in for one of my classes.

I do most of my work in the library, or really anywhere besides home. I get too distracted if I'm not out of the house and the library's never too crowded.

I find an empty desk and get started on my

work.

CHAPTER 4: SCOTT

As I open my eyes this morning, I feel ready to take on the day. I look at my phone and realize it's Saturday. Yes, Saturday means no… wait. It's a Saturday and I'm waking up ready to take on the day? I cannot remember the last Saturday I woke up without a hangover.

Then I replay the previous night in my head.

I walked into Boots with the intention to get shitfaced, like I usually do on Fridays, and possible find a girl to take home. Instead, I walked in, and my eyes landed on Rydell Rivens. She was in the same outfit from Spanish class, expect her brunette hair was now wrapped up in a hair clip.

On one side, she was sitting next to a tiny olive-skinned girl with the biggest eyes I've ever seen and on the other side sat her book. A book. She brought a book to the bar.

Every other girl in the bar was in tight dresses and mini skirt, so I'm not surprised that my eyes went to Rydell right away. She stuck out like a sore thumb and I couldn't look away. I found myself wanting her to make eye contact with me. I wanted her to notice me. But that's just because I want her to work on the project with me. I wanted to brush that hair out of her face and smell the lavender scent she had going for her in Spanish. But this is a strictly academic relationship I want, right? Right.

As if the universe was rewarding me, she turned her head, looking right at me. I smirked. She looked away.

I thought that I would for sure get her to say yes to being partners last night. For the couple seconds we made eye contact I could tell she found me attractive. Or at least interesting in some sorts.

And I know that sounds so douchey of me but 1, I know I'm hot. If I wasn't girls wouldn't throw themselves at me. And 2, I've worked hard for this killer bod.

So, it came as a bit of a shock when I got seductively close to her and she rejected me yet again. And not only did she reject me, she flat out told me that she would never want to be partnered with me.

She insinuated that she would do all the work and that I would be a freeloader.

And then some blonde came up to me. I swear I took my eyes of Rydell for one second and she was gone. I barely caught a glance of her dragging her friend out of the bar.

It threw off my whole night. Sure, maybe I wouldn't be the most hard-working partner. But Rivens doesn't even know me and she's already created her own version of me in her head. It just made me wonder if that's what everyone thinks of me.

I don't think I was even that upset about her assuming things about me. I think I was more upset that I underestimated her.

I honestly thought that she would be a bit of

a pushover. In Spanish class she let me down so politely I almost felt bad about asking her again. But her confidence in telling me that she wouldn't be used for her brain just left me so confused.

No. Not confused. Intrigued. Intrigued because I want to know the limits of her kindness. Intrigued because I want to know what makes and breaks her and all the ways she carries herself.

And since I couldn't get her out of my head, I went home and called in for an early night. Max had stayed home because he's just getting over a bad breakup, and the look on his face when I rolled in at 10 was pure confusion.

He actually started getting concerned. Asking if I needed to be taken to the hospital when I told him I only had one drink. I told him about how my night was ruined because of a certain bespectacled brunette and I swear it was like I was a stand-up comedian. He laughed through my entire story, so I flipped him the bird and went to bed.

I go down to the kitchen this morning to be greeted with Oliver Davidson.

"Cereal?" he questions.

I shake my head yes and he passes me a bowl.

"Still moody that there's a girl out there who is immune to your charm?"

Davies was there last night and saw my rejection in motion. After I told them to "watch and learn" they, like Max, had a good laugh at my set back.

"I told you man; Rydell is too smart for you to only rely on your looks."

Davies is a computer science major and apparently Rydell is as well. I learned that last night when I pointed her out and Davies told me she's been in almost all the same CS classes as him since freshman year. In fact, he said that they are kind of friends.

"Well, I still have a week to convince her, so don't count it a lose yet," I reply. "Maybe you can put in a good word for me?"

"No. Absolutely not. You're on your own for this one. In fact, I think you should just end the whole thing all together and find a different partner. Rydell is a sweet girl; I don't want to see her get hurt."

"What's that supposed to mean?"

"Don't act like you don't know Scotty," he says coolly. "Everyone knows about your reputation with the ladies: you find the most model looking girls and never go further than a one-night stand," he explains. "You told us last night that Del wouldn't resist you because you'd charm her pants off." He calls her Del. "She's not the typical girl you would go to for a hookup and she definitely isn't the type for a one-night stand. So... as soon as the project is over, and you get what you need, she'll be upset when you stop talking to her."

"You think that lowly of me?" Now I'm upset. "You think that I couldn't actually be friends with Rydell? That I'm this asshole who drops girls as soon as I get what I want?" He's not entirely wrong, but it's hard to hear out loud.

"I don't think lowly of you man, you're one of my best friends, and I know you can be a good guy. But that's exactly what you do. You need something, whether that be sex, or in this case help with a project, you find a person to satisfy that need, and then you never think twice about them. I see it happen almost every Friday night."

I stand up and dump my cereal bowl in the sink, "Fuck you." I'm not going to sit here and listen to him tell me how much of a horrible person I am. I mean he does the same exact thing. I've seen so many girls come in and out of his bedroom. Girls that I never see again because he uses them as meaningless hookups. What a fucking hypocrite.

I walk up the stairs to my room bumping into Asher, "You look like you're two seconds away from punching a hole in the wall. Still mad about last night's rejection?"

"What is it asshole day? Go find Davies downstairs and you two can gossip all about how shitty of a person I am." With that I slam my bedroom door shut and get ready for the gym.

~

After a 3-mile treadmill warm up, I walk over to the bench press station. Usually Saturday and Wednesday mornings are the only mornings without hockey practice, but I needed to let off some steam. Every other day we have gym training in the mornings and on-ice practice in the evenings.

My mind is a mess. I can't stop thinking about how everyone portrays me. I don't want to be someone who is described as an asshole. But, if I think about it, I'm not the nicest guy out there.

My whole life I grew up with a father who told me that crying wasn't manly. That expressing my emotions wasn't manly. He taught me that kindness was a weakness that could be used against you, and that being feared was an advantaged to be used at will.

So, growing up I lived that robotic life. It's hard to be something different than what you're taught.

And when it comes to the relationships, there's three reasons why I strictly do hookups:

1. I won't let anyone distract me from my hockey goals.
2. My parents have probably already arranged a girl for me to marry.
3. I haven't found a single girl that I can tolerate after the sex part.

The sex part is great. I love sex, but after I'm done hooking up with a girl, they just get so fucking annoying.

And maybe is makes me an asshole to forget about them once I get what I want, but I do tell them before-hand what they're getting themselves into. I never lead any of them on, I tell them that it will only be a one-time thing before we get in bed.

My mind is a mess. I can't stop thinking about what Rydell thinks of me.

I mean she essentially said that if we were partners, I wouldn't pull my weight.

She thinks that I'm using her for a good grade.

But who am I kidding, that's exactly what I would do.

That's why I approached her in the first place. I wanted her to be my partner so I could get a good grade. I probably would have never given her a second look if I didn't need her for something.

Don't get me wrong, Rydell is gorgeous. She has brunette hair that is usually messily pulled up, but when it's down it reaches to the tops of her ribs. I never noticed her eyes until I actually talked to her, but they are hazel and so fucking pretty. She doesn't wear a lot of makeup and has this natural look to her that I'm sure most girls would kill for. Her skin is the perfect tan-

I need to stop thinking like this.

While Rydell is not lacking in the looks section. There are reasons why I only talked to her was because I need this good grade. She does not look like the type of girl who would be into a hookup. She seems like a little bit of a nerd, which isn't a bad thing, but I don't think I'd be able to get rid of her if I tried something.

People would definitely turn heads if they saw us together. Not to brag, but everyone on campus knows who I am. Our hockey team is one of the best nationally and I'm the captain of it. Although, I'm starting to think that Rydell doesn't know who I am because she never seems fazed by my presence and, if I think about it, she hasn't called me by my actual name yet.

Anyways, I'm well known, and she is the girl who avoids attention. Not my type.

Now done with my workout, I grab my things and head to my car. I spot the movie theater that's in the same parking lot as the gym.

I really don't want to go home so I drive over to the theater.

One thing a lot of people don't know about me is that I love movies. My whole life has always revolved around hockey, but as a kid hockey was all I ever did. It's not like I could drive myself places, and my parents were never home, so I watched movies. Lots of movies.

I glance at the board with the premiering shows and see a Disney, horror, and comedy that I haven't seen yet. Not many choices, but I go with the comedy.

~

That movie sucked. It was cheesy, cringey and the acting was horrible. I would have rather gone home to endure my roommates verbal torture than watch that movie. And then I spot her, and I think maybe it was the universe giving me a sign.

Rydell and her friend from last night are standing in the concessions line surrounded by about 10 little girls.

Perfect. I'm about to walk her way when one of the younger girls starts tugging on Rydell's shirt with a pout on her face and the look that tells me she's seconds away from a tantrum. Rydell squats down to her level and after a minute of talking to her, the girl's mood does a complete 360 and she's wrapping her little arms around Rydell's neck.

Rydell stands up with the girl in her arms, wrapping her arms around the girl's waist and carrying her to cash register to place her order.

And that's when I see Rydell's shirt that says *The Recycle Crew- Massachusetts Orphanage for Girls.*

I walk out of the theater door and to my car with a smug smile of my face. I know exactly how to get Rivens to be my partner.

CHAPTER 5: RYDELL

I swear I'm about to pass out any second in this library. I'm sitting at a circle of desks with walls around them for privacy on the second floor and I think I might just give up and take a nap.

I've been sitting at this desk for about two hours trying to code the color sequence in our game to perfection, but I just can't seem to get it right and it's driving me insane.

Not to mention I'm exhausted from my day at recycling, taming wild children, and I'm running off about 4 hours of sleep.

Not only did we stay at the 106ers one too many hours late, but I couldn't seem to get the image of Prescott Bridges out of my damn head.

I know what he's doing. He's trying to get close to me so that he can get a good grade on this Spanish project.

I mean he could try harder. It's so vividly apparent that he has no interest in me other than my brain. With the way he brushed my hair behind my ear and the smirk he plasters on his face to try and get me all hot and bothered. Not to mention the model status girl he had wrapped around him as I was leaving.

I type in a new HTML color code only to hit the * instead of the #, groaning as soon as I notice the mistake. The person in the desk next to me shoots daggers and I quickly look down to avoid any more awkwardness. God, I need to get my head out of my ass and get it together.

Actually, screw it, I need to sleep, or I might actually lose my mind.

Right as I stand up from my seat, I see no other than Prescott Bridges and Oliver Davidson about to sit down at a table not too far from the desk that I'm at. And his eyes flicker to mine. And I'm on the floor.

Literally on the floor. Like sitting down underneath my desk on the floor because I don't have the mental capacity to have a conversation with him right now. It's like at school when there's and earthquake and you stop and drop and stay in place until it passes. Scott is my earthquake.

"Hello floor, long time no see. Actually you tripped me yesterday and I saw you then but you get-"

"Are you talking to the ground," of course he saw me. Scott is hunched over like how I am when I look at the bottom of a bookshelf, except he isn't looking at books, he's looking at me.

This would be so much easier if he didn't look like that. "Of course not. I'm talking to the floor. The ground is what you walk on outside, the floor is for insides only," I reply.

"Well, I guarantee the chair up here is a lot more comfortable than the *floor* down there."

"Sorry, but the floor and I have a long past and I would hate to abandon him like this," the longer I stay down here, the sooner he'll lose interest. I mean who would want to work with a crazy who talks to talks to the floor. "Plus, he gets jealous really easily, so you might want to run while you still can."

He chuckles and starts bending down squeezing into the very limited space underneath the desk with me, "I think I'll take my chances."

At this point I'm freaking out for multiple reasons. For one, he's an absolute unit. I mean he's got to be at least 6'5 and pure muscle, and there is barely enough space for me down here. Two, he's not leaving which means I'm going to have to talk to him. Three, I hate when people I don't know get close to me and I mean we can't get much closer than this, I'm practically sitting on his lap.

I start scooting into the nonexistent space away from him and my hip hurts because of how much I'm digging it into the desk. My face is probably the shade of a beet and my breathing is starting to get heavy.

Please, please, please no panic attacks. Small spaces have always freaked me out. It reminds me of things that I try to forget.

I put my hands on my pulse and try to slow my breathing.

CHAPTER 6: *SCOTT*

Davies felt bad about our morning convo and told me he'd help with my Spanish project since he already took the class.

I didn't tell him that I'm not giving up on having Rydell as my partner and that I have an offer I know she won't resist.

But I figured that Davies could help me get started with the project and I can present the work he helps me with to Rydell so that she's less apprehensive about working with me.

So, we went to the library. And thank the lord we did because right when I went to sit down, a pretty brunette popped up from her seat. I swear I've never seen someone move so fast because after about .01 seconds of eye contact, she shot back down.

And when I went over to the circle of desks to find her, I swear I thought she was a magician who just pulled a disappearance act until I saw the tips of her high tops pocking out from under the desk.

And when I bent down to talk to her. She was talking to the ground. Wait, my bad, she was talking to the *floor*. Even further confirming that

Rydell and I are two completely different people.

But here I am, crammed next to her like sardines under the desk and she smells like lavender and she's practically on my lap and I almost forget why I'm down here with her.

"Now that we've become so close... will you be my partner for the Spanish project?" I try before I pull out the big guns.

She doesn't say anything in return, just looks straight ahead. Her face is bright red and one of her hands is so tightly wrapped around her wrist that her knuckles are turning white.

I try to lighten the mood a bit, "You know, I'm a bit shocked you don't know who I am."

This makes her snort and tilt her head up to look at me. My head and neck are already craned down considering my height surpasses that of the desks, so that small movement brings are faces so close that I can feel her breath on my face as she says, "Of course I know who you are, I don't live under a rock," and shifts her face to look straight again.

"No just under a desk," I grumble as I take in her side profile, "a very uncomfortable desk that we are now going to come out from under." I scoot out and prop up on my knees grabbing her by the ankle and dragging her out with me.

She kicks her leg out of my grasp and scrambles up, "Excuse me, but I'm not some rag doll you can just pull around," I didn't think it was possible, but her face is even more red.

I smirk, "So, you know who I am?"

"Prescott Bridges. Hockey captain. School's pride and joy. Girl's fantasies."

"I'm your fantasy?" Now I'm full out

grinning.

"I didn't say *my* fantasy."

"No, but you said girl's fantasies. And you're a girl, which would put you in that category."

She groans and I realize her hand is still around her wrist as she shifts to the desk, releasing it to pack her things.

"Hey, hey, hey," I shuffle to her side, "I'll stop now, you don't have to leave."

"I'm not leaving because of your annoyance. I was about to go anyways before you showed up."

"But you had to have a conversation with the floor first?" I try to put on a serious face but fail miserably.

"Exactly," she deadpans.

"Am I really that bad to talk to Books? You'd rather shove yourself under the desk then have a conversation with me?"

Her face falls and I feel bad making her feel guilty. "I'm sorry," she sighs, "that was very rude of me. I'm not trying to make you feel bad I just had a long day and wasn't up for any social interaction."

"Maybe you could use a rant. I'm an easy person to talk to once you get to know me. Another reason why I'd be the perfect partner for this project."

She smiles and I can't look away. "Hmmm.... rant to a complete stranger or go home and catch up on sleep. I'll take the latter. Plus, I'm not lying when I say I'm too busy to be your partner, if I wasn't, I would have said yes."

"Hey, I'm not a complete stranger. You know who I am, and we've had now 3 conversations. And last night you said you wouldn't work with me even if you weren't busy so that's a lie."

"Ya, but that was after I figured out that you want to be my partner because you did research to find out I'm smart," she put air quotes around research and smart. "The first time you came up and asked you seemed genuine and I hate saying no to people, so I probably would've agreed. And if I agreed, we wouldn't have had that convo at the bar," she rambles while shoving her laptop into her bag and walking towards the stairs.

I jog to stand in front of her. "I'm sorry that you think I'm using you. And heck, maybe I am a little," I admit, and she rolls her eyes trying to get past me, but I block her way again. "Hey, wouldn't you rather me be honest? And I'm not done. Maybe I want you to be my partner because I scouted you out for your good grades. But maybe it's because I have a lot on the line, and I can't risk getting anything less than a perfect grade. I promise I won't make you do all the work. Plus, I have a proposition with you."

She stares at me before hesitantly asking, "Alright what's your proposition?"

"You work at the girl's orphanage."

"And you are creepy," I grimace. That did sound extremely stalkery.

"I saw you at the movies yesterday."

"You are not helping your creepiness case one bit, are you?"

"Will you just listen to me for a second?" I groan. "I saw you at the movies yesterday after I went to the gym, and you were wearing a shirt with the orphanage's name on it. It's not creepy because obviously I go to the gym." I lift my shirt up a bit to expose my toned abs, "I mean look at me." And she's blushing again. She makes it too easy.

"So, you know I work at an orphanage, how does that have anything to do with a Spanish project."

"The movies yesterday was a field trip of some sorts, am I right?"

"Yes. Still not getting how this is supposed to make me agree to being your partner."

"Because, if you agree to be my partner, I'll get my coach to let the girls from the orphanage come in for an ice-skating field trip." Her eyes go wide, and I know I got her but she stays silent so I add, "I'll even have a couple of guys from the team come out with me and we can teach them some things about hockey."

She chews on her thumb nail for a bit then asks, "How would that even work. I'm sure there would be a fee off some sort to rent out the rink and where on earth would we get enough tiny ice skates?"

"The rink is open to the public when we aren't practicing, so they have rental skates in all sizes, and if you agree to be by partner, it will be a completely free trip. I'll take care of it all."

"That doesn't seem very cheap. Renting the skates out for 20ish girls can add up, not to mention that renting the entire place out has to cost an arm and a leg."

"Books, I'm captain of the hockey team, do you think they'd charge me if I asked? Don't answer that, I'm telling you right now the answer is no."

"*If* I agree to this, I'm not saying I have yet, we have to set up a very strict schedule of when we meet and create a detailed timeline to track when we'll get it done," I love how she's acting like she's going to say no. "And, if you don't show up, or if I'm doing all the work, the deal's immediately off."

"Sounds good to me."

"Ok."

"Ok? Like ok you'll be my partner?"

"Yes. Ok I'll be your partner."

"Fuck yes! I knew you wouldn't be able to resist."

"Ya, ya. But I'm serious one slip up and you're on your own."

"Yes ma'am," I solute like a solider. "How about we get started now. You know Oliver from the hockey team, right? He was gonna help me come out with some ideas for the project, we can all work together for a bit."

"I love the enthusiasm, but I just spent two hours coding color sequences and I'm running off 4 hours of sleep, so my ideas won't be the best".

And she really does look like she's about to crash so I suggest, "That's cool. How about you give me your number and we can try to link up tomorrow?"

"Alright, give me your phone."

I open up a new contact and hand it over to her after I put her name as 'Books' with an emoji with glasses.

"You know, Books is a horrible nickname Prescott. And is the nerd emoji something I should be offended by?

"First off, please call me anything other than Prescott. Secondly, Books is the perfect nickname for you. And lastly, I put that emoji because you wear glasses, not because I think you're a nerd."

"If I can call you anything other than

Prescott, I think I'll start calling you," she pauses to think about it, tapping her finger on her chin, "stalker. I mean it's perfect. First you find out my name and the grades I get without ever talking to me. Then you find out where I work. Not to mention you seem to be everywhere I am. The bar, the movies, here at the library."

"You can call me whatever you want Ry."

"If I can't call you Prescott you can't call me Ry. It makes me sound like a bread."

I laugh, "Aw that makes me want to keep calling you it. It's so cute, like Ry Ry."

"Fine Prescott," she says handing me back my phone and stepping around me to head down the stairs.

"You can expect a text from me soon then."

"Ya, ya. I'm looking forward to it," she waves her hand behind her shoulder and makes her exit down the stairs.

I make my way back over to Davies silently celebrating my accomplishment.

"By the look on your face, I take it she agreed to work with you. What'd you do to make her change her mind."

"She works at an orphanage for girls and I told her I'd set up an ice-skating field trip for them if she'd be my partner," I say smugly as I take a seat across from him.

He sighs and looks back down to his laptop, "I know I promised I wouldn't say another word about it, but don't mess this up. Please."

"Why are you so protective over this one? Do you have a crush on her that I should know about?"

"No crush, but she is my friend, sort of. And

I don't know her super well, but I know her well enough that she would do anything to keep other people happy. Even if it's the expense of her own happiness." He looks up, "I'm sure she told you that she's expecting you to pull your weight, but even if you don't, she's the type of person to not complain about it no matter how much it's stressing her out because she's scared of disappointing people. I've seen it happen before on lots of different computer science group projects. Just don't abuse her kindness."

"I'll pull my weight trust me. And I'll start right now, with your help that you promised me."

CHAPTER 7: RYDELL

random number to me: *hey books :) you can add me to your phone as 'the sexiest man to walk the face of the earth'*

Great, he's even a flirt over the phone. I save his contact putting in the perfect name.

me to stalker: *I'm sorry, I think you have the wrong number. Who is this?*

I throw my phone back down to the side and pick up my book resuming from where I left off. And then my phone starts to ring. It's lit up with his contact name that I changed to stalker.

I stare at the phone hoping it'll stop ringing any second now. Why on earth would he call me? What are we in the 60s? Am I supposed to answer? Fuck that. I'll just wait until it stops ringing and then hopefully, he gets the message and texts me instead.

The phone stops ringing and me heart rate goes back down. Then it goes back up because now he's trying to Facetime me. It's 11 in the morning and Sundays are usually my lazy days so I haven't even gotten out of bed yet. I'm positive I look like a mess.

The phone stops ringing.

And then it starts again. God he's relentless.

I run my fingers through my hair a couple of times and answer.

On his side of the screen, he is shirtless and sweaty. On my side of the screen, I have bags under my eyes and unbrushed hair.

"Did I wake you up?" he questions.

I tilt my phone up to the ceiling so that he can't see my face, "No, I was reading. Why are you Facetiming me?"

"You texted me wrong number and wouldn't answer my two calls, I thought you actually gave me a fake number."

"I thought my sarcasm would carry through text."

"Put the phone back to your face," he commands.

"My hands are currently unavailable to fulfil your request. Sorry." My hands are empty but he is looking fresh out of a men's workout magazine and I look like a zombie.

"Ry. Come on. You weren't wearing your glasses; I need to make sure it's really you. And on that topic, how were you reading if you weren't wearing your glasses. Isn't that like their whole purpose."

"I'm near-sighted Prescott. I only need them to see things in the distance."

All of sudden my door bursts open, and I'm faced with a crazy looking Sam. I try to give her some sort of hint that I'm on the phone but I'm too late because she practically screams, "Sunday Funday Del! Get your cute butt out of bed and please eat something before 12 today. I know you hate breakfast, but it's the most important meal of the day."

I look down at my phone and Scott is smirking. "Actually, breakfast per say isn't the most important meal of the day. It's just whatever you eat first in the day, it doesn't matter what time it's at."

"I agree with the loud one, breakfast is important, and you should definitely be eating it. Plus, breakfast foods are like the best types of food." Sam runs and jumps onto my bed and I dive for my phone, but she grabs it before I can.

Sam looks at the phone and gives me a grin so big it looks like her face is gonna split. "Why is," she gives me a confused look "stalker.... Calling you so early in the morning?" Handing me back my phone so that Scott and I are now face to face.

"Ah, there she is," Scott is smiling, "I hope you're not going around to all of your friends calling me a stalker Ry. I thought we talked through that."

I reach over to my bedside and grab my glasses. "Actually, Prescott, I tend to not talk about you at all to my friends," I joke, "stalker is your new contact name. I thought it was fitting ya know?"

"And here I thought you looked past my stalker tendencies. Yesterday, you said you were perfectly ok with me peeking through your window."

I laugh, "I did nothing of the sorts. If I find you looking through my windows, I'm calling the police. It's bad enough that you scouted me out in the movie theaters and the library all in one day ya little creep." I look around my room noticing that Sam left.

"Please Books, we both know you love running into me."

"Mmhmm. Alright if that's all, I have important things to do."

"What like not eating breakfast and reading, those aren't impor-"

"Scotty, you wanna hit up Smoothie Palace when your done in here? Sorry were you talking to someone?" He gets cut off, I'm guessing by one of his teammates and he puts his phone in his pocket leaving me to look at a black screen.

Do I hang up? Is it weird that I'm just sitting here listening to his convo? Also, why the hell did he hide me in his pocket?

"Nah you're good and ya man, let me just finish this set."

"Cool, I'll spot you."

"Nah dude, I got it. I'm going like half max, just a cool down."

"Alright, catch ya in the lockers then."

I'm about to hang up when I'm met with him face again. "Sorry-" I hang up.

My phone rings. Stalker lights up the screen and I hit decline opening up my text messages.

me to stalker: *can't talk.*

stalker to me: *you could talk about 30 secs ago*

me to stalker: *a lot can happen in 30 secs.*

stalker to me: *answer the phone ry*

My phone lights up again, and I hit decline again. I know I am being bratty, but I can't be friends with Scott. That phone call seemed way too comfortable and that's bad for so many reasons. One, we just officially meet like 3 days ago. Two, he'll stop acting like my friend as soon as this project is over. And three, he clearly doesn't want people to know that we're talking.

stalker to me: *did I do something to make u upset?*

me to stalker: *the world doesn't revolve around you Prescott. I actually am busy.*

stalker to me: *u can finish your book later, we were in the middle of a convo*

me to stalker: *does 7 tonight work for you? We could start our project and set a schedule, meet in the library?*

stalker to me: *I have practice until 9, we can do it after?*

me to stalker: *library closes at 9 on Sundays*

My phone lights up and he's calling again. This time, I pick up.

"Finally. Glad you could unbusy yourself for a few seconds." We aren't on FaceTime anymore, just a regular call, so I feel a little more comfortable.

"Library closes at 9 tonight."

"I know, I saw your text, I find it amusing that you know the library hours off the top of your head. Can't say it surprises me though."

"Well, it's common knowledge Prescott."

"How about you come over to my place at like 9:30. If we're just getting things started and making a schedule, that should only take like 1-2 hours. Unless you're the type of person to go to bed early."

He wants me to come over to his house? Shit, this is supposed to be strictly professional. But we need to make a schedule asap, because if we don't then we might not get it done on time. And if we don't get it done on time we'll fail. "Ok, but let's try to meet at the library all the other times. More effective."

"Scared to be alone in my room Books? Are you admitting that you'll succumb to my charm?"

"Succumb? Who knew you had such a vast

vocabulary?"

"That's what turns you on Ry? Good use of SAT words? Well, I'm a hedonist, you should've told me earlier." Not gonna lie, Scott talking intellect to me is something I could get used to.

"And that's my cue to hang up. Text me your address, I'll see you at 9:30."

CHAPTER 8: SCOTT

I do feel kinda shitty for hiding Rydell away when McCombs asked me to hit up Smoothie palace with him. And I have no doubt that was the reason why she didn't want to answer my calls.

But McCombs is an asshole. As soon as he realized who was on the phone, he would've talked shit about how I scored my next 'victim' as he calls it. And that would've hurt her feelings more than me hiding her. Plus, she definitely would have called the whole thing off if she was called a victim.

Davies and Webbs are at their lockers right next to mine getting ready to leave this morning's workout, "Where's Ruddy? I was gonna ask if you guys wanted to grab some smoothies before we go home. McCombs asked me and I don't wanna go alone with the little shit."

"He already left, he's still in a pissy mood about the break-up," Davies say as he pulls a shirt over his head.

"I think Rudds just needs to get laid," Webbs jokes.

"Ya, that would work if he wasn't so concerned about Serena's feelings." The whole situation pisses me off. Max Rudderford is quite possibly the nicest human being you'll ever come across. He cares about people's health and wellbeing, he's responsible, and he's got a good head on his shoulders.

People like him don't deserve to get cheated on by their girlfriend of three years. And he definitely shouldn't be worried about her feelings getting hurt if he decides to move on. But he is.

"Well, do you guys wanna grab smoothies, we can grab one for Rudds which will give us an excuse to ditch McCombs?"

"I'm in," Webbs says as he grabs his bag.

"Ya me too."

~

We finally got our smoothies after waiting in the long ass line, "Hey McCombs, we're gonna bounce, gotta get this smoothie back to Ruddy."

"What are y'all doing tonight? There's a kick back at junior's house after practice, think you'll swing by? Lots of sorority chicks we'll be there."

"I might stop by, I'm going to convince Rudds to come out with me, get him outta this funk," Webbs says as we walk out of Smoothie Palace.

"Not sure yet, what are you doing Davies," I ask.

"I have a morning class-"

"Scotty hi, I missed you this weekend, you left boots so early Friday." I look down to see a leggy blonde whose cleavage is on full display.

"Lindsay, hey." I really don't feel like talking to her. Lindsay is one of the only girls I've slept with more than once on this campus. She's in the Alpha Delta Pi sorority, who work closely to help sponsor the hockey team. One of the most well-known puck bunnies.

The only reason she's one of my booty calls is because she never seems to expect a relationship with me. She knows that I don't want anything serious and never complains when I leave the bed in the morning.

But she is everywhere. At all the bars I go to, the gym during group workouts, the gym during my private workouts, every game, and sometimes practice.

"Why'd you leave so early, that's not like you. Feeling ok?" her arm is wrapped around mine and her fake nails are scrapping up and down my bicep.

"Fine, just wasn't in the party mood I guess."

"Well, I'll be at junior's house tonight, can I expect to see you there?"

"Not sure yet, depends on what everyone else is doing." I really just want to be done with this conversation, so I can go home and rest before tonight's practice, maybe get some studying done.

"Please come," she pouts her bottom lip out, "people are starting to think you're getting boring on us. You left Boots early Friday and everyone's mood shifted."

"I'm not responsible for other people's feelings. If they lost their party mood because I left, that's their own problem. Maybe it says more about them then me if I'm controlling their mood." Ya, I'm a dick, but I'm not going to try to make everyone happy by doing shit I don't want to do. "I left the bar early once; I don't see how that makes me boring."

"Oh, I'm not saying your boring. I totally

disagree with everyone. In fact, I was defending you. I told them that they shouldn't depend on you to make them happy." She squeezes my arm, "I think a lot of girls were just hoping you'd take them home."

"I'm sure they could've found plenty of other guys to fulfill their needs."

This makes her laugh, "Maybe, but they sure as hell wouldn't have anything on you."

"Well, this is me," I say as I open the door to my Jeep, forcing her arm to fall back to her side.

"Hopefully I'll see you tonight," she tries to say more, but I shut the door and drive away.

~

I unlock the front door to my house and am immediately bombarded by questions.

"What did Lindsay want? Begging you for that dick?" Webbs asked.

"Jesus Webbs, you really shouldn't talk about women like that," Ruddy chimes in as I pass him his smoothie.

"She just wanted to know if I was going to junior's."

"Well, I'm not going, I already told that to Webbs and Davies." Ruddy exclaims.

"Ya, and I told you that was bullshit," Webbs claps him on the back, "I'll drag you there if I have to."

Ruddy shrugs him off, "I'm not ready to get back out there. Plus Serena's in that-"

"Fuck Serena. She's the one who cheated on your ass, not the other way around. Who gives a fuck what Serena thinks," now Davies is mad.

"I care what she thinks. Just because she cheated on me, doesn't mean that the past three years just disappeared. Doesn't mean that I just stopped being in love with her."

I jump in, "Maxxy, it's been a month dude. Do you really want to go back to a girl who sleep with another guy? You're too good for her. Think of this as an opportunity to not be stuck down by a chick. This is the first time since freshman year that you've been single. Take advantage of it."

"Even before Serena, I was never the hookup type. I like long term relationships."

"Well, how do you know you don't like casual relationships, if you've never tried it," Webbs nudges him.

Max Rudderford is now genuinely considering the idea of getting a quick one-night stand. "How do I even go about it. Just go up to a girl and ask her if she wants to go home with me? That's so awkward."

"Trust me Rudds, stand close to any puck bunny there and they'll be the ones asking you to get in their bed," Webbs responds.

"Fine, I'll go. But I'm not initiating a one-night stand, if it happens, it happens."

Holy shit. "Holy shit," Davies reads my thoughts, "Oh fuck ya, now we all have to go for moral support. We'll drop by here after practice and walk from here."

All the hockey houses are down the same road, so there's no need to drive.

Now I'm racking my brain because I feel like I'm missing something.

I don't have class until 4 on Mondays, and morning practice doesn't start until 10:30. Plus I'm not planning on getting shitfaced or anything, so I should be fine.

CHAPTER 9: RYDELL

Why on earth did I agree to this.

Seriously Rydell, you should be put into a hospital for the clinically insane because there is no way that you are mental stable. You can't be mental stable because you agreed to go to Prescott fucking Bridges house to study.

Dammit, I should have just rescheduled, said I'm like a grandma and go to bed at 7. Or I could've just lied and said I had a morning class that I didn't want to be tired for.

Maybe some sadist part of me wanted to go to Scott's house. Like, maybe after our conversations, I think he might actually want to be my friend. And it doesn't even have to be a romantic relationship, I think Scott and I could be really good friends.

Fuck.

No. No. No. Strictly professional Del.

It's 9:28 and I'm pulling into his driveway.

I've seen the hockey houses before. I've been to a few of the parties thrown at them with Sam, so I'm not surprised by the sheer size of the place when I pull up.

I can't believe the school funds this. Most of

the hockey players are here on full scholarships and get to live in these ridiculous places. And I understand that they worked hard to get here, but I did too.

I worked my ass off. I had two jobs, got a 1435 on my SATs, took almost all AP of college classes, was president of two clubs, created my own club, and what do I get? A crappy grant, student loans, and a shitty apartment that I can barely afford.

Whatever.

I knock on the door.

What should I say when it opens? Oh god, what if Scott doesn't open it, what if it's a different hockey player? I bet my face would get so red. So just stick with 'hey'. Or if someone else answers, I'll say, 'hi, is Scott here, we're supposed to study'.

Oh shit. What if they think I'm one of his hook-ups? I don't look like the hook-up type. I look down at my grandpa sweater and mom jeans.

Ok, I think I can rule out the hookup insinuation.

I ring the doorbell this time.

And then I knock again after another minute.

I sit on the steps in front of the door.

His practice probably just ran late. I check my watch and the time is 9:34.

I notice noise coming from a house about three down. Maybe he gave me the wrong address. I know that all the hocky houses are on the same road, so that is a definite possibility.

I start walking towards the other house, by the time I get there its 9:38. Ok, this can't be the house. There is definitely some kind of party going on here.

"Rydell, I thought you said you didn't want to come to the party," I turn around on see the 106ers, Abby and Lily. "Did you get a ride with Sam?"

Sam asked me if I wanted to go to an upperclassman (junior and seniors only) party with the 106ers, but I told her I had to meet with Scott. Honestly, I wouldn't have gone even if I didn't have plans, who parties on a Sunday night?

"Oh. No, I'm not here to party. I'm supposed to be studying with Scott. I went to the house down there but, no one was home, so I thought maybe he gave me the wrong address." I hadn't realized the party Sam was going to be a hockey party.

Abby wiggles her eyebrows at me, "Don't worry, Sam told us all about your Facetime call with him this morning."

I roll my eyes and awkwardly laugh, "It's strictly academic. But based on the fact that I'm standing in front of a party instead of actually working on the project, it will probably end up being a very failed relationship of any sorts."

Lily's pushing me through the door. "Well, let's see if we can find him."

I'm through the door and I make eye contact with a very confused Sam.

"Lils no. Stop," I try to resist her push, "Seriously, I'm just gonna check his house one more time, maybe he stayed at practice late."

"No need, he's right there," she nods her head in his direction.

And sure enough, there's Prescott Bridges, sitting on the couch with his arms propped on each side and legs spread wide like he owns the place. On one side he has a blonde who has legs for days grasping onto the front of his shirt.

What was I thinking? I knew this was a bad idea as soon as I started thinking that we could be friends. We can never be friends.

But the girls would have so much fun on that field trip. They'd look so cute bundled up in there winter clothes, and he even said they'd teach them some hockey.

I can't jeopardize something that will make them happy. So, I'll do this project on my own and slap Scott's name on it.

Honestly that's probably what he was hoping for. We don't have to be friends. He'll get what he wants. And I'll get a fucking great field trip from those girls.

And with that, I make my way out of the door, and back to my car.

CHAPTER 10: *SCOTT*

Lindsay is annoying the shit out of me. She's being way too fucking touchy tonight, and I'm really not in the mood.

Practice sucked. The new freshmen aren't clicking with the team, so I'm stressed about that. Coach is mad at me because I haven't gotten them to the level, he wants them.

But that's his fucking job, I'm just here to get picked up by the Bruins.

At least Max is having a good time. He's leaning in close to a short, dark-haired Latina who looks extremely familiar.

"Wanna head upstairs?" I look over at Lindsay who is giving me major 'fuck me' eyes.

"I had a long day, I think I'm gonna finish this beer and head home." I take a swig.

"Leaving early again Scotty? Not a good look," McCombs says from the couch opposite of the one I'm on. He has a girl on his lap sucking on his neck.

"I don't really give a fuck about my look."

"Just saying man, also, I heard you scored that nerdy girl from Spanish. I knew you could do it."

"Rydell and I are equally doing this project-" fuck. Fuck, fuck, fuck. Holy shit. Rydell is coming over in- I pull out my phone to check the time.

9:40.

Shit, she's probably still there. I'll just say that I had to talk to some of the guys about practice.

I try to get up, but Lindsay is pulling my arm down, "Who's Rydell?"

"Someone I am late meeting. See ya."

Just as I'm about to exit the front door, the girl Max was talking to is in my face.

She's significantly shorter than me, so I'm looking down at her like she's a child having a temper tantrum.

"You were supposed to meet Del 10 minutes ago, and you're at a party drinking a beer and looking for a girl to take to bed. What the fuck is your problem?" Ooooh. This is the friend I've seen Rydell with.

"I'm only 10 minutes late, I'm going to meet her right now. She texted me like 5 minutes ago saying that she'd leave if I was 15 minutes late. I've got 5 minutes."

She laughs shortly, "Ya good luck with that, I just saw her speed walk out of here. And it's her, I want to throw myself in my bed, cocoon in my blankets, and read until I forget type speed walk."

Fuck. I jog out of the door, but before I get much farther the angry little one says, "You better fix this, Del is probably going to tell you that she'll do the project by herself but keep your name on it. I heard about your little proposition. She'd do anything for those girls. You make her do all the work, and I'll cut your balls off and shove them down your throat," she walks back into the house angrily typing on her phone.

I look towards my house, and sure enough I see a brunette in a grandpa sweater, going the pace of an Olympic speed walker back to her car.

Now I'm full-on running.

"Hey Books!"

She doesn't look back.

"Ry, wait up."

I don't know how it's possible, but I swear she picks up the pace.

"Rydell Rivens, will you stop for a second."

She turns around, "Don't use that tone with me. I'm not the one who skipped our *first* study session to party."

She spins around back towards her car. I jog in front of her.

"I'm sorry, ok. It slipped my mind; it won't happen again. I promise, it won't happen again."

"You're right. It won't happen again. Because I'm doing this project by myself."

"Wait-"

"Don't interrupt me, I'm not done talking." She doesn't even look mad when she says it, just disappointed and maybe a little sad. "I'm doing the project myself. I'll write out your part. In fact, I'll probably get it all written by the end of this week. I'll make the power point and find the outside sources we need. All you have to do it memorize it to some extent. I'll even write out your flashcards for you."

She tries to walk around me, so I put my hands on each of her shoulders. "Listen Books, I'm not letting you do this by yourself. I know you think I picked you just to have you do all the work and me get credit for it. But we would work well together. I mean, we've only known each other for a couple of days, and we are already kinda friends."

She looks down, "We aren't friends. Your friends are inside that party." She places her hands on my wrists and puts my hands back down to my side. "I'm sure they're wondering where you are."

"Rydell, it's only like 9:45, just come into my house, we have plenty of time."

"You're not going to go back on your deal, are you?"

"What?"

"The deal. The field trip? You aren't going to cancel it right? Because I'm technically still your partner." Her cheeks are red, and her voice sounds tight.

"Of course, I'm not going to cancel it. I'm an asshole, but I'm not that much of an asshole."

She opens her car door and looks back, "Alright, I should get you your part by Saturday. Enjoy the rest of the party." And then she's in her car and driving away.

And I'm sprinting to grab my keys and follow her.

CHAPTER 11: RYDELL

This is so stupid. Why am I getting so worked up over this? I knew that this was how it would play out. I just didn't know it would happen so early on. Am I really that forgettable? We literally talked this morning.

Breathe. You're driving. Don't start until you're done driving.

My hands are so tightly wrapped around the steering wheel that it hurts. My knuckles are white. My palms are clammy. My head hurts and there's a lump in my throat.

Luckily, my apartment is only about a 6-minute drive from Scott's house, so I'm already pulling into the complex.

I park. Turn off my car. And stare out the front window.

My breathing picks up but not to the point where I think I'll have a panic attack. The car ride calmed me down enough to avoid it.

I have always done a pretty good job at avoiding anxiety attacks in serious situations. I never get them in public or while driving, so that's a small blessing.

I brush a few of the stupid tears that

managed to slip down my cheeks and took a couple deep breathes, then reached over to the passenger seat to grab my backpack. Then text Sam saying I'm fine and she didn't need to leave the party because I didn't want to talk to anyone. She replies to text her hourly until I'm either asleep or she's back and if I say the word, she's there.

All of a sudden, there's a knock on my window and I fly two feet out of my seat and reach for my hydroflask in case I need to knock the shit out of someone.

"Just me, no need to make a scene," I hear the deep voice of the last person I want to see right now.

I unlock my car doors and Scott proceeds to open the door for me, "If I throw a stick, will you leave? How are you even here right now, you're really taking your stalker tendencies to the next level."

"One more chance Books. I promise you won't regret it."

I choke out a laugh and walk towards my front door, slinging my backpack onto both shoulders, "I really don't see why you're trying so hard here. You're getting exactly what you want. I already told you I would do all the work and you'd get credit for it. You just have to provide the field trip."

He grabs onto the top on my backpack and pulls me back, forcing me to turn around to face him. "That's not what I want."

I roll my eyes, "That's exactly what you want. That was what you wanted the moment you scouted me out in class."

"Maybe, but it's not what I want now."

"Alright. Why? Why are you so bent on contributing to this project?"

"I find you refreshing. You don't look at me like I'm some sort of trophy. You probably wouldn't go gossiping to all your friends if I left a party early." His hand hovers over my cheek like he's about to cup it, but then drops it back down to his side and looks down. "Were you crying? Did I make you cry?"

"I just yawned. You know, got tired of waiting for you." I turn back around and start walking again.

I open my front door, then turn around and lean on the doorframe, leaving Scott right outside the door.

"Right. I'm serious though. I don't want you doing all the work." He grabs my wrist and looks at my watch. "It's just about 10, how about you invite me it and we can work on a meeting schedule."

"You find me refreshing? You don't even know me."

"I know you don't eat breakfast. I know you like to read, but don't read with your glasses on. I know that your clumsy and like Star Wars. I know you work at an orphanage and care a lot about the girls you look after. That you're nice to just about everyone you meet and that you hate to say no. That you dress like a grandpa who likes playing chess on his free time and that you probably like lavender considering that you always seem to smell like it and there's a tattoo of it on your left shoulder."

"I knew stalker was a fitting name for you." I can feel my cheeks starting to heat up.

"I know you blush like crazy when people say nice things to you." This time when he raises his hand, he puts it on my cheek. His hands are freakishly large and he rests his palm just under my jaw and strokes my tinted cheeks with his thumb, dropping it again after he says, "I think it's cute."

I'm quiet for a second. And I know I'll probably regret it, but I say, "One more chance. And if you do a bad job, you'll be locked in here with the cockroaches, for two weeks without food and water." I quote *The Goonies*.

He laughs and steps back, "Excuse me, what?"

"Mouth. From *The Goonies?* When he translates instructions for the housekeeper?"

"What in the world is a goonie?"

This time I take a step back and gasp, "*The Goonies?* 1985, family adventure movie? Josh Brolin? Sean Austin? Only the best filmed created of all time."

He walks into my apartment, past me, like he owns the place. I lock the door, put my backpack down while taking my shoes off, and follow him to the couch. "Well, now you're telling lies. The best film of all time is *Step Brothers.*"

"How would you know? You've never seen *Goonies*, I've seen both." I sit down next to him, crossing my legs under me, leaving room for Jesus as I do so.

"Well, I guess we'll have to watch it," he says as he leans forward to grab the remote.

"We have a schedule to make."

"Do you have anything to do tomorrow morning?"

I shake my head no.

"Perfect, it's only 10." He turns the TV on.

I sigh and stand up to grab the container of

movies we have in one of the sections of our TV stand. "It's not on Netflix or anything, but I have a copy," I'll never skip the opportunity to watch *The Goonies.*

CHAPTER 12: SCOTT

"Down here, it's our time. It's our time down here," Rydell quotes, and I look at her side profile in amusement. She is totally nerding out over this movie, and I love how comfortable she is being around me.

She looks over at me, "You're not even watching," and throws her head back on the couch, then looks back over.

"Sorry," I look back at the screen trying so hard not to laugh. But a grin is poking out and I look back at her.

She points at the screen, "Pivotal moment Scott." And looks back at the TV.

She just called me Scott. "You just called me Scott."

Not taking her eyes of the movie she responds, "That is your name isn't it."

"Yes, but you've only ever called my Prescott."

She looks back over at me, head still resting on the couch, "Well, if you prefer Prescott, I'll gladly continue calling you that. Or I could just stick with stalker."

"Nope. Scott or Scotty will do. We are

friends now after all." I think back to her telling me the complete opposite. "We are friends, right?"

"I haven't decided yet." Her eyes are back on the screen, "Now stop looking at me stalker and watch the movie."

~

"No way, that can't be true," Rydell is laughing and holding onto her stomach.

"I swear to God. He didn't even ask what was going on, he just walked out of my room, and the next day my older sister is laughing at me because my dad called and asked her to put my google to private browser. It was one of his company computers and he didn't want anyone at work seeing it. Might taint his image," I chuckle.

"I can't believe he didn't say anything about you jerking off to google searched boobs," she's trying to calm herself down, but she's laughing to the point that her eyes are tearing up and her face is turning red. And I'm laughing because she's laughing so hard. And I can't take my eyes off her because my god that smile is gorgeous.

"My parents would be mortified if little 7th grade me was looking up penis pics, they'd probably lock me in the room for the rest of my life."

"Well, your parents probably actually care about you," I try to joke.

This gets her laughing to stop and she looks at me for a few seconds, still with that pretty smile on her face before saying, "What makes you think your parents don't care about you?"

Oh shit. Now it's getting serious. It's about 1 in the morning. After the movie finished, we started talking about it. Got into a heated argument about whether it's the best movie in the entire world.

It's a good movie, but not the best in the world. That statement did not sit well with Rydell.

And then we just started talking. Mainly about childhood stories since she said this movie was, and I quote, 'her entire childhood'. That's how we got on the subject of my dad walking in on me masturbating to boobs in 7th grade.

Throughout the entire conversation, everything's felt so natural. Like I don't have to try so hard to be this perfect person around her. I can just be myself without being scared that I'll be judged for it.

"They were always working when I was growing up. Going on business trips and whatnot. Never really around the house. I had a nanny up until I was maybe 13. My sister was 15 and then they fired her because they figured we were capable of managing ourselves. Plus, they didn't want their work friends to find out that their kids were being raised by another person. The chef always made meals, so it's not like we totally had to fend for ourselves," I sigh and look over at her.

She's not looking at me with pity, so I continue, "Everything's material to them. They think that buying me fancy cars and taking private jets to Cabo for vacation would keep my sister and I content. I think I really just wanted to eat dinner with them a couple times a week or go to the movie theaters with them every now and then. Maybe celebrate my birthday with me for once."

"You had a chef and private jet."

I laugh, glad she isn't just feeling sorry for me.

"Kidding," she says, "You said you have a sister, do you think she loves you?"

"I think so. Growing up we were always super close. It was hard to have friends when your parents weren't there to take you to birthday parties or playdates. So, we hung out with each other all the time. Then she got a boyfriend and started sneaking out of the house. And then she left for college. The moment she left the house was the moment I felt the most alone."

I'm looking up at the ceiling. God, why the fuck am I telling her all this. I sound so stupid right now, so I add, "Not that it matters though. I'm great fucking company, being by myself isn't bad."

"I don't think anyone ever really wants to be alone. It's not a bad think to admit that you didn't like being by yourself Scott. I don't think it makes you any less of a person to admit something like that."

I look at her for a second to find her already looking at me. Then look back up, "Really, it wasn't a big deal. Nothing I wasn't used to. I found some good ways to distract myself".

"Like masturbating to google searched boobs?" she jokes.

"No, I upgraded to the real thing by the time my sister left. I mean look at me, what girl wouldn't want to show me her boobs?"

She punches my arm, "T.M.I. Well, for a person who grew up lonely, I'd say you're doing pretty great. Everyone on campus talks about you. How you'll go pro this year, how you're like the coolest guy ever, if you're at a party, everyone else wants to be there. People really seem to love you."

"Ya, maybe not for the right reasons though."

"What do you mean?"

"People love me because they want to be me or sleep with me or use me in some type of way. They want to party with me because they want to upgrade their status. They talk about me going pro and how cool that is because they like to think that they're friends with someone famous. It's all an act."

"Well. I don't know much about hockey, and I don't really keep up with the team at all." She pauses, "Sorry. Hockey's just not really my thing. But... I think you'll do great things. People might put on an act, but you're a good guy Scott. You might not want people to think so, but I see right through you. If you were a bad person, you wouldn't be sitting on this couch with me right now."

I can't remember the last time I had such a genuine conversation. Most people would bring the conversation back to themselves. Try to say that they relate and that they had problems growing up too. Then I would have to comfort them, like I'm not completely breaking inside.

But Rydell actually seems interested in getting to know me. Not just the hockey me, but the things that make me who I am.

"How do you know I won't just stop talking to you the minute this project is over?"

"I don't. Are you going to stop talking to me the minute this project is over?" She raises an eyebrow.

I really don't think there's anything that could stop me from talking to her. I've never had a person to talk to like this. I mean I have the guys on the team, they're my friends. But they aren't like this.

"I haven't decided yet," I mimic her from

earlier. "Are we friends?" I ask for the second time tonight.

I look towards her and she rests her head on the couch to look at the ceiling, "Ya. Ya, we're friends."

CHAPTER 13: *RYDELL*

October 9th is World's Post Day, so I stick a thank you note with handmade cookies in the mailbox for our mailman as I head out to my car.

Today I'm going over to the orphanage to plan Halloween costumes with the girls.

I know October 9th seems a little early to start planning but mostly all the girl's costumes are handmade because we don't have the budget for new costumes every year.

And it's a lot of work to make 23 costumes.

As I walk into the front of the orphanage it's about 3 pm so the girls should be home from school any second. I go to the holiday closet and start pulling things out.

You know how you have that closet in your house that's filled to max capacity with random shit, well, that's what we call the holiday closet at the orphanage.

We like to make every holiday as special as possible, so we have decorations for basically everything: Halloween, Easter, 4th of July, literally everything.

And we have a lot of costumes from past years, or at least items that can be used for multiple different costumes, so I take out that box, hoping that most girls will want something that we already have.

Sexy Back by Justin Timberlake fills my ears just as I'm putting down the boxes.

I know it's Scott calling because last week during our first study session that he was actually on time for, he grabbed my phone and changed it.

So, I grabbed his phone and changed my ringtone to the *Star Wars* theme song, so that every time I called him (which isn't very often; he's usually the one calling me) people would figure out that Scott is lowkey a nerd.

And he really is a little nerd. In the past two weeks of talking to Scott, we've definitely become friends. I know I told myself that I wouldn't, but I figure there's nothing wrong with a platonic friendship.

Plus, after the night he told me everything about his parents and how lonely he's felt his whole life, I really think that Scott needs a friend. A real friend, one that he can rely on and talk to when he's feeling bad.

Anyways, in the two weeks of knowing Scotty, I found out that he not only likes *Star Wars*, but he's also read and watched all the *Harry Potter* books and movies.

"Prescott, I'm a little busy at the moment so can you make this quick."

"Ry, I could be on the side of the road dying right now, and you're telling me to make it quick, and here I thought we were besties."

"Well, are you on the side of the road dying."

"No. But this is important. Also, you didn't

deny my bestie comment so I'm taking it that I've officially surpassed Sam for that title."

Sam and Scott have a love-hate relationship. They are actually very similar personality wise, but they are always in some petty argument whenever Scott is nearby. Usually about who's my best friend. I always say Sam. "Please don't tell me that you can't make the session tonight, because I already packed all my things to head straight to the library after work." I shift the phone so that it's being supported by the side on my face a shoulder so that I can look through the costume box.

"I can make it, but we have to switch locations. The library is holding some job fair tonight, so it'll be loud and crowded. Figured we can just do it at my place."

So far, Scott and I have had two session: both at the library. And in the time span of those two sessions, we have also sat together every Spanish class, had lunch a handful of times after class, gotten coffee before class, and he even came over to the apartment to drop off my notebook he accidently took. When he came over, he ended up staying and watching the Bachelorette with Sam and I.

I mean, he complained through the whole thing, but he said that the drama was addicting and when he didn't have practice, he expects an invite to our watch parties.

And in the span of the two weeks, he has not only talked and hung out with Sam, but also the 106ers. He knows all my friends.

I have not once met his friends or been to his house. I mean, I've been outside his house, but that's not the same thing.

And honestly, his friends are a bit intimidating, so I say, "I don't mind doing it at my apartment."

"That's ok, you're all environmental right? This way, we'll be eco by not using as much gas. You have to drive anyways because you're not home. I'll already be home."

I snort, "Sounds to me like you're just lazy."

"Me? Never."

All of a sudden, the door burst open and there's three small children running my way. "Ok, I'll be over at like 7, I'll pick up some burritos or something, got to go, bye." I hang up.

"Del, tell Rosie that only one of us can be a zombie princess. There isn't room for two." Sophie exclaims as she clings to my leg.

I look down and set my hand on top of Soph's head, "Both of you can be zombie princesses. If you wear different color dresses and I do your makeup differently it won't be the same zombie."

"Nooooo," she let's go on my leg and runs towards Rosie, "we'll fight to the death. Whoever survives gets to be the zombie princess." She goes to tackle Rosie, and I catch her mid-air slinging one hand around her waist, just before she tackles her.

"Sophie Ray," oh ya, I pulled out the middle name, "that is no way to treat your friend. Don't you remember last year when you first got here, and Rosie asked if you wanted to do matching bee costumes because you were sad that the older girls didn't want you to be cats with them. You were so sad; how do you think you're making Rosie feel?"

"Sad," I let go of my grip on her.

"Right. It's not very nice to make people feel that way, is it?"

"No. I'm sorry Rosie, we can match again this year. What color dress do you want?"

They go off and I head over to Kendall who went straight to her shared room.

I lean on the doorframe, "How was school?"

She's smiling a bit, "It wasn't terrible."

"How's Ryan?" I wiggle my eyebrows at her.

Ryan is the boy that Ken has a massive crush on. And I know for a fact that those feelings are reciprocated. One time I took Kendall out to help me grocery shop and we bumped into him. Both of their faces were bright red.

She laughs a little, "His mom made cookies last night and he brought me a whole Tupperware of them. Guess what kind they are."

"Snickerdoodle?" that's her favorite.

"Yes, snickerdoodle. He said he remembered how much I liked them and asked his mom to get all the stuff for it."

"That's pretty freaking cute. I told you he liked you."

"Ya, until he finds out that I'm an orphan." Kendall doesn't tell anyone this little fact. She asked me to pretend to be her sister whenever we're near people from her school. And since she's one of two high school students we have at the orphanage, it's not hard for her to hide it.

"I don't think Ryan's that shallow Kenny. Maybe you can invite him to the Halloween carnival when we go?"

Every year the town throws a Halloween Carnival for the Halloween weekend (so Friday, Saturday and Sunday) and we always take the girls on the Friday. The city gives us free admission.

"Absolutely not, I'd rather shoot myself in the foot," she flops onto her bed.

I walk over and sit down next to her, "Growing up here isn't something to be ashamed of. It doesn't make you any less of a person."

"Like you'd know. Your parents didn't abandon you," there's the moody Kendall I know.

I ignore her comment, "What you went through. What you go through. Most people will never experience. I think it makes you all the stronger. You grew up in a non-ideal situation and turned out to be a pretty fucking cool person. A cool person who got invited to an art program at UCLA. Who got a 5 on her AP exam and 1430 on her SAT. You're going to do great things Ken."

"I'm telling Ms. Michelle that you said fucking," she jokes. The mood swings on this girl are so hard to keep up with.

"Don't you dare, that women scares me. But I'm serious Kendall. Don't let how you grew up dictate your life. Now, how about you help me make some costumes. I'll even let you have first pick. All though we better hurry because we already have fights over who gets to be zombie princess, hope that's not the one you wanted."

CHAPTER 14: SCOTT

"Come on Jacobs get your shit together. Bridges position your teams," my coach is screaming from the sidelines.

"Jacobs, get your head outta your ass and stay on Hinders," I shout. We're having a scrimmage, I'm playing center for both sides, trying to manage both teams at once, and now being yelled at by my coach.

Webbs passes to me and I shoot towards the goal that Max is guarding. He blocks it, "Nice one Ruddy," Coach Jerry cheers.

Coach Jerry is our assistant coach. He used to play for the team about 5 years ago and played pro for a couple years before tearing his ACL. He plays good cop.

Coach Michaels is head coach. He's in his mid 40s and played for the Bruins. He plays bad cop, "You could've made that Bridges."

I look at the timer right as it rings and we all skate back towards the bench.

"Jacobs, you're skating like a preschooler, what was that fall you took? That happens in a game and you could lose it for the rest of the team. McCombs, your shots are weak. Ruddy, you let some easy pucks get through you. We have our first pre-season game coming up next week and you guys are acting like you've never played together before. 20 full length sprints before you go, and Bridges I want you to work with Jacobs on passes after."

I love being captain, and I love being responsible for this team. But I fucking hate working late with people. I'm selfish. I work late by myself, but it annoys the shit out of me when I have to stay late because of another person.

It's almost 6 right now. By the time sprints are done and everyone's off the ice, I'll be like 6:30, then I'll stay with Jacobs for like 15, so by the time I get out of here, it'll be like 7.

I was supposed to be home by 6:30. Rydell will be at my house at 7.

Once sprints are done Webbs claps me on the back, "See ya at the house".

"Hey, wait. Rydell is supposed to be there at 7, but I don't think I'll get out of her until then. If I'm not there, will you tell her I shouldn't be long. I'll shoot her a text after I finish up with Jacobs."

"Ooooo, finally. The mysterious Rydell Rivens that's taking up all of my boy's free time is coming over. You gonna be a little freak in the sheets tonight? It's been a while."

I shove his arm with enough force that he trips on his skates a bit. "If you're fucking vulgar with her, or if you do or say anything inappropriate, I'll make sure you never get laid again."

"Alright, chill. I'm joking. I know you guys are just partners for a project."

"We are partners. But she's also my friend and Davies friend, so just be fucking nice."

"Ollie's friends with this chick too? No wonder he gets defensive every time she's brought up."

Like he knows we're talking about him, Oliver skates up, "Every time who gets brought up?"

I say, "no one" at the same time Asher says, "Rydell."

"What about Del?"

"She's coming over at 7 for a study session, but since I have to work with Jacobs, I'll probably be a bit late. I was just asking Webbs to be nice to her and explain the situation when she gets there."

"Oh, I can hang with her until you get back. I have a couple questions about a computer science exam anyways." I'm sure he does.

"Maybe Davies is the one who will get freaky with her."

"Will you shut the fuck up," I retort. "I don't know how many times I need to say this, but Del is just my friend."

Jacobs skates up to me, "Hey man, sorry you have to stay late because of me. I'll try to make this as quick and painless as possible for you. I just had a rough night."

Jacobs is a sophomore and being captain, I know a bit about him. I know that he tries to balance a part time job with practice and schoolwork. I know he picks up as many shifts as he can and sends most the money back to his family. And I know that the only reason he goes to this school is because they gave him a full ride to play hockey.

So, if he fucks up hockey, he loses said scholarship and then he's probably royally screwed.

Any other person gave any excuse like that,

and I'd have some not so nice things to say. But I understand Jacobs situation. "No worries man. I know you're working late shifts, but sleep is important, especially with the amount of training we do. Get more sleep."

We drill for more than 15 minutes, I give him some pointers, tell him what he needs to work on, and then give him a set of exercises he can do without me. "Maintenance will be here in like 20-30 minutes, once they get here, call it a night."

I take the fastest shower of my life, and by the time I get in the car it's 7:10, but I've already sent Ry a message explaining everything, so we should be fine.

CHAPTER 15: RYDELL

stalker to me: *Have to stay a little late, shouldn't be any later than 7:15. Oliver, Asher, and Max will probably all be there. Don't be afraid of them, they don't bite...hard. And don't just sit in your car until I get there, they know you're coming so they'll think it's weird.*

me to stalker: *ok. How do you know how hard they bite? What kinda kinky shit are you guys up to, I bet it happens in the locker room, right? Should I get them food?*

stalker to me: *oh ya, there's always orgies going on in the locker rooms. Don't buy them food, they can fend for themselves*

Ah shit. I'm in line for burritos right now. Do I get them something? I feel bad if they are just watching as we eat burritos. What am I supposed to talk about with them? Well, Oliver will be there, so it shouldn't be that bad. I'll just ask him if he's ready for the computer science exam.

I order 8 burritos. They are good sized burritos, but I don't know how much they eat, so I figure if they're still hunger after one, they could share another one.

Oh fuck, what if they don't like burritos? Should I grab some tacos too?

I go back up to the cashier and get 3 chicken tacos and 3 beef.

~

It's 6:58 by the time I pull into Scott's driveway, and their mailman is stopping at the same time I park.

Oh my gosh, I wonder if he knows it's World's Post Day. I grab the food out of the back and make my way towards the mailbox.

"Good evening. Did you know it's World's Post Day? I think mail people have such a cool job. I mean letters and packages come from all over the world and think about how happy it makes people to get said letters and packages, I know I love it. I appreciate all the work you do." I'm totally rambling, but I get nervous talking to strangers and this mailman is looking at me like I'm crazy.

"Yep, it's an interesting job. I didn't know that it was World's Post Day. Maybe I'll grab a slice of pizza on the way home to celebrate," he smiles at me.

I smile back and just kinda stand there, "Ooh, pizza's good. But I have extra food here. Do you want a taco or burrito?"

"A burrito actually sounds pretty good right now."

I hand one over and wish him a nice rest of the night and then stand in front of the door. I should ring. Or knock? No definitely ring.

Before I do either, the door flies open and very tall, very attractive guy greets me, "Did you just give our mailman a burrito?"

He's blonde and tall, "Were you watching me through the window?" I question.

"Touché come on in, Scott should be here soon. Don't worry, he asked me to be on my best behavior."

"It's World's Post Day," I blurt out and I follow him into the kitchen, setting down the bag of food.

"Huh?" he looks at me from the other side of the counter.

"Today is World's Post Day, so I was telling him how appreciative I am of postal services, and I had extra food, so I asked if he wanted a burrito."

"That's an actual thing? World's Post Day? How did you even know that?"

"Webbs will you leave her alone. Hi Del," Oliver walks into the kitchen with another super attractive tall guy who has ginger/brown hair.

"Hi Oliver and…."

"Hi, I'm Max Rudderford," he introduces himself, "And I'm sure this heathen didn't introduce himself to you."

Oh. My. God. Max Rudderford has been a pretty hot topic in mine and Sam's apartment. A couple weeks ago they hooked up and went for ice cream after. Sam deleted Tinder and hasn't had a one-night stand since which says a lot. But apparently, they both decided beforehand that it would strictly be a no strings attached, one-time thing and I don't think they've talked since.

The one who let me in sticks his hand out and in a British accent says, "Oh my apologies. How very rude of me. I am Sir Asher Webbs."

I take his hand and open my mouth to introduce myself, but Asher cuts me off, "Holy shit, your hands are so soft." He puts my hand up to his cheek.

"Ummm thank you," I slowly pull my hand back to my side. I'm sure my cheeks are tinted with some pink. "I look up national holiday's every day and write them on my whiteboard. And if it's something fun, I'll celebrate it. Oh, like September 28th was National Drink a Beer Day, so I went to the bar." They're staring at my now and it's making me nervous.

"And yesterday was National Fluffernutter Day. I had no idea what that was, so I looked it up, turns out it's a peanut butter sandwich with marshmallows. So, I went to the store for marshmallows and made one. Not my favorite, but it was fun to try," they're still all just looking at me.

I look down and realize that there's a bag of food. My rambling has mainly stopped and Asher steps in to say, "You're a weird one." Oliver punches his arm.

I continue to look down and bite the inside of my cheek, "Sorry, I tend to ramble. But... I brought you guys some food. I didn't know what you guys like but I was already at the Taco Shop and thought that you can't go wrong with burritos. I mean, what kind of psychopath doesn't like burritos, am I right? But then I was worried that you wouldn't like burritos and grabbed some tacos too."

"Thank you Rydell, that was very thoughtful of you. I think I speak for all of us when I say that burritos are the shit," Oliver says, and I'm grateful that he's here.

"Oh right. I'm Rydell by the way," I look towards Max and Asher. "Most people just call me Del though." I smile.

"Del. Perfect, I'll call you Deli, like a sandwich shop," Asher exclaims as he grabs a burrito. Great. The uber attractive hockey player nicknamed me after a sandwich shop. Yay me.

"So, what's up with you and our boy Scotty?" Max asks casually.

"We're working on a Spanish Project together. I didn't want to work with him at first because I'm super busy. But he was very persistent."

"Yep. Scotty tends to have that effect on girls," Asher chimes in.

My eyes widen and I know my cheeks are full on red now, "No. Nope, you've got the wrong idea. Scott and I are strictly Spanish partners. We aren't sleeping together or anything."

"Your cheeks say differently. Hey, I'm not judging or anything. Scott might actually like you. He tells us all the time that you're his new bestie," oh my gosh. I'm absolutely mortified.

"Webbs, will you shut the fuck up. She wouldn't stoop to Scotty's level. Right Del?" Oliver says.

"Scott and I are friends. But that's it. Friends and Spanish partners. I mean, I'm pretty sure we're friends. What do you mean by might actually like me?" I hope Scott and I are friends. I mean, the past two weeks everything has felt like a friendship.

"I'm just saying you're not the type he usually goes for."

The front door opens.

CHAPTER 16: SCOTT

I get out of my car and jog to the mailbox before I head inside. I notice that Rydell's car is parked, so I speed up to make sure she's all right in there.

Asher is a wild card. I could easily see him joking around and making her uncomfortable. I know Max and Oliver will be nice to her and for once, I'm glad that Oliver is friends with her. It probably makes her feel a bit better.

In the last two weeks of getting to know Rydell, I've learned that she's a pretty anxious person. And she has her tells for when she feels nervous. Her cheeks get red, she puts her hand on her wrist, she rambles a lot.

I'm just hoping I didn't put her in a situation that'll make her feel like that.

On the top of our letters there's a post-it note that says, 'thanks for the burrito'. Weird.

As I walk through the front door, I set my things down and walk towards the kitchen. Still looking down at the mail I ask, "Did one of you give the mailman a burrito?"

I look up, and Rydell is standing in the middle of the kitchen. Red face, hand on her wrist.

Fuck.

"You ok?" I walk over to her and brush some hair out of her face.

"I'm ok. Sorry, I gave your mailman a burrito, it's World's Post Day," of course she did. Yesterday she forced be to take a bite of her fluffy something sandwich. It was disgusting.

I look towards the guys who are watching us carefully. Davies and Ruddy are sitting at the barstools behind the counter and Webbs is leaning on the counter eating a burrito.

"I told you not to get them food," I sigh. It really doesn't surprise me that she did, but I'm mad that she spent the money on them. I walk over and grab a burrito for myself, "How much was it, I'll venmo you."

"No need, I had a free burrito to cash in on my punch card. Plus, they gave me three stamps on a new one."

"Ya but you bought more than one burrito, and why'd you get tacos? I'll send you 20."

"I wasn't sure if they liked burritos, so I got tacos to be safe. And I'll just decline the payment so you shouldn't even bother."

I groan, "Was everyone here nice to you. They didn't say anything to upset you did they." Her face isn't as red anymore and her hand has left her wrist. I shoot daggers towards Webbs who puts his hands up in surrender.

"Oh no, everyone was very nice. I probably just annoyed them a bit though with my rambling."

"You didn't annoy us, I liked hearing about your obsession with national holidays. In fact, I think we should get a whiteboard and start doing it here," Max exclaims.

I hand her a burrito, "We can take this up to my room, I'm sure they're going to the living room to play video games or some shit."

I watch Webbs wiggle his eyebrows at her and her face goes back to being red. "You head on up, walk up the stairs and my room is the first on the right, I'm just gonna grab a beer."

She nods and starts walking towards my room.

When I know she can't hear me in a whisper-yell I say, "What the fuck did you say to her?"

"Nothing, she just told us about her national holidays."

"Don't bullshit me Asher, she looked so fucking uncomfortable when I got here." I look towards Max and Oliver who are leaving to go to the living room, "Hey, you guys are a part of this conversation too."

"Dude, Webbs is the one that let her in, I was nice, I am friends with her after all," Oliver claims.

"Do you really think I said anything mean?" Max asks.

"No, but I want you here to tell me if Webbs is telling the truth. What'd he say to make her that nervous."

"I said nothing," I give him a look. "Fine. I may have insinuated that the two of you are sleeping together."

"He also called her weird," Max says with a smirk.

"What the fuck dude, that was totally unnecessary to bring up. And I meant it in a cute weird way. Not in a freak weird way."

I shove at his chest, "What the hell is your problem, I specifically told you to be nice to her and you tell her that she's weird. Ry isn't weird. She just doesn't have the personality of a cardboard box like most of the girls you're used to. If you don't have anything nice to say to her, don't fucking say anything."

He starts to laugh, "Oh god, this is so good. Scotty's got himself a little crush. I knew you were fucking her."

I'm so compelled to punch him right now, but I'm guessing that would scare Rydell and it could get me taken off the team, "I'm not sleeping with her. But she is my friend. I'm protective of her, the same way I'm protective of you three," I calm myself down, but my fist is so clenched that my knuckles are turning white, "Do you think I would sit there and be ok if someone was shit talking you. Because I wouldn't, I would be just as pissed."

"I was just having a little fun. I didn't say anything that I thought would actually offend her. She seems nice enough, but I wouldn't get attached. You two are very different people."

I'm officially done with this conversation and I've kept Rydell waiting long enough so I say, "Whatever," and stock up the stairs.

CHAPTER 17: RYDELL

When I walked into Scott's room, my eyes went straight to his desk. Underneath it, an assortment of books were poking out and around it were movie dvds pinned to the wall.

I knew Scott liked movies a lot, but I didn't realize the extent to it. As I look around, there's movie references everywhere. Not only are their dvds scattered around, but there's also posters and movie tickets all over the wall.

I sit down on his swivel desk and twirl around. I don't want him to walk in on me snooping. Plus, it's none of my business to go looking through his room.

My mind wanders to Asher thinking that Scott and I are sleeping together. Is that what everyone thinks? Girls can be friends with guys without it meaning anything. Boy-girl friendships aren't that uncommon.

And then he said I wasn't Scott's type. I'm not sure if that was meant to be an insult or not. I mean, he did call me weird.

Not that I'm concerned about being Scott's type or anything.

About 5 minutes later Scott walks in.

Without the beer he was down there for, "Where's your beer?"

His eyes widen a bit, "Decided against it."

"Alright," I shift through my bag and pull out my laptop, ignoring that he was down there for 5 minutes to grab a beer… and came back up without said beer. "So, I made the PowerPoint last night. I know we still have like 2 weeks, but I think we should get the PowerPoint done this week, that way we can focus on memorizing our speeches next week."

"Sure. Whatever you want." He sits down on his bed.

"I knew you liked movies, but your room is giving me major film nerd vibes."

"Ya well, when you have neglective parents there's not a whole lot to do. I guess I just turned to movies," he sighs and rests his back on the headboard of his bed and stretches his legs out in front of him. "The movie theatres let me escape all that shit. In fact, most years I go to the theatre for my birthday by myself. I decide which movie will be the best for my birth month, and since my birthday is on the 23rd, I see it on that day."

"What month's your birthday in?" I question.

He looks towards me with a small smile, "November."

"Well, our Spanish project will be over by then, but maybe I could go with you this year," wait maybe going by himself is tradition. I can't just invite myself to hang out with him on his birthday. "If you'd want the company. I mean, if you like going by yourself or if there's other people you want to go with I don't want to intru-"

"Ry. It would make me very happy if you came to see a movie with me on my birthday. And we're besties now. We'll still be friends once the project is over."

"Are movies the only thing you ever do for your birthday?"

"My birthday is never a big deal to me. I think my parents have remembered it maybe 4 times. My sister used to always get me a cupcake, but I haven't seen her much since she went to college. She always sends me a text though."

"Well, your parents seem like assholes so that really doesn't surprise me. You don't do anything with your teammates or friends?"

"My only friends are my teammates. Well, and now you. I've never told them when my birthday is. They know I don't like to celebrate it."

I look at him with a blank face. I never want Scott to think that I pity him. I've gotten used to those looks and they always make me feel like shit. "You don't like to celebrate it because your parents always forgot about it," it's not a question, "maybe if you find the right people to celebrate it with, it could be something to look forward to."

He looks towards the ceiling, "Maybe," we're both quiet for a few seconds, "Tell me about your parents. I mean it's only fair. You know all about how shitty mine are."

"Ok. But then we seriously need to get to work," it's already almost 8. "What do you wanna know?"

"Anything. Everything."

"Well, both my parents are pretty young. They had my older brother by the time they turned 20, they were 22 when they had me. Growing up, I always knew what a relationship should be like because I had them as a perfect example of it. They are so in love with each other," I shake my head and look down. "They've been together since high school and are still such a strong couple. My dad comes from a family who is financially very well set off for themselves. His parents gave him everything he wanted." I look up at Scott, "kinda like you. Everything was always material and not so much affection. He doesn't really have a relationship with his parents, but we see them every once in a while." I don't want to get on the topic of my grandparents because it might send me into a panic attack.

"My mom comes from a family who lived paycheck to paycheck. She had to work for everything. She grew up with 3 older brothers who were very protective of her. My mom knew from a pretty young age that she'd have to get a scholarship if she wanted to go to college. That she'd have to get a part-time job as soon as she turned old enough to get a car and save for her future. So as soon as she turned 15, she started working as a lifeguard at the aquatic center that was only about a mile from her house. That's where she met dad." I smile and look towards Scott to see if he's still interested in the story.

"Keep going," he encourages me.

"My dad went to the private school in their town. My mom went to the public school. And my dad passed by the public pool one day in high school and he said as soon as he saw her, he was in love." I laugh, "Of course, my dad wasn't allowed to go to the public pool because my grandparents thought it was dirty and there was no need since they had a pool in their backyard, so my dad would sneak out to go the pool to see her." I look back towards him and he nods.

"My dad asked her to go to a party with him one day and she said yes and that same night he asked her to be his girlfriend and she said yes again.

"And my dad was out of the house whenever he could be to spend time with her. About a year into their relationship, my dad's parents started to pay attention to him and realized he was never home. When they found out why, they were pissed. They didn't think my mom was suitable. I mean they called her trash right to her face the first time they met.

"My dad is a pretty hot-headed person, so he cursed them out and left the house. He had a trust fund from his grandparents and lived off that for the rest of high school and all through college because my grandparents told him that he was no son of theirs as long as my mom was in the picture. They only started talking to him when my brother was born and didn't want to miss out on watching their grandkids grow up. But my dad hasn't forgiven them, and he tries to keep us away from them as much as he can. I think I've seen my grandparents about 10 times in my life. And every time, it's been a disaster," I suck in a breath and try not to think about it.

"What about your mom's parents?" I'm glad that Scott redirects the conversation.

"My mom's parents are great. My grandma is probably one of my best friends. We grew up very close to them. And they were very supportive of my parent's relationship. I mean, my uncles were hesitant and lots of threats were thrown from their side. But now, my dad is best friends with all of them. My dad's trust fund ran out when he turned like 25, so my mom's dad got him a job at the car shop he worked at. And they helped them watch me and my siblings when they were working. Without my mom's parents, things would've been a lot harder for them."

"What do your parent's do for a living now?" I've never had anyone so interested in my life before and I'm definitely not complaining about it.

"My mom's a nurse and my dad is the manager at the car shop," I'm not embarrassed by my parents jobs, but I know that Scott's family owns some successful PVC Pipe company and I'm scared he'll look down on me for it.

"You have 4 siblings, right?" We've talked a little bit about my family before but not this much.

"Yep, 3 brothers, 1 sister."

"I wish I grew up with more siblings. Did you like having a big family?" he runs his hand through his hair.

I tilt my head and look at him swiveling in the chair a bit, "You're full of questions today."

I swear his cheeks turn the slightest shade of pink, "Sorry, we can start working on the project."

"No," I jump up a little, "no, I love talking about my family, I guess I'm just surprised that you want to hear me talk about them."

"I like hearing you talk. Plus, it seems like you really love them, and you get this smile I don't see often when they're brought up."

Now it's my turn to get pink cheeks. Just friends, I remind myself. "I do love them a lot. You know, I used to be so embarrassed growing up with so many siblings, but now it's something that I'm very grateful for."

"Why is a big family embarrassing?"

I sigh, "Growing up my life was hand-me-downs, thrift stores, and craigslist minivans. Nothing in my house was ever new. I had to get a job when I turned 15. And people made fun of me for it."

"Why would anyone make fun of you for something like that?"

"The schools that I went to were public, but we lived in an area that had a lot of wealthy people. So, when I came to school in a minivan that looked like it was about to shut down and everyone else was rolling up in Range Rovers, my family always stuck out. People are judgmental."

"That's fucked up".

"It is. But once I got to high school I grew out of being embarrassed. I loved having so many siblings because there was never a dull moment with them, I didn't feel lonely when I was with them. And I knew that my parents were trying their best to provide for us, I didn't ever want to seem ungrateful for that. And I fucking love my thrift store clothes. Do you know how many good, unique items I've found there? And now it's a trend to thrift shop, so I guess you could say I'm a trendsetter," I flip my hair.

Scott laughs, "Ya, your clothes are cool. Even the ugly grandpa sweater."

"Hey! My grandpa sweater is cute and comfortable."

Scott sits up and shifts so that he's sitting on the edge of his bed facing me, with his legs dangling off the side, "Sure, whatever you say."

"Take that back."

"Make me."

I smile at him, "Well, your boat shoes are hideous." Scott always wears those typical frat boy, pretentious looking boat shoes and those are actually ugly.

He gasps, "Take that back."

I smirk towards him, "Make me."

He has a mischievous glint in his eye as he jumps to his feet and lunges towards me.

CHAPTER 18: SCOTT

"Make me," Rydell mimics what I said a second ago. She's smiling and there's a small dimple poking out on the left side of her chin.

I pounce off my spot on the bed and lunge to grab her around the waist. I lift her up so that she's over my shoulder.

"Prescott Bridges put me down," she screeches.

"I don't think I should, the view is pretty great," and it really is. She's wearing a tight plaid skirt and her ass is right in my line of vision.

She pinches my side and I throw her on the bed crawling on top of her to tickle her sides.

"Scott, seriously," she's breathing heavy and her laugh fills up my room. And I wish I could record it and listen to it all the time, "I'm going to pee," she struggles to get her words out.

"Tell me my shoes aren't hideous."

"Never," her face is bright red and I continue to attack her sides. "Scott," she laughs. She tries to say more, but she's laughing too hard to get it out.

"You know what you have to say."

"Fine, fine," she exclaims, "your shoes aren't

hideous." I stop the tickling and realize the position we're in. I'm still hovering over her with my legs on either side of her waist. "Just a little ugly, apparently like my grandpa sweater," she whispers catching her breathe and trying not to laugh.

Her hair is spread out around her and the light from my bedside lamp puts a soft glow on her face. She lifts her hands up to try and push me off her.

I grab her wrists and lean down a bit further, "I was lying," my voice lowers, "I think you look pretty fucking cute in that sweater."

Her smile is slowly fading, and her breathing is still picked up. And I'm scared I've made her nervous, so I climb off her and say, "We should probably get started on the project," with a forced chuckle.

I don't want to lose Rydell's friendship. I can't lose it. And if I kiss her like I so badly want to right now, our friendship will be ruined. Because it will only be a hookup. Because I don't do relationships.

~

It's a little after 10 when we call it a night. We got most of the PowerPoint done. We just have a couple slides left and then we have to memorize are parts and we're good to go.

"You know Books, I don't think I've ever gotten a project done so quickly in my entire life," she's packing up her bag and I'm waiting by the door to walk her downstairs and to her car.

"Well, we aren't done yet."

"True, but we probably will be done early." She nods and I follow her out the door.

Walking downstairs, all three of my

roommates are sat on the couch screaming at the TV as they play Mario Cart.

"Davies, I swear to fucking god if you hit me with a banana one more time I'm going to strangle you," Webbs is fired up.

They're on Shy Guy Falls. I look over at a very amused looking Rydell as she says, "Asher you have a mushroom, if you land your glider on the top of the cliff, you can cut through the grassy section."

"Rydell, don't help him," Davies exclaims.

It's the last lap and all three of them are pretty close. Webbs takes Rydell's advice, and sure enough, he wins the round.

Webbs jumps up from his seat and does a victory dance, "Fuck yeah!" He speeds over to Rydell and her eyes grow to the size of saucers as he picks her up and spins her around.

She nervously laughs and puts her hands on his shoulders awkwardly. Her feet are off the floor. His arms are around her waist. His face is in the side of her neck. And I want to punch him in his smug looking face.

"Asher let go of her," I grunt out.

He slowly lets her back onto the ground but keeps his hand on her hips. She looks very uncomfortable and is moving her hands around like she doesn't know where to set them, "Why? Am I making you jealous Scotty?"

I put a finger through the loop in Rydell's skirt and pull her back towards me. "I was just leaving; I hope you guys enjoy the rest of your night." Rydell gives a little wave and starts walking towards the front door.

My finger is still in the loop, so she gets pulled right back into me. "Deli, you should stay and play a few rounds with us," Webbs says.

"Oh no, I don't want to intrude, plus I really should be getting home. I've got important matters to attend to."

I look down at her, "What, got a hot date with your bed and a book."

She pinches my arm as I release my hand from her, "Yes, in fact I do. And it's a very nice-looking book, wouldn't want to keep it waiting."

I tilt my head to the ceiling and laugh before looking down at her, "Come on. You don't have any morning classes tomorrow and don't go into work until 6." It's a little creepy that I know her schedule, but hey, she already calls me a stalker. "Plus, I wanna see you kick their butts in Mario Cart."

I know she'll do it too. I mean she's creating her own video game for peats sake. I'm positive she knows all the tricks to beating people in the digital world.

She considers it, "Ok, but only for a couple games and then I have to go."

CHAPTER 19: RYDELL

It's been 6 games.

"How the fuck do you know all the shortcuts," Max yells. Or Ruddy, I'm getting so confused by all the nicknames.

I think I've got them all down though. Oliver is Davies. Max Is Ruddy, sometimes Rudds. And Asher is Webbs.

"Seriously, every track we pick, there's at least one you know of," Oliver chimes in.

I shrug my shoulders, "I grew up with 4 competitive siblings, I always wanted to beat them, so I practiced until I found a way to always win."

"Holy shit, you have 4 siblings?! That's absolutely insane. I think I'd shoot myself in the head if I had to live with that many people. I bet y'all like had to share rooms and shit growing up right?" Asher blurts.

My hands are starting to get clammy. "Yep, I shared a room with my sister. I loved living with so many people though, there was always something happening. I sure as heck was never bored."

I look down at Scott who's sitting on the floor right beside my legs that are dangling off the couch. He's shooting daggers at Asher. "I think it'd be fun to have that many siblings," Oliver says before Scott can respond to Asher's comment. "I'm an only child and I always wished I had at least one brother or sister."

"Next game! Let's do Twisted Mansion," Max diverts the conversation.

Scott leans his head back on the couch and looks up at me, "You ok?" he mouths.

I give him a small smile and nod. He raises his hand and squeezes my calf. This doesn't feel friendly.

"I should get going. As much as I love beating you guys in Mario Cart, it's getting late," I stand up and Scott's hand moves down my leg to grasp my ankle.

"We could watch a movie or play a different game," Scott says as his thumb starts to rub small circles on my ankle.

I need to get out of here. He's being way too affectionate tonight. Friends don't rub each other's ankles. Boyfriends are the ankle rubbers. And Scott sure as hell won't be my boyfriend anytime soon.

Plus, that little stunt he pulled, throwing me on his bed almost gave me a heart attack. I'm pretty sure I stopped breathing at one point.

"No that's ok, I don't want to drive tired."

Scott releases my ankle and stands up next to me, "You could stay here, I have clothes you could borrow."

Oh. My. God. My heart is fluttering, and I really want to say yes. But I am not going to think with my heart on this one. My head is so much smarter and it's screaming to leave.

I look over to his roommates who are all

looking very closely at our interaction. Then I look up at Scott, "That's ok, I wanted to finish my book tonight."

He looks a little defeated so I add, "But maybe, if you're not busy, we could grab lunch tomorrow?"

"I have a class at 1," he pouts a bit, "and practice right after."

"Well, we could go at like 11?"

"11:30, I have weight training tomorrow that doesn't end until 11."

"Alright. I'll see you at 11:30 then, text me where you want to go." I walk towards my bag and then to the door.

Scott follows me to my car like a lost puppy. Before I can get fully to my car, he grabs my backpack and turns me around, "You're not leaving because of what Webbs said are you. Because if he upset you in any way, I'll fucking punch him in the throat."

My eyes widen a bit, "No throat punching needs to be done," I pat his shoulder. "I'm not leaving because of what Asher said, I actually am getting tired."

He smiles a bit, "Well I guess the grandpa sweater is perfect for you. It's not even 12 yet ya old lady. Next thing you know, you'll actually have to start using your glasses to help you read."

I laugh, "Yep, you can address me by Grandpa Rivens from now on. And you better watch out, I'll probably start ditching you for bingo night soon."

I unlock my car and Scott opens my door for me, "Text me when you get home Gramps."

CHAPTER 20: *SCOTT*

books to me: just got home. I think it's important to tell you that my book is looking extremely sexy rn. I think I made the right choice ☺

    I smile down at my phone. After a very heated conversation with Webbs about being nice to Rydell, I decided to lock myself in my room for the rest of the night.

    All three of them told me that I was acting way too desperate. That I couldn't have made it more obvious that I want to get her in bed.

    Do I want to sleep with Rydell? Fuck yes, I do. She's gorgeous, she's funny, she may have the fashion sense of an old man but I'm pretty sure that in the last 2 weeks she's become my favorite person to be around.

    Will I sleep with her? Probably not. I don't want to ruin what I have with her. Plus, everyone expects me too. I have to show them that I can be friends with a girl without having sex with her.

me to books: sexier than me?
    I send her a selfie of my shirtless self.
    She sends a selfie back holding up her book.

books to me: sorry, nothing can beat this book, it's one of my favs.

The books she's holding up in called *The Raven Boys*. I go onto Amazon and buy a copy of it with the fastest delivery.

me to books: you're terrible for my ego.
books to me: good. now honestly scott, quit bothering me, I'm trying to read

I chuckle and set my phone down reaching over to grab the remote and turn a movie on. As I'm scrolling through Netlfix, my phone dings again. Expecting another text from Rydell I grab it right away. I'm slightly disappointed when it's from Lindsay.

Lindsay to me: haven't seen you around, how about you come over

I haven't been out as much as usual since working with Rydell. I haven't had sex with anyone since meeting Rydell. I don't think I've ever masturbated this much since 7th grade.
I don't even know why I haven't been going out. When I do go out, I usually leave early, because I don't want to be hungover when I see Ry.
Maybe it wouldn't be a bad thing to see Lindsay. She isn't mega attached to me and she's a decent lay. Plus, I still have sexual frustration that I need to release from having Rydell under me.
If I go to Lindsay's maybe the guys will stop bugging me about sleeping with Rydell.

me to Lindsay: be there in 20.

I grab my keys and head to the door, "Where are you going this late, Rydell give you a call?" Webbs jokes.

"Lindsay's," I'm out the door.

~

I'm sitting on Lindsay's bed, "So, what have you been up to, you've been MIA lately. I heard you've been spending a lot of time with that Ryland girl."

"Her name's Rydell," I grind out. I hate how everyone is in my fucking business about that. "How 'bout we skip the small talk, you know what I'm here for."

"Whatever you want," she whispers as she seductively climbs on the bed to settle herself on my lap. Her eyes are hooded and she's giving me major 'fuck me' eyes.

She puts her legs on either side of mine so that she's straddling me as I sit up against the backboard. She lowers her head to my neck and starts working her way up to my ear, probably leaving small marks as she does.

When she gets close to my lips, she hovers over them for a second as she trails her hands under my shirt, scratching my abs with her fake nails.

Rydell never wears fake nails. She usually has them painted with small flowers in multiple colors, and they are almost always a little chipped. It's clear that she paints them herself, but they suit her perfectly. And she wears these rings that she's always fidgeting- fuck stop thinking about Books and think about the girl shoving her tongue down your throat.

I place my hands-on Lindsay's hips and sit up a bit, then flip us around so that she's on her back and I'm hovering over her. I lift myself off her to pull my shirt over my head and she lifts herself up a bit to do the same.

When she plops her head back down, her hair fans out around her. But it doesn't look nearly as pretty as Rydell's did when I had her in this position not too long ago.

I lean back down and start kissing down her chest, strategically moving my hand to her back to unclip her bra.

Her bra's across the room and I make my way to unbutton her skirt and she pulls off my belt.

Her skirt doesn't have belt loops like Rydell's did.

"Your condoms still in the drawer?" I ask. No way I'm taking any chances.

"Mhmm," I go to grab one and she follows me, attaching her lips to my neck.

CHAPTER 21: RYDELL

Sexy Back fills my ears and a jump to turn it off considering that I'm standing at the bus stop with a bunch of parents to pick up the elementary school girls. I slide my phone to answer Scott's Facetime, "Scott now's not a good time".

"It's never a good time for you Books. But I'll make it quick. Practice got out early, I was thinking sandwiches for lunch, but we can do whatever. Where are you?" His eyes are scanning the area.

"Oh shit. We were supposed to do lunch today. I'm sorry Scott. I got called in to help with the afterschool shift. On Wednesdays they get out at 11:30 and someone asked to switch shifts with me, so I told them I'd help out."

He drops his head back and lets out a groan, "Ugh, Ry, we never get out of practice early, and the one day we do, you're switching your shifts. Just leave, I'm sure the girls can walk home. Have you even eaten anything today?"

I did skip breakfast, but I grabbed an apple on my way to pick the girls up. "I had an apple, that should hold me off until my shift ends."

"What time does your shift end?"

"3, put I have a class at 3:30."

"Books, that isn't healthy. You need to be eating more than that. And how much sleep did you get, there's bags under your eyes."

"Thanks for pointing them out," I sigh, "I couldn't put my book down, I was at a pivotal point."

"But you've already read that book."

"Yes, but it just gets better each time I read it."

I look up and notice the bus driving up, "Gotta go Scotty. I'm sorry again, I'll make it up to you."

Tessa is the first one out of the bus and is running towards me. She's out of breath when she looks up and says, "Ms. Angie was supposed to pick us up, what are you doing here," placing her hands on her hips.

"Ms. Angie was busy, what, am I not good enough?" I put my hands on my hips to mimic her.

"DELLLLLLLLLL, I WAS #1 ON THE STAR CHART," Violet is tugging on my pants.

"Awesome Vi. Did you get a prize?"

She lifts up a slap on bracelet and smacks it onto her wrist, "Very cool. Alright everyone, grab your buddy and single file please."

The orphanage is only about a 5-minute walk from the bus stop, but the buddy system is always the way to go, especially when you're in charge of 10ish elementary school girl.

~

I'm braiding Rosie's hair while the other girls work on their homework at the dining room table when Ms. Michelle walks in. Ms. Michelle is the head of the orphanage. I swear, the woman is a saint, and like an aunt to me, but she can be scary when she's serious. "Del, there's someone at the door for you."

That's weird, no one has ever visited me at work except for Sam. And if it was Sam, she would've just walked in, "Did they tell you their name?"

"It's a tall boy. I think his name started with an S, I was a little distracted, he's very handsome."

My eyes widen, "Scott?"

"Yes! It was Scott."

I'm in the middle of this French braid and I know Rosie will throw a fit if I don't finish it. "Um, can you just have him come in, if that's ok. I'm kinda in the middle," I tilt my head to Rosie.

"Sure, but if he's going to be a distraction while they work on their homework, he has to go."

"Of course," why the hell is he here? Oh my gosh, my hair is all over the place and probably looks unbrushed.

And sure enough, there's Scott, looking perfect like he always does. He's holding a bag that says Sammy's on the side. Sammy's is a sandwich shop on campus.

I give him a 'really?' look and finish Rosie's braid.

He has the stupidest smirk on his face, "Hey Books, figured you might be hungry."

"How'd you even find this place? And that's completely unnecessary, I told you I had an apple."

Rosie stands up on her chair so that she's at my level and leans in to whisper in my ear, "Is that your boyfriend?" But it's not really a whisper and Scott defiantly heard because he looks like he's about to start laughing.

I shake my head no and then Violet looks up from her homework. Her eyes go wide, and I know what she's about to say before she even says it, "DEL'S BOYFRIEND'S HERE. OH. MY. GOSH. HE'S SO CUTE!!" I swear that girl has the biggest freaking mouth.

She jumps off her seat to stand right in front of Scott. "OMG. ARE YOU LIKE A GIANT OR SOMETHING?"

Scott chuckles. Now half the girls are standing in front of him. Only the elementary girls are off school early on Wednesdays. Thank goodness, the older ones would be drooling.

He looks over to me and I just raise my eyebrows and give him a small smirk. I'm not helping him out of this one, he bombarded me at work, he can deal with the consequences.

"He could be like Hagrid from Harry Potter, only half giant," Tess exclaims and then looks towards me, "is he half giant?"

"I don't know, why don't you ask him."

Now it's Scott's turn to give me the 'really?' look. "Well, are you half giant?"

He squats down to Tess's level, but still slightly towers over her small frame, "I'm only a quarter giant."

Tess gasp, "I knew it."

"What's your name?"

"Tessa. I heard that your name's Scott."

"Who's your favorite Harry Potter character Tessa?" he asks her.

"I like Hermonie. She reminds me of Del."

Scott looks up at me with a smile, before bringing his attention back to Tessa, "Good choice. I like the Weasley twins, they're pretty funny."

"You like Harry Potter? Does that mean you're a nerd? All the people at school say I'm a nerd because I like to read it at lunch."

"Oh ya, I'm a huge nerd. But nerds are the best type of people. I mean, look at Rydell, she's a nerd and she's pretty fuc- freaking cool right?" Ok burn.

"Yes! Do boys have cooties?"

"Only some of them," he replies and all the girls take a little step back.

"Do you have cooties?" Rosie asks.

"I don't know. What do you think Ry, do I have cooties?"

"Oh ya, he's definitely got cooties, see those little marks on his neck?" Scott is sporting some hickey and my stomach drops a little at that fact. Wrong move. Now the girls are running around and screaming.

"Shit," I curse under my breathe.

Ms. Michelle comes in, "I hope this means that all the homework is done with all the noise coming out of this room," as if a light switched, all the girls are back in their seats to finish up.

She gives me a stern look and I mouth a quick 'sorry'.

"That's my bad, I shouldn't have gotten them all riled up."

"No worries sweetie. If they were done with their homework, I would be glad for the excitement your bringing," and Ms. Michelle has a sweet spot for Scott. Although, that doesn't surprise me, he's quite the charmer.

Ms. Michelle leaves the room and Scott walks up to me. "A sandwich for my favorite little nerd," he hands me one from the bag and it's a caprese, my favorite.

"Thank you, you didn't have to do that. Don't you have a class in like," I check my watch to see it's 12:15, "45 minutes."

"Ya, but campus is only like a 10-minute drive, I've got plenty of time." He looks around at the girls, "figured I could start getting the girls shoe sizes so I can start setting some aside for the field trip. Do Saturdays work for you guys. I was thinking maybe this weekend, my coach said any Saturday."

I honestly kind of forgot about the field trip. Scott and I's relationship hasn't really felt like a deal. It makes me a little sad to think of it that way, but this field trip will be super fun for the girls.

"Yes, Saturday's work. We do our recycling in the morning and usually finish around 10:30. Maybe we could do 11?"

"That should work, I'll let my coach and a few of the guys know."

I open my mouth to say something else but then Sophie speaks up, "I need help."

I walk over to help her with her 1st grade level math problem she's working on. Her problem is 9-7.

"Alright, we can use our hands to help us, right? Can you show me 9 fingers?" She lifts up the correct number of fingers, "Ok, now can you put 7 down?" She counts to 7 as she puts her fingers down. "Good, now count how many you have left."

"2!", she yells as she goes to pick up her pencil and write down her answer.

"Very good, easy peasy, right?"

"Mhmm," she pokes her tongue out of the side of her mouth as she concentrates on the next question. I look up to find Scott staring at me, which a soft smile I haven't seen before.

One of my other coworkers is in the room helping out with homework, so while no other girls have questions, I walk back over to Scott. "You're really good with them you know?" he comments.

"I try. I'll get all the shoe sizes to you tonight. When they have screen time, I'll get them all."

"No rush," he grabs my wrist and looks at the time on my watch. "I should probably head out; I need to stop by my house to grab my backpack before class."

He puts my arm down, but his hand is still wrapped around my wrist. One thing I've noticed about Scott is that he is very touchy. Not that I'm complaining.

"DEL'S BOYFRIEND IS HOLDING HER HAND! DEL YOU HAVE TO LET GO YOU'LL GET COOTIES!" Violet screams.

I look over to Scott who is silently laughing. He let's go of my wrist, brushes some hair out of my face and leans into my ear to whisper, "Better watch out Ry. I'm gonna give you all my cooties." He leans back to look at my face which I'm sure is bright red.

"DEL YOUR FACE IS RED! HE IS GIVING YOU COOTIES," I swear I'm going to give this girl one less Oreo when it's snack time.

Scott is smirking down at me, "Enjoy the sandwich Books," he walks towards the front door and I shove my hands under my glasses to put my cold hands on my cheeks.

CHAPTER 22: *SCOTT*

Practice is coming to an end, and the team is finally starting to click a little more. It's clear that Jacobs has been putting in the work and the guys are finally starting to listen to me. I guess they got tired of sprints.

"Not bad today boys. Remember we have our first pre-season game on Sunday and the girls from the orphanage are coming tomorrow. Those of you who can make it, please come. I'm sure the girls would appreciate it," Coach Michaels says.

With that everyone makes their way to the locker rooms. "Going to the party tonight Scotty? Maybe you'll stay for most of it this time," McCombs voice is like nails on a chalkboard.

"Ya, I'll be there. If it's fucking boring like most of them have been lately, I'll leave early. Unlike some people, I have no problem finding other ways to entertain myself."

"Right. I almost forgot about your pretty little nerd from Spanish class."

"Watch your fucking mouth," I know if I punch him, I'll have to sit out for the game on Sunday, so I keep myself busy by grabbing my clothes from my locker.

"No judgement here, I bet she's got a cute little body under those overalls," he snickers.

I shove him into his locker and put my forearm against his chest leaning in to say, "I said watch your fucking mouth. One more word about Rydell and I'll make sure you sit out of the game on Sunday."

"You wouldn't do that. I'm one of your best defensemen," he has a smug look on his face.

"Fucking try me," Ruddy pulls me back a bit and I shrug him off and grab my towel to head to the showers.

~

"Come on Books, you never go out. I've only been to the bar with you once. You're never at parties. Plus, you owe me from ditching me on Wednesday," I just got home from practice and am now on Facetime trying to convince Rydell to go to the junior's party tonight.

The junior house is the main party house, sometimes the sophomores will throw it, but for the most part, the junior's is the way to go.

"Technically twice. That one time you bombarded me begging to be my partner. Anyways, we have an early morning tomorrow Scott," she looks at me with a 'remember?' type look. "Field trip with the girls at 11? Plus, I have to be at the orphanage by 7:30 for recycling."

"It's only 9:30. Just stay for a couple hours. It's not like you have to drink much."

"What's the point of going to a party if I'm not gonna drink?"

"Oh, I don't know. Maybe to hang out with your bestie. Come on Gramps, you're killing me here."

"Del! I need your expert fashion advice. Leather skirt or black mini dress?" Sam bursts into her room. She's definitely going if Sam is.

"Will you look at that. Even Sam's going, your second bestie will be there too."

Sam's face fills my screen, "Nice try Prescott," she looks to Del, "Who's your best friend Del?"

"You know you are Sam. Leather skirt."

"Dammit Books. First, you're refusing to come to the party and now you're telling lies. What am I gonna do with you," there's a lot of things I want to do with her. Things that I won't tell her because they aren't friendly. "Now you have no excuse to not come. Sam also has to be there for recycling in the morning. If I don't see you at the party within the next hour, I'm going to kidnap you. See you in a bit." And with that I hang up and jog down the stairs.

"Convince Deli to come out tonight?" Webbs asks.

"I think so. I don't need to tell you to be nice, do I?"

"No sir," he stands up straight and solutes.

~

The party is packed. The music's loud. People are making out on every couch. And I'm in about to win this game of beer pong.

I shoot. I score. And everyone around me is cheering, some people are clapping me on the back, and Rudds is chugging the last cup, "Good game Rudds, you never had a chance."

He flips me off and sets the drink down and looks towards the door. And his eyes stay on whatever's at the door with a predatory gaze so I turn my head to look.

And there's Sam in the leather skirt Rydell told her to wear. I'm pretty sure Max is crushing on Sam, but he's been in hookup mode still trying to get over his breakup.

I start walking towards Sam because if she's here either Rydell's with her, or Rydell stayed home.

A skinny ginger wraps herself around my arm, "Good game Scotty. I could give you a winner's prize."

I pry her off me, "No thanks."

And then Rydell walks through the door to stand next to Sam.

Holy fuck. This was a bad idea, because Rydell is looking way too hot right now.

She's in a black corset top that puts her tits on display and jeans. Her hair is slightly curled, like she rushed it, but fuck it looks sexy. Her lips are tinted red and it's like the forbidden fucking apple, because I want to bite that bottom lip so badly. She isn't wearing her glasses, and her eyelids have a little bit of smokey looking eyeliner. Just looking at her makes my pants feel a little too tight.

She's looking around the place like she's looking for someone, holding her hand on her wrist and then her eyes find mine. And all of a sudden, the party doesn't seem so loud.

She does a cute little wave. That fucking dimple on the left side of her chin is poking out as she smiles and she's walking towards me. I on the other hand, am currently stuck in my place.

"Hey handsome, I was hoping you'd be here," my perfect view is blocked by a blonde head. Lindsay grabs the hem of my shirt and starts to fiddle with it. "How many drinks do you need to have before we take this party to your place."

I look up to find Rydell, but she's disappeared so I look towards Sam. Max has made his way to the feisty little one, and is whispering something in her ear, causing Sam to put her hand on her hip and roll her eyes.

"Well?" Lindsay says. I forgot she was there.

"Do you see a brunette in a black corset top anywhere?" I ask her, ignoring her question.

"The one who was wearing Doc Martens. Total fashion disaster if you ask me, but she went towards the kitchen. So party at-"

I walk towards the kitchen leaving Lindsay behind, and sure enough Ry's in the middle of it throwing back a shot.

"Easy there Gramps. You've got an early morning," I walk so that I'm standing right in front of her.

"Figured I'd get the alcohol down before I have to socialize with anyone," she goes to grab a hard cider from the cooler.

Someone bumps into Rydell from behind shoving her into me. I look towards to guy who did it, "Hey, watch where you're going asshole. Apologize to her."

The guy turns a little red, "Sorry," he mumbles out as Rydell turns around.

"Oh, it's really no problem. I shouldn't be standing in the middle of everything," she grabs a beer from the cooler and hands it towards him. "Beer?"

He grabs for it lingering his hand on her wrist for a bit. He's staring at her boobs and Rydell walks back a little causing her back to fully bump into my chest. "Thanks, any chance I could snag a dance with you?"

I put my hands on Rydell's hips, "No," I tell him, taking one hand off Rydell's hip to grab a beer and then slightly pushing her towards the living room.

I push us so that we're next to a wall and a little away from all the craziness. "Hey, what if I wanted to dance with him?"

"Did you want to dance with him?" I question her. I know she didn't by the way she backed into to me, but it makes my heart speed up at the thought of her wanting to dance with someone else.

"Well, who else am I supposed to dance with? Sam is dancing with... who is that Sam's dancing with?" I follow my eyes in the direction she's pointing.

"Hinders. He's a junior on the team," and they are really going at it. His hands are guiding her hips over his dick and she's already looks a little wasted.

"Jesus. She pregamed a bit before we came. Girl does not handle her liquor well."

"I'll dance with you," I blurt out. I just really want an excuse to touch her.

"What," she takes her eyes off Sam to look at me.

I take a long drink of my beer, "You asked who you're supposed to dance with. You could dance with me."

"I think I need a little more alcohol in me for that. If I try to dance right now, I'll end up looking like a slightly cooked spaghetti noodle floppin around out there, and that's a sight that no one wants to see," she goes to down half her drink.

"You'd be the sexiest slightly cooked spaghetti noodle out there," I lean into her ear to make sure she can hear me over the music as I say, "you look fucking stunning." I pull back, she's looking up at me with that dimpled smile.

"Alright then. One dance," she puts her cider down, grabs my hand and leads me to where everyone is dancing. I silently do a little cheer as she does so.

Once we're in the middle of it all you spins around and says, "Sorry, but I won't be twerking on you. This is a friend's dance," damn ok subtle friendzone there but that's ok because that's what I want too.

Sexy Back by Justin Timberlake starts to play over the speakers and we both stare at each other before we start cracking up.

I'm looking down at her and her head is tilted up to the ceiling as she laughs. She looks so fucking gorgeous. I stop laughing and just smile down at her as she pulls herself together.

"What are the odds. Your favorite song," she grabs my hand and gestures for me to twirl. "Wait, twirl and then dip! I've always wanted to dip someone," she looks so happy and I'm the reason for it. I'm thinking that if nothing else works out in my life. If my hockey career ends. If I'm forced into a loveless marriage. If I'm stuck running a company that I don't want for the rest of my life. As long as I can keep her looking this happy, nothing else would matter.

She tries to dip me but I'm much taller than her and those SpongeBob-like muscles cannot hold me up. I try to break my fall, but it's no use because I'm going down and I'm taking her with me.

And she's laughing again. And she's on top of me. And it's fucking turning me on. Her face is close to mine, her laughing is dying down, and I put my hands on her hips. "I don't know why I thought that was a good idea," she says. She looks down at my lips and I'm moving my hand to the back of her neck to pull her down to them. My eyes flicker to her lips and my hand is now tangled in her hair. She's moving a little more and her hips push down a bit on my dick. Fucking hell, she's driving me crazy. I can feel her breath fanning my face and I lift my head off the floor to connect our lips but before I can we're interrupted.

"Y'all ok down there?" Rydell jumps a little and stands up. I groan and let my head fall back to the ground. Or floor, as Rydell likes to correct me.

Rydell is brushing herself off then looks down to me and holds her hand out. I'm so tempted to take her hand and pull her back down here with me, but I let her help me up.

"Sorry, I should've known I couldn't hold your weight."

"Calling me fat Books?" I try to lighten the mood because she looks really uncomfortable.

"You could cut back on the burritos," she jokes back.

"Scotty is one of the best hockey players in the nation. He's in the perfect shape," I look over to the fucker who interrupted us. And I'm not at all surprised when I see Lindsay moving towards me.

"Oh right, ya. I was just joking I don't think he's actually fat or anything. And if he was a little bit overweight, it wouldn't matter. Because it's his body and I'd never judge anyone for their body. Because all bodies are beautiful and no one should ever feel ashamed about how their built," she's rambling.

"Riiiight," Lindsay draws out, then looks towards me, "I was thinking maybe we could grab a drink and then replay Tuesday night." She's running her hand up my chest, "I had a good time."

Fuck. I shouldn't have slept with her. I didn't even finish. As soon as she released, I pulled out and left. The whole time I was thinking about how much I wished she was Rydell.

"I feel like I might be interrupting something. I'm gonna go grab a drink," Rydell starts to walk towards the kitchen.

"Wait, I'll come with you, that was hardly a dance".

"Don't worry about it, you guys can keep talking, I'll be back. Do you want anything?"

"No, but really Ry, I don't want to leave you alone." Almost all the guys in here have been staring at her and I don't want any of them getting any ideas.

"I'll be fine." And before I can even respond she's gone.

Lindsay hand is now curled on my neck and she's forcing me to look down at her.

I grab her hands and push her away. "I told you I don't want a relationship; I don't even want a booty call. Tuesday shouldn't have happened."

"Why? Little Ry would've gotten jealous. For a guy who doesn't do relationships, you're sure close to that one."

"Rydell's my friend. And stop fucking talking about her. What goes on between us, is none of your business, it's no one's business but mine and hers." I walk away only to be stopped by McCombs.

"The captain made it," I am not in the mood for his bullshit. "I saw your ticket to an A, now I understand why you spend so much time with her. She's fucking hot when she tries to be."

"Just stay the fuck away from her," I shove past him and go to find a drink.

CHAPTER 23: *RYDELL*

I saw the hickeys on Scott's neck when he came to the orphanage on Wednesday, so I really don't know why I'm upset to hear that he slept with the blonde.

I throw back a shot and make my way back to the living room to see if Sam's done dancing. I'm looking around trying to look like I fit in, but I probably look like a lost puppy.

Maybe I could just hide in the bathroom for a bit. I can't leave Sam by herself here and I promised we could stay for a couple hours. It's only been about 30 minutes.

"Hey Ryland, right?" It's the blonde from earlier.

She's smiling at me, so I smile back, "Hi, uh, Rydell actually."

"I'm Lindsay. Those shoes are killer," I look down at my Doc Martens. They're my favorite pair of shoes.

Now I'm smiling a bit more naturally, "Thanks, they were my mom's when she was in high school. Isn't it crazy how good the condition is for being that old?" I love bragging about how vintage they are.

"Yep. Crazy. You and Scott are cute together, I mean it looks a little like a charity case, but from girl to girl, just be careful with that one. You guys are just hooking up right? You know since he doesn't do relationships."

"Oh. Um... Scott and I aren't sleeping together. We're just friends, and working on a Spanish project together," I found myself wondering why Scott doesn't do relationships.

"I see, you're not one to kiss and tell right? Well, if you don't want people knowing you're fucking, you should tone it down a bit. I mean you're all over him tonight, it makes you look a little desperate. But I'm just trying to help you out here," it doesn't seem like she's trying to help me out.

"Thanks for the tip, but I swear, our relationship is strictly platonic," she's being rude, so I add, "not that I have to explain myself to you. It's really none of your business."

She looks taken aback that I'd stand up for myself. That's right blondey, I know how to handle your type. "Will you look at that, she bites back," she's smirking a bit. "Next time Scott gets you in his bed, tug on his hair when you kiss his neck, it drives him crazy."

My stomach drops. I mean I knew they slept together but I didn't *know* they slept together. "Right. Well, if that's all you wanted to say to me, I'd rather be literally anywhere else," I reply. I just want to go home.

"I was just trying to be friendly," sure she was. "I came over because Scott's waiting for you in the room over there. He asked me to take you to him."

Scott's waiting for me in a room. Did he ask

me to the party because he just wanted to sleep with me? I mean everyone here assumes we already are.

And he started pulling me in for a kiss when we tripped. Not that I was rejecting it or anything. Because if we hadn't been interrupted, I definitely would've kissed the shit out of him. And who knows what would've happened from there.

It probably would have made this extremely awkward. And then we wouldn't be friends anymore and that would make me upset. Because I like being friends with Scott. I don't even want to think about what would've happened with the Spanish project.

Dammit Rydell, how could you be so stupid. Kissing him would have ruined everything. Ok whatever he wants to do in this room, I'll just dodge it. I'll pretend that nothing happened, and I'll tell him that I need to go home soon. I do have an early morning tomorrow.

Lindsay opens the door for me, and I step in, only for her to close it the second I do. It's dark in here and it's making me nervous, so I put my hand on my wrist.

"Scott, if this is some prank it's not funny. It's really dark in here." I feel around the room and find out soon enough that it's not a room. It's a closet. And my chest hurts, and my eyes are tearing up.

"Scott can we please get out of here," my voice is shaky as I say it. He isn't responding and even if he was, I'm not sure I would've heard him. I go to sit on the floor and put my hands over my ears while lifting my knees to my chest.

Oh fuck. I can't breathe. I can't breathe. All I can think about is the trip we took to my grandparent's house for Thanksgiving break when I was in 3rd grade.

Every year, my grandparents throw a Thanksgiving party with a bunch of their friends. This year they invited us. It was only about the 4th time I'd ever seen my grandparents, so I was already nervous about it. Especially since the last time we visited my grandpa came into the room I was staying in super late at night and put his hand down my pants. He told me if I said a word or told anyone he would go into my sister's room and do the same to her. Then he kissed me on the lips and left. That was my first kiss. He stole my first kiss.

I cried myself to sleep, woke up the next morning and told no one.

But the worst thing that ever happened during any visit to their house was that Thanksgiving party. Throughout a majority of the evening my grandpa and one of his friends were tracking my every move. So, I stayed next to my dad for most of the night. My dad always made me feel safe.

My grandma called me into the kitchen to get dessert, and when I was walking back to my dad, my grandpa and his friend blocked my path.

My grandpa said, "Come with us, we have a game for you to play."

I told them no thank you and said that I didn't really want to play a game. He grabbed my upper arm and told me that if I didn't want to play, he was sure that Andromeda would. So, I let him guide me with his friend following.

And they took me to a closet far from the party. Told me to take my dress off and both watched as I did so. Then my grandpa's friend kneeled to my level and whispered in my ear to be quiet and started kissing down my chest and stomach. He put his hands in my underwear, pulled his pants down and started stroking himself with his other hand. He just stared at my naked body and jerked himself off, occasionally leaning in to kiss me.

It was dark in the closet, and I couldn't see much but that just made the situation even scarier.

When the friend finished pleasuring himself, they left with the threat of doing the same to my sister if I said a word.

I scrambled to put my dress back on and just sat down. I have no idea how long I was in there for, but I know at one point I started crying. I felt so numb I couldn't walk; I couldn't even stand.

Then my dad opened the closest and picked me up telling me he was starting to worry. I guess my grandpa told him that the kids were playing hide and seek, and that's why no one could find me.

I'm trying not to think about it but all I see is their eyes following me and their hands touching me.

I'm hyperventilating so badly, and my vision is starting to spot. And I feel like I'm about to pass out. Maybe I should try to stand up and get out of here. I try standing up but fail miserably and grip onto something only to pull it down with me.

CHAPTER 24: *SCOTT*

I watched as Rydell and Lindsay start walking off somewhere. That's a recipe for disaster.

I make my way towards them to make sure everything's ok, but am stopped by a very drunk, very emotional Ruddy. "What if I'm unlovable. What if I jump into a new relationship and the same thing happens? Maybe I'm not supposed to do serious. I think I'm just meant to have meaningless hookups for the rest of my life," and then he chugs the rest of his drink.

"Alright Maxxy, I think you've had enough," I grab his empty bottle and set it aside, then clap his shoulder, "You just haven't found the right person buddy. Serena? She wasn't your person. Hookups are fine. But one day, you're going to find a girl who's worth the possibility of being hurt by," I think about Rydell.

Shit. Rydell who was just with Lindsay, I need to evaluate that situation. I spot Oliver. "Davies, will you take Rudds to get some water?"

I pass him off and walk to where they were headed. Lindsay is standing by a closet door laughing with the ginger who came up to me earlier.

Rydell is nowhere to be seen.

"Where is she?" I approach them.

"I'm right here. Now can we please go to your place," Lindsay goes to grab my hand, but I jerk it back.

"Rydell, she was just with you," I hear crash from inside the closet and go to open it.

"We were just having a little bit of fun."

And there she is, with tears in her eyes, surrounded by a coat rack that must've fallen. Her hands are covering her ears and she's breathing way too fast.

I drop to my knees and go to cup her cheeks, "Hey. Hey, what's wrong? Are you ok? Are you hurt?" I scan her face and body for any signs of injuries.

She's looking up at me with blank eyes and the tears won't stop streaming down her face and she's going to pass out with how fast she's breathing.

And then it hits me. She's having a panic attack. When I went over to Rydell's apartment to drop off her notebook that I purposely took, I ended up staying to watch the Bachelorette with her and Sam.

At one point, I went to grab a beer from the fridge and taped to it was a list of things to do to help her get over a panic attack. I took a picture of it, just in case, and I'm fucking glad I did.

I whip out my phone and scroll through until I find what I need. I look up at her and she's staring off into space.

"Alright pretty girl let's calm you down."

Put her hands on her wrist. I grab her hands and take them off her ears and position them, so her

143

right hand is wrapped around her left wrist.

She looks towards me and I nod, "Good now try to count your heartbeats," she's still just staring at me, tears are still running down her cheeks and her breathing hasn't slowed down at all.

I brush some tears out of her face and let my hand rest cupped on her cheek. "Ok, try counting with me gorgeous."

I put up one finger, "Come on Books. One," I start off, but she's not counting with me.

Fuck. Why isn't this working?

She squeezes her eyes shut and takes her hands of her wrist and puts them back on her ears. She's sobbing uncontrollably and I can feel my eyes start to water up at the sight of her.

"What's wrong with her. She was only in there for like 30 seconds, is she afraid of the dark," Lindsay nervously laughs.

"Shut the fuck up," I've never felt so compelled to punch a girl.

I grab Rydell from under the knees and lift her to my chest. The closet is right next to the front door, so I stand up and easily slip out without anyone noticing that she's breaking down.

And I speed walk to my house, "It's ok Ry. I'm gonna help you. Try to focus on your heartbeats, put your hand on your wrist."

She does as I say. Thank god. I rush her up the stairs and into my room as soon as I reach the house and then sit her on my bed. "That's it. You're doing so good Ry, just keep trying to count those beats."

I'm scrambling around my room, looking for my air pods. I grab them from my nightstand and put them in her ears. Then I grab my phone and go to her Spotify profile, clicking on the playlist that's supposed to calm her down.

I wipe some more tears and let my hand stay there to stroke her cheek with my thumb hoping it'll calm her a bit. After about 5 minutes, her breathing is starting to go back to regular, but still a little fast for my liking.

I pulled up my desk chair to sit across from where she is on the bed. And we're just staring at each other. I don't know what else I'm supposed to do.

The tears have stopped, but her eyes are still glassy, red, and puffy. She takes her hand off her wrist and goes to put her hand over the one I have over her cheek. But she doesn't take it off like I expect her too, she just holds it there. "I'm sorry," her voice is raspy, and it comes out as barely a whisper. She looks down to her lap.

I put my other hand on her opposite cheek and lift her face to look back up at me, "Don't apologize. I shouldn't have left you alone. What happened? Are you hurt? Did someone say something to make you upset? Give me names. I already have some choice words picked out for Lindsay."

She just sits there. She looks so numb, like she's not even processing what I'm saying to her. I stand up and go to sit next to her on the bed, grabbing one of her hands in both of mine. "Talk to me Books," I whisper.

She turns to look at me, then drops her forehead on my shoulder and takes a shaky deep breath, "I hate closets," and my shoulder starts to feel damp.

I put my arm around her waist and adjust

us so that I'm leaning against the headboard of my bed and she's in my lap. She wraps her arms around my shoulders and stuffs her face in my neck. I can hear her sniffling and feel her tears. And it's breaking my heart. I shouldn't have pushed her to go to the party.

I rub up and down her back, trying to calm her back down, "Shh. You're ok. I'm here, I'm not going anywhere. Just talk when you're ready."

~

About 20 minutes have passed. Rydell has the side of her head rested on my chest like she's listening to my heartbeat. I'm still slightly rubbing her back. Her breathing is officially back to normal and she's not crying anymore.

"Why do you hate closets?"

She shakes her head, "Long story," she's whispers.

I brush her hair out of her face and tilt her chin to look up at me, "Good thing I don't plan on leaving this spot anytime soon. It's obviously something bad if that's the reaction it got out of you. I think it would help for you to tell someone about it."

She looks back down, "I don't want you to look at me differently. I- I can't tell you this one."

"I don't want to push you. But I do want to help you, and I don't think it's healthy for you to hide all this, hoping that'll go away. It's not just going to go away Rydell."

"It's a burden I promised myself I wouldn't tell anyone. I haven't told my parents, I haven't told Sam. I can handle it myself."

"You obviously can't. I just spent the last 45 minutes trying to get your hyperventilating to stop.

Rydell you were on the verge of passing out. Do you know how that made me feel? Seeing you that upset? I wanted to beat the shit out of Lindsay for putting you in that situation."

She climbs off my lap and sits down next to me pulling her legs up to her chest and resting her head on the bed frame.

"I'm sorry," she sighs.

"Stop apologizing. I'm glad I was there to help you, and I'm not upset with you in any way. I'm worried about you. And I just want you to talk to me. Please, just talk to me," I whisper the last part.

She looks at me for a second with a pained expression on her face. Then she looks up at the ceiling and closes her eyes. "What I'm about to tell you stays between us. I'm not going to tell you names, and I'm going to leave a lot of things out. But this is more than I've ever told anyone, ok?" she looks back at me and I nod.

She looks back up at the ceiling and says, "I was sexually assaulted in elementary school. 3 times. Two out of three of those times, it happened in a closet."

My heart is beating so fast right now. And all I can think about is finding the mother fuckers who touched her and making sure they regret it.

"Why haven't you told anyone Del, that's a big fucking deal."

"Because it happened when I was so young. And the people who did it threatened doing the same thing to my sister if I said anything," if she had any tears left in her, they would be running down her cheeks. "I didn't understand what was happening, but I understood that I didn't want my little sister involved in it."

"You can still do something about it. You can go to the authorities-"

"What and sit in a court room for months and months waiting for them to make a decision. They don't have evidence. I didn't speak up when it happened. The people who did it to me were rich and powerful men. Whose side do you think they'll choose Scott? Cause I can tell you right now, that it won't be mine."

"You don't know that."

"I do. Because I've seen it happen time and time again. I won't say anything. And neither will you. Please Scott. It's in the past. You promised you wouldn't say anything. Don't make me regret telling you."

I sigh, "I'll testify. I can tell them about how you get panic attacks just being in a closet. How I've seen first-hand how it's affected you."

She grabs my hand and slides hers in to intertwine our fingers, "I love that you'd do that. But it won't make a difference. Please don't tell anyone. You're the only person who knows about this."

"Ya me and the fuckers who did it to you," I look back at her and she's looking down at our hands that are situated on her lap. "Your secrets safe with me. It's not my story to tell. But I think you should do something about it. And if you do choose to do something, I'll be with you through the whole thing. I'll do whatever you need me to do."

"Thank you," she moves to her knees and wraps her arms around my shoulder, and I lift her so that she's sitting back on my lap.

CHAPTER 25: *RYDELL*

I'm jumped awake by the sound of my phone ringing. This doesn't feel like my bed. I pat the space that I'm lying on. But it's not a space it's Scott's arm, "What!" Scott jumps to a sitting position, and I fall off his chest. He looks down at me, "Are you ok? What's wrong?"

Everything comes rushing back to me and I'm a little embarrassed. But Scott was so good throughout the whole thing. He never made me feel like a burden which was the thing I was most scared of.

"My phone's ringing," I grab my phone from my back pocket and sit criss cross. Before I answer I look at the time to see that it's almost 1am. It's Sam.

"Sam," I rub the sleep out of my eyes.

"Del, where the fuck are you? I've been looking for you for the past 20 minutes and you haven't answered any of my text."

"Shit. I'm sorry Sammy. I had a panic attack and Scott took me back to his place to help me get over it."

Scott takes my free and looks down at it as he starts to play with my fingers. Physical touch is definitely his love language.

"Dammit Del. You should have found me. We could've left."

"It's a long story that I will tell you when we get back to the apartment. Do you want to meet at the car?"

"Ya, see you in a bit."

I hang up and look towards Scott who's still focused on my hand. "I need to get going."

"Ya," he says. Neither of us make an effort to move. He looks up and we just look at each other for a bit. Now it's my turn to look down.

"Thank you for staying with me and helping me get over it," I say quietly. I shift myself off the bed and start making my way towards his front door. He follows.

When we get to the door I turn around and wrap my arms around his torso. "I mean it. Thank you," I mumble into his chest.

He wraps his arms around me and brushes the back of my head with one of his hands. "You don't need to thank me. I like taking care of you," my heart flutters at that. "You need anything, say the word, and I'm there Books."

I nod, "Ok, Sam's waiting."

He walks me to my car and a very concerned Sam throws her arms around me. She's still a little tipsy, "Del, thank goodness, you scared me," she lets go and looks towards Scott, "were you the one that caused the panic attack, huh?" she jumps towards him and I block her path.

"Scott didn't cause it, he found me and helped me stop it."

"You're lucky buddy. I would've knocked you the fuck out," she looks at me, "you say goodbye, I'll be in the car," she stumbles to the passenger seat.

Scott puts his arms around my waist, and I put mine around his neck. He breathes deeply, "I'll see you tomorrow. Call if you need me," and with that he opens my door and I start to head home.

~

"So, you literally feel asleep in his arms. Hate to break it to you Del but that doesn't sound like just friends to me," Sam says as she sorts plastic bottles into the bin.

"Ya, it didn't feel like just friends either," I sigh and grab a new bag of bottles to sort. "I wanted to grab his cheeks and kiss the fuck out of him like 5 times last night, I need to get my shit together."

Sam chuckles, "Can't say I didn't see this one coming because I totally did. I just can't get over that blonde bitch. Next time you see her, point her out. I'm gonna knock a bitch out."

"No need, I don't think Scott's going back to her anytime some. Or anytime at all for that matter. He was pissed." I think back to Scott telling me he wanted to 'beat the shit out of her'.

I also think about how he slept with her. And how she told me that when she tugs on his hair it drives him crazy. And it hurts a little to think that they slept together.

Scott's entitled to his past, anything he did or does isn't something that I can hold against him. I mean we aren't even a couple. We aren't even a thing, we're just friends.

And as much as I wish we were more than friends; I have to think about this relationship long term. I know Scott doesn't do relationships; I don't know why but I've heard it on multiple occasions. I want to change his mind about it, but I don't want him to resent me for it. Because no one should have to change who they are for a relationship.

And I sure as hell am not going to change into a person who is ok with a friends with benefits relationship, because that's just not the type of person I am. Not that I have anything against it, but casual sex isn't for everyone. I tried it before, and it sucked.

"I finished my bag, can you pass me a new one Del?" Kendall walks up to me and I hand her the bag I just picked up.

"Wow Kenny, this is the most enthusiastic I've seen you for recycling. Excited for ice skating?" I tease her.

"Of course, I am. I get to spend my day with college hockey boys," she wiggles her eyebrows at me a bit.

"Hey, don't get any ideas. And poor Ryan's going to be jealous."

"Oh please, Ryan has no competition. But I won't be complaining at the idea of being surrounded by cute boys. Plus, the little ones can't stop gushing about how cute your boyfriend is, I'm excited to meet him."

"He's not my boyfriend," I mumble.

"Keep telling yourself that Del," she walks back to her bins to sort.

~

"Everyone grab your buddy please," Ms. Michelle announces. "Del, you take elementary with Sam," Sam and I make our way to our group while Michelle announces where everyone else needs to be.

Kendall and Ava, our two high school girls,

152

come up to Sam and I. "Figured we'd help out here since we don't need chaperoning," Ava says, "Plus, I want to witness your boyfriend coming up to you Del."

I groan, "Will you guys quit it. Scott is not my boyfriend," we walk into the hockey rink.

On the bleachers there's a handful of guys from the hockey team. They all look towards us the minute we walk in. And most of the girls are looking very shy right now.

"Hey Deli, cute beanie," Asher is the first to greet us.

Rosie tugs on my pants and I squat down to her level, "Are they all part giants like Scott?"

Asher is bent down too now, "Don't worry, I'm a gentle giant. That's the one you have to look out for," he points over his shoulder at Oliver. "What's your name?"

"Rosie, what's your name?"

"Asher. But you can call me Webbs if you want."

"Like a spider?"

"Exactly. Wanna go try on some skates Rosie?"

Rosie shakes her head yes and Asher stands up, holds out his hand for her to take it, and leads her over to the bleachers. The rest of us follow.

Some of the guys start helping the girls find the right size skates. I've seen Oliver, Max, and obviously Asher, but there is no sign of Scott. I look around the bleachers. Maybe he decided not to come. Oh shit. What if I scared him off last night? Maybe he doesn't want to be my friend any-

Arms are thrown around my shoulders from behind, "Looking for someone Books?" I almost sigh in relief of hearing his voice.

He cranes his head down to look at the side of my face and I turn my head so that I'm looking at him, "Hey." Oh, thank god. Good to know that he still wants to be around me, even after I turned completely psycho last night.

He turns me around and starts rubbing his hands up and down my arms, "How are you feeling?"

"Better."

"SCOTT! KENNY THAT'S THE BOY WHO GAVE DEL COOTIES," Violet screams and all the guys start laughing a bit.

I cover my face with my hands and Scott chuckles, "Aw, don't be embarrassed Ry, you love my cooties."

I shake my head and turn to make sure everyone is getting their shoes ok. Scott walks over to Tessa.

"Hey Tessa. Read any Harry Potter lately?" he starts tying up her laces and the sight melts my heart.

"I'm on *The Goblet of Fire* right now. Harry just fought the dragon!" she exclaims.

"Very cool," once he's finished with her skates, he pulls his out of his bag and starts putting them on. "Do you like Cedric Diggory?"

"Yes. He's in Hufflepuff, and I'm also in Hufflepuff so I'm pretty sure we would be friends if we met."

"I'm sure you would be. Ready to get on the ice?"

"If I fall, will it hurt?"

"Not too badly. Plus, I won't let you fall."
He takes her hand and leads her to the ice.

He lifts her up a bit and sets her in the rink. She wobbles, but Scott continues to hold her upright under her armpits and goes to stand behind her on the ice.

Soon enough everyone except for myself and a couple of the other employees are on the ice.

Sam did figure skating growing up, so she's out there helping a couple of the girls. I look over to her right and see Max helping her with the group she's with. And I don't miss the way he's looking at her.

There's a handful of girls who already know what they're doing, mainly older ones, and the players are teaching them how to shoot the puck into the goal.

Scott's still with Tess, but he's got her skating all by herself. I mean she's going very slow and her hands are braced out in front of her like she's going to fall any second, but it's progress.

"He's good with them," I look over at Ms. Michelle who tilts her head towards Scott.

"He is. Doesn't surprise me though. He's good with everyone." And it's true, Scott is the most charismatic person I've ever met. I don't think there's a person who doesn't like him.

"He's good with you," she looks towards me. "I think he's exactly what you need. He'd get you out of your shell a bit."

I huff, "I do not have a shell."

"Oh, you totally have a shell. It's not a bad thing. You just guard yourself. You don't let people in easily. I mean it took me like three months to get to know the real you. You've known Scott for what? Close to a month now? And you're already completely comfortable with him. I know it probably scares you, but it's a good thing."

And she's right. It terrifies me how close to Scott I am. Because if I lost him or if our friendship fell apart it would devastate me. I don't know how I'd ever let another person in if he decided he didn't want to be my friend anymore.

"What if he decides that I'm not worth it. What if I've showed him too much of the real me and it scares him off?" I whisper.

"I think if you were going to scare him off, it would've happened by now," she looks back towards Scott who is skating circles around a laughing Tess. "I don't think he'd be this invested in the field trip if it weren't for you. And if he does leave, he's a fucking idiot. And you'll pick yourself right back up. Because you're stronger than letting some boy break you. The way people treat you, the number of friends you have, none of that determines your worth Del. You're a fantastic human being who's going to do great things. If a boy decides to leave, that doesn't lessen that fact one bit."

I nod, "You said the f-word. $2 in the curse jar," we both laugh and when we settle down, I look towards her. "Thanks Michelle, I think I needed to hear that."

"I know you needed to hear that. I could see it weighing on you, you don't fool me Del."

"Ah, I forgot, nothing gets past Ms. Michelle."

"And don't you forget it. And that's my cue to find something else to do."

I give her a confused look as she walks towards some of the other employees.

I look straight to find Scott walking towards me like he's on a mission.

CHAPTER 26: SCOTT

I'm on a mission.

Rydell has be sitting on the bleachers this whole time, and I am going to get her to put some skates and get on the ice with me. It'll give me an excuse to hold her hand.

"What size shoe do you wear?"

"Not happening," she deadpans.

I grab her hands and pull her to stand up with me, "Don't worry Books, I won't let you fall." Even though she let it happen to me.

"Maybe I don't trust you," that's what I'm scared of.

"If you don't put skate on, I'm going to throw you over my shoulder and take you out onto the ice like that. Your choice, but either way, you're getting into that rink."

"You're here to help the girls skate. Not me," she crosses her arms around her chest, and I move towards the skates.

"You've got some klonckers on you. I'd say, what?" I gaze down at her feet. "10?"

"Excuse you," she laughs a little. "I have perfectly normal sized feet."

"Whatever makes you feel better Big Foot,"

she now standing next to me and goes to punch my arm. Before she can I grab her by the wrist and pull her a bit closer to me. "Come one Books, let's get you outta that shell of yours."

She visibly freezes. Like I've said something I wasn't supposed to know. I brush a bit of her hair back to get her to regain focus. She clears her throat, "Um. 7. I'm a size 7."

She sits down and starts to take off the converse she's currently wearing. I smile when I see that she's wearing sushi-cat socks. "Cute socks," I hand her the skates.

"Right?! They're sushi-cats!" she's struggling to pull the skate on.

"Sure, you don't want to reconsider the size 10?" I tease her.

"Fuck off," she laughs.

"Who knew the innocent little bookwork had such a filthy mouth?" Dammit Scott, don't think about her mouth. Too late, I'm definitely sporting a semi.

I kneel down in front of her and start lacing up the skate that she got on. Then going to do the other one once she's pulled it on her foot.

I tie it up and put my hands to cup the back of her calves. "Think you can keep up Gramps?"

I stand up and put my hands out to her. She grabs them and I pull her off the bench to walk to the ice.

"If I fall, I'm taking you down with me."

"That wouldn't surprise me. I mean you did it last night when you tried to dip me."

Her cheeks go slightly red, and I don't think it's from the cold, "Ya, well I can't help it that you weigh a million pounds."

She steps on the ice and I grab her waist as she starts to slip. "Careful old man, you'll break a hip."

"This was a bad idea Scott. I'm gonna freaking crack my head open."

I stand on the ice, keeping my hands on her waist, rubbing my thumbs in circles to calm her down, "I'm not gonna let that happen Books. Just trust me."

She nobs a little. "Ok, now think of it like you're sliding on the tile in your sushi-cat socks. Glide your right foot, then you left."

She does as she's told and starts to move forward, "Good. Just like that. Keep going Ry."

"Del's on the ice! Del! Look at me! Look at me! I'm ice skating all by myself!"

"Awesome job Tess. You're a natural," right as she says it, Tess falls right on her butt.

"Oh shit," Rydell mumbles and she starts skating towards Tessa. She's looks like a newborn horse, but she's not falling. So, I go to stand next to her and grab her hand.

"Scott, you're supposed to be helping me. Not holding my hand!"

"Careful Rydell, you're making me think that you like my hands on your waist."

She huffs.

By the time we get to Tessa she's already back on her feet. "You ok Tess?" Rydell brushes the top of Tess's shoulders to get the ice off.

"I'm ok. Falling doesn't even hurt that bad. Right Scott?"

"Right. Try convincing Del though, she's being a big baby. She's about to squeeze my hand off," and she really is. The girl has got quite the grip.

Rydell shoots daggers at me and Tessa laughs, "Come on Del. Don't be a baby. I'll help you." She sticks out her little hand and Rydell lightly grabs it, still gripping onto mine.

The three of us skate a couple of laps around the rink and Rydell has it down so I release her hand.

Or I try to release her hand. As soon as I let go, she grabs right back on and intertwines our fingers. "Don't you dare. Why don't you just take me back to the bleachers?"

"Come on Books. You have the movement down on your own. Mind over matter Ry."

"Ok, but stay close to me just in case," she slowly releases her hand and starts to skate on her own.

"Look at you go," she starts to pick up her pace a little. "We've got a little speed racer on our hands," I skate backwards so that we can stay face to face.

She's laughing her intoxicating laugh. And she has her dimpled smile. And I think that if I were to die right now, I'd die a very happy man.

"I'm doing it all by mysel-"and her words are cut off by her falling on her ass.

"Fuck," I go towards her, expecting her to be mad at me for not catching her. Her bodies shaking and I think she might be crying.

But when I bend over to see if she's broken anything, I find that she's not crying. Instead, she's laughing so hard that she has to clutch her stomach.

"You ok down there Books. Any broken hips?"

"I'm fine, help me up will ya?" I reach my hand down and pull her up, then put my hands on her hips to stabilize her. And because I like putting my hands on her hips.

She grabs my hand and starts skating laps again, "You let me fall," she says, still with that fucking smile on her face.

I raise the hand that's not holding hers to rub the back on my neck, "Sorry. In my defense, you're very distracting."

"How so?" I skate in front of her so that I'm holding both her hands and skating backwards.

"You probably have the most contagious laugh. You get a dimple on your left chin when you smile," all of a sudden it feels very hot in this ice rink. "You look fucking adorable in that beanie. When I look at you, I forget about everything else going on around me."

Now we're both blushing. She bites her lip and I want to tell her that it's driving me fucking crazy. But before I can even think of doing so there's a small human tugging on my pants.

"Will you teach me how to skate backwards like you," I think this one's name is Rosie. She looks at Del, "Violet asked me to ask you to skate towards her so she can show you her twirl."

"Duty calls," she looks towards me. "Thanks for the lesson Scotty. I think I can take it from here."

CHAPTER 27: RYDELL

He forgets everything around him when he looks at me? I don't know how to process all the shit that he's laid out for me this past week.

He almost kissed me yesterday, he sat with me for hours to help me get over a panic attack, he brought me a sandwich to work.

But, when he brought me that sandwich, he had hickeys on his neck. And when I came to the party yesterday 5 seconds in, he had a pretty ginger wrapped around him.

He's confusing me.

I need to just stick to being friends with this one. It will end badly if I start crushing on him because then whenever I see him out with other girls (which will inevitably happen) I'll be upset.

"Finally, Del, you're like a snail!" Violet exclaims. "Now watch this," her tongue is poking out and she has the most focused looking face. She does a very messy looking twirl and then sticks her hands up in the air as if to say 'ta-da'.

I clap my hands, "Awesome job Vi! Are you having fun?"

"YES! I don't think any of these boys have cooties. Except maybe Scott."

I look over at Scott who has already got Rosie skating backwards. Like he knows my eyes are on him, he looks up and gives me a wink.

I look back at Violet, "Oh ya, Scott definitely has cooties." Or some type of disease that he's made me catch because as much as I want to deny it, my feelings for Scott are more than friendly.

"Not your boyfriend my ass. He's looking at you like he's in love with you, and you're looking at him the way Kendell looks at Ryan," Ava says as her and Kendell skate up.

"Hey, I hide my feelings for Ryan very well. Rydell blushes every time he does literally anything."

"Ha says the one who got beet red in the grocery store when Ryan said hi. I thought you forgot how to use your tongue with all the stuttering you were doing," I retort.

"Not true!"

"Oh, it's so true," Ava jumps in.

I stick my tongue at Kendall, and she mimics me.

"Well, are you guys having fun?" I turn on mature mode.

"This might be the coolest field trip we've been on yet. It definitely helps that we're surrounded by cute boys," Kendall says.

"I think the Halloween Festival is the coolest field trip, but this is a close second," Ava claims.

"Oh, come on, this is so much cooler than a Halloween Festival," I turn around to see Scott holding on to Rosie's hand. "Right Rosie?"

"Sorry Scotty, but the festival is the best field trip. Rydell made me a zombie princess costume for it!"

"If you could wear your zombie princess costume here then this would be the best field trip then?"

She looks up to him and smiles, "Suuuuureee."

"Well now I think I should go to this Halloween Festival if it's so cool."

"Yes, yes, yes! Please go with us Scott!" Rosie exclaims.

Shit. Fuck. Shit. They're getting attached to him. That wasn't supposed to happen. I mean I'm not surprised I got attached, but the girls weren't supposed to.

What if he doesn't want to be my friend after the project and I'm stuck with a group of little girls asking where he is and why he doesn't want to see them anymore. Dammit.

"Oh, I'm not sure if that's Scott's sort of thing. He probably wouldn't want to dress up," I try to talk him out of it.

"And you're dressing up? I'd love to hear what your costume idea is," he's smirking at me.

"That's for me to know and you to never find out."

"She's being a holy cow!" Violet screams. Fucking big mouth.

"A holy cow?"

"I have cow print pants and I'm gonna wear a halo," I mumble giving Violet the stink eye. "Really Violet?"

She just laughs and then takes Rosie's hand from Scott so that they can skate together.

"So, when are you guys going to this festival, I have the perfect costume."

"Oh ya, and what would that be."

"I'm going to dress in all brown and then put a halo on."

I give him a weird look.

"You can be holy cow, and I can be holy shit."

I laugh, "You can't be serious."

"I'm dead serious gorgeous, we'll be the best dressed people there."

"Who says I want you there?"

Kendall and Ava are whispering to each other as they watch the interaction go on. "Plus, I'll be two busy hanging out with Ken and Ava, right you guys?"

"We go the Friday before Halloween every year. This year it's on the 28th," Kendall says as her and Ava skate away.

"Traitors. I'm surrounded by traitors."

Scott laughs. "You should get used to not hiding things from me Ry."

"Hmm."

Before he can say anything, Ms. Michelle yells, "Alright girls, we need to get going. Come to the bleachers please."

I start skating towards the bleachers with Scott right behind. As I make my way over, I trip a bit on an ice chip. Before I can face plant, arms are around my waist and holding me up right.

Scott's breath is tickling my ear, "Careful Books," he moves to my side and grabs my hand until we get to the bleachers.

"Did you do any sports growing up?" Scott asks as we take our skates off.

"I tried soccer for one season, but I was scared of the ball and the other girls made fun of me for it, so I quit," I look up at him and he's smiling.

And I love it when he smiles, especially when I know I'm the one who put it on his stupidly handsome face. "I was the kid who got distracted by butterflies on the field."

"I would've loved to see little Rydell chasing butterflies and ducking every time the ball came around."

"So, you could laugh along everyone else?" I joke.

"I would've laughed in secret. But if I saw anyone bullying you, I'd like to think I'd tell them off for it."

"That's sweet. But if younger you met younger me; we wouldn't be friends."

I tie up the laces on my converse, "Why's that?"

"I'm getting major Prom King vibes from you. Right?"

"Well. Ya, but I don't see how that has anything to do with us being friends."

I huff, "You wouldn't have even noticed me in high school. I spent my lunch in the library and didn't go to Prom."

"Why didn't you go to Prom?"

"Nobody asked me."

"You could've asked someone."

"I did. I asked my boyfriend. And he said it was lame. So, I watched Prom through snapchat stories."

"Sounds like a shitty boyfriend."

"Can't disagree with you there."

"Alright, find your buddy. Leaders, same groups," Michelle announces.

"Well. That's my cue," I stand up and Scott walks me to the van.

"Thanks for making this happen. I think all the girls had a really good time."

"A deal's a deal," my heart drops thinking that this is just a part of a deal.

"Right. See you in class then," I look at Sam who has a sympathetic look on her face like she knows exactly what I'm thinking.

I'm thinking that I'm being stupid. And that I need to start distancing myself before I get hurt. "I'll drive Sam."

Scott opens the door for me, and I climb in, "I have a pre-season game tomorrow at 5:30. You don't have to come, but I thought maybe if you're not busy you could stop by," he pauses and looks down. "I know you're not a hockey fan or anything, but I'd really like it if you were there," his cheeks are pink.

I stay silent having an internal battle with myself. I don't know what his intentions of asking me are. Did he ask Lindsay to come or the ginger? It seems like something friends do but it also seems like a girlfriend type thing and Scott doesn't do relationships as I've been told twice now.

I guess I take too long to respond because now Scott is blurting, "Sorry, I've never really asked anyone to come to my games before. My parents never come and my sister's always busy. And I thought it might be nice to have someone's in the stands for me. You know what, forget I asked I-"

He's never asked anyone to a game before. But friends support each other, I shouldn't be reading into this too much, "I don't get out of work until 6:00, so I'll be late. But I'll try to catch the end of it if that's ok."

"Ya. Yes, absolutely that's fine. Players get

saved seats, so I'll put your name down then and I'll have them add like 3 more seats in case Sam and your old neighbors want to come too."

"Alright. See you tomorrow then."

"See you tomorrow," he has a genuine smile on his face as he closes the door to the car, and I drive off.

CHAPTER 28: SCOTT

"Get your head out of your ass McCombs," I yell over as he lets the other teams center pass him and take a shot towards the goal. Ruddy blocks it and passes it over my way.

Sprinting to get towards that direction, I get the puck and make my way down to the other team's goal post. I can see their left center coming towards me from my peripheral vision, so I pass off to Webbs.

He shoots but their goalie blocks it. "Weak shoot Webbs," I hear coach yelling from the sidelines.

I'm not that concerned about winning, the last period only has like 15 minutes and we are winning by a lot. But the games not over. And until it is, everyone on this team should be playing like we're about to lose. If we get cocky, we get lazy. I don't want this team getting into lazy habits.

Our first pre-season game is always against University of Massachusetts, probably since they're so close to us, and they are usually pretty good competition, but they lost a lot of players last year so they're a little unorganized.

15 minutes pass and the ref blows the

whistle indicating the end of the game.

After games we have a quick huddle with the coaches and then we get to see the people who came to watch us. Then we'll have an actual evaluation of the game in the locker rooms.

I usually go straight to the locker rooms because I never have people come to see me. Rydell was late to the game but during the last period I spotted her in the bleachers. I think she brought two other people with her, but I wasn't really paying attention.

So right after coach's small chat saying good job for the win, I made my way towards her, still in my skates. I texted her earlier to not leave right away and she doesn't because I'm approaching her and my cheeks kind of hurt because of how hard I'm smiling right now.

Her backs turned so she doesn't see my approaching her, and I take that as an opportunity to wrap my arms around her waist from behind and pick her up.

"Guess who?" really, guess who? God I'm so fucking lame. I need to pick up my game.

"Prescott put me down right now, you are way too sweaty to be touching me."

I put her down and turn her around, keeping my arms slightly wrapped around her waist.

"Ah. Come one Books, I've been told on multiple occasions that I'm extra sexy when I'm sweaty."

She huffs, "I'm sure you have," she grabs my hands to take them off her waist. "Good game. I didn't understand anything that was going on, but I figured it was good when you got the puck thingy in the goal and you did that a couple of times."

"Yes, it's definitely good when the puck thingy goes into the goal," I laugh. I look around and notice that her friends left. "Didn't you come with a couple people?"

"Ya, Sam and Lily tagged along, but they said something about going to the bathroom."

Before I can reply I hear coach yell, "Bridges, lockers."

"We usually get some pizza and beers after games. You should come with."

"I have an early morning so I probably shouldn't."

"A slice of pizza won't kill you Gramps, I'll make sure you get home at a reasonable time."

"I carpooled with Sam and she has a date at 8:30 so I can't even if I wanted to."

"Bridges come on," I wave my hand behind my coach indicating that I'll be there in a sec.

"I'll drive you home."

"No, I don't want you to have to leave early. You should stay out and celebrate with your team. This is your first win of the year, kind of an important one."

"I really don't give a fuck about celebrating if you're not there to celebrate with me. Like you said, it's an important one, so you should be there."

"Why would I need to celebrate, I'm not on the team."

"Because I'm captain of the team and I want you there."

She contemplates it for a second. "One slice, and I'll uber home. Now go before I get you in trouble."

"We'll talk about the uber. Stay in the

stadium and I'll come get you when we're done. I don't want you waiting in the parking lot by yourself."

I walk into the locker rooms, "It's about damn time Bridges," Coach Michaels says.

Coach Jerry walks up to me, "I'm glad you had someone in the stands for you tonight. Looked like she makes you super happy," he claps me on the back and walks to stand next to Jerry.

"You guys won. But that doesn't mean that you played well. Bridges tell them what they did wrong."

I go to stand in front of the guys. "You played like you already won the game. You were lazy by the second period and stopped playing to your fullest potential. If we start getting into that early on in our season, it'll become a habit. And it's a bad fucking habit to have. Ruddy, you had solid blocks. Jacobs, I can tell you've been putting in the work, you played well today. Everyone else needs to start taking things seriously."

I go to sit on the bleachers with the rest of my teammates and listen to the coaches break down of the game.

~

I walk towards the rink with my bag slung on my shoulder, spotting Rydell sitting on the bleachers with her face stuffed in a book. Not surprised.

"Ready?" she jumps a little at the sound of my voice.

"Yep. I had about 5 people come up to me asking who I was here for. When I told them your name, they were all very surprised. Not sure why though, I figure at least half the fans are here to watch you specifically."

"Maybe. But you're the first person that I've had sit in the family and friends' section."

She stops walking. "You've never had friends or family come watch you?"

"I wasn't lying when I told you you're the first person I've ever asked to a game before."

"I know. But I just thought that your parents or sister or maybe some friends have watched you play before."

"Well, my sister's always busy, my parents don't give a shit about me, and until you, my only friends were the guys on the team."

I grab her hand to get her to keep walking. Instead of letting go, I keep a hold of it and start swinging our arms back and forth.

"You've never had a girlfriend that you've wanted to get tickets for?"

I open the passenger's door of my car for her, closing it, and then jogging to the driver's seat.

"I've never had a girlfriend period," I start the car and look over to make sure she's buckled. When I see that she is, I start driving towards the pizza place.

"Why?"

"You're full of questions tonight," I notice.

"Sorry," she goes to turn the radio up. "We don't have to talk, where's your phone so I can pick a playlist."

I hand her my phone. She's been in my car before and has used my phone to play whatever she wants so she already knows the passcode.

I slightly look at her then put my eyes back on the road, "I'm not the relationship type. I don't necessarily want to be held down by one girl."

"Well, what if you found the right one?" she's looking down at her lap and playing with her fingers.

"It wouldn't matter. I would ignore it. My parents probably already have someone lined up for me. I need to marry a respectable girl if I'm to run the family business," I say sarcastically but also slightly seriously.

She bursts out laughing. "You can't be serious. You're not serious right? Because we're in the 21st century and that would be completely ridiculous. Plus, you don't even like your parents, why would you do something so life changing to please them?"

"They may be shitty parents but that doesn't mean that I don't care about them."

"Shit. I'm sorry Scott, I wasn't saying you don't. It's just. Marriage is a big deal. I mean, you spend your whole life with that person. I think you should have a say on who it is."

"Don't apologize. You're probably right. But I owe them something. They are the ones who got me into hockey. And hockey is the one thing is this world that I actually love," I look over at her and she looks at her window. It's dark so I can't read her facial expression, but she doesn't look happy.

"But you said that the only reason you started hockey was because they needed you to have an afterschool activity so that they could work more. And sometimes people come into your life when you least expect them to. Who's to say you won't fall in love with them?"

She sounds almost shy as she says it. And she's right. Because I don't know what love is and I never thought I would. But she unexpectedly came into my life and if I did know what love felt like, I think it be what it feels like to be around Rydell.

"If they didn't work so much, I wouldn't have needed an afterschool activity."

She's quick to respond, "I don't think that means you owe them anything. Them getting you into hockey to neglect you shouldn't be something you reward them for. Especially if you're marrying her for the image of a company I don't think you even really want."

She's bringing up a lot of good points. "You don't know what I want."

"I guess not," her voice is tight.

We pull up to the pizza place and as we're walking to the entrance she says, "Lily said that she could pick me up, so I think I'm just going to get my slice to go. I'm really tired and I do have to be up early tomorrow."

She's wrapping her arms around herself like she's trying to warm herself up and I have to impulse to wrap my arms around her, but I don't think she'd be too into that at the moment.

"Is it because I told you about my relationship situation."

"No." But she won't look me in the eye. Of course, this is why I don't open up to people. But I don't want to close myself off when it comes to Rydell.

"Hey. I'll think about what you said, ok? You're right, I don't want my family's business. And I don't owe my parents anything. But it's complicated."

I put my arms around her, and she just stands there, still with her arms wrapped around herself. I pull back and start rubbing my hands up and down her arms to warm her up.

She looks up, "I just want you to be happy Scott. You know I care about you, right?"

I don't think I've ever had a person tell me that they care about me before. And I don't think I really cared. But it's everything to hear it from Rydell.

"I know. And I appreciate it probably more than you realize. Thank you for coming to the game by the way."

"Mhmm. I'll make it to them whenever I can. I can't promise I'll be at all of them though."

I grab her hand, which is freezing, and walk to the door. "One slice with me? I gotta warm you up, you're freezing."

"One slice."

CHAPTER 29: RYDELL

We order our pizza and have just found a spot at a table with some of the other hockey boys and girls that Scott calls puck bunnies.

He's still holding my hand, claiming that he's warming it up. But I can't stop thinking about what he said in the car.

I almost started crying. Not because I want to be with him. Ok maybe slightly because I want to be with him, but more so because I'm sad that he has to live like that.

Live thinking that he owes his shitty parents something. He doesn't owe them anything. And I hate they are taking away marriage for him. And not just marriage, his whole life.

If he starts running that company, it will become his whole life. And he doesn't even want the fucking company. It'll make him miserable and that makes me want to cry. Thinking about Scott being stuck in a situation that makes him miserable.

Then he asked me if I wanted to leave because of his relationship situation and I said 'no'. But if I'm being completely honest, maybe it was because of it. He said that even if he found the right girl, it wouldn't matter. That even if by some extraordinary miracle, even if he could come to have feelings for me like I'm having for him, it wouldn't matter. Fuck. I really have dug a hole with this one.

I'm brought out of my thoughts when Scott grabs my other hand off my lap. "Jesus Books, you're freezing. You should really have worn mittens." He brings my hands up to his face and warms them with his breath.

Which is a little gross in hindsight and I've never understood why people do it because his mouth germs are getting all over my hands. But I don't mind Scott's mouth germs. He was right, I love his cooties.

"Deli! I knew I saw you in the stands. You know, you're the first person Scotty Boy has ever had in the family stands. You must be pretty special," Asher says.

He definitely already has a couple beers in him. And so many people are looking at me now, waiting for my response. Scott puts my hands down to his lap.

"Well, it was a very exciting game. You guys all played well," I really have no idea if they played well, all I know is that they made more goals than the other team.

"Oh ya, we really know how to get the puck thingy into the goal. Right Ry?" Scott's making fun of me.

I grab my hands out of his grasp and punch his shoulder lightly. "Sorry Prescott, not all of us are hockey experts like you."

"Nope, just everyone at this table," he smiles down at me.

"You guys are so cute together," Asher gushes. And then runs up to order another beer. He definitely has had one too many.

"I'm gonna go check on him. You ok for a minute?"

I nod yes and watch him go take care of Asher.

"Hi. I'm Dylan Jacobs. But everyone just calls me Jacobs."

He has dark hair and brown eyes and is definitely one of the younger players.

"Rydell Rivens," I put my hand out to shake his. Do people still shake hands? That's a thing, right? Oh shit, my hands are probably so clammy. "But everyone calls me Del. Sorry, my hands are probably super clammy right now. They're always like that." God, why can't I just keep my mouth shut.

He laughs a little, "You're good. You're a computer science major right?"

"Yes. Are you a comp sci major too?"

"No. Mechanical engineering actually. But I had to take a cs course, and one of my professors spent an entire lecture going over a code you did for a project of his."

"Oh ya, Professor Bahri. He told me he was going to show it to his class. I've been in a couple of his classes. I'm in one of his advanced color sequencing classes. He's helping me proof code for a video game I'm creating."

"You're creating a video game? That's fucking dope."

"It's pretty cool right? My friend Sam is doing the graphics for it. It's meant to target kids with behavioral problems. Studies show that violet games for kids with autism or anger issues cause violent behavior. So, we're creating a game that helps build motor skills and activates positive brain stimulation. It will hopefully help them with things like problem solving, creativity and possibly communication skills," I could literally talk about it all day, but I don't want to bore him.

"That's so cool. What kind of sequence are you using for it?"

"It's a custom code, but I'm using C programing language. And some 3-D code engine mainly for graphics which seems to give me the most trouble."

"Makes sense. But the 3-D engine is necessary right? Especially for graphics."

"Exactly. What do you want to do with mechanical engineering?"

"I want to go into aerospace engineering eventually. I know it's a little ambitious, but ever since I can remember, I've wanted to work for NASA. Not as an astronaut or anything but work on the machines that are taken up into space to help us get a better idea of what else it out there."

"I think it's good to be ambitious. That sounds super cool. You seem like a pretty well-balanced guy. Not many people ask me questions about the mechanics of the coding I'm working on. You did. I think that says something about your intellect."

He's blushing. "Thanks Del."

"Your welcome Jacobs. What grade are in?"

Scott sits down next to me, with my pizza in hand. "M'lady".

"Thank you."

"Sophomore. You're a senior like Scott?"

"Yep, almost out of here."

"Ry, you made a new friend. I'm so proud

of you. I thought you'd feel awkward just sitting here," I roll my eyes at him.

"Yes, you better watch out, Jacobs might take your spot as best hockey friend."

"I'm your best every kind of friend Books. You and Sam both know it. You're being nice to her Jacobs right?"

"Of course, Cap. Enjoy the rest of your night Del. I'm heading out Scotty, I have a night shift at the bar tonight."

"Jacobs, it's only a couple hour shift right?" he says as they do their little dude handshake.

"Yep, don't worry cap, I'll be nice and rested for practice tomorrow."

"You better be."

I'm already about halfway done with my pizza by the time he leaves. "Good lord Ry, you're inhaling that pizza. What did you eat today?"

"I usually eat after my shift, but I came straight to your game, so I didn't have time to eat."

"You should've gotten something at the snack bar."

"I didn't want to miss anything."

"You didn't even understand what was going on, it would not have matter if you missed a couple more minutes of it."

I just shrug. "No wonder you get cold so easily. You have no meat on your bones. I need to fatten you up."

"You shouldn't talk about a ladies weight Scotty," Max chimes in.

"Ya Scotty," I tease him.

He mumbles a 'sorry'.

Not too long after, I've finished my pizza. "Ok, I'm going to order an uber and get out of here."

"Noooo. Aren't you still hungry? You only had one slice; one more will be good for you."

"The slice was big Scott, plus if I'm still hungry I'll just eat something from home."

"But pizza's better than you're food from home. Plus, if you ate at your house then you'd have to make it. If you filled yourself up here, you wouldn't have to make it. Think of the dishes you won't have to wash."

"I'm not even hungry."

"Fine, we'll get one to go then. And if you really don't want to eat it tonight you can eat it for breakfast."

"I don't eat breakfast."

"Well, you will tomorrow."

"God, you're annoying. Fine," I stand up and start walking to the register to order my to-go pizza. "One slice of cheese to go please."

"3.50," I go to hand to swipe my card but before I can Scott hands her a $5.

"Keep the change," he grabs my hand and takes me to the to-go waiting area.

"That was totally unnecessary. I could've paid for it," hell ya I could've, I'm an independent woman.

"Think of it as payback for the burritos and tacos."

"Whatever," I cross my arms over my chest. I pull out my phone to order my uber. Before I can do so my phone is taken out of my hands and into Scott's pocket.

"Hey, give me that back. I need to order an uber."

"No, you don't. I'm driving you home."

"Scott. The whole point of you coming here

was to celebrate. You've hardly celebrated."

"Yes, and I'll come back after I drop you off. I have to make sure Asher gets home. But I'd rather drive you home than have a stranger do so."

"Careful Scotty. Keep saying things like that and I'll start think you care about me."

He turns fully towards me, "Rydell Rivens. I don't think there's a person in this entire world that I care about more than you."

What the fuck. I don't even have words. How am I supposed to respond to that? I mean, he knows I care about him. I made it pretty clear earlier tonight. Fuck, he's so confusing.

"You are my bestie after all." Right. Friends. That's what I wanted though. But if that's what I wanted why am I so disappointed to hear it?

"Right."

"Order 28," I walk up to the counter and grab my food with a thank you to the employees before walking out the door.

Scott moves in front of me and I take this as an opportunity to grab my phone from his back pocket.

"Ha ha. I'm too speedy for you Scott. You never saw it coming," I'm speed walking away from him because if I can avoid running, I tend to. And I'm trying to order this uber so he doesn't have to go through the trouble of driving me home.

And 2 seconds later, he has me thrown over his shoulder. "Go ahead Rydell. Order your uber. But you won't ever be getting into it. I'm driving you home whether you like it or not. And think about how sad the uber driver will be when he drives all the way here only to be stood up."

"Dammit Scott. You are the most stubborn

person I've ever met."

He pats the back of my thigh, "Not fast enough Gramps."

I flip him off but realize he can't see my hand, "Just so you know, I'm totally flipping you off right now."

He laughs, "I'm sure you are."

CHAPTER 30: *SCOTT*

"Scott, you missed the turn."

"I know, I'm not taking you home."

"What do you mean you're not taking me home. Oh god, I knew your stalker tendencies were a red flag. You're probably driving out to the middle of the woods to kill me. I just want you to know, that I am carrying pepper spray, one wrong move, and you'll regret it."

I start laughing. "I thought we came to an agreement tonight that I am way more stealthy and faster than you. I'd dodge it."

"First of all, I don't remember agreeing to that. Second, you wouldn't see it coming."

"Of course I'd see it coming, you just told me your plan of attack. You would so be dead if I was an axe murderer."

"I have other tricks up my sleeve."

"Oh ya, like what?"

"Well, obviously I'm not going to tell you. You know just in case you are planning on murdering me."

I pull into the McDonald's drive through. "Good to know you're learning."

"What are we doing here?"

"October 14th is National Dessert Day. I know how much you like the sundaes from here, so I figured it was fitting to stop for one."

I look at her, and she's looking at me with her fucking dimpled smile, "You've been looking up national holidays?"

"I figured I should prepare myself. I don't want to get roped into eating another fluffy sandwich."

"It's called a fluffernutter."

"Sure, and it's fucking disgusting."

"Welcome to McDonald's what can I get for you."

"One hot fudge sundae please."

We roll up to the window and drive away when we get her sundae.

She holds her spoon out to me to take a bite, "I didn't order one for a reason Del."

"Yes, a stupid reason. Just take one bite Scott, it's not going to kill you."

"It might. You know I don't like sweet things."

"Your favorite food is pancakes. Hate to break it to you, but that's a sweet food."

"That's an expectation."

"Well, I'm not eating any of this until you take a bite, so up to you."

"Stubborn woman," I let her feed me a bite.

"Says the one who refused to let me order an uber."

"That was for your safety."

"Yes and taking a bite of this is for your well-being. Good right?"

"Oh soooo good," I drawl out sarcastically.

"I think I need to put you into a mental

hospital. There's no way you're sane if you don't think that tastes good."

I laugh and shake my head, "Whatever." We sit in a comfortable silence until I ask something that I've been wondering for a while. "What about you and relationships. You know I've never had a girlfriend. Have you ever had a boyfriend?"

She laughs a bit, "That came out of nowhere."

"Sorry, I was just wondering, you don't have to tell me if you don't want to."

"No. I've had two boyfriends. My first one was Danny Fitzgerald in 6th grade. I had the biggest crush on him, so I made him a friendship bracelet and told him I liked him. And then he kissed me on the cheek and asked me to be his girlfriend."

"Ah young love," why do I feel so jealous of a boy she dated in fucking middle school?

"Only lasted about two weeks though. He gave the friendship bracelet I made him to another girl, and I cried myself to sleep for like I week and told myself I'd never date another boy again," she laughs and shakes her head.

"What a little asshole, if I ever meet this Danny Fitzgerald, I'll beat the shit out of him for hurting 6th grade Rydell."

"Oh, trust me, my brother took care of it. The day after it happened my older brother, who was an 8th grader at the time punched him in the face and got suspended for a week."

"Sounds like my kinda guy."

"And my only other boyfriend I dated all throughout my junior year and most of senior year. Trey Handson. He's the one who wouldn't go to Prom with me. He was captain of the surf team and thought he was too cool for it. He was popular and a lot of people were confused about why he'd want to be with me. But we knew each other because our parents are friends. His family was always at our house or vice versa. I had multiple people telling me it wouldn't work out, but I fell in love with him anyways," she looks down at her lap. I pull into her driveway and give her my full undivided attention.

"I thought he would be the person I ended up marrying. My family loved him. He was one of my only friends at school. And we were different in a lot of ways, but he never made me feel- I don't know, unworthy of having him I guess."

She looks up to see if I'm still listening, so I nod, encouraging her to continue.

"I was always very scared of sex. Because of," she clears her throat a bit and lowers her voice, "because of what happened with the whole sexual assault thing. I mean when it happened, they never actually went all the way. They just got me naked and touched me. But the concept of losing my virginity and being that vulnerable with someone was still terrifying," her voice is tight, and I can tell she's struggling so I grab her hand and intertwine it with mine. And I squeeze it to give her some comfort. My blood is boiling as I hear specifics about what happened to her.

"Take your time," I tell her.

She shakes her head. "I applied to all the colleges that he applied to. I only applied to Daxton because it had been my dream school for forever, considering they have one of the best Comp Sci programs. But I applied with the intention of not going. I just want to see if I could get in. None of the schools he applied to had a good computer science program, but I didn't care. Because I thought that as long as I was with him, nothing else would matter," her eyes are watering and she's sniffling a bit and it's breaking my heart. "Because he made me happy. And I wasn't really sure why someone like him would want to be with me so when he told me that he couldn't be with me anymore if I didn't sleep with him, I let him take my clothes off and do whatever he wanted to do with me. I thought that was what love was supposed to be like. Making sacrifices and doing whatever you could to make the other person happy, even if it was at the expense of your own."

A tear runs down her cheek and I cup her face with my free hand to wipe it off.

"But the morning after he took my virginity, he told me that he didn't feel a spark anymore and that he didn't want to be tied down when he left for college. And I spent so much time hating myself for it. That maybe if I had sex with him sooner, he wouldn't have left me."

"Rydell. He's a shitty person. None of what happened is your fault. And it's probably a good thing you're not with the asshole anymore."

"I know that now," she nods her mind. "But it took me a couple years to figure it out. I had a lot of meaningless hookups my first year of college because I thought that maybe if I got more experience, my next relationship wouldn't end so badly. There was a period of time when I thought I'd never be happy again. Like I didn't deserve to be. I forced myself out of bed and I started this endless cycle of nothingness. But one day something clicked, and I started to pull myself together. I think a lot of it had to do with starting to create the video game and finding purpose. And working with the girls at the orphanage."

"And are you happy now?" there's a lump in my throat. Like I might start to cry thinking about how shitty this asshole made her feel.

"Most days."

"What do you do the days you're not?"

"Focus on the good things I have going. Remind myself that I have a purpose. Try my best to make other people happy in case they're feeling the same way I am."

"Rydell Rivens. You are most definitely the best person I've ever met. I wish we knew each other in high school. You said we wouldn't have been friends, but I think we would've been. And I wish I had been there to help you through the Trey situation. Because you are the last person who deserves to feel anything less then worthy. The world doesn't deserve your kindness, and if I could shield you from every bad feeling in this world I would."

"I wish I knew you in high school too. I think we both could've used a friend." My hand is still rubbing her cheek and before I can start leaning in, she says, "Well, thanks for the sundae. It's getting late but, I'll see you in class," I shake my head at her abruptness. I can tell that it was a lot for her to tell me and I don't want to push her so I don't mention it.

She goes to exit the car and I walk her to her doorstep.

"You didn't need to walk me to my doorstep."

"There could be an axe murderer on the loose."

She turns around from unlocking her door, "That's exactly something an axe murderer would say."

Once she unlocks it, she leans on her doorframe. "Thanks again, for the pizza too," she holds up her to-go bag. "And the chat. Have a good rest of your night Scott."

She looks so pretty, and I don't know if it's because of the conversation we just had but, I lean down and lightly kiss her cheek, letting my lips linger there for longer than I should have. Her breath intakes a bit and I smile at the affect I have on her. "Sweet dreams gorgeous."

She nods absentmindedly "Mhmm," and with that she walks into her apartment and shuts the door.

~

When I get back to the pizza place, I spot Asher swapping salvia some random puck bunny. Jesus, he's going to get himself kicked out for public indecency with the way her hand is pulling at the hem of his shirt.

I internally vomit and make my way towards Ruddy and some of the other guys who are chilling in a booth.

"Get Rydell home ok?" Max asks.

"Yep. Took a bit of effect, but I got her there," I smile thinking about her stubbornness.

"I'm glad you have her man. I think she's really good for you. It's about time you start to seriously settle down with a girl."

"Thanks, but we're just friends. If I slept with her, I'd fuck everything up."

"You really think you'd fuck her and then leave her? Because I don't. I don't think there's

191

much, if anything, that could keep you away from that girl."

"I can't lose her man. My future? It's already planned for me. And I want her in my future, but there's things I don't want to rope her into, that's why she can only be in it as a friend. Especially when my parents inevitably introduce me to the girl they want me to marry."

"That's all bullshit Scott. You're one of the most independent people I know. You don't take shit from anyone and you sure as hell don't let people boss you around. I don't know why the hell you'd let your parents control your life like that. Especially when you have a fucking good thing going with Rydell."

"It's complicated."

"No, it's not. I was on the verge of being black out drunk, but I remember you telling me not too long ago that one day, I'll find a girl, and she'll be worth the possibility of being hurt," he pauses to clap me on the shoulder. "You've found your girl man. And sure, maybe you'll get hurt. But I don't think you will. And if you do, I think it'll be worth it. Somethings are worth it, and Rydell is one of them. I can tell by the way you look at her. And the way she looks at you."

"And how does she look at me," I'm practically on the edge of my seat waiting for his answer.

"Like you're the only person in the room. And that first interaction I had with her when she came over to our house with burritos… she was fucking uncomfortable. But as soon as you walked into the room, she was so visibly relieved. She looks at you like you're safety. It takes a lot of trust and connection to feel completely safe with someone Scott."

"And what if she doesn't want to be my friend after this project?"

"I really don't think that's something you need to worry about", but then he adds, "I think if she does distance herself after the project, she'll do it because she thinks you might want that. And in that case, you reassure her that you want her in your life. You guys are gonna be fine man."

"I really fucking hope so."

CHAPTER 31: RYDELL

A week and a half pass and it's already October 28th. There are three important things about today:

1. It's National Chocolate Day
2. Field trip to the Halloween Festival
3. Scott and I present our project

That last one scares me the most. Not because I think we'll get a bad grade. We'll fucking ace it. I know because this past week we've done multiple practice presentations and most of them went very smoothly.

stalker to me: *stop freaking out, we're going to be great. No negative emotions Books, we gotta manifest this shit.*

me to stalker: *don't forget your flashcards*

stalker to me: *already packed and ready to go. See you in a bit.*

~

As I walk up to the lecture hall, I spot Scott standing in the front reading his flashcards. He looks up, making eye contact with me and walks the short distance towards me.

We walk in to find our seats, "I can practically feel your nerves Ry," he's walking behind me since the rows are narrow and puts his hands on my shoulders, rubbing them lightly.

"Sorry. I hate public speaking."

"Don't apologize. I happen to love public speaking, so if you need help during any of it, I'll jump in. I have most of your notes memorized."

"I said I hate public speaking, not that I'm bad at it."

He laughs, "There she is."

We sit down as the professor walks in. Scott's eyes are burning holes in the side of my face. I look at him, "What?"

His tongue pokes at the side of his cheek, "Nothing," he looks forward.

And then I feel his hand cover my thigh. I hadn't realized it was shaking until he did so. He starts rubbing small circles with his thumb then looks over at me again, "Relax," he whispers.

"Alright, any volunteers to go first?"

My hand shoots up. I always prefer to get it over with. "Alright Ms. Rivens come on up. Do you have a partner?"

As I stand up, I point my thumb back at Scott, "Yes. Scott Bridges," as I say Scott's name, I can practically hear the girls in the class swoon which makes me internally roll my eyes.

After I set up the PowerPoint, I go to stand next to Scott, take a deep breathe, and begin.

~

Walking out of the lecture hall, Scott picks me up into a hug and twirls me around. After class, we got our grade from the Professor which just so happened to be an A+.

"I knew we could do it! For someone who hates public speaking, you're really fucking good at it," he sets me down but keeps his hands on my waist, and I keep mine wrapped around his neck.

I'm laughing and say, "We make a pretty good team don't we?"

"Fuck ya we do! We have to celebrate, I have practice soon, but maybe after we can go somewhere?"

"Halloween Festivals tonight and I have to be at the orphanage early to help them get ready," I say as we unwrapped ourselves and start walking to the parking lot.

"Right, I totally knew that. And I'll definitely be there. I mean, I already got my costume."

"You don't have to come."

"Trying to get rid of me Books?"

"No, it just doesn't seem like your scene. Also, don't you need to be walking the other way?"

"As if I'd let you walk to your car by yourself. And I'm actually very excited for this festival, Tess and Rosie talked my ear off about it the other day."

Scott brought me lunch again a couple days ago. Well, more like a dinner/lunch, it was at like 4. And the girls adore him, so he stayed a bit to hang out during screen time.

He opens my car door for me after I unlock it. It the poshest accent I can muster up I say, "Why thank you kind sir."

He mimics my accent, "You're welcome, fair lady," he puts his arms on the top of my car and leans down to my level, "See you tonight Books." And he kisses my cheek. And my heart stops. It always does when he kisses my cheek, which has been his way of saying goodbye ever since the night we got pizza.

It confuses the fuck out of me, and we still haven't talked about it. But I'm so scared to bring it up because I don't want him to stop doing it.

~

"ME NEXT!!!!" Violet screams. I'm in the bathroom doing the younger girls' hair for the festival tonight. Sam is sitting next to me doing their makeup. Kendall and Ava are also helping out with hair and makeup.

"Alright Vi, pig tails or braids?" she's being a cowgirl.

"Braids please," I start brushing out her curly hair with my fingers, so it doesn't get too fizzy and begin my work.

"How'd the project go?" Sam asks.

"A+ baby," I gloat.

"That doesn't surprise me. So, what happens next? With Scott."

I sigh, "I mean, I hope we still friends. He's coming tonight, that has to mean something right? And it's not like we finished the project and I felt detached from him. We still feel like friends," or maybe more than friends. He kisses me on the cheek, holds my hand sometimes, and when he looks at me I wanna grab his cheeks and kiss the shit outta him. But I keep that little fact to myself.

But he also told me that he doesn't do relationships, not even if he found the right girl. And I don't know if it's healthy for me to be around him as much as I have been. Because I told myself that I only to be his friend, but I'd be a liar if I said that's still what I want. And I don't want to get anymore attached to a person that will never be with me long term.

"Del. I know you're overthinking all this shit-"

"CURSE JAR!" Violet exclaims.

"Sorry. Stuff," she lowers her voice so that the girls can't hear as much. "And I know you're thinking about distancing yourself. I've seen you do it with just about every person at this college. But I think what you have with Scott is a good thing. I hate to admit it, but he's one of your best friends now. Second to me of course. But I think you could also possibly be more than friends. And I think if that's the route you decided to take, it would work out pretty well."

"I can't be with him like that. He doesn't do relationships," I finish tying up Violet's second braid, "All done Vi."

"THANKS DEL!" she exclaims as she runs off.

"Well maybe you can change his mind."

I huff and throw my head back to look at the ceiling. "I don't want to have to change his mind for him. I want him to do it willingly. If it's something I have to force out of him, I don't want it. And I don't want him to change himself for me," there's a lump in my throat. "I like him how is."

I look down and cover my eyes with my hands. "If I'm not good enough for him to want to be with, there's nothing I can do about it," I whisper. "So, if I start detaching myself now, I'll be less hurt when he inevitably leaves me."

"Del," whoever's makeup she was doing has left and Kendall and Ava are in a different bathroom doing hair and makeup, so we're left alone. She wraps her arms around me, pulling me in for a hug. "You're such a fucking awesome human being. If Scott can't see that, then he's an idiot. And I really don't think he's going to leave you. I've seen the way he looks at you."

I snort, "Oh ya, and how does he look at me?"

"Like he wants to push you up against a wall and kiss the living daylights out of you. Like you're the only person in the world that matters. You need to stop treating every relationship like they're going to end it the way Trey did."

"I'm trying."

"I know. Just don't be scared to let yourself be happy. You'll end up regretting it when you let a good thing slip through your fingers."

~

I'm holding the hands of two zombie princesses and making my way over to the goat pen. The elementary girls love the petting zoo aspect of the carnival.

"Goats! Goats! Goats!" Sophie is chanting.

"I hope we get to feed them carrots!" Rosie chimes in.

"Finally! I've been waiting for forever!" Scott says as we approach the pen. I texted him that we go there first.

"SCOTT!!" Rosie runs to him and jumps in his arms.

I start laughing realizing the costume he's in. "I can't believe you actually did it," I take in his 'holy shit' attire. And then look down at my 'holy cow' attire.

"I told you I was going to Books. I wanted us to match," I'm pretty sure my heart just flipped.

"Awesome princess zombie costume Rosie."

"What about mine?" Sophie stomps her foot and crosses her arms around her chest.

Scott bends down to scoop her in his other arm so that he's balancing each of them on his hips. "Very cool Soph. Your hair is on point."

"Del did it!" she exclaims, then points to the goats. "Now take us to feed the goats Scott!"

The other girls who wanted to see goats are already in the pen feeding them. Sam took her small group to the face painting, the middle schoolers and high schoolers get to go off by themselves as long as they check in every hour. The remaining are with me and Ms. Michelle at the petting zoo.

Scott scoops up some of the goat food into his hands and transfers it into Rosie and Soph's tiny hands.

I look over to the other girls who are with Michelle to make sure that they're doing ok and then walk over to Scott and the girls bending down to pet the goat that Rosie is feeding.

Another goat comes up from behind me and starts chewing on my angel wings. "No bad goat, that's not food." The one Rosie is feeding jumps so its hooves are on my shoulder, sufficiently causing me to fall on my back.

And Scott is having a field day with it. His phone is out and he's snapping a pic of me shielding myself as two goats attack me, laughing like it's the funniest this he's ever seen.

"Come here goaties. Don't worry Rydell, Rosie and I will save you!" Sophie exclaims. She manages to distract the goats with food for enough time for me to stand up.

"I'd say the goats like you Ry," Scott's still

laughing.

"Asshole," I mumble. "Some help would've been nice."

"Aw. Did the goats scare you Rydell?" he teases.

"Prescott, I was attacked!"

He's still chuckling, but wraps he's arms around me. One around my waist and the other angled so that his hand is brushing my hair. I keep my hands at my side but put my cheek to his chest and listen to his heartbeat.

"Such a traumatic experience."

I push him off me, "I'd like to see you go up against two goats."

He laughs at little and then starts to brush the hay off my back and out of my hair as I watch the girls pet the goats.

Ms. Michelle walks up, "Well, if I ever have to bet money against who would win in a fight: you or goats, I know who I'd pick".

Now both of them are laughing at me, "Ha ha. Yes, let's all laugh at Rydell."

"Kidding, kinda. Del you don't have night shift today we just need you until we leave, so if you and Scott wanted to stay later, you can do that," she gives me a knowing look and then walks off.

"What do you say Ry. I doubt the girls are going to want to go through the haunted maze. We could hit it up when they leave. I can drive you home."

"I hate haunted mazes."

"Don't worry, I'll keep you safe," he puffs his chest out a bit.

"Scott, I can barely handle goats. Imagine how I'd be in a maze where the goal is to get scared!"

"Come on Gramps, I'll be fun. And I'll buy you a funnel cake after."

"Dammit Scott, I can't resist carnival food."

"Great, I take that as a yes then. Does Sam have night shift?"

"Ya, we drove separately to the orphanage. So, instead of taking me to my house, can you take me there to get my car?"

"Mhmm."

"Can we go on the bumper cars now Del?" Soph asks.

I'm in charge of Sophie and Rosie for the night so I just go wherever they want to, "Sure Soph. Rosie, that's what you want to do too?"

"Yep, I call holding Scott's hand!"

"No, I want to hold his hand," Sophie pouts.

"My hands aren't good enough?" I huff.

"I think Rydell's just mad because *she* wanted to hold my hand," he grabs Rosie and Sophie's hands and starts to swing them.

"Del, you can hold my free hand," I grab onto Rosie's open hand and she starts swinging are arms like Scott's doing to hers.

"Don't worry Books, you'll have plenty of opportunities to hold my hand," Scott looks over at me and winks and I curse myself for letting my cheeks heat up.

~

"Hey Ken!" We just got off the bumper cars and I've just spotted Kendall so I figured I'd check up on her.

She's giving me the 'shoo, go away hands' and I'm very confused until I see Ryan pop out and hand her an ice cream.

"Ice cream for the lady," he looks up and sees me. "Hey. You're Kendall's sister. Rydell right?" he then looks at Sophie and Rosie. And there's no way that those two can get away with being Kendall's sister.

I look like Kendall. We both naturally tan, but obviously white, with brown hair and hazel eyes.

Sophie is Latina with black hair. And Rosie is a pale skinned ginger with blue eyes.

"Sister?" Scott whispers to me. I'm dressed as a holy cow, but I'm wearing my cow print pants with my white Massachusetts Orphanage Recycle Crew shirt. All the employees wore them, in case one of the girls lost us.

"Hi Ryan. I didn't realize that you were coming to the carnival."

He's clearly read my shirt. Shit. "Ya, my mom is doing a bake sale and I saw Kendall walking around so I thought I'd say hi." He looks at Kendall. Then back at me. "You work at the orphanage?" he nods towards my shirt and now it's my turn to look at Ken.

"Yep. Umm, we're here on a field trip," I gesture to the girls who are staring wide eyed at the whole situation.

And then Sophie opens her big mouth, "Kendall, when we get home, before it's lights out will you paint my nails again? You have the best nail polish there and mines chipped?"

Fuck. Kendall looks like she's about to start crying. Ryan is chewing the inside of his cheek than looks at Kendall, "Rydell's not your sister, is she?"

She shakes her head no. "So what? You just lied. Straight to my face. And what if we did get serious and I wanted to meet your parents? What would you have said to me then? You really think I would stop talking to you because you're an orphan? Fuck, Kendall. How do you really see me then if you think I'd be that shallow?"

"Ryan," she tries.

"You know what? I don't even want to hear it," he starts walking away.

"Kendall," I go to give her some sort of comfort but as soon as my hand touches her arm she pulls away.

"God. You just had to open your big mouth didn't you Sophie? Well thanks a lot for that," she has tears running down her cheeks and runs off to god knows where.

"Shit," I put my hands in my hair.

"Go on. Make sure she's ok. I can stay with the girls."

"Scott I-"

"Del, Ava's with me. We can handle it. We'll sit over at the benches over there until you're done."

I look to Ava who gives me a nod and make my way to Kendall.

CHAPTER 32: SCOTT

Sophie's crying. And I'm not sure how to handle it.

I look over at Ava for some help, but she's looking down at her phone texting someone.

I pull Sophie onto my lap and start to brush her tears away. "You're ok Soph. You're going to mess up your makeup."

That just makes her cry harder. She wraps her little arms around my neck, and I pull her into a hug. "Shhhh. It's ok. You're ok. How about you tell me what's wrong."

"Kendall yelled at me," she gets out between sobs. "I just wanted her to paint my nails. I didn't mean to make her upset," I can feel her tears soaking through my shirt. And probably her snot too because she can't control her nasal canal, I guess.

"She's just upset because she got into a fight with her boyfriend. It's not your fault."

She brings her face out to look at me, "It's not?" and sure enough she has snot all over her nose.

I'm a little grossed out by it, but I pull her back, lift the bottom of my shirt and wipe it off for her.

"No. And hey, maybe Ava will paint your nails. Right Ava?" I give her a look that says, 'you better fucking say yes'.

"Oh ya. Totally," she looks back down at her phone.

"Ok. Thanks Ava!"

"Mhmm," she hums and I roll my eyes.

"How ya doin' Rosie," she's sitting down next to me on the bench, swinging her dangling legs.

"I'm boreddddddd," she complains.

"Well, as soon as Rydell comes back, we can go do something else. Maybe we can go to the trunk or treat section?"

"No, that's last. We have to pick out pumpkins first. We're carving them tomorrow," she explains like it's the most obvious information ever.

I look around and spot a cotton candy stand not too far from where we are. "Do you guys like cotton candy?"

~

Everyone is now happy and there's not complaining being done as we sit back down in our seats with cotton candy.

Not too long after we sit down, Rydell and Kendall come walking up. I hold out a cotton candy to Kendall and she shyly accepts it, "Thanks, sorry for taking Rydell away on your date."

I say, "No need to apologize" at the same time Rydell mumbles, "Not a date". And it stings a little.

Rydell looks at me, "How much was the cotton candy? I'll pay you back for it. Also, thanks for watching them. It's not your job, and I know for a fact that Halloween parties start tonight. Those are always the best parties of the year; you should go.

Have some fun."

"And what if I said that this carnival is way more fun than any frat party?"

She gives me a 'really?' type look. "Then I'd say your full of s-h-i-t," she spells shit out.

"Well, I am dressed up as it, so makes sense, right?" she laughs a bit and I'm glad she doesn't look as stressed anymore. Then I add, "It doesn't really matter where we are Ry, I always have fun with you. Plus, I can't leave until we go through the haunted maze."

"I just don't want you to feel like you're obligated to be here. I mean I'm technically working, I'm in caretaker mode. This probably isn't your ideal night. And all your roommates are probably out now. You might regret staying here when they tell you about how much fun they had."

I grimace a bit, "If you don't want me to be here, just say it Books."

"No!" she exclaims immediately. "I love your company, of course I want you here."

Before she can say anything else, I say, "Then I'll be here. Rydell, I promise you, there's no place I'd rather be."

She nods.

"Del, can we go pick pumpkins now? Ava and Kenny said they'd go with us too!" Rydell looks over at the older girls and raises her eyebrows.

"You two want to go with us to pick pumpkins?" she questions.

"We did just have a conversation about me accepting my family. You're right Del, I shouldn't be hiding them," Rydell looks like she just won the lottery and I smile at her happiness.

"I'm right?" Rydell mimics here. "Well, I

could get used to hearing that. Say it again Ken, tell me how right I am?"

"Oh shove off," Kendall laughs then looks down at Sophie, "I'd love to paint your nails later. And I'm sorry for yelling at you."

Sophie stands up on the bench and wraps her arms around Kendall. "That's ok Kendall. I'm sorry your boyfriend yelled at you."

Kendall mumbles, "He's not my boyfriend."

"Yes, he is. He looks at you the way Scott looks at Del," that little fucking big mouth.

I look over at Rydell who is hiding her face in her hands. "Look, Scott's blushing!" Ava exclaims.

Now she gets off her phone. Of course. "I am not blushing. It's just really warm outside right now."

Now Kendall jumps in, "Ya because 65-degree weather is so warm. Del's blushing too! Oh my gosh aren't you guys the cutest," she patronizes us.

"I'm not blushing, I just have a naturally red complexion," she's fanning her face down.

I go over to Rydell and sling my arm around her shoulders, tucking her into my side, "I look at Rydell the way I do, best she's my best friend. And hands down my most favorite person to walk the earth."

"Scott, you can't say things like that, it only brings out Del's red complexion more," Kendall jokes as I look down at Ry's bright face.

Rydell claps her hands together, "Alright, let's go pick some pumpkins."

CHAPTER 33: RYDELL

We have successfully loaded all the girls into the vans with their pumpkins and candy. The first bus already took off and Michelle is getting into the driver's seat of the second one.

"If you guys need any help, just call. You know I never mind coming in," we just lost a couple employees so we're a little short staffed.

"Del, don't worry about us, we're fine. Enjoy the rest of your night." She looks towards Scott who's saying bye to Sophie as her shuts the van door, "You better get her home safely young man."

"Yes ma'am."

Bidding our final goodbyes, I watch the van drive off. Then turn on my heels to face Scott. It's just the two of us now. And we've done plenty of things with only the company of each other, but it feels different this time.

It feels a lot like a date. And it scares me how much I wish it was.

Scott grabs my hand and starts walking me back to the carnival. He looks down at me and says, "Lucky you, both my hands are open now."

"Who says I want to hold your hand?" I

raise my eyebrow.

He lets go of my hand and puts both of his up, "Fine, but when we're in the haunted house and you get scared, don't except the comfort of my expert hand holding."

I roll my eyes and cross my arms around my chest. "I'll be just fine. If I can be alone with a potential axe murderer, I'm sure I can handle a haunted maze."

~

"AHHH," I cannot handle the haunted maze. "Ok, stay where you are!" one of the workers is dressed as a creepy clown and coming straight at me. "Please stay away!"

I grab the back on Scott shirt and rest my head on the center of his back to shield me from everything.

Scott is having the time of his life. You would think it's a comedy show with all the laughing he's doing.

Scott grabs my arm, forcing me to stand next to him, "Oh no you don't. You wouldn't hold my hand early, now you get no comfort."

I flip him off. A prop jumps out in front of us and I scream while grabbing for Scott's arm on instinct.

"Now you not only want to hold my hand, but you want to hug my arm too," I look up and he's smirking but instead of moving his arm out of my grasp like I expect him too, he shuffles closer to me.

"Will you save being an asshole until we're out of the maze. I think I might pee myself Scott, this is not the time to joke."

He just laughs and guides me towards the next section of the maze.

This one has your classic operation table with a zombie surgeon and pregnant women giving birth to some hideous looking monster. The zombie surgeon comes running at us with his operation saw and I bury my head into Scott's chest.

I feel Scott wrap in arm around my shoulder and walk us towards out of the room.

He leans down to my ear "You alright?"

I take my face out of his chest to see where we're going, but keep myself tucked under his arm, "Peachy," I deadpan.

He just chuckles a bit as we walk through a hallway with body bags hanging around us.

After a couple more rooms I spot the exit and step out from under Scott arm to jog out of it.

"Oh, praise the lord. Free at last," I look back expecting Scott to be right behind me, "Scott?" I call out when I realize he isn't right behind me.

Shit. What if he got lost in there or didn't see the exit? I take a deep breath and walk back into the maze. "Scott?" I call out again.

I am looking around when all of a sudden, I feel arms wrap around my waist to pick me up off the floor and out through the exit.

I scream, naturally, "Stop, put me down, workers aren't allowed to touch the people going through!"

And then I hear Scott's laughing his ass off as he puts me to the ground. I turn around to face him. "Prescott Bridges, that was not funny. I think you just gave me a heart attack. I go into save you because I thought you got lost and this is how I'm repaid," I put my hand up to my chest and slow my breathing.

He pulls me into a hug, but I do not

reciprocate, "Sorry Del, I couldn't resist. But it's good to know that you would go in to rescue me," he stops and pulls me in front of him so he can look at my face. He rubs his hands up and down my arms as I cross them. "Round two?" he says with a straight face.

"Fuck off," I mumble. "You so owe me funnel cake for that."

"As you wish milady," he says in a British accent as he put his arm around my shoulder again and nudges me in the direction of the funnel cake stand.

As we make our way over, he starts laughing again. "What?"

"You were so scared in there! You should have seen your face," he can barely get his words out he's laughing so hard.

I shove his side causing his arm to fall off my shoulder. "You asked them to stay away from you! You even said please!" he's laughing like it's the funniest thing in the world.

"Well, I'm glad you enjoyed yourself asshole. I'm sure you were taking notes for all your axe murdering and stalking."

He looks down at me, "Oh ya. I was for sure. I think I'll invest in one of the chainsaws, those seemed to scare you the most. Might fuck around and get a clown mask."

I roll my eyes, "Done making fun of me?"

"For now," we get in line for funnel cakes. "Which one do you want?"

"That's a stupid question. Obviously, I want the strawberry one."

He puts his hands up in surrender, "One strawberry funnel cake coming right up."

The sun's gone down now, and I'm starting to get cold. I'm in my cow print pants and a thin white long sleeve.

As if he's reading my thoughts, Scott walks behind me to take off my angel wings. Holding them between his legs, he takes off his brown jacket and puts it around my shoulders.

"That's completely unnecessary Scott, you'll be cold," I say. But at the same time, I slip my arms in the jacket to put it all the way on.

He helps me put my wings back on and then moves in front of me. "Arms up," I put my arms up in front of him like a zombie and watch as he rolls up the sleeves so that they aren't covering my hands.

"I spend essentially all my time in an ice rink Books, it takes a lot to make me cold."

I nod, "Thank you."

"You guys make such a cute couple! I love your matching costumes," the older lady behind us in line gushes.

I'm about to correct her but Scott beats me to it, "Thank you, it took a lot of convincing to get her to match with me, but she has a hard time resisting my charm," he takes it a step further by pinching my cheek and saying, "isn't that right darling?"

I internally glare at him as I swat his hand away, "I wouldn't say it was the charm as much as it was the tears. He's very sensitive, you should see when we watch movies together. He cried during the *Gonnies!* Can you believe that? Is that not the sweetest thing ever?" I look at him with a smirk as I pat his cheek.

"Awe, like a big teddy bear!" the lady exclaims, and it takes so much for me not to burst out laughing. Especially when I look over at Scott's sour face.

"Exactly!"

"Next in line," Scott turns around orders my funnel cake.

"$4.50," the employee says.

I had my money prepared and stick out a $5 at the same time Scott does.

"Take mine, he paid for the cotton candy," I tell her.

"No, take mine, I forced her to go through the haunted maze and bribed her with funnel cake to do it."

She takes Scott's money, "Dammit," I mumble as I shove my money back into my pocket.

We get our funnel cake but before we can leave the older women touches my arm and whispers in my ear, "Don't let that one go, I can tell he's really in love with you."

And I feel like grabbing Scott and kissing him. But I also feel like crying and throwing up, thinking that we'll only be friends. Especially now that the project's over, who knows what's going to happen.

I just nod and walk back over to Scott, "What was that about?"

"Nothing," I shake my head and walk over to a picnic table to eat the funnel cake.

I grab the fork out of his hand as we sit down and take a bite. If food could give you an orgasm, this funnel cake would've definitely gotten the job done.

I scoop some more up onto the fork and put it up to Scott's mouth. "Come on Scott, it's kinda like pancakes."

"Will accept no as an answer?" I shake my head, "Always so stubborn," he complains as he accepts my bite.

"Sooooooo? Good right?"

"Not bad, but it's nothing like pancake."

"Oh my gosh, you totally like it!"

"No, I don't, I just said it wasn't bad."

"Whatever makes you feel better Scotty."

He rolls his eyes at me, so I stuck my tongue out at him like the mature person I am. As I do so, Scott takes out his phone and snaps a picture of me.

"Hey! Delete that right now, I probably look like a crazy person."

"Oh, you definitely look like a crazy person. But I think it's cute. You're the psycho to my stalker."

"I am nowhere near your stalker-axe-murderer level."

"Don't worry crazy, stick with me and I'll get you there."

I stand up and start walking in the direction of the psychic/medium after we finish the funnel cake.

"Where are we going," Scott asks as he grads my hand and starts swinging our arms back and forth.

"I want to read your palm."

Our arms stop swinging, "Excuse me?"

"The psychic stand has a chart that helps you read palms; I want to read yours."

"Ohhh, so you can find all the secrets my hands hold. You could just ask me; I'll tell you anything you want to know."

My heart flutters a bit at that, but I ignore it and find the palm reading chart. Then I cup his hand in one of mine and open it so that I have a good view. His hands are so nice. They're very large and super manly looking and I really need to stop thinking about how attracted I am to them.

"Ok," I trace one of the lines on his hand. "This one is your line of heart," I move to the next. "Line of head," and then I trace the last, "Line of life."

I look up at him to see that he's very intensely looking at me. I look back at the palm chart but can feel him watching my every move. I lift his hand up to take a good look, "I'd say your hands look most like fire hands." I look down at his hand and start tracing the lines again.

"It's said that people with fire hands are passionate, confident and industrious. They're goal oriented and can lack empathy on bad days."

I look back up at him, not surprised to see his still staring at me. The little perv.

"Sounds pretty accurate, most of my actions are taken in terms of achieving a goal. I'm kind of an asshole, so the lack of empathy makes sense."

"I think your definitely confident. You probably have the biggest ego out of everyone I know. But I don't think you're an asshole. Actually, I think you're pretty far from it. Lack of empathy could just mean that you can easily turn off your emotions. Which you can, and I think you might have learned that from your parents. But you're certainly not an asshole, you wouldn't be standing here with me right now if you were."

He hums an agreement, "Ok, your turn," he switches the position of our hands so that he can read mine. He starts to trace the lines on my hand, and I shiver a bit at the feeling. "Are you still cold?"

he looks up at me.

"No, it just tickles," he chuckles but continues to trace the lines on my hand.

Then he looks at the palm reading chart, "I would say you definitely have air hands," he starts reading the description, "Hands of the intellects. People with air hands are smart and often make both good students and teachers. They're patient, curious, but are often overthinkers." He looks to me, "That's pretty accurate."

"Well, I definitely overthink everything," I mumble.

"Maybe, but I don't think that's always a bad thing. You're obviously patient. I mean you wouldn't have stuck with me so long if you weren't. You're hands down the smartest person I know, but not just book smart. Mentally, you're a genius, you always have the right thing to say. I mean I saw that happen tonight with Kendall. You're gonna do great things one day Books."

He's still holding onto my hand, but now he's slowly bringing it down to our sides and intertwining our fingers. "You're gonna do great things one day too Scott."

We are just standing there staring at each other, and that might seem weird, but it doesn't feel awkward at all, just comfortable.

Just as he starts raising his other hand, we're interrupted. "How about a card reading for the lovely couple?"

Scott gives me a grin and starts pushing me towards the chair sitting across the psychic. I start shaking my head because I don't want to do it. Scott knits his eyebrows together and nods his head yes and mouths 'oh ya'.

"Alright, this is very simple. Both of you pick a card that speaks to you and I'll tell you what they mean in terms of your relationship."

"You first sweetie," she says to me. I look at the stack of cards and pick a random one out.

"Ahhh, The Hermit. It looks like you have some baggage that you need to let go of. Maybe there's a past relationship or a past experience that is holding you back from going all into a new relationship. But when you are in a relationship, you become the other person's rock. You like deep and meaningful relationships and do anything to make the people you love happy, even if it's at expense of your own."

Fuck. That was accurate. I can't help but think about Trey and my grandpa, and how I let their actions control how I take my own. I mean, that's one of the main reasons I haven't grabbed Scott by the face a kissed the life out of him.

"Your turn dear," she nods at Scott who is standing behind my chair with his hands on my shoulders.

He points to a card and the lady flips it over, "Wheel of Fortune. Maybe this relationship was unexpected to you. But when it happened it was exactly what you needed. This person you're pursuing is an unlikely perfect match, and you feel strongly for them, but it scares you. You're scared that you might not be able to live up to certain expectations and that you'll let down the people you love. But this card is one of success, so it's best to rid of any worries."

Scott's thumbs are rubbing slow circles into my shoulders now and I can't help but wonder if he relates to his card as much as I did to mine.

CHAPTER 34: SCOTT

After a couple hours at the carnival, we decided to call it a night. As I'm driving Rydell home, my mind shifts back to the psychic's tent.

First, she grabbed onto me in the haunted house and I loved feeling like I was protecting her. I also loved how her hands were on me basically the whole time because it gave me an excuse to put my hands on her.

Second, she was tracing the lines of my hand and it took so much restraint to not sling her over my shoulder, take her to the back seat of my car and show her just how into her I am.

And then to put the cherry on top, the fucking medium told me essentially exactly what I feel in terms of Rydell.

Like spot on. I would have never thought that Rydell Rivens would come creeping into my life and that I would feel as strongly as I do for her, but she did. And the psychic is right, she is exactly what I need. Maybe exactly what I've always needed.

But I am also terrified that I'm not good enough for her. I don't want to let her down and I'm scared that I might not be able to love her the way she deserves to be loved. Especially with everything she's been through.

She needs someone who is strong and deserving, and as much as I want to be that person, I'm scared that I'm not.

And I really want to know if her card reading was as accurate as mine was.

I stop at a red light and glance over at her in my passenger's seat and smile when I find her loudly singing the lyrics to Bestie Boys Paul Revere, "HE TOLD A LITTLE STORY THAT SOUNDED WELL REHEARSED, 4 DAYS ON THE RUN AND THAT HE'S DYING OF THIRST."

She looks over at me, catching me staring at her, "What?" she turns the volume down a bit.

"Don't stop, I'm enjoying your show," I tease her.

Honestly, the first time she put on Beastie Boys and knew just about every single lyric to every song I almost passed out. Just when I thought she couldn't get any more perfect, she does.

I find myself constantly surprised with her. I mean, she fucking breathes and it's the most interesting thing to me.

Fuck. I'm pretty sure I'm in love with her. I mean I've never been in love with anyone before, but this has to be what it feels like.

And I don't know if this carnival made me realize it or if I've always kinda subconsciously known. But I'm sitting here at this red light staring at this perfect girl thinking that she's the sun and I want to be in her orbit. In fact, I want to be the only thing in her orbit. And maybe that's selfish of me but I want to be the only thing on her mind, because she's sure as hell the only thing on mine.

Rydell gives me a weird look and then looks

back out the front window, "The lights green stalker."

I practically force myself to look back towards the road. I clear my throat, "Right. I knew that."

"Suuuurrrre," she turns the radio back up. "Now be quiet and listen to the music. I'll sing Mike D's parts, you take Ad-Rock and MCA".

And so, we spent the entire car ride putting on our own mini Beastie Boys concert. And I know for a fact that I'm in love with Rydell Rivens. Like fully, deeply, genuinely in love with her. And I'm so fucking scared.

Scared that I can't give her what she needs. Scared that she'll never love me back and find someone better than me. Scared that I'll lose my best friend if I tell her.

I've never had a problem asking girls out. And maybe it's because I knew they wouldn't say no, or maybe I just didn't really care if they said no. But if Rydell said no, I don't think I'd recover from it.

Because I'm convinced that she's the only person in this world that I'll ever come to truly love.

I pull into her apartments parking lot and turn off my car. And shift in my seat to look over at her. She looks over at me.

Should I kiss her? I look down at her lips for a split second and then back up to her eyes. I should definitely kiss her. I should ask her if it's ok first though, right?

"I had fun tonight. Even though you almost made me pee my pants in the haunted house," she laughs a little and tucks some hair behind her ear.

Fuck. What do I say? She just talked about

peeing her pants that doesn't sound like something someone who wants to be kissed would say.

I guess I've been quiet for too long because she says, "You ok?" with a confused look on her face.

"I'm ok. I had a lot of fun tonight too. I think I just might invest in one of those chainsaws we saw in the haunted house."

She tilts her head back a little and laughs, "I'm sure you will ya little creep."

She looks back at me and her laughs gradually stop. And we just look at each other. And I swear she looks down at my lips. So, I look down at hers, then back to her eyes. I unbuckle myself.

As I start to slightly lean in I look back down at her lips and say, "Rydell, I really want to-"

And then her fucking phone rings. She jumps in her seat a little and mumbles out a 'sorry'.

She pulls it out and looks down at it with a very confused expression. "It's my mom. She knows it's late here." She looks up at me, "I should probably take it."

I nod as I turn my body back to face the front and lean in my seat.

"Hey Mom," she answers. There's a long pause before she talks again.

"Your side or Dad's?" I'm guessing her mom responds because then she says, "when?"

"Um. Ok. Ok. I'll see what I can do. Ya. Ok. I love you too. Bye."

She hangs up the phone and stares at the window. She has the look that she had after she had her panic attack, so I straighten myself up. "Everything alright?"

She's still staring out the window, "Rydell?"

"My grandpa died," she looks over at me.

"Fuck, Rydell I'm sorry."

"Ya. Um. He had a heart attack," she doesn't necessarily look sad about it.

"Mom's or Dad's side?"

She's looking back out the front window again with a blank expression on her face, "Dad's," it comes out as barely as whisper.

"Ok. And how do you feel about it?" I question slowly, knowing that she wasn't close to him.

"I- I think I should go. This is- it's just something to process." She looks back over at me.

"Maybe you should talk to someone about it. You can talk to me about it Del."

She shakes her head no and starts unbuckling, "That's ok. I just need to think by myself. I'm sorry. I totally just ruined the night."

She opens her door and climbs out as she starts speed walking to her apartment. I jog to catch up to her. "Hey, Del. You look like you did when you had your panic attack. Why don't we just sit down for a little bit. You can process it, and I'll sit here if you need anything."

She's shaking her head and fumbling with her keys to open the door. Her hands are wobbly and it's so clear that she's slightly panicking. "No. No, I'm ok. Really. But I'm tired. I'm tired and- and I think maybe I need to sleep this off and process it in the morning."

I take the keys from her hands and unlock the door for her since she's struggling. "Rydell, it's ok to be upset about this," I grab her hand to stop her from walking into the apartment and brush away some of her stubborn hair that won't stay behind her ear. "You don't have to hide from me. I want to help you," I caress her cheek.

She looks at me with watery eyes, "I'm not hiding. I really just want to be by myself."

"Finally, you're home. Can we please watch *Hocus Pocus?*" Sam walks into view and pauses when she sees how upset Rydell looks. "What's wrong. I swear to god Prescott Bridges if you hurt her in any way, I know how to cover up murder."

"No one needs to be murdered," Rydell turns towards Sam. "We had a good night. I'm the one who ruined it."

I hate how she is always blaming herself. "You didn't ruin anything. How could that possibly be your fault?"

"I'll see you later Scott. I have Sam with me, I'll be fine. Thanks again for tonight though." And with that, she shuts the door.

CHAPTER 35: RYDELL

I shut the door and my breathing immediately starts to pick up. I'm hyperventilating and I don't even know how to begin to process the information that has just been given to me.

I feel relieved. And I feel like it's shitty of me to be so glad that someone's dead. But at the same time, it's just bringing up so many memories. I'm expected to go to this funeral and to their house within the next couple of days and it fucking terrifies me.

How am I supposed to go to an event celebrating the life of a man who sexually assaulted me? A man who gave me off to his friend to sexually assault.

I can't fucking breathe. I'm in full panic attack mode. I'm not sure how I got to the couch but I'm sitting on it with my knees up and arms wrapped around them.

Sam's saying something to me, but I'm not sure what it is. I can feel his hands on me, and my skin feels like it's on fire.

I start rubbing and itching everywhere on my body, hoping that it will rid the feeling. My nails are digging so deeply into my skin, but the feeling won't go away. I don't want it. It hurts. It hurts so fucking badly.

All of a sudden Sam is grasping on to my wrists and I'm trying to pull them out of her grip because I need to get rid of it. "Let go. It hurts. I don't want it. I don't want to feel it. Please make it stop. I don't want to feel them," I can barely get my words out because of how badly I'm sobbing.

"Feel what? Del you're hurting yourself. What don't you want to feel?" I look up at Sam and see a worried expression on her face.

"His hands. I don't want to feel his hands. Please. I- I can't breathe," I feel my vision start to spot and I feel like I'm about to pass out.

"Ok. Ok stay right here. I'm getting your medicine." In emergencies, when I can't calm myself, I have anxiety pills to help. The one I take is Xanax, but I only take it if it's a very serious situation because I never want to be reliant on it to function.

Sam leaves and I start ripping at my skin again.

"Fuck. Del stop." She takes my hands again and puts the pill in my mouth a little forcefully. I swallow it.

After about 5 minutes, my breathing is finally evened out. I look down at my arms to see noticeable red scratches. Some of them are bleeding a little. "Sorry," I whisper to Sam, figuring that I might have scared her a little bit.

"Don't apologize. But what the fuck is going on Del? Did Scott do something. Did he put his hands on you, because I fucking swear-"

"No. No, this had nothing to do with Scott," I feel so exhausted.

"Whose hands were you talking about Rydell?"

I look up at her and I can feel my eyes start to water a bit and I feel a lump in my throat. The Xanax is definitely starting to kick in because without it, this conversation would be a whole hell of a lot harder.

"My grandpa's."

"I don't understand. Why were you feeling his hands on you?"

"He died. I just got the call from my mom tonight."

Sam puts her hand on my shoulder and starts rubbing it, "Fuck Del. I'm sorry. Why'd you start scratching yourself though?"

I look down and laugh. But my throat is so raspy from the panic attack that it barely comes out. "I'm not sad about it. In fact, I'm very relieved."

And that's how Sam found at about what my grandpa did to me. I told her everything. Every small detail about it and it felt so fucking good to tell someone. But, if I hadn't taken the pill, there's no way I would've told her anything.

After I finished up with my story Sam looked mortified, "Why didn't you tell anyone. Someone could've helped you."

"I wasn't going to take any risks. If I told someone, he might've done the same thing to Andy. And I couldn't live with myself if she had to go through it. So, I dealt with it. And by the time I was old enough to fully understand what happened, it was too late. No one would believe me. Plus, it doesn't matter anymore. He's dead."

"Is his friend dead too?"

"I have no idea, it's not something I'd like to

think about."

"And now, you want to go to his funeral?"

"I think I need to," I look over at her. "I don't think I'll ever get any closure if I don't see his body go 6 feet under."

She nods her head slowly, "And the only other person who knows about this is Scott?"

"Scott knows bits and pieces of it. He knows I was sexually assaulted. He knows that it happened in a closet. But he doesn't know the context of it or who did it."

I get another slow nod. "Ok then. Let's clear up your schedule, book you a flight, and get you some closure then."

CHAPTER 36: SCOTT

It's November 4th. I haven't heard from Rydell in a week and I am losing my mind.

I've tried calling, texting, facetiming. I've message her on every single social media. I even emailed her.

When I thought she might be dead on the side of the road, I finally went to their apartment, ready to knock down the fucking door.

Sam answered and told me she wasn't there but that she was ok. And that's about all that I got.

I mean at least I know she's not dead, but fuck. I don't know what to think. Did I do something that made her not want to talk to me? Is it because of her grandpa's death? Does she not want to be friends with me now that the project is over?

I've played so many so many physically excruciating hockey games, but I've never felt as out of breath than I do at the thought of losing her.

"Dude you look like shit," Ruddy announces as he walks into the kitchen.

I'm at the island eating cereal. I don't say anything back.

"What's going on man. You're walking around like a zombie, you barely talk to anyone, and you've been off your game at practice. Coach is starting to think that you're not going to be focused for the game tomorrow."

"I'll be fine."

"What is it? I'm worried about you Scotty?"

I sign and put my forehead on the cool counter. Then look back up, "I haven't heard from Rydell in a week."

"I thought you guys had a good time at the carnival. You came home saying that you wanted her to be your girlfriend."

"I thought so too. I don't know what I did, but she's completely shut me out and I'm losing my shit."

"Has she been in class?"

"No. But I talked to Sam who said she was fine but wouldn't be in town for a little."

"Oh. If she's out of town, she's probably just busy."

"Too busy to pick up the phone and tell me that she's alive? I was genuinely scared for her health."

"Just wait it out a bit dude. She'll talk when she's ready. And if she doesn't then when she's back in town you force her to talk. Tell her how you feel."

I just sigh.

~

Today's game day. I've sent Rydell a text and tried to call her. I heard nothing back.

Coach Terry comes up to me in the locker rooms as I'm getting ready, "I don't know what's been going on this week Scotty but try to block it out for the game. You're our best player. I know you'll do what you can to lead your team to victory. If you need to talk to someone about whatever's happening, you know you can come to me, right?"

I nod, "I know. I'll be fine coach. Don't worry about me."

~

I'm not fine. My shots are weak. I've gotten hit by the opposite team way too many times. I can barely even get my team together. The first quarter ends and we skate to the bench. We're down by 2.

"Get your head out of your ass Bridges. You guys should be up by 2, not down. Go to the lockers and try to shake it off, I don't even want to look at you right now," Coach Michael's says.

I put on my skate guards and walk to the locker's rooms. Sitting down on the bench, I put my elbows on my knees and head in my hands.

The door opens and I expect it to be a teammate or coach, "I know. I'll get my head in it it's only the first quarter."

"I don't know hockey terms, but I assume that means it's early in the game." My head shoots up immediately at a voice I don't think I could forget even if I tried.

And there she is. The person who has me playing like shit. I stand up from the bench and wrap my arms around her waist and up into a hug, putting my head in the crook of her neck. Her arms wrap around my neck and her hands brush through my hair. I swear I feel a weight lift off my chest.

"I might be hugging you right now. But I'm so fucking mad at you Rydell Rivens."

She doesn't say anything but continues brushing at my bottom neck hairs. I pull away and drop my forehead down to rest on hers. My eyes closed. "Where the fuck have you been? And why the hell weren't you answering my calls?"

"I had to go back to California for the funeral. I turned my phone off because I had some things I need to sort out without distractions. Sam's the only one who knew," she says lightly.

"I was losing my fucking mind Rydell. I didn't know it you were alive," I start choking on my words, "I didn't know if you got hurt. I thought maybe you didn't want to be my friend anymore and that the only reason you talked to me was for the project."

She cuts me off and pulls her face back a bit to caress my cheek with one hand. "I'd never not want to be friends with you Scott. I just had so much shit I had to deal with."

"That's fine. But as your friend and someone who cares a lot about you, I want you to come to me with these things. I want to be able to help you. If you're hurting, I want to hurt with you and find ways to take that hurt away."

Before she can answer, the lockers open up and she drops her hands to her sides. "Back on the ice Scott," Terry says.

Rydell starts walking towards the exit. And I grab her hand to pull her back, "You better not fucking leave. As soon as this game is over, we are going to talk. Please stay in the stands. I want you here."

"I'm not going anywhere."

"Good," I kiss her cheek and head back out to the rink.

CHAPTER 37: *RYDELL*

Our team won 4-2. Scott played a lot better after our chat in the lockers. I know it was wrong of me to not tell him where I was, but I did actually turn my phone off.

The night I broke down to Sam, I booked a flight to go back to California the next day and dealt with all my shit.

I went to the funeral. Watched them put his body under. Got some closure there. And then I stayed for the rest of the week to be with my family. I hadn't seen them in a couple months.

I told them everything. About how I was sexually assaulted and how I was threatened to not say anything.

My dad looked like he was going to kill someone. My mom started crying. My siblings were speechless.

And they helped me heal some wounds I thought I would never close. And now, they're helping he figure out who the other man was. It's difficult since I don't really remember anything about him. Just his eyes and the feeling of his hands.

As bad as I feel for keeping Scott out of the loop, it's something I really needed. Just being with my family and having their support fixed a lot of broken pieces in me.

I spot Scott as I walk down the bleachers now that the game is over. When he reaches me he pulls me into another hug. He holds me like he can't believe that I'm here, and that if he lets go, I'll be gone. But I meant it when I told him I wasn't going anywhere.

He pulls back, putting his hands on my shoulders and scanning my body. When his eyes land on my forearm he holds it up and traces the scar that formed after I scratched too deep.

"This wasn't here before. What happened?" His eyes are boring into mine as he continues to rub soothingly up and down my arm.

"I promise I'll tell you everything. But you should get to the locker rooms. I don't know if you were planning on going out tonight-"

"I'm not going out. And neither are you. As soon as I'm done in there, we're going to my house. It's non-negotiable. Did you drive here?"

"No, Sam did."

"Good. Tell her I'm taking you. No waiting in the parking lot. Stay on the bleachers over there please."

I nod and watch him walk off.

~

I'm now sitting on the edge of Scott's bed as he shuffles around his room to put all his things up.

Well barely said anything to each other on the car ride over. I half compelled to put on Beastie Boys to cut some of the tension, but I decided against it.

Scott sits down on his desk chair to sit directly across from me.

"I've never heard of a week-long funeral."

I sigh, "The funeral didn't last a week. I just needed to be with my family for a bit."

"I thought you weren't close to your grandpa on your dad's side. I know death sucks, but I just am confused at how it affected you so much to the point where you had to cut off contact with everyone for a week."

I look down at my lap and fiddle with my fingers. "Do you remember when I told you I was sexually assaulted?" I look back up.

His jaw locks, "It's hard to forget," he grinds out.

"My grandpa, the one who just died, was the one who did it. Well and his friend one time."

Scott's staring at me with the same type of face my dad made when I told him. "How many times?"

"3. One time he invited his friend to accompany him. That one happened in the closet and was why I freaked out that one time."

He nods slowly and scoots the chair over so that he's right in between my legs. He takes my hands in his. Looking down and messing with my fingers he asks, "Why'd you go?"

"I needed closure. I feel shitty for saying it, but the second they covered his casket, I felt so relieved."

He looks up at me, still holding onto my hands. "Don't you dare feel shitty about that. What he did to you was fucked up, and if he was still alive, I'd hunt down the fucker and kill him myself."

My eyes are glossy and there's a lump in my throat. "I'm sorry."

He wipes the tears that I didn't even realize

escaped, "Baby, don't apologize. I just wish I was there for you."

This past week I've cried more than I ever had in my entire life. And I really thought I didn't have any left in me. But the comfort I feel from Scott is overwhelming.

I'm full-on sobbing now and Scott climbs onto his bed, scoots to the headboard and grabs my arm to pull me onto his lap. I stuff my face in his neck and wrap my arms around him as he rubs up and down my back.

"You're ok. I'm here," he's whispering affirmations into my ear.

Once I've calmed myself, I pull back so that I can look at him, "I was gone so long because my family was trying to help me find the other man who molested me," I take a deep breathe. "Not only that, but I needed them to help me fix parts of me I've been trying to glue together for as long as I can remember."

"And did it help."

I sigh, "To some extent. They helped me in a lot of ways I never thought I could be helped. But there's still so many parts of me that feel so broken," I whisper the last part. "I just don't think I'll ever be normal. I mean I can't even go a month without having a severe panic attack. I feel so pathetic."

I bring my hands up to cover my face, but he catches my wrists. "Rydell Rivens, you are the strongest person I know. If you need help picking up the pieces of you that you think are broken, I'll be here to hold that glue together for you. But you can't fix something that's perfect. And I'm not just saying that because your upset. I never thought the perfect person existed until I meet you."

"I don't want to be a burden to anyone though."

"If I could take away all your worries and every bad thing that's ever happened to you, I would. I would carry all your hurt for you without hesitation, no matter how overwhelming it got. Fuck Rydell, I think I'd do just about anything for you." He's still caressing my cheek, "It's more of a burden to not have you in my life. I need you in my life. All of you. The good, the bad, all of it."

Honestly a week without Scott was too long. The whole time I missed him, and I finally feel like myself again now that I'm with him.

I am so undeniably in love. I spent so much time thinking about him leaving me I didn't realize I was so scared of that possibility because of how in love with him I am.

I snuggle back into Scott, resting my forehead on his shoulder.

"Promise me you won't shut me out again. Promise me you'll come to me when you're hurting," he whispers as he rubs circles on my back.

"I promise."

"If you break this promise Rydell Rivens, I'll kidnap you to keep you in my line of vision at all time. You know I would."

That gets a breathy laugh out of me and I lift my head to look at him, "Ya you would. I still don't know why I'm friends with a psycho axe murdering stalker."

"Best friends," he corrects.

"Sam's my best friend. But you might be my favorite friend."

He has the biggest grin on his face, "Hell yeah I am. I'll get to best friend and favorite friend soon enough."

I smile back at him and shake my head, "And what am I to you? Do I hold the best friend title?"

"You hold every title. Best friend, favorite friend, person I care most about. In fact, you might be the only person that really matters in my life. I could have no one in my life but you and I'd be content. You make me really happy."

I can feel my face heating up, so I hide it in the crook of his neck. I take a deep breath through my nose. He smells like his woodsy cologne and if I could get high off a scent, it would be his.

"You make me really happy too."

CHAPTER 38: SCOTT

The light from my window is coming in directly at my eyes. I groan and drape my arm across my face to cover it.

And then I feel pressure on my chest and realize that my legs are tangled with someone else's.

I look down and see Rydell whose head is rested on my chest. She's got one arm slung around my middle and one of her legs is in between mine.

The arm of mine that I wasn't using to cover my eyes is pulling her onto me. I push the hair out of her face.

Fuck. Bad idea. I already have morning wood and touching her is not helping. She's so fucking pretty.

She fell asleep not long after she told me that I make her happy. I could tell that she was exhausted so I didn't wake her up. It's a Sunday and I doubt she's working since she just got back.

Shit, I have morning workout. I look over at the clock to see that I still have an hour until I have to be at practice, so I relax a bit.

Last night I was so close to telling Rydell that I was in love with her. She told me that I'm her favorite friend and I can't think of anything that's made me happier.

Seriously, not more than 24 hours ago, I didn't think I was her friend at all anymore. But that reassurance from her was so comforting.

And then she told me about her asshole of a grandpa and if I could bring the fucker back to life I would, just so I could be the one to kill him. She's just going through so much right now. I don't want to push all my feelings on her at once when she's got so much shit to think about.

I'll wait until her mind clears up a bit. And in the meantime, I'll be by her side and help her with whatever she needs.

I look down at Rydell. Her face has a soft glow from the morning light, and I'm pretty sure she's drooling a bit on my chest. She's so perfect.

As if she knows I'm staring at her, she shifts closer to me, if that's even possible and opens her eyes. She flinches a little, probably from realizing that she's not in her bed.

"Morning sunshine. Did you know that you drool in your sleep?"

She groans and stuffs her face in my neck. "Why were you watching me sleep stalker?"

"It's hard not to, you're the one who latched themself to me while we were sleeping."

She starts to scoot away from me, and I turn on my side so that both my arms are around her now holding her in a hug. I'm not letting her get away from me that fast, I'm thoroughly enjoy these morning cuddles. "Not that I mind," I add.

She shifts a little more, "I'm sure you don't mind. Do you always get this hard in the morning, you little perv?"

Fuck. Down boy. "Only when I wake up to a

pretty girl in my arms."

She snorts, "Alright time to let go, I have to pee."

"Hold it, I'm so comfortable right now."

"Scottttt," she groans as she wiggles to try to escape. But she's rubbing up right on my already hard dick and it's turning me the fuck on.

I roll us so that she's fully on her back and our chest are pressed together as I hover over her. "Keep wiggling around like that, and you'll find out just how hard I can get in the morning."

She unintentionally bites her bottom lip. "Don't fucking do that," I bring my hand up to bring her bottom lip back out and let it linger there.

"I might pee in your bed it you don't get off me," she says.

Well, I can count on Rydell to ruin the moment. I roll off her and watch as she walks to the bathroom.

When she's done doing her business, she comes back on the bed to sit next to me. My back is against the headboard and she's sitting criss cross in the facing towards me.

"Do you work today?" I ask her.

"No, I don't go back until tomorrow. What time's your practice."

"I have to be there in like an hour."

She nods, "When you go to practice, I'll just go with you and have Sam pick me up from there."

I look down at her arm that she's rubbing. Leaning forward, I grad it and inspect her forearm, tracing the scar that she's acquired since I saw her last.

"What happened here?"

She signs and runs her free hand through

her hair, "Panic attack gone wrong. That night of the carnival, after you left my apartment, I was in full blown anxiety attack mode. I vividly remember not being able to get the feeling of his hands off me. Sam said I was scratching at my arms and one of my nails went too deep."

I raise her arm up to my mouth and brush my lips over the scar. "I shouldn't have left that night," I whisper.

"There's nothing you could've done. I'm the one who shut the door on you. Plus, I had Sam with me, and she helped a lot."

My heart is breaking at the fact that she was in that much pain. "Still, I wish I was there to help."

"Scott, it's ok. Really. You're here now."

I kiss her scar one more time and then put her hand in mine, "Damn right I am. And I'm not going anywhere. Neither are you; I'm not letting you push me away again."

Rydell gets a ding on her phone and reaches for it. "November 5th is National Redhead Day! We should get Max a cupcake or something."

I laugh and shake my head, "Don't call him a redhead, he refuses to believe that he's a ginger. He says its brown with a light tint of red."

"Do you have pancake mix; we can make him breakfast," she shifts off the bed and looks at me with a look that says, 'come on'.

I sigh and follow her out the door, "I'm only making pancakes because they're my favorite food, not because it's redhead day."

~

The guys start trickling into the kitchen not long after Rydell and I start making breakfast.

"Happy National Redhead Day Max! How

many pancakes do you want?" Rydell exclaims as soon as she sees him.

"Del, good to see you again. But I'm not a redhead, my hair is brown with a tint of red."

"Whatever you say ginger," Webbs chimes in. "Deli, I missed you!" he crosses the kitchen to pull her in a hug that lifts her feet off the ground.

He's so fucking touchy. When he puts her down Davies goes to pull her into a hug as well. "Class was fucking boring without you. Professor Bahri about lost his mind that his star student was missing."

"Sorry, I had something I had to deal with, but no more boring classes for you, now that I'm back." She smiles up at him and I roll my eyes.

"Watch out Scotty, your jealousy is showing," Ruddy whispers to me as I flip a pancake.

"I'm giving you all the burnt ones."

He just laughs and opens the fridge to grab the orange juice.

I look over at Rydell who is still talking to Davies, so I put the spatula down and grab the belt loop on her jeans to pull her into me. "You're supposed to be helping me make pancakes. Also, how the hell did you sleep in these?" I motion to her jeans as she turns around to face me.

"I was tired, I could've been on concrete and I would've slept like the dead," she picks up the spatula and gets to flipping.

Davies and Webbs look at me with smirks and I flip them off. Walking back over to the stove I put my hands on Rydell's hips so that my chest is slightly against her back. "I have some sweats you can change into if you want."

She shakes her head, "That's ok, we're

leaving soon anyways."

I wrap my arms around her middle and drop my chin to her shoulder, "I really missed you, ya know."

"I really missed you too," I kiss her cheek and move to grab some plates down from the cabinet.

CHAPTER 39: *RYDELL*

"They're interested in looking at the work you guys are doing," Professor Bahri says to Sam and I. He asked us to come into his office hours because he had exciting news.

"Ubisoft?" I say with uncertainty.

"Yes."

"As in one of the biggest video game distributors Ubisoft?"

"Yes," Professor Bahri has the biggest grin on his face.

Sam cuts in, "They want to see more of our work and possibly help us develop the video game?"

"You guys have to finish it up which will take maybe another year to work out all the logistics. But they want to set up a meeting so they can hear all your ideas and see more of what you guys have already. If they like it enough, they'll sign a contract with you guys."

I don't even know what to say. I'm standing there staring at nothing with my mouth open like a fish out of water trying to process it.

I think Sam is doing the same because Bahri adds, "Well, is that something you guys would be interested in?"

"Yes!" Sam and I exclaim at the same time.

"Yes, that is definitely something we'd be interested in," I reassure.

"Great, I'll set up the meeting then. They said they have an opening in early December, so I'll reserve it for you guys. Congratulations ladies, this is such a big accomplishment."

We profusely thank him and walk back towards the parking lot.

"Holy fuck," Sam says after a while.

"Holy fuck," I agree.

We look at each other with matching smiles and let out a squeal and hug each other while jumping up and down.

"Fucking Ubisoft is interested in our work. We might actually be able to develop this game," Sam pulls back and puts her hands on my shoulders. "We need to get to work on what we want to show them ASAP. Let's grab our things from the apartment and go to the library."

"As much as I would love to do that, I have a shift in 30 and after I'm going to the art museum with Scott. Remember? I asked you if you wanted to go since it's National Art Museum Day?"

"Right, well I have some sketches I'm behind on and you have a lot of the coding, at least for the next sequence done, so we should be fine."

"I actually finished the next five sequences; I got a lot done when I was in California. Helped me clear my mind."

"Oh shit, I'm very behind then. I'll get them done by the end of the week though."

"Don't rush it, we have a meeting with fucking Ubisoft, if they like the tiny bit that we submitted, they'll love seeing the whole plan."

"True. Ok after the museum no getting distracted with Scott, we are going out to celebrate. You can bring him with you if you want, I'll text the 106ers and maybe you can see if Scott roommates want to come. We can grab pizza and beers or something."

"Oh, I'm sure you'd love me to invite the roommates. Especially a certain redhead."

"He's not a ginger. It's brown with a tint of red."

"I never said a name, funny how you knew exactly who I was talking about."

"Fuck off," she rolls her eyes at me, but the smile stays on her face.

~

We met for office hours at 7:00 and now at 8:00, I'm helping some of the girls get ready for school. Rosie and Tessa run to grab their uniforms with the 10-minute warning being called out.

Sophie wraps her little arms around my torso as I lift myself up sitting criss cross on the floor. "But I don't wanna go to school."

"Sorry Soph, but we gotta fill that brain of yours up so you can be super smart."

"But I don't wanna be super smart," she whines.

"Heck ya you do. Being smart is like only the coolest thing ever," I counter, "Because when we're super smart there's so much we can do. Like help other people, read lots of books, get a job that makes you happy."

She still looks unimpressed, so I add, "You know, Sam and I go to school too," I smile thinking about the news we got earlier.

Her pupils dilate and she heads to her trunk grabbing her school uniform and running towards the bathroom.

It gets them every time. You know at the elementary school age when you would go to the mall and see older kids hanging out and hope that one day that would be you? Well, some of the kids have that mindset when they look at Sam and I. For some reason, unknown to me, they think that we're the epitome of cool and wanna do everything just like us.

Once everyone's dressed and fed, we make our way to the bus stop, Soph and Rosie each holding one of my hands.

Arriving at the bus stop I feel a little nudge on my hand, and I squat down to Sophie's level.

"You're smart, you're brave, you're kind, and you're just as good if not better than them." Every time I drop them off, Sophie and I do affirmations. After her first week at the private school, some of the other kids made fun of her for being a scholarship kid and the affirmations is something that seems to calm her down.

"I'm smart, I'm brave, I'm kind, and I'm just as good if not better than them," Soph mimics.

"Good," I say straightening her coat, "don't let them get you down kiddo."

"Just kick them in the privates if they make fun of you Soph," Rosie pitches.

"No! No, absolutely no kicking in the private, or kicking anywhere for that matter."

"Right, biting is so much better."

"NO," I smack my forehead with the palm of my hand. "Violence is never the answer, that'll get you in the principal's office. Just use your words and tell me if they are bothering you so I can try to handle it. Alrighty, I won't see you guys for a couple days so give me a hug."

With a hug goodbye I start walking back to the house with a couple of other employees. There's still a handful of girls who are too young to go to school, so we treat the day with them like preschool. Learn alphabets, colors, animals, all that jazz.

SexyBack fills my ears and my coworkers wiggle their eyebrows at me knowing exactly whose calling. I flip them off jokingly and answer.

"Hey stalker."

"Hey Books, what time did you want to go to the museum?"

"Mmmm I don't get off until 12:30, so maybe 1?"

"Ok, have you eaten anything this morning?"

"No, but I have a granola bar for later."

"Dammit Del, that's not enough. I'll pick you up at your place at 1 and then we can go grab something to eat. Start thinking about what you want now, because we'll be in the car for an hour waiting for your indecisive ass to choose something."

"You can pick."

"You said that last time and then everything I mentioned didn't sound good to you. You pick. Flip a coin if you can't decide."

"Alright, if that's all, I just got back from dropping the girls off. I'll see you at 1."

"Wait, Rydell."

"Yes…"

"Ummm"

"What is it Scotty, I don't have all day."

"Nothing, sorry. See you at 1."
Weird.

CHAPTER 40: *SCOTT*

I hang up the phone. Really Scott? Fucking idiot, I tell her to wait just to say, 'umm bye'. When it comes to Rydell, my game is shit. Sometimes I can barely get out a fucking sentence.

And what the hell was I thinking. I was about to tell her that I love her over the fucking phone? I'm such a dumbass. But it's been on the tip of my tongue since she's been back and driving me insane.

But I still don't think she's ready to hear it. We've had a lot of late-night talks not only talking about all her shit, but also about all of my shit.

We both have things that we need to work out.

I walk into the gym to start morning practice. Today we're working legs, so I go over to the squatting station.

"Lindsay's been asking about you. She says you won't answer her calls," I look over at McCombs as I put the amount of weight I want on either side of the bars.

"Well, she can keep on waiting if she wants. Or you can tell her to fuck off because I don't want anything to do with her."

"You're really going to choose glasses over Lindsay?"

"I wouldn't choose Lindsay over anyone, she's a piece of shit."

"Fuck, the nerds got you whipped. Lindsay is the most popular girl on this campus. She can get you places. What's going to happen with glasses? She'll just pull you down."

I keep my cool, "I don't need Lindsay's help to get me anywhere. I'm perfectly capable of doing it myself, maybe unlike you. As for Rydell, keep her name out of your fucking mouth. In fact, don't even think about her. If there's one person that can help me be a better person, it's her."

"Fucking whipped," he laughs and starts walking away. Ya he better fucking walk away.

"What was that all about," Webbs comes up as I start my set.

"Give me a sec," a workout probably isn't the worst thing right now. Especially with McCombs nagging me.

When I finish, I turn to Webbs to see both Ruddy and Davies also standing with him. We usually stick together as a group, so it doesn't really surprise me.

"McCombs started running his mouth about Rydell so and told me to go back to Lindsay. I told him to shut the fuck up."

"I swear to God, if that asshole says one bad thing about Deli, I'll give him a piece of my mind," Webbs claims.

Over the couple months of mine and Rydell's relationship, she's become friends with the guys. I mean it's hard for her not to considering that we're with each other all the time. And I've found that all of them are pretty protective over her. Also not surpising though. I'm convinced that there isn't a person out there who wouldn't like Rydell if they got to know her.

Which is kinda a scary thought considering all the guys who would want to be with her the minute they have a real conversation with her.

Fuck, there's probably so many guys who want to be with Rydell. Especially all those little computer science nerds. They're probably all in love with her. Not many girls are computer science majors, not to mention she's fucking gorgeous.

"You don't think he'd actually say anything to her face, do you?" Davies asks.

"If he does, he won't be playing in our next game. You think coach is going to stand for some asshole bad mouthing the only person who comes to sit in the family section for me?"

Not only do the guys love Rydell, but the coaches also love her. They met her a couple games ago, and always make a point to say hi to her when she's at the rink.

Plus, they've told me multiple times that she's exactly the type of girl that I need. Not only is she what I need but she's probably the only thing I've ever really wanted.

Sure, I want to get a spot playing hockey pro. But if that didn't work out, I'd be happy as long as I had Rydell.

As if I've hit some sort of epiphany, I walk outside and pull out my phone to dial my mom's number.

"Scott now is not a good time, I'm about to be in a meeting."

"I'll make it quick. Don't bother finding a

girl for me to marry, I've found one. And I don't particularly care if you like her or not. You guys can take my trust fund away, I still have the one from grandma and grandpa, and no one can get rid of that," it's true contracts were signed so that one is legally mine.

"Also, I'm going to be a pro hockey player, that's going to make me more then set for life. I won't be running your company, but I know Penelope would love to," also true, my sister has always had a bone for business, and she would do a fucking good job running the company. Way better than me. But my misogynistic parents would give it to me even though she's older.

"She's already working there for you so train her for it because I won't take it. Hope that was fast enough, you can go to your meeting now," I don't even wait for her response as I hang up.

My phone starts ringing, and I turn it on silent as I get back to my workout.

~

After securely picking up the package, aka Rydell, we decided on Sammy's for lunch. I open the door for her, and we walk to the register.

We give our order, "Alright that'll be $12.95".

Before I can even process what's happening, Rydell's card is in the machine and she's paying for the meal. "Ha. You're too slow for me Scotty." She has a big smile on her face.

"Oh, I'll get you back for that Rydell Rivens. I wanted to pay for it."

"I know you did. But you always pay even against my protests and I'm a strong, independent, working woman who can pay for a meal thank you very much."

The worker is looking at us with amusement as she hands Rydell the receipt, "You're order number 4."

"Thank you," Rydell responds with a smile as she goes to find a seat.

We find a booth and sit across from each other. "So," her fucking dimpled smile is still on display.

"So...."

"I have some news," she seriously cannot wipe the grin off her pretty face. Not that I'm complaining, I love her smile.

"Ok, are you gonna tell me or are you just going to sit there smiling at me?"

She laughs a little, "You know how I told you that Professor Bahri sent out a demo of mine and Sam's video game to the comp sci board?"

"Yes...." I start smiling myself waiting for what I know she's about to tell me.

"Ubisoft is interested, and they set up a meeting with us to discuss the details of it so we can possibly set up a contract with them."

My eyes widen. I may not be a coding nerd, but even I know how big of a company Ubisoft is. "Shut the fuck up. Are you serious?"

My nods her head super-fast. I get out of my seat and sit in her booth putting my arms around her and lifting her so that she's on my lap. "That's fucking amazing. I'm so proud of you," I pull back a bit so that I can look at her face. "Can't say I'm surprised though. Didn't I tell you someone was going to pick it up."

"Ya, you did."

"Fucking Ubisoft is huge though. Should I

get your autograph now or later hot shot?"

She laughs and climbs off my lap. I don't make an effort to move, instead I wrap my arm around her shoulder and kiss the top of her head.

"Well, it's not set-in stone yet, but they said they really liked it, and we barely showed them anything," she looks up at me, and sure enough that dimple is poking out on the left side of her chin.

I raise my hard to brush my thumb over it, making her smile a little bit wider. I move my fingers to brush across her blushing cheeks and then leaning in to kiss her right one.

"Order number 4," and there goes that moment.

CHAPTER 41: RYDELL

Today will be the day I tell Scott how I really feel.

Ever since our day at the museum I've been trying to find the perfect moment to tell him how much I care about him and that I know he doesn't do relationships but maybe he might want to try one with me.

I'm not expecting anything though. And sure, I'll be a little disappointed if he flat out rejects me, but I've gotten to a point where I don't really care if he rejects me.

Yes, it would hurt but we're so close that I don't think his rejection will end our friendship. And I'd rather try to be with him and hope that it turns out, then not try at all.

Anyways, our museum day felt a lot like a date. We held hands the whole time, he kissed my cheek when I told him about Ubisoft, and he told me I was 'prettier than any of the art pieces in there'.

And I ran that through my head for weeks.

It's November 23rd, aka Scotts birthday, and I have it all planned out. I'm going to go over to his house with a cupcake as a surprise and then take him to the movies.

He told me that he always goes to the theatre on his birthday, so I figured after the movie well go wherever he wants. We'll chat. Then I'll grab him by the cheeks and kiss him.

Wait. No, I won't. I'll grab him by the cheeks, and then ask him if I can kiss him because consent goes both ways. Then, if he says yes, I'll kiss him and tell him that I'm pretty sure I'm in love with him.

My heart is excited just thinking about it. I'm not even scared. I respect his decision to not go into relationships, but I honestly think he might want one with me just as much as I want one with him.

Anyways, today is the day that I need to tell him because I fly out to California tonight for Thanksgiving break.

Thanksgiving is always a difficult time of the year with me, and now that my family knows about the situation, it will be nice to have their support this year.

Plus, I figure, if I do get rejected, I'll have those few days out of town to recover from it. Dang, I'm so good at making plans.

"Hey Sam, I'm about to leave. Wish me luck," I lean on her door frame.

"Good luck!" she comes over to give me a hug. "If he hurts you in anyway, call me and I'll hunt him down, chop off his balls and feed them to him."

"Totally unnecessary," I pull back. "I won't hold it against him if he isn't feeling it. He did tell me he doesn't do relationships, so this is kinda a long shot."

"Tell him I say happy birthday."

"Will do," and with that, I grab the cupcake, candle and his present and head out the door.

~

"Ok Rydell, you've got this. It's ok if he says no. You don't need a man in your life to be happy. Plus, he'll still want to be your friend. I mean hopefully he'll want to be your friend still. Oh my gosh what if he doesn't want to be your friend? No, he definitely will, Scott isn't a shitty person." I'm giving myself a pep talk before as I pull into his neighborhood.

There's a lot of cars here. Maybe the juniors are having an afternoon party. All the houses have pools so sometimes they throw pool parties. Which I never understood because it's freezing outside, but I guess they heat it. Usually, Scott tells me about them.

I hope he's home. But he would've told me if he was going because he always tries to drag me to them.

Plus, I know he doesn't have practice for the rest of the day. He got out at 11, and its 12. And he's usually home at this time. Maybe I shouldn't have made it a surprise. Maybe I should have called to make sure he was home.

I stick the candle in the cupcake and light it when I get to the front door. My present to him is in the tote bag that I have slung on my shoulder, maybe I'll give it to him later. It's the second book in the *Raven Cycle* since he read the first one and said he liked it. I annotated it for him, leaving small drawings, notes in the margins, underlining's of my favorite quotes. It took me hours. I also found matching necklaces from Claire's. One says 'best' and the other says 'friends' and when connected they make a heart. But I figure that Scott can buy himself anything he wanted so I decided to get him something less material and more personal.

Ok, there's definitely something going on at their house. I think it might be a party of some sorts because there's music and lots of people talking.

Fuck. This was such a bad idea. But I'm already here so and I can't back down. I've been trying to find the perfect time to tell him for weeks. I ring the doorbell.

Shit. Maybe I should leave before he answers. Oh, fuck this is so stressful. No Rydell, you can do this, Scott is your friend. Everything is going to be fine.

The door opens and I'm faced with a shirtless, soaking wet Davies. They must be in the pool.

"SCOTT! RYDELL IS HERE!" he looks back and yells. "Hey Deli. What brings you here?" I look past him. There is definitely a party happening.

Oh my god. There's a party happening. On his birthday. I am so stupid.

I feel my eyes start to sting at the fact that he didn't invite me to his birthday party and there's a lump in my throat. "Um, I was actually just going to leave. You don't have to tell Scott I was here. You guys are busy and I um-"

"Ry, hey. I was just going to call you," sure he was. I notice that he isn't in his bathing suit.

"Hi," I stick the cupcake out that still has the candle lit. I'm trying so hard not to cry right now. "Happy Birthday, I know you don't like sweet things but it's the principle, right?" I do my best to say it without my voice sounding shakey.

"You remembered my birthday?" he says

slowly. I shove the cupcake in his hands. I need to get the fuck out of here.

"Of course, I did," I shake my head. I'm about to lose it, I can feel my breathing pick up. "I saved it to my phone after you told me. I thought maybe we could go to the movies but I'm clearly intruding here. I'm sorry, I really should've called. But I'm gonna go. Enjoy the cupcake."

This is a disaster. I start speed walking back to my car.

CHAPTER 42: SCOTT

When I got home a whole sorority was here with a bunch of my teammates yelling happy birthday.

"Dude, we finally find out what day your super-secret birthday is. Why'd we have to find out through the sorority?" Davies claps my shoulder.

"What the fuck is going on?" I am so confused. I have never told anyone my birthday for a reason. In fact, I was planning on coming home from practice and calling Rydell to ask if she wanted to go to the movies with me.

I know I said I always go by myself, but if there's anyone I would want to spend my birthday with, it's her.

I had a plan. I was going to go to the movies today. Tell her it's my birthday. She'll feel bad that she didn't get me a gift. And then I'll tell her that I know a gift she can give me. When she asks what, I'll say a kiss and she won't be able to refuse since it's my birthday.

After that, I can finally tell her that I'm in love with her and that I know I don't do relationships, but I want to try it out with her.

Damn, I'm so fucking good at making plans.

But now my plan is getting fucked up. I don't even know how the hell they found out it was my birthday.

"How did you find out?"

"Some of the girls from Alpha Delta Pi suggested that we through a surprise pool party for you."

Oh, there's a party all right. And it's in full swing. Most of the people here haven't even acknowledged my presence, they're too busy getting wasted or messing around in the pool. Most of them probably don't even care that it's my birthday, they just came for a good party.

"Of course, we knew when your birthday is Scott. You do realize that when you google search your name, there's a whole page about you," I turn around to see a person I swore I'd never talk to again.

"Get the fuck out of my house Lindsay. You're not welcome here."

"What, you're going to kick everyone out," Davies has left, and I need him to tell me what the hell is going on right now.

"I don't really care what everyone else does. I'm not staying here for whatever the fuck this is. If you're still here when I get back, I'll call the fucking police and filing a restraining order."

I faintly hear Davies calling me to the front door over the music and walk towards him to tell him I'm leaving.

When I get to the door, I see the only person who I want to spend my birthday with, holding a cupcake that has a candle lit. She remembered my birthday. Oh my god. We talked about my birthday that one time, but I didn't think she'd actually remember.

But she did. She remembered. On her own. Not with the help of a google page. Of course she did, I don't know why that surprises me. I could literally cry right now, no one besides my sister has ever remembered. I got a happy birthday text from her saying that she'd call me later and there's a 50/50 chance I'll hear from my parents.

I look at Rydell's face and she is visibly upset. "Ry, hey. I was just going to call you," sometimes I swear it's like the universe has connected us. It's like whenever I think about her, she appears in some way. Either through messages or in person. That has to mean something right?

"Hi," she sticks the cupcake out probably prompting me to blow the candle out. "Happy Birthday, I know you don't like sweet things but it's the principle, right?" I don't like sweet things, but I will eat this entire fucking cupcake to make her happy. And she put all the effort into getting it for me, I'll just make her share it with me.

"You remembered my birthday?" I say slowly because honestly it feels like I'm having the best fucking dream. She shoves the cupcake towards me, and I grab it from her hands. Then I notice that her hands are slightly shaking.

"Of course, I did," she shakes her head. I scan her face and she has one of the fakest looking smiles I've ever seen. I can tell because there's no left side dimple. Her eyes are a little bit glossy and I'm trying to figure out what's wrong. "I saved it to my phone after you told me. I thought maybe we could go to the movies but I'm clearly intruding here. I'm sorry, I really should've called. But I'm gonna go. Enjoy the cupcake."

She's doing her Olympic speed walk down the porch stairs and to her car. Oh shit. She thinks she's intruding. She thinks I'm having a party and didn't invite her. She has no idea that she's the only person I want to be around on my birthday.

"Hey! Wait a second!" I jog up to her. "I want to go to the movies with you," I say as I stand in front of her, blocking the path to her car. "Just let me grab my keys and wallet, I'll drive."

She's looking at me, her eyes filled with tears that are threatening to spill over. She laughs a small humor less laugh, "What, and leave your party?" She tilts her head to the side a bit. "It's ok that you didn't invite me. I just thought... I thought that we-" she shakes her head. "I don't know what I thought. But clearly, I was wrong. It's fine though. Really. I understand, this is a different group of people that I don't really fit into, so it's probably good that you didn't invite me."

"Rydell, I didn't even know that this party was happening, I swear," I don't want her to think that I wouldn't invite her. Especially, when in reality, she's the only one I'd invite to a birthday party.

"It's fine," she says but her face is saying something entirely different. "I didn't think you'd be doing anything because you said no one ever celebrated it with you. And I know your sister isn't here to give you a cupcake, so I thought that I'd fulfill that duty. But look," she jerks her thumb back at the house, "you have a house full of people to celebrate with now. You don't need me," I need her more than she fucking knows.

"I don't want to celebrate with any of them though," I raise my hand up to her cheek. "I only want to celebrate with you. Plus, it's like my own mini tradition to see a movie on my birthday, and I want to add you into that tradition. Let me just grab me things ok?"

"I'm not letting you leave a party thrown for you. All these people are here for *you*. You should enjoy it. I think you'd have a better time," her voice catches and she swallows thickly, "with them. Put your swimsuit on and have fun. You deserve to have an actual birthday party for once."

She takes my hand off her cheek and puts in back down to her side, then walks around me to her car. I follow her to the driver's side of her car. "Rydell, I swear, I didn't know that this was going on. Some of the guys threw it. I'm not lying when I say I was just about to call you. I was going to ask you to go to the movies with me. That's all I want to do for my birthday. The people in there don't give a shit about me. I'm convinced that most of them don't even know it's my birthday."

"Scott, really, it's not that big of a," she looks past my shoulder and her eyes flash with hurt, "deal," she whispers the last part. That prompts me to turn around finding Lindsay and a ginger walking towards me.

"Come on Birthday Boy. The parties inside. Oh, this is awkward. Ryland, I don't think you're invited to this one. Scott only wanted his close friends here. Scott said you guys were just Spanish partners. Sorry."

"What the fuck," I look back to Rydell who is failing to keep her tears back. I go to grab her hand, but she jerks it away. "Books, I swear that's not true. I-"

"It doesn't matter," she wipes at the tears on

her cheeks and her sniffles are breaking my heart. Then she grabs a wrapped present out of her tote bag and shoves it in my hand.

She's trying to act like she's not crying but definitely struggling with it. She looks at Lindsay, "It's ok. I was just dropping something off." Then she looks back at me, "Wouldn't want any unimportant people at the party, it might ruin it. We were just Spanish partners after all," she's at a point where she's not even hiding her tears. And I so badly want to reach out and wipe them off. I want to pull her into a hug and beg her to believe me.

I feel like I'm losing her. This was not how the day was supposed to go.

"Happy Birthday Scott," with that she hops into her car and drives away.

CHAPTER 43: *RYDELL*

"He had a whole party going on," I can't stop the tears from falling down my face and I can barely get my words out. "It was only for his close friends. They said I was just his Spanish partner. Like nothing happened between us. I'm so stupid. How could I think he actually liked me?"

Sam has her arms around me and she's brushing hair on the back of my head. "Wasn't Lindsay the one who locked you in a closet? Are you sure you can trust her word? I just can't see Scott using you for a Spanish project."

"You should've seen his face. He looked so guilty. Like he was caught in a lie. I don't know why I thought this would end any differently," I'm choking on my words.

As soon as I got home I full on lost it and Sam was there to comfort me. I've been trying to explain the situation to her for the past 30 minutes.

"Maybe I could ask Max what-"

I cut her off, "No! No, I don't want anyone else getting involved. I have a flight that leaves tonight, and I'll distance myself. I knew there was a possibility that he just thought of me as his Spanish partner. I just didn't think it would hurt this badly to hear it in actuality."

If I'm being honest, after about a month of knowing Scott, I ruled out that possibility. I thought there was no way he was just using me. And I think there's a part of me that still thinks that.

It's hard for me to believe that he could've acted the way he did with me without it meaning anything.

And maybe I read into the whole relationship thing wrong. But I do think that we were friends at one point. Maybe I just thought it was a more serious relationship then it was.

"Rydell," Sam brings me out of my thoughts. "I've said your name like three times now. Did you hear anything I just said?"

"Sorry. What?"

"I said, I don't think you should just ignore the situation. I don't think you should go on acting like you guys never knew each other. Go home, have a good time with your family, sort out all your feelings, and then sit down with him and have a conversation. I mean, this morning you were prepared to tell him you're in love with him. Those feelings aren't just going to go away overnight."

"I don't know how I'm even supposed to talk to him anymore. I think the moment I see him, I'll probably start crying. I couldn't even fucking hold myself together as I was leaving. It was so embarrassing and I'm sure Lindsay had a field day with it."

"Ya, well Lindsay's a fucking bitch so who cares what she thinks," Sam puts her hands on my shoulders. "You've been through a lot. Especially this past month with your grandpa dying and all those memories resurfacing. And with the whole

Trey experience I know it's hard for you to let people in. But you're so much stronger than letting this break you," I look down.

"Hey. Rydell Rivens, you're going to get through this. We aren't having another Trey situation. And if we are, if Scott really did blindside you, then it's a good fucking thing that you didn't tell him how you feel. Because if he was just using you, he doesn't deserve you or the love that you could give him. In fact, it's a major loss on his part."

"What if... what if I never find someone who wants my love? What if this is the best it gets? Sometimes I really feel like I'm not meant to be loved, just to love," I look back up at her. "I really thought Scott might be the one who changed that. And I wanted it to be him. It just hurts thinking about how wrong I was."

"It'll hurt for a bit. I know that sucks to hear, but you care about him, so it's not going to be easy. Just think everything through and talk to him. Hear his side of the story and then decide what you want to do."

I just nod my head. "I should probably finish packing. Make sure I have everything ready for the trip. I want to go early and see if they can fit me on an earlier flight now that I don't have plans for the day."

~

I ended up getting put on an earlier flight and I was so grateful for it.

I've always loved airports and flying. There's something about being in a building with people going literally everywhere and anywhere that brings me some sort of peace. I think it also puts how small our lives are into perspective.

I mean that sounds a bit depressing. But I guess it's true. Makes me wonder how important my love life problems are in the grand scheme of things. Sure, it's a solid point of pain for my life right now, but it's really not that important on a large scale.

There's what? 7 billion people on this earth. When I put it that way, my problems just seem so small. I mean, who cares, besides me?

Being in the airport let me clear my mind a bit. Instead of focusing on what happened a couple hours ago, I basked in the idea of seeing my family soon.

I'm just getting off the plane and walking over to baggage claim. The airport is packed considering that it's Thanksgiving week.

After about 20 minutes of weaving through people and waiting for my bag, I finally go out to the pickup area, spotting my sister's car right away.

Andromeda, or Andy, is a senior in high school and uses every opportunity she can to drive so I wasn't surprised to find out that she was the one picking me up. She is driving the car that I used to drive in high school.

Before my older brother, Chris, went to college, we used to share it which caused lots of fights. And more fights when he left, and my younger brother Liam got his license and started sharing the car. Now Andy and Oliver share it.

"Finally, I've only been waiting for forever!" Andy exclaims after I put my bag in the trunk and climb in the passenger seat.

"Nice to see you too," I reach over the center console to give her a side hug. "Hi David," I turn and wave to the person in the backseat.

"Hey Del, how are you?"

Oh, you know, just got my heart broken. Scared I'll never find someone to truly love me. "I'm doing alright. How are you. How's wrestling?"

"Good and good." All my siblings, including Andy, were/are on the wrestling team. I'm the lone one out who decided I didn't want to break any bones. My parents made me take classes for it all throughout elementary school, but I hated it. I'm just not aggressive enough for it. I love to watch it though.

That's how Andy and David met. They've been in the same wrestling class since kindergarten. One class together and they become best friends. Best friends who are too scared to admit their feelings for each other.

They go to every school dance together, they are practically glued to the hip, and they've never dated anyone. But they claim that they are just friends.

"David made captain of the boys' team," Andy butts in.

"That doesn't surprise me. You guys have only been training your whole lives. They honestly probably would have made you captain freshman year if they didn't like to keep it a senior."

And it's true. David is a great wrestler. He's ranked 4th nationally. Andy is ranked 3rd nationally. But they train at one of the best places in the country, and a lot of the long-time wrestlers there are ranked high. Lots win state.

"Ya well Andy is captain again. But I'm sure you already knew that."

"Of course I knew that. I'm proud of both of you though. What colleges are you looking at? Andy mentioned that Oklahoma was interested in picking up her and a couple of others from the team."

"Ya I've heard from Oklahoma. Also, Montana and Iowa State. It would be cool if Andy and I went to the same college though. Right, Ands?"

"Mhmm. You would be lost without me."

"Probably," he agrees. God they are sickingly cute. If they don't end up together, I'll be convinced that love in the modern day isn't real.

As we pull into the driveway, I spot my parents on the porch bench. Both with books in their hands. I get my reading addiction from them.

Andy honks the horn, and their heads shoot up. My mom jumps down the steps and starts flailing her arms around like one of those inflatable things that are in front of car shops. You can see where I got my awkwardness from. My dad stays on the top on the steps leaning on the beam watching my mom with a smile on his face.

As I climb out of the car, my mom tackles me in a hug. "I know it's only been a couple of weeks, but I missed my sweet girl." She puts her hands on both my cheeks. "What's wrong lovie?"

I can't get anything past this woman. "Nothing. I'm just tired from the flight."

"Rydell Catherine, you might want to come up with a better excuse then that because I'm not buying it from one second."

"Leave the girl alone for a second will you Goosey," my dad has had the nickname 'Goosey' for my mom ever since they met. He said she was always a mother goose. To everyone she met.

When my dad approaches me, he sticks his index finger out, and I touch the tip of my index finger to it. I really don't know how that tradition started, but that's always how we greet each other. Then he pulls me into a hug.

"Ollie! Will get down here and greet your sissy? Grab her bag and take it to Andy's room."

I pull back from my dad, but he keeps his hands on my shoulders and scans my face with a small frown. "You know you can't get anything past us. But I won't bombard you for questions until later."

I give him a small smile, "It's nothing I can't handle. You know me. Always the independent."

He chuckles, "That you are Ryles."

CHAPTER 44: *SCOTT*

Fuck. This is such a stupid situation. They fucking stalked my google page for this birthday party? "You need to get the fuck out of here before I do something I'll really regret," I tell Lindsay and the ginger as I head back into the house to kick everyone out.

She tries to follow me up the stairs, "One more step and I promise you, there will be a restraining order made." She doesn't come any close, but instead cries off to her car. Fucking bitch.

"Where'd Deli go, she didn't look very happy," Webbs says.

"Everyone needs to go. I'm serious, get every person out of this house right now or I'm going to fucking lose it," I can't get the image of Rydell crying out of my head. She looked so sad and it's because of me. I never want to be the one making her feel that way. She's already been through enough; she doesn't need this drama piled on top of it.

I unplug the speaker that's blasting music and head up to my room to grab my keys. I'm shuffling through all my shit, but they are literally nowhere to be found.

Going back downstairs, Davies and Webbs are getting the people to leave but there's still a big crowd gathered around. "Everyone out! Parties over!" I shout to the people lingering.

"Have you guys seen my keys anywhere?" I ask my roommates.

"No, did you check your bag and pockets?" Ruddy walks up.

"Yes, I looked fucking everywhere. I need them. Now. Like right now," I'm losing it.

"Alright calm down, I'll help you look, Davies and Webbs can get everyone out."

I walk to the kitchen to look, but there's alcohol and solo cups scattered everywhere, making it hard to find anything.

I'm knocking cups over as I scramble to find my keys, "Dude take a breath. What happened?"

"I didn't want this fucking party. I never asked for it. In fact, I purposely don't tell people my birthday because I hate it. But this year, I was actually excited for it because I was going to ask Rydell to go to the movies with me. But she came over and she remembered my birthday from the one time I told her. I only very briefly told her once and she remembered. And she brought me a cupcake and a present and wanted to take me to the movies. But she saw the party and thought I didn't invite her and then fucking Lindsay told her that it was for close friends only not Spanish partners and she was crying and-"

"Ok, ok," I probably look like I'm about to pass out. I have never been one to ramble, but my mind is such a mess right now. I am not about to lose Rydell. I'll do whatever the fuck I have to, to keep her in my life.

"Let's check a couple move places for your keys. Your spare isn't in your desk."

"No. No I was using my spare this morning," I couldn't find my keys for practice and I woke up too late to look for them.

"Alright, if we can't find them in the next 5-10 minutes, you can borrow my car. But you need to chill for a second. You shouldn't drive when you're this upset."

"I'll do whatever the fuck I want. I need to see her Max. You should've seen her face. She looked so fucking sad. I need her to know that it's just a big misunderstanding."

"Maybe try calling her."

"She won't answer. She doesn't think we're friends. She thinks I was using her for a good grade."

"Ok, I'm going to look in your car, maybe you left them there."

~

I finally found my keys in between the couch cushions. About 30 minutes later. Ruddy was scared that I would get into an accident if I drove in my 'state of mind'.

I tried to tell him that the longer I wait the more upset I'll be, but he didn't buy it. Asshole.

I'm jogging up to Rydell's apartment door.

After knocking, I'm faced with a very angry looking Sam. "You have some fucking nerve showing up here."

"Where is she?"

"Why should I tell you? Do you know how upset she was? I had her crying in my arms for about half an hour telling me that you only talked to her for a good grade. How she's scared to ever let anyone else in again because she always ends up getting hurt. That she's only meant to care about people, and never have anyone care for her back."

Fuck. "It's a misunderstanding. I swear. I would never do anything to hurt her. I didn't even know that the party was happening. Lindsay stalked me on google and found out when my birthday is. I wanted to spend the day with Rydell, I'm not lying when I say I was going to call her right when I got back from practice. And then I was bombarded with all that shit. Are you really going to trust the girl that locked Rydell in a closet?"

"All I know is that she was devastated. And I don't really know why I should trust you."

"Because I'm fucking in love with her. Ok? I'm in love with and I was going to tell her at the movies today. I had it all planned out. I was going to tell her it was birthday because I didn't think she'd remember. But of course, she did because she's a fucking angel. And I didn't think she would have a present so when she felt bad about it, I was going to tell her that she could give me a kiss. And then I was going to confess my feelings for her," I blurt out.

Sam looks at me with slightly wide eyes. "Trust me now?" I ask.

"Rydell's not here. She took an earlier flight to California. I just got back from dropping her off at the airport and her flight already departed."

"Fuck," I can't wait a week to see her. "Do you have her sisters' number?"

"Yes, but I don't see how that has anything to do with your situation."

"Because I'm going to fly out to California, and I don't have her address. It's also probably not a good idea to go completely unannounced and her sister likes me. I've talked to her when Rydell has her on FaceTime."

"You know, all the flights are probably pretty booked considering that Thanksgiving is tomorrow."

"It doesn't fucking matter Sam. I'm not waiting a week to explain the situation to her.

CHAPTER 45: *RYDELL*

"Rydell, stop eating the mashed potatoes, you'll spoil your appetite!"

"Dad's eating them too!"

"Oi, don't drag me down with you Ryles."

I'm feeling a lot better today. My whole family is here. My mom's parents and all my siblings finally made it. It's very rare to have all my siblings here at once. Andromeda and Oliver are still in high school. Liam and I are in college. And Chris is graduated from college but lives about an hour away from my parents' house with his wife.

After lots of talking with Andy last night, I decided to not make any assumptions about what happened yesterday. Andy kept saying that she knows Scott didn't know anything about the party and that I need to trust her on that one. Whatever that means.

But I'm going to call him back after dinner and hopefully clear it up. I just don't know if I'm necessarily ready to confess my feelings for him.

"The Handson's are here!" Oliver shouts from the living room.

My mom warned me that they would be here. We've spent Thanksgiving with them for as long as I can remember. Since our breakup, Trey has never been to the Thanksgivings. Freshman year, he didn't come home from college, sophomore year he went to his girlfriends, and last year he was working. Not sure if those are real excuses, but I was glad for them.

Trey's mom walks into the kitchen. "Oh, look how pretty you are Rydell! You look so much more grown up every time I see you!" she goes in for the hug.

"Hi Nancy. It's good to see you," as I look pull back, I look over her shoulder and see the face of someone I haven't seen since high school graduation.

"Hi Del. You look good."

I put an awkward smile on my face, "Hi Trey. I didn't think you'd be here."

"Well, no girlfriend and I got work off, I figured it's been awhile. Thought it'd be nice to see everyone. I thought it'd be nice to see you, I was hoping you'd be here."

"Of course, I'm here. I would never miss Thanksgiving dinner. Mom's mashed potatoes are too good."

He laughs a little, "Good to see you haven't changed. I remember the mashed potatoes being your favorite."

He's moved to stand next to me while are moms are talking at the stove.

"Ya, well, some of us stick true to ourselves. Some don't," I look up at him with a suggestive look.

"I tried to call you a lot freshman year. To apologize for the whole situation. I really fucked up Ryles."

"Don't call me that," only people I'm super close with call me that. "And ya. You did fuck up. But there's really nothing you can do about it now. I got over it eventually."

"I didn't. Rydell I've really missed you."

I force out a laugh, "I'm sure you did," I say sarcastically. "But I haven't missed you since I left for freshman year of college. I don't know what your motivation for coming here was, but I'm completely over you Trey. I don't even really want to be your friend."

"What do you want me to do Rydell? Act like we don't know each other? Are parents are best friends, you can't avoid me forever."

"I'm not avoiding you, but I'm not going to rekindle our past. You hurt me, and I can forgive you for it. But I'm never going to forget it. I'll be friendly, but I can't let you back into my life. Not the way you want me to." Our voices have dropped down to whispers.

"Hi Ryles. Everything ok over here?" David comes up to us with a protective look. He must have just got here. His family usually comes over for Thanksgiving.

"It's fine," I move to give him a hug. "Is the rest of your family here? Where's Andy?"

"My families here. Andy had to pick something up."

Mom probably asked her to make a last-minute grocery trip. "I should probably go say hi to them. Excuse me," I mumble as I walk away from Trey.

After saying hi to everyone, I walk up to my sister-in-law, Savannah. "You alright Ryles. Your chat with Trey didn't seem very fun. Chris was two seconds away from going up to him to tell him to fuck off."

"He said he's missed me. I mean, what kind of bullshit is that."

"And what'd you say?"

"What do you think I said?! I told him that I'd be friendly, but nothing is going to happen there. I told him I don't even really want to be his friend."

"Good. I'm team Scott anyways."

I groan. Scott has been with me throughout many FaceTime family calls, so just about everyone in this house knows about him.

"What's with the groan. Trouble in paradise?"

"Long story," I mumble. I look down at her pregnant stomach and put my hand on top of it, almost immediately being reward with a swift kick. "How's this one doing?"

"Well, she definitely likes her Aunt Del. This is the first she's kicked all day," I smile at that.

"Heck yeah she does. I'm going to be the best auntie."

"It's good though, she due just about any day now. I swear if she gets any bigger in there, I'm never getting off the toilet. I have to pee all the time. She also likes to kick in the middle of the night, I have to take naps throughout the entire day because I'm up all night."

I laugh, "Already a little troublemaker."

"Mhmm, just like her daddy."

I smile thinking back at Chris's rebellious high school years. Now he's still got that fun spirit, but he's also a lot more responsible. He's going to be the best dad.

"I heard my name. Babe, I thought we

agreed that you can only call me daddy in the bedroom," he jokes.

"Ewww. I think I need to bleach my ears after hearing that."

"Fuck off. You have the dirtiest mind," Savannah says as Chris kisses her cheek and rubs her belly.

"You need me to have a chat with Dickwad over there Ryles?" he gestures to Trey.

"Nah, I have it handled. If you see him alone with me though, have someone interrupt."

I look over to the front door as it opens and see Andy walk in with a small smirk on her face. She doesn't have any grocery bags.

When she walks up to me, she says, "There's someone at the door for you."

I give her a confused look and glance over at my brother and his wife who look like they know exactly who it is.

"Okayyyy. Who is it?"

"Why don't you go find out."

I huff and make my way towards the door. I feel like everyone in this house is staring at me as I do so.

Opening the door, I see the last person I expected I would.

CHAPTER 46: SCOTT

"So, she's the only one who doesn't know I'll be here?"

"Yep, mom is so excited to meet you. Dad will probably give you some sort of warning. And Chris, Liam and Ollie will all try to intimidate you but as long as you play family football with us, they'll like you. David will be nice to you though. He's nice to everyone."

"David's your boyfriend, right?" her cheeks go a little red, like how Rydell's do.

"We're just friends."

"Right. Rydell told me you guys were in denial about your feelings for each other."

"I'm sure she did, sounds like some other people I know," she mumbles. "So, this Lindsay girl is obsessed with you and doesn't like how close you are with Ryles, so she sabotaged you."

"Pretty much. I should've called her in the morning to plan the movies. I was running late though and it slipped my mind. I don't know how much of the story you heard, but I promise you I'm not using your sister."

"When I first heard the story, I was obviously pissed. But you wouldn't have gotten an expensive, last minute plane ticket if you were just using her for her brains. Plus, I've heard the way she talks about you, and you always seem to be together. Not to mention, this Lindsay character seems like a bitch."

"Well, thank you for picking me up and making this happen."

"Mhmm. If you do hurt her though, I'll run you over with this car. I'm sure my brothers wouldn't hesitate making you regret it either."

"The last thing I want to do is hurt Rydell. I'll keep your warning in mind though."

As we pull up to what I assume is their driveway I feel my heart rate start to pick up. From what Andy has told me, it seems like Rydell is more than willing to hear me out. That fact alone lifted about 10 pounds off my shoulders, but I'm still nervous.

When we walk up the porch stairs Andy turns to me and says, "Stay here. There's a lot of people in there and I think you want to have a private convo. Plus, Del has no idea you're here."

I nod my head as I watch her step into the house.

Holy shit. I can't remember a time I've been this nervous. I've sure as hell never been nervous about the idea of talking to a girl before, but I've learned with Rydell that there's a first for everything.

The door opens and I raise my gaze to see the person who's been driving me crazy.

She's in a very Thanksgiving looking out. It's a dark red dress that has a floral pattern. She doesn't have her glasses on, and she looks so fucking pretty. But she always looks pretty so I'm not really surprised.

Her mouth is agape like she's the last person she expected to see.

"Hi," really, that's all you can come up with? Hi?

She steps out the door and closes it behind her. "Scott," she rubs at her forehead. "What are you doing here? How did you even get here?"

"After you left yesterday, I kicked everyone out of the house and grabbed my keys to stop by your place and explain everything. But I couldn't find my keys anywhere and by the time I got to your apartment you had already left."

She slowly nods her head. "Ok. That still doesn't explain how the hell you got to California and why you're standing on my parents' porch."

"Rydell. I couldn't wait a week to explain what happened. I can't lose you," I whisper the last part.

She walks over to the railing of the porch and leans her back against it. I move to stand in front of her. "I swear, I didn't just use you for a good grade. Rydell, you're my best friend. If I were to invite anyone to my birthday party, it would be you. And I wasn't lying when I said I wanted to add you into my movie-birthday tradition. I planned to take you to the movies yesterday but when I got home, I was bombarded with all that shit."

"And Lindsay?" she questions.

"Lindsay stalked my google page to find out it was my birthday. As soon as you left, I told her I would filing a restraining order if she stepped inside my house again. Everything she said was a lie. I don't know if she's jealous, but she's got some serious problems. I hadn't even talked to her since the whole closet thing. In fact, after that happened, I texted her that she needed to stay the fuck away from you and me."

She just nods.

"Books," I say gently. I don't know what I'm supposed to do if she doesn't believe me. "The minute I first came into your apartment and watched you recite essentially the entire *Goonies* movie, you became more than a Spanish partner. Plus, the project has been over for what, a month? And I still can't stay away from you. I'm convinced that there is nothing in this world that could keep me away from you," I raise one hand to cup her cheek and I reach the other one to brace onto the railing slightly trapping her to me. "Please believe me. I would never do anything to hurt you. I promise."

She reaches towards my neck and right when I think she's about to strangle me, she picks up the necklace that's lying on my chest. It's my half of the best friends' necklace that she got me for my birthday, "Nice necklace."

"I'll have you know, I finished like half of the book on the plane. Your annotations are the best part. Does this mean you believe me?"

"I believe you," she tilts her head up to look at me.

"Oh, thank god," I waste no time to pull her into a hug, wrapping an arm around and putting a hand on the back of her head to keep it on my chest.

She wraps her arms around my torso and all of a sudden, my heart feels a lot less heavy.

"I can't believe you flew out to California. I was going to call you tonight to hear your side of the story you know. "

"I don't think I could've waited until tonight. I tried to get a flight for yesterday, but it was all packed."

She pulls back but keeps her arms around my waist. I move my hands to rub up and down her arms. "How did you arrange all of this then? How'd you get Andy to pick you up?"

"When I went over to your apartment, I explained the situation to Sam and when she told me you already left, I didn't hesitate to book a flight. I asked her for Andy's number, and we worked it all out."

"I knew that little shit was up to something. When I was talking to her about it, she kept saying, 'trust me, I know Scott didn't just use you' and that I need to hear your side of the story. Now I know why she was so instant on it."

I laugh a little. When she moves her hands off my waist, I bring both my hands to the railing behind her to cage her in. Looking her right in the eye I say, "You know I'd never hurt you. Right?"

"Ya. I know. I shouldn't have left without letting you explain. I just- I've been hurt in the past and-"

"You don't need to explain anything to me gorgeous. I'm just glad that you heard me out now."

"So, I'm your best friend?" there's that dimpled smile I missed so much.

"You're my only friend."

She laughs a little, "Don't tell your roommates that."

"Ok let me rephrase it. You're the only friend that I need. I could lose everyone in my life, and it would suck but I'd eventually get over it. I would never get over it if I lost you."

She's still smiling. God, I will never get over how much I love seeing her happy. "We should probably head in. I bet you anything all my nosey family members are talking about what's happening."

"Alright," I lean down and kiss her cheek. Then I remove my hands from the rail and grab her hand.

CHAPTER 47: *RYDELL*

My family loves Scott. My brothers and parents all gave him warning that if he hurt me, he'd regret it, but they also welcomed him with open arms. I've barely talked to him since we've walked into the house, I've barely even been by his side and that was like an hour ago. Everyone wants to talk to him.

And he's so good with them. Not that I'm surprised. Whenever I looked over at him from across the room, it's like he knew my eyes were on him. Because he'd look over and either give me a little wink or smile.

We just got split up into groups for football. Scott and I are on opposite teams. "You're going down Bridges," I actually hate playing football because I'm scared of getting hit by it, but my dad says that we need to 'fight the patriarchy' since most families only let the boys play. Can't argue with that.

"I'm not so sure, I'm quite the athletic."

"Hockey skills won't help you here Scotty," he just laughs and goes back to his team.

Their team starts with the ball first, Trey acting as their quarterback. Trey has been giving

Scott dirty looks all day and I'm really hoping that doesn't turn into something.

When I pass the ball to Andy, she takes off. But not too long after she has the ball, David wraps his arms around her waist from the back and lifts her up. "Nice try Ands."

"You couldn't have let me get a little farther?" they've always been very competitive with each other.

The game goes on like that for a while and we are approaching the end. My team has the ball and we've got my dad as quarterback. We're huddled, this is the last play. "Ryles get yourself open. I'll throw it right into your arms. You're pretty fast and they won't expect it."

"I have only caught the ball about twice in my entire existence. I don't think that's the best idea. Next?"

"Just get open. Break."

Oh shit. As soon as he says hike, I take off sprinting and turn around when I think I'm at a good distance.

The ball is flying through the air, so I stick my arms out and close my eyes, preparing to be knocked in the head with it.

And it fucking lands in my arms. I open one eye, keeping the other one slammed shut. When I realize what happened I put it in my hands and jump up and down. "I caught it! I actually caught it you guys! Oh yeah! I should go pro-"

"Run! Go to the end zone!" all my team members are yelling at me.

Right. I start running towards the end but before I can get there, I'm lifted off the floor by a pair of strong arms.

Dammit. I was so close. I do not like the way these arms feel. "Gotcha," of course fucking Trey would ruin my moment of victory. I wiggle my way out of his arms as soon as my feet touch the ground. Everyone looks visibly upset, even his parents. My siblings are all shooting daggers at him and look like they're seconds away from coming over here to give him a piece of their minds.

I'm pulled back by the tie on my dress and comfortable arms wrap around my shoulders. I don't need to look back to know that it's Scott. He has a comforting touch.

"You didn't want to give her that one man, we weren't even keeping score," Scott voice sounds tight. I reach my hands up to rest them on his arms.

"Just playing the game, *man,*" he replies.

"Sure," Scott turns me around to face him and kisses my cheek. "Good catch Books, if someone from the NFL saw that they'd definitely sign you."

I smile up at him and as I do so, he brings his hand to cup my jaw as his thumb traces the dimple on my chin.

"Alright! Time for dinner everyone!" my mom shouts. Most people have already made their way inside, I guess they retreated from their attack when they saw Scott take charge of the situation.

Not that I really care about not getting a touchdown. I think it's just the fact that it was Trey who had to stop it. Having his hands on my body made my skin crawl. Trey was wrong. I did change. Because there was a moment in time when I use to feel the safest in his arms, and now, when he touches me there's so much discomfort.

Scott takes my hand and leads me to the table with all the food. Whenever we have a big gathering of people, we never eat at the table. We set it up like a buffet and finding a spot to eat is a free for all. We set up tables in the backyard, so most people go there.

I go straight for the mashed potatoes. I have my priorities in line. Scott shakes his head and chuckles but follows me. "You're going to turn into a potato one day with the amount you eat."

Scott knows my love for potatoes, we've talked about it before. He picked it up when he noticed that I order fries with just about everything.

"Potatoes are a gift from God Scott."

After grabbing our food, we find a seat at a table with Chris, Savannah, Andy and David.

"Holy shit, your mom's food is so good," Scott says after a couple bites.

"Mhmm. She always makes the best food on Thanksgiving," I say as I shove food into my mouth.

"What does your family do for Thanksgiving Scott?" my chewing slows down when Chris asks. I don't want Scott to feel awkward about his family situation.

"Nothing. My parents always work on Thanksgiving. My sister and I used to watch *Home for the Holidays* every year when we were younger. In fact, this is the first time I've had a Thanksgiving meal."

"Oh. Well, I'm sure it's made up for in Christmas dinner, then right?" why must my older brother be so stupid.

Scott looks a little bit uncomfortable, so I grab his hand and intertwine it with mine on my lap under the table. "Mom makes us watch *Home for the Holidays* practically every year, I'm sure she'd love to put it on tonight," I butt in.

"Ah you don't have to do that. And we don't celebrate Christmas either. My parents gave us a credit card when we got to high school so just told us to buy ourselves presents. My parents weren't home much and when they were, we didn't have home cooked meals like this."

I squeeze his hand. "Well, this is the perfect first home-cooked family meal then. Mom goes all out for Thanksgiving," I'm glad Chris finally caught some sense to divert the conversation.

CHAPTER 48: SCOTT

Rydell's family is amazing. I've never really had family time like this, but they are so welcoming. I could see myself getting used to this kind of life. But I wouldn't want to do it with anyone other than Del.

Trey's family is getting ready to leave as the night comes to an end. When Liam pointed him out and told me who he was it took so much restraint to not go over there and punch him in the jaw.

I bonded with all her brothers over a shared hatred for him. Her brothers threatened me, as did her sister, David, her parents and her grandparents. But all of them also told me that they were rooting for me. Especially after I confronted Trey for not letting Ry get the touchdown.

I mean, what a dick move. She was so excited, and it was fucking adorable. I didn't even make an attempt to tag her out, so when I saw the asshole running for her, I was furious. As was literally everyone else here, even his own family. I didn't do anything drastic because he already embarrassed himself enough.

Rydell is saying bye to Trey's parents and I'm standing next to her telling them it was nice to meet them.

"Rydell, can we chat in private for a sec?" I scoot a little closer to her as Trey asks.

"No. I already told you everything I had to say earlier Trey," hell yeah she did. I'm so proud of her for standing up for herself.

"Come on Ryles. Just give me a minute."

"I told you not to call me that," she's visibly upset. "Your parents are leaving Trey."

"One minute-"

"She said no," I go to stand a little bit in front of Rydell.

"I don't see how any of this is your business," I step a little bit closer to him. He's probably 5'11. I tower over him.

"Maybe not. But I'll make it my business if I have to. I'm not going to stand by and watch you make her uncomfortable. She said no, does it look like she wants to talk to you?"

The second he came up to her, she put her hand on her wrist.

"Whatever. Rydell, when you realize that I'm the best option you have, come find me. If I haven't found someone better by then, I'm sure we can work something out."

"Watch your fucking mouth," Liam says as him, Chris and Ollie walk up.

"I think it's time for you to leave," Ollie adds.

"Whatever," he walks back to his parents who look so disappointed. His mom slaps his arm as soon as he reaches them. How fucking embarrassing.

"You good Ryles," Chris asks her.

"Fine. Thanks you guys."

~

Chris and his wife, the grandparents, and David's family have all left and we are just finishing up *Home for the Holidays.*

Liam is staying at the house until he has to go back to MIT, David drove separate from the rest of his family so that he could stay later, and Ollie and Andy still live here so they are obviously here as well.

One thing I've learned about Rydell and her siblings is that they are all extremely talented. Chris graduated top of his class at University of Washington for paramedic school. And after that he joined the fire academy. Now he works as a dual firefighter/paramedic.

Liam goes to fucking MIT and wants to be a petroleum engineer. He got nearly a perfect score of both the SAT and ACT.

Andy is ranked 3rd nationally for wrestling and has already gotten offers for full wrestling scholarships.

Oliver is not only ranked 2nd nationally for wrestling, but he will also probably graduate as valedictorian of his class.

And then there's obviously Rydell who graduated as valedictorian and is about to sign a contract to develop a video game with fucking Ubisoft.

I don't know what their parents did, but they created some fucking perfect human beings. I can't imagine how proud of them they are.

And I have no doubt that their parents are a big reason why their children are so successful. They have created such a loving atmosphere. They support every part of their children, they welcome their flaws, and help them learn from their mistakes.

They aren't very strict, but you can tell that they raised their children in a way were there's a mutually respect for one another.

The end credits for the movie start to roll and I look over at Rydell who is tucked under my arm, trying so hard to keep her eyes open.

I'm so comfortable right now, and her body is so warm pressed against mine, but I don't want to overstay my welcome here. So, I start to stand up.

Rydell's hand shoots up to mine. "Where are you going?" I look down at her.

"I should probably find a hotel to check into."

"Hotel? What the hell are you talking about?" Rydell's mom questions. "We aren't letting you stay in a hotel; you're staying here sweetie. You can share the guest room with Rydell. I trust you both are mature enough to share a bed?"

"Oh, I don't want to intrude-"

"It's not an intrusion at all Scott. Please, we'd love to have you," I look back down at Rydell who's playing with my fingers. She looks up and smiles with a nod.

"Ok. Thank you Victoria."

"You're staying for the same amount of time as Ryles right?" her dad asks.

"Ya, Sam actually helped me book the same flight back as Rydell, so we should be on the same plane back Sunday."

"Perfect, that gives you guys all of tomorrow. Del can show you around and maybe take you to the beach!" Victoria exclaims.

I look down at the couch. Rydell is still holding onto my hand but she's shifted to a laying position and looks like she's passed out.

"I swear, when that girl is tired, she sleeps like the dead," her mom gestures towards her sleeping figure.

"I'll take her up to the room. Which one is it?" I start to grab Rydell from under the knees and cradle her to my chest.

"Second door on the right," Victoria smiles at me.

CHAPTER 49: *RYDELL*

I wake up with a jump because I am definitely not on the couch anymore.

"Go back to sleep pretty girl," I hear Scott say as I'm lowered onto the bed.

"Pjs," I mumble as I get off the bed to grab clothes from my bag. When I come out of the bathroom from changing, Scott is stripping his shirt off. I avert my eyes, so I don't give myself away too much and climb back onto the bed.

I go back to closing my eyes, expecting the bed to shift from Scott getting on the other side. But I never feel his weight.

Opening my eyes, I see him grabbing a pillow and going over to the couch in the corner of the room.

"What are you doing?" I ask, still half asleep.

"I was planning on going to bed, why? Do you have other plans?" he says with a suggestive smirk.

"Well, if you're going to bed, you should probably get back over here. Right now, you're going to couch."

"I figured I'd let you take the bed; I don't

mind sleeping on the couch."

I scoff, "Don't be ridiculous. Get over here, there's plenty of room for the both of us."

Without protest, he shuffles his way over and I lift up the corner of the comforter so he can climb in.

As soon as he's settled. I gravitate towards his body warmth, positioning myself so that my head is practically on his chest, and throw my arm around his torso. "Thanks for flying out. I'm really happy you're here."

He's stiff at first but I can feel his body relax as he puts his arm around my shoulders and pulls me so that I'm practically all the way on top of him.

Our legs are tangled and he's brushing my hair back with his hand and I'm thinking that I wouldn't mind getting used to this.

~

I wake up with arms wrapped around my waist and my back pressed up against a warm chest. I smile to myself when I remember Scott flying out and spending Thanksgiving with my family.

Crazy to think that less then 48 hours ago I thought he was playing a game with me. And it kind of scares me that almost losing Scott was way worse than losing Trey all together.

It took a while, but I eventually got over Trey. If Scott blindsided me, I think I'd be broken beyond repair. And I hate to think about my happiness depending on a man, but I'm so in love with him that it hurts.

I have to pee so badly. I can feel Scott's hot breath on the back of my neck and his nose is slightly grazing the space behind my ear.

I start to very slowly inch my way off the

bed, but the moment I move I'm pulled closer to Scott by his arms around my waist. "Don't get up yet," as he says it, his lips brush my neck causing my to slightly shiver.

"I didn't mean to wake you. I'm about to pee myself though," I try to move again only causing Scott to wrap his arms tighter.

"Squeeze any tighter and I won't be able to hold it," he automatically loosens his arms, but still keeps me comfortably against his chest.

"You didn't wake me. I've been up like 15 minutes," so he's just been lying there with his head in the crook of my neck this whole time. Consciously?

I turn my head to look over at him and sure enough, he looks fairly awake. "I've been up for like 5 minutes; did you realize?"

"Of course I noticed. I could feel your breathing pattern change on my chest."

"Why didn't you say anything? I thought you were still sleeping."

"You need as much sleep as you can get, I didn't want to disrupt that," I turn around in his arms so that we are face to face. He lifts his hand and brushes my bed head back. Then starts tracing my jaw with his index finger. "Plus, I like cuddling with you. You're warm and soft and you smell good."

His index finger goes on a journey across the planes of my face. The slope of my nose, my cheek bones, the bags under my eyes, and then my mouth, lingering on my bottom lip. "You're so fucking pretty."

I can feel my face start to warm up. And as much as I want to kiss him, our first kiss won't be with morning breath. I need my mouth to taste good so that he'll want to do it again.

Having him in this trance like state allows me to slip out to use the restroom. After I'm done emptying the tank, I look into the mirror.

I have mascara smeared under my eyes from last night, my hair is stuck up in multiple directions, and I've got major bags. Not quite sure what Scott was talking about. Ok I need to start putting on the moves. I've never been the best flirter, but Sam was texting me some tips during the movie last night. I decide to quickly brush my teeth, just in case, and head back to the bed. I'm supposed to expose my neck to him, twirling the hair helps, tilt my head down when I look at him.

We took a step back after the whole birthday party thing, but then we took like 10 steps forward when he flew out and spent Thanksgiving with my family.

I've decided that I need to just go for it. Life is short and I need to start taking risks. Even if they end up hurting me.

Scott is laying with his hands under the pillow and his chest to the bed giving me the perfect view of his toned back.

I didn't realize that he slept in his boxers last night and thinking about it makes me blush. His head shifts so that he's look at me. "Quit staring at me and get back over here."

Him asking me to come back to bed only makes me blush harder. I slowly start to walk back, hyper focused on the fact that he's watching my every move. Ok think sexy Rydell, you brushed your teeth, so all moves are a go.

Should've known that wouldn't work.

Whenever I'm aware that people are looking at me, I somehow forget how to walk functionally, so I'm not completely surprised when I trip on my own feet.

I catch myself before I completely face plant and when I look back over at Scott, he has his head propped up on his elbow and is looking at me with an amused smile.

"Shut up," I tell him before he says anything.

"I didn't say anything," he puts his hands up in surrender as he shifts so that he's on his back with his hands behind his head. The comforter is sitting right at the top of his boxers, so now instead of a toned back, I have the perfect view of his toned abs.

"Dang Del, how long are you going to check me out for?"

As soon as I go to sit on the bed, Scott grabs my hand and pulls to lay on top of him. He shifts his arms to wrap around my waist as I wiggle mine to wrap around his neck. Stuffing my face into the crook of his neck, I inhale deeply. He always smells very woodsy.

"I think that might've been the best sleep I've ever had I usually wake up at least twice in the night," Scott says as he runs his hands up and down my back. "You probably shouldn't have invited me into the bed last night, now I'm never going to want to sleep without you."

My pj shirt is slightly ridden up and his hands keep brushing against the exposed part of my lower back.

I hum a bit, "I don't think I'd be very opposed to that."

"Yeah?" I unstuff my face from his neck and prop my hands on either side of his shoulders as a sit up. My legs are on either side of his hips, so I'm almost straddling him.

"Yeah. You're a personal heater and a very comfortable pillow," I'm going to do it. I'm going to kiss him. But I should ask him first.

"However, we need to see if we can do something about your drooling problem. Seriously, I wake up drenched."

I gasp, "That is such a lie. I might drool a little, but it's not that bad."

"It's that bad."

"Well, then we need to do something about your snoring problem."

"I don't snore," he doesn't snore.

"And how would you know? You're unconscious in your sleep. Have you recorded yourself?"

"I'm quite a hot commodity, no girl I've ever slept with has said anything about me snoring."

I'm not going to kiss him. Fuck. I look off to the side a little bit and start to climb off him. His hands reach for my waist to keep me in place.

"If my dad walked in, he'd probably kill you," this makes him loosen his grip allowing me to slide off him and sit criss cross in the space next to him.

I know Scott has had lots of hookups. That's nothing new to me. It just makes me wonder when his most recent one was. And if all he wants is hookups. Because that's not what I want. I want him to myself. Exclusively, and it scares me.

"I bet if we go downstairs my mom will be making breakfast burritos. It's one of the only times

I'll actually eat breakfast."

I feel like whenever I gather the courage to kiss him, something comes in the way of it. Maybe that's a sign from the universe.

I start walking down towards the door as Scott gets off the bed and pulls a pair of sweats and a t-shirt on.

Before I can walk down the stairs, I'm pulled back the waistband of my pajama pants. Scott's hands find my waist as he turns me around. Keeping one hand on my waist, he uses the other to tuck my hair behind my ear. "We're good right? I shouldn't have mentioned the girls' I've slept with in bed. That was stupid of me." He leans down to kiss my cheek, "You're the only girl I've been in bed with that matters," he whispers.

"We're fine," I say as I look up at him.

"You guys look comfy," Liam says as he passes by me to walk down the stairs. I take a step back from Scott. "Better hurry before Andy eats all the burritos. That maniac could eat the entire house and would still be hungry, especially since we've started having practice twice a day."

"Leave enough for the rest of us?" I ask Andy when I walk down to see her double fisting burritos.

"We're doing a morning surf and I'm a growing girl."

Surfing is a big part of my family. My mom's dad taught her from a young age and when my dad started dating her, my grandpa taught him as well. Obviously, my dad's parents thought that surfing was for barbarians, but he fell in love with it almost as much as he fell in love with mom.

We've been on surfboards for as long as I

can remember. The moment my siblings and I turned old enough, my parents got us out in the water and on boards.

My dad walks into the kitchen with his hair still wet from the ocean, I'm guessing he's already been out this morning. "Ryles, I thought it might be nice to let you and Scott sleep in this morning, but I'm sorry to say that you are not getting out of this late morning sesh. You're lucky I didn't get everyone up for sunrise."

Dad and mom used to always get us up at the crack of dawn every Saturday for sunrise surfing. I loved it in elementary school but hated it in middle and high school. Not so much fun waking up at 5 in the morning on one of the only days I could sleep in.

"Have any experience surfing Scott?" my mom asks.

"No ma'am. I know how to water ski but that's about it."

"How about snowboarding or skating?" my dad chimes in.

"Ahh, my parent's never let me. When we went to the slopes it was always strictly skiing."

"Mmmm. What do your parents do for a living?"

"They run a pvc pipe company."

"Oh my god. Bridges. As in Bridges and Co?" Scott nods his head yes. "I don't know why I didn't put that together. My parents own a plastics company that works closely with them. Your grandparents were always at our house for events. I used to be schoolmates with your parents."

Ok. Small world, I guess.

"I wish I could say that I know what

company you're talking about, but I really don't pay too much attention to my parents work."

"I remember when your parents got married and your dad took over the business. I was meant to do the same for my parents, but life took a much better turn for me." He looks over at my mom and gives her a soft smile before looking back at Scott. "So, you don't want to follow in their footsteps?"

"Much to my parent's disliking, no. I don't want the company. Trying to convey that to them."

My eyes widen as he says it. Last time we talked about this topic it seemed like he was willingly to give up everything to please his parents.

"The best advice I can give you is to find something or someone that makes you happy and stick with it. Don't live your life fulfilling other peoples' expectations. You're the mediator of your life. Not your family members, not society, not anyone other than you. Trust me, that's something I struggled with a lot. And it's only harder coming from families like ours. If you have any worries about it, you can talk to me, I might understand where you're coming from."

Scott clears his throat and I grab his hand from under the table we moved to sit at. "Thank you, sir. I have been trying to defy their expectations in a respectable way, but it is very difficult."

"Alright," my mom claps her hands together. "Enough family pressure talk. Let's eat our burritos before the swell goes down."

CHAPTER 50: SCOTT

Rydell's hometown in California is only about a 10-minute drive away from the beach, and since I'm from Massachusetts and haven't been to many California beaches, she told me to we had to go. And I guess her family already had it all planned out.

They said something about not going to beaches being a crime against humanity. I've been to a couple of California beaches; my grandparents have a house in Malibu.

But Andromeda said that Malibu didn't count because it was where all the rich people went and there weren't enough locals. She claimed that beach bums are the best type of people.

That's how I've found myself in the water absolutely embarrassing myself with how much wipeouts I'm currently getting.

Rydell and her family, however, are all making it look so much easier than it is. That doesn't surprise me though. When I walked into their garage it looked like a mini surf shop. They had all kinds of surfboards and wet suits.

Rydell told me that the long board would be the easiest and that she'd stick with me at the whitewater.

After about 20 minutes of Rydell trying to explain it to me, her dad took over. Which was for the best because Connell doesn't laugh at me the way Rydell does.

And after about 15 minutes with Connell, I finally am starting to get the hang of it. Granted, all the waves I catch are whitewater and I still look like an idiot riding them. But it's progress.

When I look over at Rydell, she looks so in her element. I can tell that she misses California and as happy as it makes me to see her enjoying herself, it does scare me a little.

I don't know if Rydell's plan is to move back here when she graduates and as much as I don't want her to, I think it might be best for her. And I don't know how that's going to work since I want to play for the Bruins.

I know we could make long distance work, but I think I'd go insane not being able to see her for long periods of time. I mean, she's like 30 ft away from me right now, and I want her right next to me.

When she left for the funeral, I could barely function.

I've become so dependent on her constant presence that I don't know how I'm supposed to live without it.

"Everyone has to pay their dues before they get comfortable on the board," Connell says as he paddles up to me. We're both sitting on our boards as we wait for a set to come in. "She's been through a lot you know," he nods his head towards Del.

I look over at her. She is laughing with her siblings. From the looks of it, Andy pushed Liam off his board because he's swimming over to her and yanking her off hers. David also made his way out to the beach today and Andy is reaching over trying to hold onto him for stability.

"I know. She's so relaxed here. I'm happy she has such a good support system as her family."

"I think you've become a big part of that support system too. I can tell you make her really happy. I wouldn't be out here in the water having a civil conversation with you if you didn't."

"She's hands down the kindest, most selfless person I've ever met. I care a lot about her."

"Do your parents know about her?" He gives me a knowing look. It's kinda nice to have someone who's been in the same situation as me to talk to.

"They know I won't marry someone of their choosing and that I won't run their company. They know it's because of a girl, they just don't know who. I'm scared to introduce her to them. I mean I barely see them in the first place, but they've been nagging me about meeting her ever since I told them."

Ever since I gave my mom a call, they've been constantly harassing me to introduce them to the girl who tainted me.

"Have you told her that you're in love with her?"

My head whips to look at him, "Don't try to deny it, I see the way you look at her. I see the way you're protective over her."

"No. I haven't," I admit.

"Why the hell not? You guys aren't getting any younger. And before you give me some bullshit response that you don't want to ruin the friendship because you think she'll reject you; I can tell you right now she feels the same way. I raised the girl; I know her mind and heart, and I'm telling you right now, she feels the same."

"I'm scared I'm not good enough for her. She deserves someone who has their shit together. Someone who doesn't have as much baggage as me," I sigh.

"What she needs is someone who will make her happy. Someone who will make her feel safe and loved and wanted. I think you're the perfect guy for that. Listen man, how often are you going to find a girl's dad who is rooting for you? That doesn't just happen. But I think you're exactly the type of man my daughter needs. Grow some balls son," With that he paddles over towards his family.

He called me son. "Come one then," Connell calls over his shoulder gesturing me to follow him.

CHAPTER 51: *RYDELL*

As I'm laughing at Liam yanking Andy off her board, I can't help but wish I was living in California again. I don't want to leave my family.

There are so many things I love about Massachusetts. I love Sam and the 106ers. I love all the girls at the orphanage. I love that it's opened up such a great career opportunity for me. And I love Scott.

I look over at him to find him in a somewhat serious looking conversation with my dad. Dad's a much better surf teacher then I am. I was just trying not to laugh at him the whole time.

"Liam and Andromeda will you two cut it out," my mom's voice snaps me out of my thoughts. I look over to see Andy shoving Liam's head under water.

David is paddling closer to Andy and grabbing her arm to stop her from drowning Liam. "You were supposed to help me, not help him knock me off my board!"

Andy flips David's board over and shoves his head under the water as soon as he's overboard.

"Andy will you try not to drown David. How will you ever get married if he's dead?" my

Dad jokes as he paddles up to us with Scott.

Andy groans and let's David up. "Jesus woman, are you trying to kill me?" he splashes her as soon as he catches his breath.

I lay down with my back to my board and let the sun soak into my skin. It's late November so I'm obviously wearing a wet suit, but even though it's cold outside, it definitely beats Massachusetts weather. We're far enough out that we won't get caught up in whitewater and we can just float out here.

I can hear the light chatter of my family around me but I'm not really paying attention to the conversation. "Your dad's a much better surfing teacher then you," I can feel Scott's presence next to me.

Shifting my head to look at him, I block the sun with my eyes, "Yeah. I saw you catch a couple. Are you having fun?"

"I can't remember a time I've been so relaxed. Your families awesome. I wish I had something like this growing up."

I sit up on my board and look over at my family as they joke around with each other, "They're pretty great," I have to move back here once I graduate.

"What are you thinking about?"

I look back over a Scott and the mere sight of him is breaking my heart. I know his dream is to play for the Bruins. It always has been, and nothing will change his mind. Not even me.

"Earth to Rydell," I have completely zoned out and probably looked like a weirdo just staring at him.

"I'm thinking that I like having you here

with my family," I know that sounded selfish of me. I don't want him to give up anything for me and I don't expect him to, I just don't want to lose him.

He hasn't responded so I ask, "What are you thinking about?"

"I'm thinking that I like being here with you and your family."

"Yeah?"

"Yeah. I'm expecting an invite to all family holidays from now on. I would so fly out with you from Mass to hang out."

"What if I move back here once we graduate? I mean, I don't know if I will for sure yet. Would you still come out for holidays?"

"If you wanted me there, I'd be there."

I nod slowly, "So, we'd still be friends?"

"Books, you're my best friend. The distance between us will never change that. Hate to break it to you, but you're kinda stuck with me now. Because I'm not letting you go, whether you like it or not."

I look down at my hands and start to chip at my nail polish. "It would be kinda hard not being so close to each other though. You don't think we'd eventually lose touch," I look back up.

"I don't. I think we have a strong enough relationship. Since the second you walked into my life, there hasn't been a moment I've thought about not having you there. You're probably the most important part of my life."

"Hockey's the most important part of your life."

"It used to be." Used to be?

"Alright let's head back, Scott and Del only have the rest of the day, they leave early tomorrow morning. You want to show Scott around right Ryles?" my mom asks.

"Yeah. Well, only if that's what you want?" I look towards Scott.

"Sounds good to me."

~

I decided to take Scott to the Santa Cruz boardwalk. Growing up, it was always the cool hang out place, and I've been countless times. It was always a happy place for me. I never really had friends to go with, so it was usually either by myself or with my siblings. And Trey never wanted to go because he complained that there were too many tourists.

I've always wanted to have a person to go to the boardwalk with, besides my family, and Scott's the perfect person for it. In fact, he's really the only person I care about taking here.

"What do you want to do first?" I ask Scott as we walk up to enter. Andy and Ollie both work at the boardwalk. I used to work there in high school as did Chris and Liam. So, we get free tickets.

"What is there to do? I've never been to a boardwalk like this before. I've never really been to any carnival type thing actually, besides the Halloween one."

When Scott says things like that, I can't help but feel bad about the way he grew up. I want to be the one to show him all the great things he missed out on as a kid.

"Well, we could mini golf, go on some of the rides, go to the arcade, eat," I list some of the things I usually do while here.

"What's your favorite thing to do?" he asks as he subtly moves to hold my hand. Now I'm

317

smiling like an idiot.

"Ummm," I'm so distracted by his thumb that is rubbing circles on the back of my hand. "Mini golf. I've always liked the mini golf section."

"Lead the way," he looks down at me with a smirk that tells me he knows exactly the type of effect he has on me.

CHAPTER 52: *SCOTT*

I know exactly the type of effect I have on Rydell. It's pretty easy to read her when she smiles a certain way or when her cheeks start to get a rosy blush on them.

That's why throughout our entire time her at the boardwalk, I've been grabbing her hand, or brushing her hair out of her face, or wrapping my arms around her from behind. I love seeing her get flustered from it.

And as flustered as she gets, she also seems so calm about it. At least that's how I hope she feels. I never want her to feel nervous around me. I want her to feel safe and protected.

We've done a lot at the carnival so far. We started with mini golf, which she extremely destroyed me at. She claimed that she was just naturally that good, but then also said that in high school, she came here all the time with her sister because they get free tickets.

And I know how Rydell is when it comes to competition. She loves to win. So, I wouldn't be surprised if she memorized the course and how to beat it with the best score.

I bought her a strawberry funnel cake after

much resistance from her. She likes to say that she's a 'strong independent woman who doesn't need a man to pay for everything'.

And I know she is just that, but I like taking care of her.

Now we're in line for one of the rollercoasters. I look over at Rydell who is chewing on her thumb nail and very visibly fidgeting around.

"Are you scared of rollercoasters?" I question as I take in the worried crease between her eyebrows.

She just shakes her head no as she stares at the group of people before us buckling up.

"We don't have to go on it if you don't want to," I reach my hand up to smooth out the line between her eyebrows. That makes her look up at me.

"No, it's ok. You said you wanted to go on them. So, we'll go on them," she responds with confidence.

"I know you said we could do whatever I want, but what I want is for you to have fun. And you're not looking like you're having fun right now."

"I always have fun when I'm with you," I swear the things she says fills a hole in my heart that I thought would be open until the day I died. She pauses before she adds, "I'm just not the biggest fan of heights."

I grab her hand and start to tug but she stays rooted in her spot. "Come on Books, I'm not going on it if it scares you."

"But I want to go on it. I'll have fun once I'm actually on, it's just the waiting that makes me nervous. I'm fine though."

"Have you been on it before?"

"Yes, lots of times. Andy loves the rollercoasters and always drags me straight to them when we come."

The gates open, prompting us to sit into the seats. Now it's Rydell's turn to tug on my hand moving us to get on the ride.

"Just don't laugh if I'm screaming," she says as she secures her buckle.

I reach over and tighten the buckle for her, making sure it's fully protective, "No promises," I reply.

She reaches over and does the same for me: making sure my seat is fully tightened. I watch her every move, taking in the way her eyes slightly lose worry as I joke with her. Once she's finished checking my buckle, I grab her hand to intertwine our fingers together.

"I might break a couple of your fingers," she warns.

"It'll be worth it," I reply right away.

The coaster starts moving forward and her hand starts to squeeze. As the coaster reaches its highest point it stops for a few seconds and I look at the view.

Then I look over at Rydell and watch her watch the view. She doesn't look as scared anymore and as she takes in the scenery, I find it hard to look away from her. "It's pretty. Right?" She asks as she looks at me.

I continue looking straight at her. "Yeah. Really fucking pretty," I hope she understands that I'm talking about her and not the view, but I don't get the chance to clarify that because the next thing a know, we're dropping at full speed and my hand feels like it might be broken because of her grip on it.

She isn't screaming but when I look back over at her, she has her eyes squeezed shut like she's just waiting for it to be over. Note to self: no more rollercoasters for Rydell.

When the rollercoaster is over, I can't help but laugh. Rydell's eyes are still glued shut, her hair is sticking up in a million different directions, and her nose and cheeks are rosy from the cool air.

"I told you not to laugh," she pouts as she unbuckles and climbs out.

"And I told you no promises," my laughing dies down. "You were right though; I think a couple of my fingers are broken."

She frowns and inspects my hand as we walk towards the arcade. She then brings my hand up to her lips and peppers kisses all over my fingers. I almost drop dead. The feeling of her lips sends fire to my skin and she needs to stop because my pants are way starting to tent. I swear she has the strongest effect on me.

I start walking us over to the token machine, but I feel a tug on my hand in the opposite direction. Rydell holds up a rewards card, "Nice try, but you can't pay for this one Scotty, I have left over tokens on this card from the last time I was here."

"Jesus Books, how often did you come here if you have a rewards card that still has tokens on it?"

"In high school, obviously I worked here, but even if I wasn't scheduled to work, I was usually here or the beach."

"Fun spot to hang out with friends?" I question, mainly because I want to know everything about her. I want to know what she did on her free time growing up. I like that I get to see the place she worked at in high school. I like seeing the beach she surfed at. I like that I got to sleep next to her in her childhood home and go surfing with her family like I was a part of it.

I've been on so many extravagant vacations in my life. Summers were Paris, or Greece, or Bora Bora. Literally anywhere we wanted. But being here in Santa Cruz, California with Rydell Rivens is hands down the best vacation I've ever been on.

Rydell's nervous chuckle breaks me out of my thoughts, "I didn't really have friends to go with. Trey only ever wanted to go surfing or to parties. I mainly just came with my siblings. David and Savannah tagged along a lot too."

"Chris and Savannah meet in high school, right?"

"Mhmm. They had Spanish class together freshman year, and the rest is history. She became an honorary part of the family basically the second we met her. Kinda like you now. And now she's an actual part of the family. Along with Andy and Sam, she's one of my best friends," I get excited at the idea of being an actual part of her family.

"And me, I'm also one of your best friends," I include hopefully.

"And you," she responds with no hesitation.

"And I'm still your favorite friend," I say it as a fact not a question but, I'm a little nervous for her response.

"Yeah. You're my favorite friend," I start swinging our arms back and forth and look over at her the same time she looks over at me. And I'm rewarded with the sight of that dimpled smile I love so much as she stops in front of the air hockey game.

"You're good at ice hockey, but I bet I could take you down in air hockey," she challenges.

CHAPTER 53: RYDELL

Scott and I had our plane ride back to Massachusetts. It took off at 5:30 this morning, and my dad dropped us off.

Last night, we went to have dinner at one of my family's favorite local taco shops. Chris and Savannah, David, and my grandparents all tagged along for our last night there and it was very bitter-sweet.

It felt so fucking good to be around all of them. I fell right back into sink with my life there. Going to the boardwalk, taking morning surfs, eating at the cheap taco shop downtown. I could practically feel a burden lift off my shoulders the whole time I was there. And I know I have to move back when I graduate. There's really nothing that could hold me back from that.

Except maybe Scott, but if he's willing to make it work, then so am I.

Scott paid to have his car stay at the airport while we stayed in California, so after getting off the plane we went straight to where he parked. Both of us only had carry-on bags, so we didn't have to deal with baggage claims.

By the time the plane landed it was about

3:00 in the afternoon, Massachusetts time, but we hadn't really eaten since a quick snack this morning, so we decided to pick up a pizza and take it back to mine and Sam's place.

"Alright, you've been way too quiet today. Tell me what's wrong," Scott breaks the silence as I set the pizza box on the kitchen counter.

I shrug my shoulders, "Just tired."

"Bullshit."

"Prescott, we had to be up at 4:30 this morning, I'd say that is a pretty justifiable answer," I am tired. But I've also just been so deep in thought about moving back to California.

"Books, I'd like to think that I know you way better than that. There's something on your mind. I won't stop bugging you until you tell me what it is." He walks over to the couch and sits down.

I sigh and start pacing back and forth in front of him. "I am tired," I stop to look at him. His legs are spread out and his hands are behind his head like he owns the place.

Scott always has that effect though. He tends to be the center of attention in any room. He has no problem making himself comfortable wherever he is and always has this relaxed persona.

It's the same at parties. Everyone that I've been to, since Freshman year, that he's also been at, my eyes have always gone to him. Everyone's eyes are always on him though.

And that's another thing that scares me. I hate having the attention on me. For anything. That's why I slightly dread my birthday, I feel so uncomfortable with everyone staring at me.

A relationship with Scott will mean having

eyes on me at all times. Everything I do, everything I say, all of it will be judged.

"Ry, I can practically see the gears turning in your head. You know you can tell me anything."

Right. But can I? I can't just flat out say, 'oh hey, just you know I'm in love with you and it scares me half to death and I don't know if you feel the same and even if you did, I don't know if I could do it with the constant judgement of everyone around us. Also, I'm moving back to California and I know you'll never move there because your dream is to play for the Bruins.' God, I ramble even in my thoughts.

"Ryde-"

"I'm moving back to California," I blurt out.

"That's what you've been stressing about? Books, I knew that the moment I saw you with your family. Why was that so hard for you to say?"

I don't know how to take that. Does he not see how that could be a big deal? "Because I have another life here that'll be hard to leave. Sam's here. The orphanage is here," I take a deep breathe. "You're here," I whisper and start pacing back and forth again.

I can feel his gaze watching my every move. I've gotten used to have Scott constantly looking at me. If it were anyone else, it would make me nervous, but I like it when he looks at me.

"Rydell, the happiest most care-free version of yourself is when you're in California. The support your family gives you, the familiarity of everything there is good for you. And it's not like you're just forgetting about everything here. 5 hours on the plane isn't that long."

"Not all of us have an endless supply on

money Scott. It's not as easy as hopping on a plane and staying for a couple days at a time. When I go, I'll probably barely see you," I don't even try to bring up anything else. He's probably the hardest thing I'd have to leave. And I feel slightly like an asshole for comparing our financial statuses, but it's true.

"Well then, I'll come to you. I already told you Ry, you can't get rid of me that easily. Plus, we can Facetime all the time. And I can spend all my off season with you. There are plenty of ice rinks in California."

"But you'll eventually get tired of it. All the back and forth."

"I won't," he replies without hesitation.

"And Facetime isn't the same. It's different when we're together. When everything's tangible."

"Are you saying you'll miss holding my hand?" he says with a slight smirk.

"Scott I-"

"Why are you making this so difficult? You're my best friend. I thought we talked about the whole trust thing. Trust me when I say I won't stop this," he points back and forth at the space between us.

But what is us? "I do trust you. It's just- it's just that," it's just that I'm in love with you and I'm scared to leave you is what I want to say.

"It's just that what? Would you stop talking to me?"

"No, but-"

"But what?"

Why can't he just see that I'm in love with him, why does he have to make it this hard? I sigh, "Fuck it," I plop myself down right on his lap, put both of my hands on either side of his face and kiss him.

His lips are soft and warm and basically exactly how I thought they'd be. They also aren't kissing me back. Oh shit, I should've asked for consent. This was a mistake. I pull back and look at his confused face.

Oh my god. Oh my god. Fuck. What did I just do? "Sorry," I whisper. He still is just staring at me. God I am such an idiot.

I climb off his lap and slide into the seat on the couch next to him. I put my hand up and brush my fingers against my lips. "I'm sorry. I should've asked. Actually, I shouldn't have done anything at all. I know you don't do relationships and I don't do hookups. But I thought- I thought that you might like me and might want a relationship with me. Which is so stupid because you told me even if you found the right person you wouldn't do anything. Oh fuck. Not that I'm the right person or anything, I just thought that maybe you liked me. I'm sorry," I'm rambling so hard right now. Why isn't he saying anything?

I quickly stand up from the couch and make my way for the front door.

CHAPTER 54: SCOTT

"Fuck it," I hear her mumble and the next thing I know she's sitting on my lap kissing me.

Her hands are cold as they rest on either side of my face and her lips feel so good on mine. But it's hard for me to register what's happening.

I mean one second, we're talking about being best friends and her moving to California and the next the girl that I've secretly been in love with for months is attacking me in the best possible way.

I feel like I've won the fucking lottery, I'm so shocked that it's happening because I was planning on being the one to initiate our first kiss.

Right as I start moving my hands towards her waist and start tilting my head to kiss her back and finally get a good taste, she pulls away.

What.

Just.

Happened?

"Sorry," I barely hear her whisper because I'm still in some sort of trance from feeling her lips on mine.

She's moving off my lap and I want to grab her to keep her in place, but my body is frozen.

"I'm sorry. I should've asked," asked? Why

the hell would she ever have to ask? It's only been something I've wanted to do basically since the moment I meet her.

She's going full on ramble mode, "Actually, I shouldn't have done anything at all. I know you don't do relationships and I don't do hookups. But I thought- I thought that you might like me and might want a relationship with me," of course I want a fucking relationship with her, I thought I was doing a pretty good job at conveying that to her.

"Which is so stupid because you told me even if you found the right person you wouldn't do anything. Oh fuck. Not that I'm the right person or anything, I just thought that maybe you liked me. I'm sorry," she is the right person! How could she not be? She more than the right person. She literally everything I've ever wanted and she's definitely way too good for me, but I'm a selfish mother fucker.

I'm sitting here thinking about how completely wrong she is and trying to find the right words to tell her that I want to be with her. But I'm scared that she'll think I'm lying. I mean I've told her on multiple occasions that I don't do relationships.

She's standing up now and walking out of her front door.

Where does she think she'll escape to, it's not like she can go home? She's already here.

I jog after her, "What's your plan here? Just escape all of it and leave me here? At your house?"

"I clearly haven't thought it through. But I'm going to leave somewhere. And you're going to go home. And then tomorrow, we can pretend like none of this ever happened. We'll treat it how it as it is. As a mistake."

"A mistake?" I mimic her.

"Yes Scott. A mistake. Don't act like it wasn't I saw the look on your face," she is so visibly upset, and I can tell she's trying her best to not show it.

"Ok, why was it a mistake then? I'm actually very interested in hearing you explain that."

"Did you not just hear a single word I said? You know, on the couch, when I kissed you and you didn't kiss me back?!" she's raising her voice now.

"You didn't give me a chance to respond! You up and left out the door Rydell! Is that what you're always going to do? Run away from your problems?" my tone is matching hers now. I'm not even mad at her. I'm just so frustrated that she can't see that I'm in love with her.

I know I should probably just say it straight up, but I'm so bad at expressing my feelings. I grew up being taught that it was a sign of weakness. Plus, I've never been in love with anyone up until now. It's hard for me.

"Oh ya, you would know all about running away from problems, wouldn't you?" she's patronizing me.

"Me?! You leave every time something gets hard Rydell. Remember my birthday? You left before I could get a word out to explain the situation!" I throw my hands up for exaggeration. "I had to fly all the way to fucking California to keep whatever the hell is going on between us together!"

"I never asked you to come. If it was that big of a deal you should've just stayed here, because look where's it's gotten us! I'm sorry I caused you so much fucking trouble," she takes a breath and continues. "I mean, you're so fucking confusing Scott! You say you don't want a relationship but then you do shit like hold my hand or kiss my cheek and I don't know what I'm supposed to think!"

"Of course, I wanted to come out! I don't regret flying out to see you, but it would've caused a lot less drama if you just let me explain the situation in the first place! You're first instinct is to always leave; I don't know how I'm supposed to get you to trust me!"

"I trust you, you know I do. But clearly, I thought our relationship was something more than it actually is. We'll only ever be friends. Noted. Just stop fucking leading me on!"

"I'm not leading you on," I respond immediately.

She laughs without humor, "You're joking right. You say one thing, but your actions say something entirely different Scott! What is it that you want from me?"

I stay quiet. This is turning into a shit show and I don't know how I'm supposed to switch direction.

"Whatever," she mumbles and starts walking towards her car.

"Wait!" I try.

She turns around to look at me again just as she reaches the driver's door, "No! If you can't figure it then I'm-"

"Rydell, I'm fucking in love with you!"

Her eyes go wide, and she freezes in place, so I take that opportunity to start walking slowly to stand in front of her.

"What?" she whispers.

I bring my hands up to cradle her face in my

hands, "I'm. In. Love. With. You." I emphasize every word, so she fully understands what I'm confessing.

She slightly shakes her head back and forth, "I don't- I don't under-"

I lean my forward to rest against her, "Books, I'm so fucking in love with you," I whisper to her like it's my most secure secret.

My heart is particularly beating out of my chest and I'm looking into her eyes trying to read her, but I have no idea what she's thinking.

I can feel her warm breath on my lips as she says, "Say it again," she whispers back and closes her eyes.

My lips start to curl at the sides, "I'm in love with you," I mumble as I brush my lips against hers.

She breathes me in, "I'm in love with you too," I can feel her lips move against mine and I don't waste any more time. I press my lips fully against hers and move one hand to thread my fingers through her hair to get a deeper angle.

Her lips are warm, and they taste like strawberries, probably from her chapstick. She's not kissing back though. She's just standing there with her arms at her sides. I pull back, keeping my forehead pressed to hers and my lips are still lightly brushing against hers. Her eyes are still closed, and her lips are slightly parted and the image of her makes me smile.

I shake my head back and forth against her forehead and move my hands down to grab hers, lifting them up to wrap them around my neck.

She responds immediately by gripping onto the hair against the base of my neck. I try not to flinch at the feeling of her cold fingertips. Holy shit, I don't think she understands the effect she has one me.

I move my hands down to rest on her waist, "Now would be a good time to kiss me back Books," I mumble against her lips.

CHAPTER 55: RYDELL

I'm kissing Scott. Scott's kissing me. Scott and I are kissing each other.

I was so shocked with it all that at first, I didn't really know what to do. I was just relishing in the feeling of his lips on mine until he told me to kiss him back.

I certainly didn't need to be told twice. He's pressing his hands on my waist causing me to take a couple steps back until I feel the cold metal of my car. I feel him slightly nip my bottom lip, giving him the chance to explore my mouth with his tongue as I gasp on instinct.

I pull harder on his hair with one hand and move the other one to cup the back on his neck and bring him closer, which isn't by much because we are already practically glued to each other.

I can feel his hands start to move under the shirt I have on under my hoodie, and his cold hands on my bare stomach makes me jump a little.

"Let's go back inside," he says against my lips. He pulls back enough so I can see his entire face but keeps his hands on my bare waist. I'm suddenly more aware of the 40-degree weather.

He gives my lips another small peck and

then removes his hands, grabs my hand and starts leading us back to my front door.

I'm coming out of my daze and now I'm starting to freak out a bit. He told me loves me. Actually, he said he's *in* love with. And I told him that I'm in love with him too.

But I still don't know what that means. I don't want to get my hopes up until he explicitly tells me that he wants to be in a relationship with me.

As we walk through the door, I remove my hand from his, and go straight to the kitchen. He doesn't hesitate to follow me. On the counter, I see the pizza that is probably slightly cold now and move to grab a slice. I turn around to face him as I lean my back on the counter and start eating.

He's looking at me with an amused expression and stocks towards me. His eyes never leave mine as he puts his hands on the counter behind me, caging me into him. I hold his gaze as I continue to eat my pizza.

I actually am very hungry, but I also am not kissing him again until I get a definitive, straight up answer. No matter how much I want to.

"Hungry?" he asks with a smirk.

"Mhmm," I agree.

He slowly nods his head and looks down, training his eyes on my mouth. If anyone else were watching me eat this intently I would feel so awkward and probably put my food down. But I refuse to lose this silent battle with Scott. Plus, I don't ever really feel awkward or uncomfortable around him.

He moves one hand back under my shirt and starts moving his thumb back and forth across the skin on my lower stomach. My toes curl in my shoes and my core starts to tingle. But I hold my ground, taking the last couple bites.

As soon as I finish, Scott raises his free hand, putting his thumb to the corner of my mouth wiping off what I assume to be pizza sauce and then sticking said thumb in his mouth to get it off. He finally takes his eyes off my mouth to look me in the eyes.

"Took you long enough," he complains as he caresses my cheek and leans in.

Before he can kiss me again, I put my hand on his chest and push him away. "Easy tiger," I grab another piece of pizza and stick it out for Scott to eat.

"Ry, I'm not hungry for pizza right now."

"Eat the pizza Scott. We need to talk," I demand.

He groans, takes the pizza and gives me some space.

I exhale a breath I didn't realize I was holding as he takes a few steps back, and hop up to sit on the counter, letting my legs dangle.

I watch Scott take the smallest bite of his pizza, put it back in the box and make his way over to me, nudging himself in between my legs. "All done. Talk so I can kiss you again," he commands as his hands move to either side of me on the counter.

"What if I say I don't want to kiss you again?"

He chuckles, "Then I'd say you're full of shit and the worst liar. Tell me you don't want me to kiss you again Books."

"Of course I want you to kiss me again-"

"Good," he starts leaning in again.

"But," I put my hand to his chest again and let it rest there before moving it up to cup his shoulder. "But I need to know what this is first," look at me putting down my foot.

"What do you mean you need to know what this is? Rydell we just confessed our love for each other. What do you think this is?"

"I don't know, that's why I need you to tell me. Because I know you don't do relationships and I'm confused."

Scott sighs and looks down for a second. I expect him to pull back. Fuck. This is the moment when he tells me that he won't be in a relationship with me.

Don't cry. Don't cry. Don't cry. He's staying silent, still looking down and I go to move down off the counter and away from him.

He grips both sides of my waist, keeping me pinned to the counter. "Don't fucking leave. We just talked about you running away. Don't you dare fucking move."

"You're scaring me with how quiet you're being," I admit softly. He's right, I need to work on confronting my problems.

"I'm just trying to find the right words to say," he's looking back at me now. Hands still gripping my waist. "I'm going to be as clear with you as I can be, so you better listen up."

I nod, prompting him to continue, "Rydell Catherine Rivens, I'm telling you right now, that you are the only person I'll be with until the day I die. You're it for me. I want you to be my girlfriend. I want us to have an exclusive relationship. And I promise you, one day, I'm going to make you my wife," my eyes are starting to water, and he brings one of his hands up to cup my cheek.

He starts to soothingly run his thumb across my cheekbone, "My parents, their company, none of it matters. And if you think for one second that I'm going to tell you that I don't do relationships you're so fucking wrong," he leans his forehead to rest on mine and closes his eyes. "I do relationship, but only for you. Only ever with you."

I don't even try to stop the couple tears that run out of my eyes. My silence prompts him to pull back and open his eyes. He has both hands on my cheeks wiping the stray tears away.

"Say something," he whispers. He sounds a little scared.

"Ask me then."

"Ask you what?"

My lips start to curl into a soft smile, "Ask me if I want to be your girlfriend," I wrap my arms around his neck to keep him close to me.

He matches my smile, grabs my legs to wrap them around his torso, and then wraps his arms around my waist, "Rydell Rivens will you be my girlfriend?"

I give him a face like I'm thinking, "I don't know, I've gotten a lot of offers, but I'll review and get back to you in 3-5 business days," I joke.

He nudges his nose against mine causing me to let out a little laugh, "Rydellll," he draws out.

"Prescott Bridges, I will be your girlfriend."

"Hell yeah you will," I can feel his smile on my lips as he impatiently moves in to kiss me.

CHAPTER 56: *SCOTT*

Rydell's my girlfriend. I'm Rydell's boyfriend. Rydell and I are in a boyfriend-girlfriend relationship and she's in love with me.

I move my hands to grip her thighs that are wrapped around my torso, and then slowly move them up lingering on her ass and finding my way up her shirt to touch her bare skin.

Her stomach feels warm in contrast to my hands and it makes me want to wrap my entire body in her. I want her everywhere. I want her lips on my lips all the time. I want her hands on me and I want my hands on her. I never want this moment to end.

We are both clearly running out of oxygen because the kiss is getting rushed, and I pull back to breathe but keep my lips brushing against hers. I want to take my time with her. I don't want her to think that all I'll leave her if she doesn't sleep with me like Trey did.

She's had such a bad experience with all things sex related and I want our relationship to be a steppingstone in fixing that. Helping her be comfortable in terms of being intimate is something that I want to do right.

I take a deep breathe, "You have no idea how long I've wanted to kiss you."

She laughs softly, "Oh, I think I have a pretty good idea," as she says it, I fall in love with how her words feel against my mouth.

I press a kiss to her mouth, then another, and another. Then I start to pepper kisses all over her face. On her cheeks, her nose, her forehead. And she's smiling, so I lean in to kiss that fucking dimple on the left side of her chin. "I'm so fucking obsessed with you."

"The feeling's mutual," with one hand still wrapped around my neck, she moves the other to cup my jaw, moving her thumb back and forth along it. My hands are lightly gripping her bare waist.

She leans in and kisses me slowly. So slowly that it's like the slower and longer she does so, I can feel my heart fill more and more with her. My heart is her's. Every bit of it belongs to Rydell Rivens. If I could label it with her name, I would.

"Fucking finally," Rydell pulls back and looks at something behind me, her cheeks are red. I look over my shoulder to see Sam giving us a smug look. "It's about damn time. I've been watching you guys tiptoe around your feelings for months now."

"Oh shit, what did I miss?" Max fucking Rudderford walks in with grocery bags. Why the hell is he carrying Sam's groceries?

"What did you miss? More like what did we miss?" I raise an eyebrow at him darting my eyes back and forth between him and Sam. At the same time, I turn around, leaning my back against the counter as Rydell drops her chin to my shoulder and drops her arms to wrap around my torso in a hug from behind. Jesus, I love the feeling of her touching me.

"No. No changing the subject, I just walked in on the two of you swapping spit!" Sam exclaims.

Rydell's arms squeeze tighter around me and I put my hands on her thighs that are still wrapped around my middle.

"I'm allowed to kiss my girlfriend Sam," I respond. I feel Rydell hide her face in my neck and I can image the blush that is probably sporting her cheeks.

"You're lucky. If I heard one more time that you don't do relationships, I would've strangled you."

Max sets the bags down. Rydell takes her face out of my neck and I miss the feeling on her nuzzled there. "What brings you to our apartment Max?" Rydell asks my next question.

"Sam and I went grocery shopping," he states bluntly.

"Why were you and Sam grocery shopping together?" I interrogate.

"I'm allowed to go shopping with my friend Prescott," Sam mimics me from earlier.

"I wasn't aware that you guys were friends. Is this a new establishment?" I am actually very curious to hear the answer to this. I'm pretty sure that they hooked up at a party a couple months ago, but I didn't know that they still talked.

"I don't see how that's any of your business," she fires back.

I raise my eyebrows at Max. He sighs, "Sam and I have been friends since the ice-skating field trip. You and the guys on the team aren't my only friends Scotty."

I remove my hands from Rydell's thighs and

put them up in surrender, "I'm not saying we are. Ry's my best friend and she's not on the hockey team," I declare with a smug smile. "She's also my girlfriend, future wife, the woman who will carry all my babies," Rydell is my new favorite thing to brag about.

I feel her lean in to kiss my cheek at the same time I put my hands to rub up and down her calves.

"You guys are going to be one of those disgustingly cute couples, aren't you? You know the ones that make single people want a relationship?" Sam questions.

"Most definitely. Kinda sucks for everyone else. No one will be able to accomplish a relationship as perfect as ours."

Sam puffs out some air before looking me straight in the eyes, "If you hurt her in anyway, I will rip your testicles off and shove them down your throat to make sure you never reproduce."

God, for someone so small, she is very scary. "You don't need to worry about that ever happening," I never want Rydell to feel hurt, especially not by me.

"Good," Sam replies.

"There's plenty of pizza if you guys are hungry," Rydell redirects the conversation. The box is set right next to her on the counter and she releases her hands from me to grab a piece. More specifically, the piece that I took a bite out of.

She shoves it in my face, "You should eat more, it's been a while since we last ate," I take it because I actually am very hungry. I was just too distracted by wanting to kiss her to realize it. And with Sam and Max here now, I don't necessarily want to make-out in front of them.

When I enjoy her, I want it to be just the two of us.

As I start to eat my pizza, I'm hyperaware of Rydell staring at my side profile. Chin propped on my shoulder.

"Enjoying the view," I tease her.

"Mhmm. You're very pretty," there's something about her calling me pretty that makes me feel all melty.

I turn in her arms; she still has her legs and arms wrapped around me. I give her a quick peck on the lips and continue eating my pizza, basking in the feeling of her fingers playing with the ends of my hair.

CHAPTER 57: RYDELL

Scott and I both ended up eating more pizza and are now in the middle of watching *Grown Ups* with Sam and Max.

There's definitely something going on between the two of them. I have a feeling they are more than friends. I'll bring it up to her later.

Scott and I are cuddled on the love seat, while Sam and Max occupy the couch. They have a gap between them but are sharing a blanket. I also think that they are slowly gravitating closer to each other. Mark my words, those two will be a couple one day.

My legs are swung over Scott's lap as my head rests on his chest. He has one arm wrapped around my shoulder pulling me close to him. The hand of his free arm is roaming everywhere. It's rubbing up and down my thigh, or squeezing my calf, or going under my shirt to leaving goosebumps on my stomach. Every now and then he'll grab onto my ass, causing me to jump and him to laugh.

It's a good thing I've seen this movie a million times because I'm not paying attention at all. The feeling of Scott's hand on me makes me want to drag him up to my bedroom and have him touch me all over.

But at the same time, I don't want to rush things with him. Sex is obviously something that we'll have to discuss. Don't get me wrong, I definitely want to have sex with Scott, there's probably not many people who wouldn't.

And I'll get there with him probably pretty quickly, but I've been so hurt in the past. I know he won't hurt me, but it's not something I want to just jump right into.

Scott leans down and kisses my neck once, keeping his face nuzzled in my neck. I'm pretty sure he's smelling me. Little stalker.

I breathe deeply. He is not going to make this easy. I squeeze my thighs together and hear him chuckle. His nose trails up the length of my neck and he starts pressing small kisses across my jaw.

He follows the path up to my ear, biting my earlobe softly when he gets to it. Holy shit. To say I'm turned on right now would be an understatement.

"I love you," it's so soft that if he wasn't literally saying it into my ear, I wouldn't have heard it.

I move my head to look up at him. He closes the very small gap between us and brushes his nose back and forth against mine.

I let out a small, breathy laugh, "I love you too," I reassure him.

"Hell ya you do," he mumbles it against my lips before fully pressing his mouth on mine. His hand is making a journey down and stops when it finds my butt.

Pulling back, he looks at me with a smirk, "I'm totally touching your butt right now," I tilt my head back and laugh. When I look back at him, I shake my head back and forth.

I love his smile. Especially the one that seems crafted just for me. One that I don't see when he's around the hockey team, or the people at parties. And it makes my heart warm that I'm the one who gets to see it. It's like my most special secret that I wish I could always carry around in my pocket.

I move my hand down under him so that he's essentially sitting on my hand, "I'm totally touching your butt right now too," there. Now we're equal.

He laughs. "I understand that you too are in the midst of the honeymoon stage, but some of us are trying to watch a movie," Sam groans.

I mimic zipping my lips shut and throwing the key. Then Scott leans down and whispers the hottest thing into my ear, "November 28th is National French Toast Day. Wanna go to my place and make some?"

I don't even like breakfast foods, but I have the biggest smile on my face. I nod my head and he kisses the dimple on my chin. I don't know what his fascination with that is, but I love it.

Scott lifts both of us off the couch and grabs onto my hand to lead me out. "I was just kidding. You guys don't have to leave," Sam states. At the same time, she's wiggling her eyebrows at me suggestively.

"We're going to make French toast," I giggle. Oh god. I did not just giggle. I feel like I'm drunk. Or floating. Or in some sort of unrealistic dream. I'm so entranced that this is really happening.

"Have fun," Max says as he scoots closer to Sam. I wiggle my eyebrows back at her.

"You too," Scott says as if he's reading my mind.

~

"No, I did not!" I laugh and cover my hands in my face.

I'm sitting on his kitchen counter as I watch him flip his pancake. I don't like breakfast foods. Scott doesn't like french toast. But his favorite food is pancakes, so I suggested that he just make that instead.

Right now, he is totally exposing me. More specifically, a couple days ago when I epically failed at flirting with him. You know, when I came out of the bathroom channeling my inner sexy and totally ate it.

"You so were! You twirled your hair, and when you came out of the bathroom you tripped over your feet when you tried to sexy walk," I'm mortified. "Plus, you were giving me major psycho eyes," he's laughing at me.

"That's rich coming from the pro stalker! You knew my name, my place of work, and my grades before even talking to me! And they weren't psycho eyes, they were supposed to be flirty eyes," I cross my arms over my chest.

"Aha, so you admit it, you were flirting with me!" he points the spatula at me before turning back around and putting the pancake on a plate.

"Of course I was flirting with you. I was trying to hint that I liked you, but you were so oblivious!"

"You don't just like me," he walks in between my legs and wraps his arms around my waist. "You love me."

I wrap my arms around his neck as he starts attacking my neck with kisses. When I start laughing, he looks up at me and pecks my lips. Then pulls back and does it again. And again. And again.

"You were the oblivious one. I didn't know what else I was supposed to do. I held your hand at any given opportunity, I told you you're the only person I cared about, I kissed your cheek. You didn't see any of my advances."

I raise an eyebrow out him, "All of that is good and nice. But you also kept calling me your best friend and constantly told me that you," I put air quotes around the next part, "don't do relationships."

He unwraps his arms from my waist and grabs my hands as they're in the air, intertwining our fingers together, "You *are* my best friend. And I didn't do relationships before you."

That kind of sends my mind into a whirl. Because he didn't do relationships before me. And there was a reason for that.

"You didn't. Because of your parents," I state. I'm sure he has a perfectly responsible answer to my next question, but I can't help but get a little nervous. "What are you going to do when they find a suitable girl for you to marry?" I ask it in a small, almost sarcastic voice while looking anywhere but at him.

He lets go of my hands, putting one hand on my counter and the other one up to grab on to my chin, forcing me to look at him.

He presses a long, hard kiss to my lips and as he pulls back says, "You don't have to worry about that."

I puff out air from nose, "Well, I am worrying about it."

"Well don't."

"You telling me not to worry isn't going to magically get rid of said worry Prescott."

"Rydell, I thought I made it pretty fucking clear that you're the girl I'm going to marry. I literally told you like 2 hours ago that you're the only girl I'll ever be with. So, don't worry about it."

I feel a little guilty about even bringing it up. I just am so scared of being hurt again. And I'm almost positive I don't have to worry about being hurt with Scott. But I didn't think Trey would break me, and he did.

"I'm not Trey," he always knows exactly what I'm thinking. He moves his hand from my chin to cup my cheek, running his thumb back and forth. The hand on the counter goes to my hip. I love the way he looks at me. It sounds weird, but when we're liking this, just staring at each other, moments like these are the times when I feel most comfortable. Like all the loneliness that I've ever felt goes away. Like every bad thing that's ever happened to me doesn't matter because I get to experience having Prescott Bridges look at me.

"I know," I respond after a while.

"Do you? Because I don't know how else I'm supposed to convince you."

"I do. I promise I do. It's just hard for me to think that I can really be this happy. Because you make me so indescribably happy and it's hard for me to realize that this will last forever. I'm not sure I deserve it."

"You deserve every good thing in this world Rydell. And I'll tell you that every day until you

351

believe me if I have to. Every day I'll try to give you all the happiness I can. All of my happiness is now yours too. Ok?"

"I don't want you to sacrifice your happiness for me. *You* make me really happy Prescott Bridges."

"You make me really happy too Rydell Rivens."

CHAPTER 58: SCOTT

I can't keep my hands off Rydell. I mean it was difficult before, but now that she's my girlfriend, I never want to stop touching her.

She's so soft. And she feels cold compared to me. I love the idea of keeping her warm. And she smells so fucking good. It's intoxicating.

If I could glue us together and keep us permanently attached, I would.

I know she's a little hesitant going into this relationship because of her past, but I'd like to think that I'm doing a pretty good job reassuring her that I will never hurt her in anyway.

Rydell hops off the counter and walks over to the stove to keep making pancakes. Pancakes that she probably won't even eat because she doesn't like breakfast foods.

"Do you want me to make you something else?" I open the fridge; we really need to go grocery shopping. "We have… well let's see." Closing the fridge, I go to check the freezer, "We have frozen burritos and hot pockets. Either sound good to you?"

"That's ok, I'm still full from pizza," I close the fridge and walk over to the stove. I wrap my arms around her waist, putting my hands under her shirt and splaying my fingers flat on her stomach. She took her hoodie off when we got here, giving me easier access to her skin.

"Are you sure? I can order you something or we could go out and get you something. I don't want you to be hungry," I kiss her neck a couple of times before dropping my chin to her shoulder.

She puts the last pancake onto the plate, turns of the stove, and turns around in my arms. Her hands are rested on my chest, "I swear, I'm not hungry," she raises to her on her tip toes to press a kiss to my lips.

I pull her body flush against mine, dropping my hands to her ass and pulling her closer. I feel her sigh against my lips, giving me the opportunity to slip my tongue into her mouth.

I switch positions with her so that she isn't right next to the hot stove and start backing her up to the counter opposite of the heat.

My hands leave her ass as soon as her back hits the counter and they very slowly travel up. My fingertips explore her hips and waist. Then move on to her hands and up her arms, feeling the goosebumps they leave as I continue my journey.

I start to lose oxygen as my hands cup her neck. She feels so delicate in my hands. My tongue continues to taste her mouth and the feeling of her slightly fighting for dominance is so fucking addicting.

She pulls back, but not by much. Her hands are fisting my shirt, her forehead is pressed against mine, and I feel her lips brush my lips as she says, "The pancakes are getting cold."

My hands move to her hips and I lift her up

to sit on the counter, rubbing my hands up and down her thighs, "I think I'm hungry for something else," my voice is raspy as I say it.

She wraps her legs around my middle and closes the small gap between us, moving her hands to cup the base of my neck, thumbs resting on my jaw. Our kisses are getting fast and desperate. Like we'll both die if we slow down or stop.

She nips at my bottom lip, eliciting a groan out of me. We haven't even gotten to the good stuff and I already feel like I'm going to explode. It's seriously embarrassing because I'm not even inside her and I'm not sure how much longer I'll last. Especially now that she's at the very edge of the counter, pressing herself right against my pelvis.

I tear my mouth from hers, her lips following as I do so. Before she can complain, I start trailing wet kisses all over her neck and collarbone, leaving small marks as I do so.

She's breathing heavy and as I find the spot just below her ear, a soft moan escapes her. And it almost kills me. I think I'd do just about anything to hear it again. I bite her earlobe, "I love you so fucking much," before she can respond, I smash my lips back into her's and move my hands under her shirt. Her skin feels slightly colder than my hands, looks like I gotta warm her up.

"Can we take this upstairs?" I mumble against her lips.

She nods absentmindedly before she slowly comes out of a trance, "Wait," she pulls back.

"I- I don't want to have sex yet. I'm sorry," she's still panting a bit from the kiss. "I'm sorry, I just-"

I peck her lips to shut her up, "Don't

apologize. I want to take things slow with you. I wasn't going to take you upstairs with the goal of sex, I just didn't want any of my roommates walking in on us. I want you to trust me."

"I do trust you," her thumbs brush my jaw. "And don't get me wrong, I really want to go all the way with you, it's just... I see this relationship as a long-term thing, and I've had only bad experiences with sex. Not that I think it would be bad with you, in fact I think it'd be really really good," I smirk at that. "It's just that with my grandpa and Trey and meaningless hookups, I'm a little scared of having it in a healthy relationship, because what if I find out that I'm the problem," her hands drop down to her lap. A rambling Rydell is a nervous Rydell and I don't want her to be even a little bit nervous about sex with me.

I put my knuckle under her chin, forcing her to look at me, "I promise, you're not the problem. I don't want you to be nervous about being intimate with me. I want it to be something you enjoy, not something you worry about," I drop my hand and kiss her cheek. "Rydell, we could go our entire lives without having sex, and I'd still want to be with you. Only you. I'm not with you to have sex with you. I'm with you because I'm in love with you. Ok?"

She nods her head and pulls me in for a slow kiss before moving her mouth to my ear and softly nipping my earlobe, "I love you too." Fuck, that was hot. She pulls back to look at me, wrapping her arms around my neck, "I said I didn't want to have sex, but that doesn't mean I don't want to do other things," she kisses me again and mumbles against my lips, "I think we should go upstairs."

Her legs are still wrapped around my torso, so I grip her thighs and start making my way up the stairs. As soon as I do, she starts to kiss my neck, sufficiently distracting me. I swear, I've been on the verge of black out drunk, but I've never had so much trouble walking up a set of stairs before now.

She continues exploring my neck as I walk into the room, shutting the door behind us.

When I get to the bed, I set her down gently and scoot us up so that our entire bodies are on the bed. Her lips have detached from my neck and we are both breathing heavy as I hover over her. She lifts her hand to grab the chain of my 'best friends' necklace, pulling me down to meet her swollen lips. Ever since my birthday, I very rarely take said necklace off.

One of my hands is propped on the side to keep my weight from crushing her and the other one is roaming up her shirt. Taking that as a cue, Rydell lifts her body up a little bit and takes her shirt off. Holy fuck. I'm pretty sure I blush like a fucking school kid as she says, "Your turn," grabbing the hem of my shirt and helping me take it off.

She's held up on her elbows, eyes roaming my body as my eyes roam hers. "You're so fucking gorgeous," I whisper as I lean down to kiss her neck.

"You are too," her voice is raspy. As my mouth works at her neck and collarbone, one of my hands smooths down her stomach until my fingers reach the waistband of her jeans. I stick my hand under both her jeans and the band of her underwear and lay my hand flat against her bare hip, right at the side of her ass.

"Is this ok?" I whisper as I place a soft kiss right about the top her bra.

She nods her head. I don't know if her breathing's fast because she's nervous or because it feels good.

"I need to hear words Books."

"Yes. Yes, it feels good."

"Do you want it to feel better?" I ask as I start to kiss down her stomach.

"I definitely wouldn't be opposed to it," I smirk against her skin and pull back, using both hands to unbutton her pants.

"Hips. Up," she lifts her hips and I take my time peeling her jeans off.

When they're on the floor, I trail my fingertips over the entirety of her smooth legs, digging them into her hips once they reach that point.

I hover back over her and lean down for a slow kiss, "Say the word, and we stop. If it's too much, tell me and I'll stop. Ok?"

"Ok," she breaths into my mouth.

One of my hands goes back under the band of her underwear and my index and middle finger slip between her folds, teasing her entrance. She's already so fucking wet and it takes everything for me not to devore her right there.

I slip one finger in and smash my lips into hers, eating the moan that comes out of her mouth. Bringing that finger out, I pull back and look at her pretty face, "Good?"

"Yes," she breaths. I go to put two fingers in her, until she says, "Wait," I stop immediately, fearing that I took it too far. "Your rings are still on, what if they get lost up there," I can't help but let of a laugh.

I kiss her cheek and say, "I love it when you

talk dirty to me," I take my rings off to rid her worries, "Do you want me to stop?"

"No. Please don't."

With her confirmation, I give her mouth a soft kiss and ease two fingers inside her, feeling her warmth to the comparison of her usually cold body.

I kiss down her body towards her exposed naval, pressing my mouth to the area right above the hem of her underwear. As I continue working my fingers inside her, I press my thumb to her clit. "Fuck Scott," I love how my name sounds on her lips.

I move my face in between her legs and use my free hand to lift her leg over one of my shoulders. I take my time kissing her thigh, biting and sucking her soft skin, traveling closer and closer to the spot I want to taste the most.

The closer I get, the heavier Rydell breaths. Her hands travel to my hair and I momentary look up at her for confirmation that I can start removing her panties. She looks at me with hooded eyes and does a small nod as she continues to tug at my hair.

Once I have them all the way off, I replace my thumb with my mouth, pressing a couple feather-like kisses to her clit. She lets out a long sigh before I fully devour her with my mouth sucking on her point of pleasure. "Oh my god," she's comparing me to god, I'll take that as a good sign.

"You taste so fucking sweet," I mumble against her, then swirl my tongue over her clit. My fingers are still pumping and she's starting to get squirmy. I lay my free hand flat against her bare stomach, pinning her to the bed. This causes her hips to lift, slightly grinding against my tongue and fingers.

Looking up, I have the most ideal view of her arched body. She is so perfect. The image of her, paired with the taste of her is almost painful. I seriously don't think I've ever been this hard. But I want this to be all about her. I don't want her to think that she has to return the favor. I'll just take a cold shower later.

I can feel her start to tighten around me, so I start to pick up the pace with my tongue and fingers. "Let go baby," I mumble. Right as I say it, she lets out a sound that I note to memorize, and I feel her release. I remove my fingers and move my mouth to where she's the most soaked, cleaning up the mess.

CHAPTER 59: RYDELL

I really had no doubt that Scott would be impressive in the bedroom but holy shit. It's embarrassing how wet I was before he even started touching me down there. But then he added his fingers and his mouth and oh my god. It was like the fucking Niagara Falls down there by the time I released.

My eyes are still closed, and my breathing is still a little heavy as I feel him start to move his way back up. I can feel his hard on against my stomach as he presses into me, I should probably help him take care of that.

I open my eyes and move my hands from his hair to cup his cheeks. "Hi," I say as he hovers over me.

He chuckles a bit, "Hey. How was that?"

"So good. Final review is a solid 10/10."

His lips brush against mine, moving against them as he says, "Glad you were satisfied," before pressing a long, soft kiss to my mouth. "Way better than pancakes," he whispers as he pulls back.

My hands move from his neck and feel down his hard chest, traveling to trace the lines of his abs, then reaching the top of his pants, fumbling with the button of his jeans.

"No, it's ok," he pulls back a bit propping up both hands on either side of my head.

I lean up, keeping my hands near the zipper, "Scott you're very visibly in need of release," I kiss the spot under his ear then whisper, "Let me help you."

I sit all the way up and force him to switch positions with me. He's sitting with his back against the headboard and I'm straddling his thighs as I unzip his pants.

He snatches my wrist right before my hand goes under and places a kiss on the palm of my hand. "I want you to be comfortable when we're intimate. I don't want you thinking you have to repay me in anyway. I'm fine, I'll take a shower in a bit," he runs his free hand through his hair.

I take the hand not held in his grip and palm down on his extremely hard dick causing him to groan and tilt his head back, "You're telling me that this isn't bothering you at all?"

"Nope," he can barely form his words.

I move my hand to cause friction, "Not even a little bit?" I whisper as I lean in to kiss his neck.

"Fuck Rydell. It certainly doesn't help the situation when you're touching me," he puts his hands on my hips and lifts me off his lap.

I'm about to protest, but he sticks his hand down his pants and starts stroking up and down his length, letting out a throaty groan. He pins me to my spot with his eyes, "Just let me look at you gorgeous," his voice is raspy and so fucking sexy. His eyes roam around my body, I'm only in my bra now and I feel very exposed, but not uncomfortable.

I figure I'm basically naked, so I reach my

hand to unclip my bra, letting the straps run slowly down my shoulders before completely taking it off.

I watch Scott watch me, eyes lingering on my chest, "You're so fucking pretty," his hand movements speed up and I crawl back over to him, cupping his cheek with one of my hands and pressing a kiss to his swollen lips. His free hand reaches so that it's wrapped around my neck, not squeezing, just resting there.

As I move my lips to kiss down his neck, he moves his hand to smooth the slop of my bare back. His fingertips are rough and calloused and every time they touch me, they leave goosebumps. His hand moves to my waist then up to my breast, slightly massaging it. We let out synchronized groans.

"I'm so close. Let me see you baby," I move my head out of his neck and he moves his hand to grip onto my hip, keeping me in place.

"Holy shit Rydell," my name sounds like a prayer on his lips as he ejaculations, pumping up and down a couple more times as he rides off his high.

When he gets himself under control, he leans off the headboard, cups the back of my neck and kisses me. I swear, our lips are going to be bruised in the morning. Can't say I'd be upset about it though.

"Well, better than the googled boobs you looked up in 7th grade?"

That gets a hearty laugh out of him, "So much better," he pecks my lips.

"Good. Ok, bathroom break," I grab his shirt off the edge of the bed and throw it over my head, then grab my underwear before slipping into the restroom.

As much as I'd love to stay there curled up in Scott, peeing after sexy time reduces the risk of STD's and UTI's.

After I do my business, I look in the mirror to see my hair completely messed up and my lips very swollen. I smooth my hair down and wash my hands before I exit.

Scott's laying on the bed in nothing but his boxer's, with both hands under his head, watching my every move.

"Try to sexy walk again, let's see if you can do it without tripping," he smirks at me. I flip him off.

"Rude. You should be flattered that I was flirting with you in the first place," I retort.

He just smiles at me and shakes his head, pulling me so that I lay flat on top of him. I put my hands on his chest and my chin on my hands, so that I'm slightly propped up and can look at his pretty face.

He keeps one hand behind his head and the other one moves under my (his) shirt to rub up and down my back. "I like seeing you in my clothes almost as much as I like seeing you with nothing on."

I can feel my cheeks heat up. As I go into kiss him the door bursts open.

"Hey, Scotty I can't find my-"

Faster than I can comprehend it, Scott flips me off him and covers my bare legs with his comforter.

"It's about damn time. So, how was it releasing all that sexual tension?" Asher jumps on the bed right next to me, causing me to clutch the comforter a little tighter.

"Get the fuck out Asher," Scott grits out.

"Oh sorry, was I interrupting something? Davies get in here!" he yells. Asher looks down out my disheveled figure and smirks.

"I swear to god Asher, if you don't stop looking out her I'm going to rip your eyes out," Scott says in all seriousness.

"Lips might be bruised tomorrow Deli. I could kiss it better for you though."

I raise my eyebrows at him, "You must have a death wish Webbs," Davies says as he enters the room. "Fancy seeing you here Rydell," he grins at me.

"Alright, you two have overstayed your welcome," Max walks in a grabs Asher by the back of the shirt, dragging him off the bed. I wonder when he got back.

"Use protection!" Asher yells as Max closes the door behind them.

"Fucking asshole," Scott mumbles. "Did they make you uncomfortable? Because I'll have a serious-"

I cut him off, "It's fine. Honestly, I thought it was a little funny," I smile up at him. I shift from laying on my back to lay on my side, towards Scott.

He scoots down and lays on his side facing me. He raises his arm to pull me closer to him so that our noses are practically touching. "I was two seconds away from strangling Webbs. He couldn't take his fucking eyes off you. I'm seriously considering suffocating him in his sleep."

I lean in to brush my nose against his, "You know he just does it to annoy you."

"That's not the only reason. Rydell, you're

fucking gorgeous, it's hard for guys to not look at you."

"Well, I guess it's a good thing that I'm only looking at you," I lightly kiss him.

"Damn right," he cups the back of my thigh to lift it to wrap his legs, letting his fingers trail up and down. So touchy.

I grab his necklace between my fingers, fidgeting around with it. Our foreheads are pressed together, and I don't think I've ever been this comfortable in my entire life. Laying here with Scott, it's like nothing else in the world matters.

"I told my parents about you," he whispers. What. The. Fuck.

I pull back a little so I can look him in the eye, "What?" I'm so confused.

"Well, I guess just my mom. But I'm sure she relayed the message to my dad."

"And what was this message exactly?"

His hand is still rubbing up and down my thigh. "That I won't marry a girl of their choosing because I already found one."

I probably look like a fish out of water gaping at him as he says it. Before I can even process, he drops another bomb, "And that I won't run their company because it's not what I want to spend my life doing."

Holy shit. I don't even know what to say. He brings his hand up to run his fingers through my hair, "Say something," he sounds a little worried.

What am I supposed to say to that? He scrambled up his entire life for me. The first time I asked him about relationships, he had it all planned out. It seemed like nothing could change his mind, no matter how unhappy that life would've made him. I'm not sure how I was able to change his mind, but I'm so fucking glad that I did. I say with all seriousness, "I'm really proud of you. I can't imagine that being an easy call."

"It was actually probably one of the easiest calls I've ever made. I never really even needed to think twice about it. As soon as you came into my life, their plans were ruined. You're the easiest decision I've ever made. I'd give up anything to be with you," he caresses my cheek.

I raise my hand to his hair, brushing back a piece that's fallen near his eyes. Then I trace the edge of his forehead with my index finger, trailing down to his cheek bone, then to line the shape of his jaw. His eyes flutter close as I continue my path. "Anything?" I question.

"Anything," he whispers back without hesitation.

"You don't have to give up anything for me. As long as I have you, I'll be happy."

"Then I guess you'll always be happy."

CHAPTER 60: *SCOTT*

Rydell slept over last night. In my bed. Wearing my shirt. I can't believe this is my reality right now. I honestly don't think I've ever been this happy.

She's still sleeping, but I have practice in like 30 minutes, and as much as I want to stay like this forever, I should start getting ready. My chest is against her back and I've propped myself up on my elbow to get a good look at her sleeping face.

I brush her hair out of the way and press a light kiss to her neck. I keep peppering small kisses all over the side of her neck, behind her ear, and across her jaw until she starts to stir, and her pretty eyes flutter open.

She rolls to her other side so that we are face to face. I'm still held up by my elbow. Looking down at her sleepy face gives me so much comfort. She scoots in to tuck herself into me, throwing one of her legs over mine and setting one of her hands on my chest. "Go back to sleep," she mumbles. It's so tempting, but I can't be late. I caress her cheek and lean down to press my mouth to her's.

"I have to get ready for practice. You stay right here and keep sleeping, then when I get back, we can stay in bed for the rest of the day," I peck her lips again, brushing my fingers through her hair to soothe her back to sleep.

"What time is it?" she keeps her eyes closed as she asks.

I grab my phone to look. "9:32. Go back to sleep gorgeous."

She breathes in deeply before rolling to lay on her back, looking up at me with tired eyes, "I can't. I have a meeting with Professor Bahri at 11. If we leave a little early, can you drop me off at home? If not, I'll just Uber back."

"Of course, I can drop you off. I'm not letting you get in a fucking Uber."

She shakes her head back and forth and looks at me with a dimpled simple. I brush a kiss over her dimple because I'm her boyfriend and I can kiss her casually now.

"Alright, time to pee," I swear she has the bladder of a small child.

I open the bathroom door when I hear her flush and grab both our toothbrushes as she washes her hands. Rydell already has a toothbrush here from the last time she spent the night.

I wet the toothbrushes and spread toothpaste on both, giving one to her when I finish.

As we stand there brushing our teeth together, I stare at her through the mirror. Every time her eye catches mine, she smiles and looks away. I don't look away, instead I wrap my arm around her waist and pull her to move so that she's standing in front of me, keeping my gaze on her the entire time. "Stalker," it sounds jumbled coming out of her mouth and toothpaste drips down her chin as she says it.

I bring my hand up to wipe the toothpaste off her chin, then wipe my hand on my leg to get rid of it.

I put my free hand under her shirt, well my shirt, and use my thumb to rub small circles against her skin. She leans her head back to rest on my chest. I think brushing my teeth with Rydell is my new favorite activity.

When she bends over to spit and rinse her mouth, her ass rubs right against my dick. Fuck. I was doing pretty good keeping my thoughts pure this morning, but when I look down to see her panties peeking out the bottom of the shirt, I can't help but feel turned on.

When she's done, she scoots to the side so that I can spit. She smacks my ass as she leaves the bathroom, "No getting distracted Scotty, you've got a practice to get to," god, I love her so much.

I rinse my mouth as fast as I can, to follow her back into my bedroom. I spin her around and throw her over my shoulder eliciting a squeal from her, "Prescott put me down," she laughs.

I do as she says and throw her onto my bed, crawling on top to hover over her. "Practice can wait," when I kiss her, she sighs a little and I don't waste any time to explore her mouth with my tongue. She tastes minty from the toothpaste.

She puts her hands on either side of my neck pulling back a little. "I don't want either of us to be late," she's looking at me with those pretty hazel eyes and I groan thinking about our responsibilities.

I look down at her neck, seeing a mark that stayed from last night. I raise my hand to brush my fingers over it, then move them to the neckline of the shirt pulling it down slightly to see one that I left on her collarbone. I kiss both of them before getting out of bed, lifting her up with me.

~

I swear, I feel like I'm floating on a fucking cloud. I didn't think life could be like this. I didn't think I could be this happy. But I am. Because Rydell Rivens is my girlfriend.

"What's got you grinning like an idiot today Bridges?" Coach Michael's asks as we go to take a water break.

"I convinced Rydell to be my girlfriend," I say, smiling growing. My cheeks are actually starting to hurt.

Coach laughs a bit and shakes his head, "Well, I like seeing you happy. And you're playing really well today, let's keep that up yeah? As glad as I am for it, this is the most important part of the season, scouts will be out at these next games. Just make sure you leave room to think about that."

"No need to worry about that coach," I know Rydell plans to move to California once she graduates. If the San Jose Sharks take interest in me, that's who I'll play for. I don't want to say anything to her yet because I've always preached that I want to play for the Bruins. But the Sharks are a fucking good team, and it's a huge plus that San Jose is only 45 minutes away from Santa Cruz.

It's really early into the relationship so I don't want Rydell to get scared that we're moving too fast when I tell her, but I'd follow that girl anywhere. I told her long distance would work, and I would make it work. But I like having her tangible. I always want to be touching her or looking at her. I'm happiest when I'm in her presence.

~

Practice ended with a pep talk from the coaches regarding our next game. We play in the next couple of days and the game after that is in Oregon. I'll be gone for 3ish days and I'm really hoping I can convince Rydell to fly out with me.

"What happened to glasses not being your type? You said nothing was going to happen there, that she was just your ticket to an A. Does she know that?"

The smile that was previously on my face is knocked off as soon as McCombs opens his big mouth. "That changed the second I actually talked to her. She knows how I feel about her. What's your fascination with our relationship? You always have something to comment about it when it's none of you goddamn business."

"I don't understand it. Here you are, the captain of one of the best college hockey teams, a shoo-in for the pros. You could have any girl you want. Fuck, you could have any girls' plural. I don't see why you'd tie yourself down to anyone, let alone the little nerd from Spanish class."

"You don't the first thing about Rydell because, if you did, we wouldn't be having this conversation right now," I get in his face backing him into a corner to get my point across. "Don't say another fucking word about her. Don't even think about her. If I hear that you've said one bad thing about her, or to her, you'll fucking regret. Understand?"

"Whatever man. But one day, you'll wake up and realize that I'm right. You'll see yourself trapped in this little box and find out that she's not worth it. And when you do, you'll break her heart.

It'll be fun to watch this blow up in your face."

I laugh humorlessly, "I feel sorry for you. I'm fucking in love with her. There's nothing that could ever make me not want her. No other girls, no fear of my reputation, nothing. I'm going to marry her one day and have kids with her, if that's what she wants. And as long as I have her, not a day will go by were I'm not happy," I back away from him a bit and look at his pathetic figure.

"You on the other hand," I continue, "You'll live a miserable fucking life. You'll go around having meaningless sex because you think it makes you look cool. You'll surround yourself with people who pretend they like you, when in reality they don't give a shit about you. It'll be fun to watch you realize how miserable you are."

With that, I turn around and leave the locker rooms.

CHAPTER 61: RYDELL

"They want to move the meeting to next week through Zoom. If they want to continue, which seems to be the case, you'll be invited to a banquet. They are picking up a couple of other developments and are showcasing them to sponsors December 10th."

I take a deep breath and look at Sam before looking back to Professor Bahri. "Well, we're ready. We have more than enough coding and designs done and have been working on it a lot lately to fine tune details."

We really have. Even when I was home for Thanksgiving, most of the nights I spent up with Sam on FaceTime to coordinate sequences. Much to Scott's dismay. He kept telling me how unhealthy it was to stay up late.

"Great. They should be sending you the Zoom link within the next couple of days, so keep an eye out for it. I also want to know all about the meeting so come see me sometime after please."

"Will do. Thank you, Prof," Sam says before we walk about.

"This is getting very real," I state once we're out the door.

"Agreed. We got this though, there's no way they turn us down. Especially since our video game specifically targets to help people. That will make it stand out from the others."

I nod my head. When we round the corner to head to the parking lot I bump into a figure. "Oh, sorry I wasn't looking where I was going and-" I look up to see Lindsay. "Um. Sorry."

"Ryland, should've know you'd be one to not watch where you're going."

"Hey," Sam pitches in. Oh shit. "How about you shut the fuck up Linda."

"It's Lindsay. And you are?" she says with a snarky look on her face.

"I'm the person who won't hesitante to wipe that stupid look off your face if you don't apologize to Rydell right now."

"Ooo, I'm so scared," Lindsay really does not understand who she's messing with.

Sam opens her half-filled smoothie cup from before our meeting and looks down at Lindsay's shoes. "Those look expensive. Wanna rethink that answer?"

"Crazy bitch," Sam dumps the smoothie on her shoes, then grabs mine out of my hand.

"Ya, I'm a crazy bitch. You're a jealous bitch. Glad we got that out of the way. Apologize, or this crazy bitch is going to make your shirt match your shoes."

"God, ok. Rydell, I'm sorry. However, word from the wise, you're not going to last with Scott. I heard all about your guy's new relationship. He's going to break your heart when he gets tired of fucking you."

Sam throws the smoothie all over Lindsay's

shirt then pounces at her with her fists ready for a sucker punch. I grab Sam's arm to hold her back before she gets herself arrested for assault. "I'm fine Sam. She's not worth it."

Sam cools off a bit as I look at Lindsay and say, "I feel sorry for you. I know you're probably used to relationships that are nothing more than meaningless hookups and status quo, but that's not how all of them are. I feel sorry that you haven't experienced what it's like to be genuinely in love with someone and know that their feelings our reciprocated. I'm in love with Scott. And I know he's in love with me. You can go around spreading whatever shit you want about me; I really don't care. But if you say a bad thing about Scott or try to hurt him in anyway because he doesn't want you like he wants me, you'll have more than ruined shoes to worry about." With that, I start pulling Sam towards my car.

"Damn Rydell, that was so badass. The look on her face was priceless. I hope that smoothie stains her clothes," she links her arm through mine.

"I might vomit. That was so mean of me," I put my hands down on my thighs and lean over to catch my breath.

"She was the one being mean. Everything you said was stuff that she needed to hear babes. Don't feel bad for putting her in her place," she rubs my back a bit.

I nod my head, "Yeah. You're right. Hopefully that gets her to back off and leave Scott and I alone. Thanks for helping me with the situation."

"I'd never sit there and let someone talk to you like that Del. But I'm really proud of you for standing up for yourself," she says, causing me to smile.

"It did feel kinda good."

"Hell, yeah it did," she says as we get into the car to drive to the orphanage for our shift.

~

I'm sitting in the middle of my bed, criss cross, as I try to code the speed of the CPU for our video game.

It's a bit frustrating because I can't seem to get it right and don't know what I'm doing wrong.

I faintly hear Sam answer the front door as the bell rings, but I'm too invested in getting this code done to care who it is.

I read over the code. Nothing's wrong with it. So why the hell isn't it how I want it to be. I read it again. Then again. Then again and see that I have an extra space in it. "Mother fucker," I mumble.

"Do you kiss your mother with that mouth?" My head shoots up and I see Scott leaning against my bedroom door frame.

"When did you get here?"

"Hello to you too," he says sarcastically.

He walks over to my bed and moves my laptop out of the way, ignoring my protests. He puts his arms around my waist, pushing me down so that I'm on my back. His weight is fully on me as he stuffs his face into my neck, breathing me in.

I reach my hands down to thread my fingers to play with his hair. "Hi," I did miss him, even though I saw him this morning. God, I'm going to be one of those girlfriends who always wants to be near her boyfriend.

He places a soft kiss to my neck before lifting his head and kissing my lips. "Hey pretty girl.

How was your day?" He flips us over so that I'm flat against his chest and his back is to the bed.

I prop my chin on my hands and look down at him. "Let's see. Sam and I have a Zoom call with Ubisoft next week. They are most likely going to develop our game and if they do, we'll be invited to a banquet to get sponsors," I love the smile that he has on his face as I say it. Like he's genuinely proud of me.

"That's awesome Books. There's no way they don't want to develop it. What else happened?"

"Mmmm," I don't know if I should tell him about the whole Lindsay situation, so I skip it and say, "Violet and Rosie almost got into a fist fight over who got to help me do dishes today."

"Why on earth would they fight over chores?"

"They like to dry the dishes. I think it makes them feel mature, I really don't know."

"They probably just like spending time with you," his hands travel under my shirt to rub up and down my back.

"Maybe," I bite the inside of my cheek. Scott takes one hand to brush my hair out of my face, then tangles his fingers in it to play with the ends.

"I feel like there's something else. Come on Ry, you have to tell me since I'm your boyfriend," I sigh deeply and he adds, "Sorry, you don't have to tell me, but I would like it if you did."

"I had an interesting chat with Lindsay earlier," his hands stop playing with my hair.

He sits up so that his back is to the headboard and I'm now sitting on his lap. Well, more like straddling it. "What'd she say?"

"Well, it started with her bumping into me

and insinuating that I'm stupid and clumsy. When she didn't apologize, Sam dumped her smoothie on her shoes. Then took my smoothie and threw it on her shirt when she told me that you'd break up with me when you got tired of fucking me," I look down to avoid his intense gaze.

"Rydell," he sticks his knuckles under my chin to maintain eye contact.

"I'm not done," I guarantee his mind is filled with the insane idea that I believed her.

"I told her that I'm in love with you. And that I know you're in love with me. That she can say anything to me that she wants but if she tries to hurt you, I'll personally make sure she regrets it."

I stuff my face in my hands as a grin starts to breakout on his face, "I was very mean. But she kinda deserved it."

He grabs onto my wrists to reveal my face. "I really wish I could've seen that. Look at you. My little badass girlfriend. I'm proud one you for standing up for yourself. I don't have to tell you that everything that came out of her mouth was bullshit, do I?"

"No, you don't," I reassure him.

"Good," he guides my wrists up to wrap them around his neck as his go to wrap around my waist.

He leans in but before kissing me says, "I think it's super hot that you told her off," I feel his words against my mouth. When he fully presses his lips to mine, I don't hesitate to reciprocate.

CHAPTER 62: SCOTT

She's so fucking pretty. After our chat about Lindsay, I felt a lot of relief. I think she actually trusts me to protect her heart. She knows that I love her and that's a really good feeling.

She let me kiss her for a little bit before pulling back and telling me that I can't distract her until after her coding sequence is finished. And as much as I want her to pay attention to me, I know how important getting this done is to her.

So, I'm lying on my back with my hands under my head watching her as she codes sitting criss cross in the middle of her bed.

Every now and again she'll look over at me, notice I'm already looking at her, smile, and mumble 'stalker'. I love her pet names.

I watch her scrunch her nose when she's stuck on something, her eyebrows furrow when she's confused, her eyes light up when she figures it out. And I fall even more in love with her, if possible.

"Don't you have something more important to do than stare at me?" she asks after she catches me looking at her for about the 8th time.

"I can't think of anything more important

than admiring my gorgeous girlfriend."

Her cheeks start to bloom with pink and I silently applaud myself for still having that effect on her.

"How about the Spanish annotations, have you finished that yet? They're due on Friday."

We only have a couple more weeks of Spanish before the semester ends. I hated Spanish when I first started it, but now it's hands down the best class I've ever taken. I mean, I met Rydell through the class, how could it not be? And I'm a little sad to see it come to an end. Rydell and I will never have another class together. Maybe I'll just try to sneak into some of her computer science classes.

"I finished it during Thanksgiving break," I say smugly.

Her head shoots up, like she doesn't expect my answer. "When?"

"When you were on FaceTime with Sam working on the video game. I didn't want to go to sleep without you next to me, so I found something to occupy my time."

"That's very sweet of you," I'm rewarded with a dimpled smile.

"Yeah, having you curled up right against my dick is like the best feeling," I can't help myself.

She rolls her eyes, "Moment ruined," the smile stays on her face.

I lean up and sit criss cross, facing her and lean my lips down to her neck to kiss it. I lift my head to bite her earlobe, "Don't pretend you don't like the feeling," I whisper.

"5 more minutes," she pushes my chest. I listen to her request to stop distracting her and go back to watching her.

~

I feel a weight against my chest and small pressure on my neck. That small pressure is Rydell giving me soft kisses. Shit. I must've fallen asleep.

She's straddling my thighs and hovering over me. I can smell her intoxicating lavender scent, and my hands don't hesitate to find her hips. She continues trailing her kisses from my neck, up to my earlobe, biting it and whispering, "I love you."

I smile to myself and go to cup her cheeks to pull her head out so that I can kiss her properly. When I pull back, I look at her tired eyes and shift her so that I'm still on my back but she's on her side resting her head on my chest. Her hand is slowly drawing circles and her leg is thrown over my hip.

"How long was I asleep?" I brush hair back from her face.

"Mmm, close to an hour. I'm sorry, once I figured out the right code I was on a role and didn't want to lose momentum," she yawns.

"No worries, I know how important it is to you. Are you tired?"

"A little bit," she props up on her elbow to look down out me, raising her hand to gently move my hair back. Her fingers are cold, and I close my eyes as I indulge in the feeling of her playing with my hair. "But I feel bad that you came over here only for me to pay attention to something else. Tell me about your day."

"Books, if you're tired, let's go to sleep," I put my hand under her shirt and rub up and down her back.

She sighs deeply and lays back down, scooting impossibly closer to me. I'm pretty sure both our love languages are physical touch and I'm definitely not complaining. I love how touchy she is with me, especially now that she's my girlfriend.

"Please tell me about your day. I want to know. Plus, I like listening to you talk."

"Ok, but don't feel like you have to stay awake, if your eyes start to close, keep them closed and go to sleep."

She nods against my chest. My hand continues to lightly scratch her back. "Well, this morning I woke up with the prettiest girl in my arms. She does drool a bit, but its ok because I like her cooties."

I feel her vibrations as she laughs. "I don't drool that much," she looks up at me, keeping her head rested on me. I kiss the top of her head.

"Whatever you say Books."

"Ok, keep going," she encourages me.

"Alright. Like I said, I woke up to a pretty, drooling girl in my arms. I brushed my teeth with this girl, even though I wanted to stay in bed with her all day but, we both unfortunately had things to do."

"Mhmm," she hums.

"Anyways, we brushed our teeth, and I didn't think I'd ever be addicted to something like brushing my teeth, but I kinda want to do it all the time. Only if it's always with her of course."

"Of course," she mimics.

"And this pretty girl is such a tease. I mean she bent over to rise her mouth, rubbing right against my dick and I wanted to take her back to bed and show her how crazy she drives me, but she's responsible and has self-control that I lack. I was rewarded with a couple of very nice kisses though. She was also wearing my shirt which rode up a lot;

that was a major plus."

"Perv," she mumbles. I can hear the sleepiness starting to lace her voice. I raise the hand I have around her to start brushing my fingers through her hair to lure her to close her eyes.

"I dropped her off at her apartment so that she could be a superstar video game developer who goes to important meetings and signs with major companies. And I missed her all day."

"Yeah?" her voice is just above a whisper.

"Yeah. I'm pretty sure I might be addicted to her. Not that I mind. I would be a junkie for her any day."

I look down at her. Her eyes are closed, but she has a sleepy smile on her face.

I continue playing with her hair. After staying quiet for a bit, I say, "I always want to be next to you Rydell Rivens. And I'll follow you anywhere. If you go to California, I'll go to California. Nothing else matters more than you."

Her breathing pattern has slowed and becomes rhythmic, and I know she's sleeping because her mouth is slightly open and any second, she'll start to drool. Maybe I knew she was asleep and that's why I said it. Maybe I said it with the hope that she might hear it.

Whatever it was, all of it was true.

CHAPTER 63: *RYDELL*

"Well, that settles it, I guess. The next step is the banquet which will happen December 10th. We'll send you all the information for it, but it does take place in New York, so just make sure you're ready for it. Your flight and all other accommodations will be taken care of though, so don't worry about that. And we look forward to working with the two of you."

"Thank you so much. We are very grateful for this opportunity," I exclaim.

"Yes, we are very excited to work with you guys," Sam adds before we say our goodbyes and end our meeting.

Sam and I look at each other. I can't even begin to describe the feeling that consumes me. I feel so proud of both of us. I mean this is 3 years of work finally paying off.

"Holy shit, we did it," I wrap my arms around Sam and pull her in for a hug.

She doesn't hesitate to reciprocate. "We're going to New York to get sponsors for our video game that's going to be developed by Ubisoft," Sam exclaims as she pulls back. "I need to call my mom!"

She runs to her room to make her calls, and I

go to do the same. I hit on the number of the first person I want to tell. It only rings a couple of times before he picks up. "Hey gorgeous girl, how'd the meeting go."

"It was ok," I play it off.

"Just ok? Well, did they tell you if they were going to move forward, do they want to set up another meeting? What'd they say?"

"They said they were going to fly us out to New York so that we can get sponsors for our game that they are going to help us develop," I'm smiling so hard right now.

"Fuck yes, that's my girl! I knew you guys would get it; they'd be idiots not to develop it. I'm so proud of you baby, we can celebrate tonight after the game. I would come to drive to you right now, but coach wants us here until the game starts. Will you be here tonight?"

"Of course I'll be there. We can have a double celebration tonight: for the game development and your win."

"We haven't won yet."

"I'm manifesting it," I respond.

I hear Scott's coaches yell at him in the background, "Alright, I won't hold you up any longer. I don't want to get you in trouble."

"I don't mind getting in trouble if it means that I get to talk to my favorite girl," my cheeks heat up. "Are you blushing right now?"

He knows me way too well, "This room is just a little warm."

He chuckles, "Rightttt. Seriously though Books, I'm so fucking proud of you. You're going to do great things with this video game, and I feel really luck that I get to watch you in your success."

"Thank you Scotty. I feel really lucky that I have you by my side through it all," his coach yells again. "Ok, ok, you better go. I'll see you at the rink."

"Will you find me for a good luck kiss before the game start?"

"Absolutely."

"Good, I'm looking forward to it. Ok, bye pretty girl. I love you."

"Bye pretty boy. I love you too."

After I finish up my call with Scott, I call my parents, Chris, and my grandparents who all are very excited for me.

Finally done with my calls, I walk into the kitchen to find Sam on FaceTime with Max.

"Oh look, here's Del," Sam points the camera to my face.

"Hi Del, congrats on the video game. I'm super excited for the both of you."

"Thanks Max. Are you ready for the game tonight? How's Scott, he's not too nervous for it is he?"

"I think we'll do good. Scott's going over game plans with the coaches, he never shows his nervousness, but I think he's fine."

"Ok cool. I'll let you guys finish your chat. Good luck tonight. Sam and I will be cheering you guys on."

I let them have their privacy. I wonder if she called him or if Max called her. I don't know, but there's definitely something going on there. I'll ask her later.

~

After Sam and I took a trip to Professor Bahri's office to tell him the news, we went straight to the game.

The team is warming up when we walk in, and the stands are already super packed. Probably since their next couple games are away.

As I walk towards the players' bench, my eyes scan the arena for my favorite person. It's not hard to spot him. Maybe because I love him so much or maybe because he looks so natural on the ice. Like he's meant to be there.

"I promised Scott I'd see him before the game, but he looks busy right?" I lean into Sam so that she can hear me over the crowd.

"I wouldn't say he looks that busy," when I look back, he's taking off his helmet and skating over to us. "I'll meet you at the seats," Sam says as she walks away.

"Hey number 15," I call out as Scott walks off the rink. He sets his helmet down and scoops me up in a hug that lifts my feet off the floor.

"Hey superstar. I feel so honored to be in the presence of a hot shot video game creator," he sets me on the floor, and cups my cheeks. My arms move to wrap around his torso. "Congrats baby, I'm so fucking proud of you," he starts to pepper kisses all over my face causing me to giggle like I'm a freaking schoolgirl. He has the strongest effect on me.

"Thanks. I have no doubt you'll make me just as proud during this game, regardless of the outcome. How are you feeling? Nervous at all?"

Before letting go of my cheeks, he places a sweet kiss on my lips and then moves his hands to rub up and down my arms.

"Dartmouth's team is pretty good, but I'm not very nervous. Are you warm enough, it's cold in here and outside," he takes my hands and raises them to his lips. "Where are your mittens Ry?"

"I forgot them in the car. I hate driving with them on," he gives a kiss to the back of both my hands cupping them in between his to warm them up.

He shakes his head and releases my hands, "Stay right here."

He moves on the ice to the benches. After about a minute, he's back in front of me, grabbing for my hands.

When he has them, he starts slipping on his mittens that I assume were in his gym bag. They are extremely oversized, but I can feel them already start to warm me up. "There. Now you'll be warm. Keep forgetting your mittens and you'll get sick Books."

"Well, it's a good thing I have you then," he leans down to kiss the dimple poking out of my chin.

"Damn straight."

"Bridges, wrap it up!"

"That's your queue," I tell him as his coach shouts at him.

"Good luck kiss?"

I raise on my tippy toes and cup the back of his neck to pull him down to my level. When our lips meet, he cups my cheek to tilt my head and deepen the kiss. His other hand moves down to slap my ass as he pulls away.

I squeal and slap his ass as pay back. "Go get 'em 15," I peck his lips one more time.

He leans down to bite my earlobe before moving his mouth to my ear and whispering, "I love you."

"I love you too," he smiles and kisses me one last time.

"Meet me on the bleachers after?"

"Yep," with that he skates towards his team and gets ready for the game.

~

Our team won 3-1. It was an exciting game, and both teams' player really well. We just played better.

As the players start to trickle out of the locker rooms, fans start to accumulate around them to congratulate them on the win. "I'm going to tell Max good job," Sam says.

"Oh yeah, give him a kiss for the win," I wiggle my eyebrows at her. She flips me off as she walks over towards the crowd.

Scott isn't out yet, and I stand back to let him celebrate his win. He'll find me when he's ready.

As soon as he walks out, the crowd gets a little louder. Which makes sense considering that he's the captain. People are clapping his back and going in for high fives, but he just scans the crowd until he finds me away from it.

He smiles and suddenly it feels like we're the only people in the rink. It's like laser focus. It takes me back to one of the first times we talked at the bar. He was on a mission to talk to me and everyone parted for him so that he could get to me.

As soon as he reaches me, he cups the back on my neck and kisses me right in front of everyone. This kiss is hard and feels full of love. It's the kind of kiss that makes your head dizzy. I have to put my hands on his hips to stabilize myself.

He pulls back slightly and then goes in for a

couple more pecks. In between kisses he says, "I'd say that good luck kiss worked."

I tilt my head back to laugh and he bites my earlobe causing me to squirm a bit. "Alright Books, where do you want to eat?"

He grabs my hand that is still covered in his mittens and starts swinging our arms back and forth as we make our way out to the parking lot. Most of the girls are glaring at me as we walk past the crowd. "Scott, are you going to Boots to celebrate the win?" one of them yells?

He just ignores it and keeps walking. "Um. We can go to Boots for a bit with the team if you want," I don't want him to think that he can't go because of me.

The cold hits hard as soon as we open the doors to leave the rink. Scott notices and wraps his arm around my shoulder, curling me into his side. "I don't want to celebrate me and the team Ry, I want to celebrate you."

"But you guys won. I don't want to put my success over your's. You deserve to be celebrated just as much as me. Plus, people will be upset if you aren't there."

"I really don't give a fuck about other people," we reach his car, and he opens the passenger's seat for me. Sam knew that I was going with him after the game, so she drove us in her car.

Once I sit down, he raises his hands to the top of the car and leans down to me slightly, "You're too sweet Books and that's one of the reasons why I love you. But I've won a countless number of games. In fact, I very rarely don't win. It's not every day you sign with a company as big as Ubisoft. We are celebrating you whether you like it or not," with that he checks to make sure my seat belt is secure and closes the door.

CHAPTER 64: SCOTT

"Ok, ok," Rydell exclaims, "This time you have to throw it backwards!" she's so cute when she's excited

I'm not quite sure how we got here, but we ended up at a bowling alley eating pizza with my roommates, Sam, and Rydell's old neighbors.

Rydell said that her and Sam were drunk at a bowling alley when they came up with the idea for their video game and left the bowling alley before the game was over to start working on it.

Sam called Rydell not too long after we got in her car and sprung the idea and Rydell was all for it. And I'm all for whatever Rydell wants to do. Sam invited Max, and Oliver and Asher overheard and wanted to celebrate their signing as well, so they all skipped Boots with the team. Rydell called the 106ers who happened to be there the night Rydell and Sam came up with the video game idea.

Instead of playing conventional bowling. Rydell and Sam said we had to play their way. Their way is doing a challenge each round. For example, the last round we had to use our non-dominate arm. This round we have to throw it backwards.

Rydell stands up to take her turn and I

lightly smack her ass as I say, "Go get 'em Books."

"Save that for the bedroom Bridges," Webbs jokes.

As Rydell takes her turn I can't help but feel like I'm in a trance. I suppose that's how I always feel when I'm around her. She's so fucking radiant that it's hard for me to take my eyes off her. Especially when she's like this: carefree, happy, surrounded by people she cares about.

The sight of her jumping up and down after getting a spare knocks me out of my thoughts and I start to clap to cheer her on.

"Did you see that?!" she plops down right on my lap and wraps her arms loosely around my neck. "I should go pro," she adds.

"Good job gorgeous," I give her a quick peck on the lips before pulling back and tucking some hair behind her ear. "Are you have a good time?"

"Mhmm. Thanks for coming with. I'm glad you're here to celebrate," she kisses my cheek, and my heart melts a bit.

I lean in to bite her earlobe and whisper, "We could celebrate more tonight. Just the two of us," my hand rubs up and down to caress her thigh as I feel her squirm on top of me.

She stuffs her face in my neck to hide her blush. I feel her warm breath hit every time she exhales and her lips brush against my skin. She places a soft kiss there before moving to my ear, "You're up."

I look to the board, and sure enough it is, unfortunately, my turn. She slides off my lap to sit in the seat next to me and it takes so much for me to leave her side, even if it is just for a minute.

Before going to the lane, I peck her on the lips, "For luck," I wink at her and smile at her cheeks that are sporting a pink flush.

~

"No offense, but you kinda suck at bowling," Rydell claims as we walk into my house and take off our jackets. Sam and Max went out for ice cream so who knows how long they'll be out, or what's even happening there. And Webbs and Davies went to Boots and won't be back until late, if at all tonight.

"I'm usually pretty good, I was just very distracted tonight," I give her a knowing look. I truly don't think I've ever bowled so badly. But every time I went up to take my turn, all I could think about was sitting back down and having Rydell sit in my lap.

Rydell plops herself down on the couch, "Oh yeah. And what was so distracting tonight," she looks at me with a smirk.

I smile and shake my head as I sit down next to her. As soon as I sit down, she throws her legs over mine and my hands automatically find their way to knead at her calves and thighs.

"A very, very pretty girl."

She hums and lets her head drop to my shoulder, "If pretty girls make you distracted, you must be out of it all the time."

"There's only one girl who has that effect on me. She's the only one who's ever made me feel this way."

"And what way are you feeling?"

I move my shoulder so that she lifts her head, and I can make eye contact with her as I say softly, "Like I've got everything I thought I didn't deserve. Like I won't ever go a day unhappy since I have you in my life. I'm so fucking in love with you Rydell that sometimes the mere sight of you is overwhelming. I look at you and I don't understand how I ever got this lucky. And sometimes I'm not sure that I deserve it. I'm not sure I deserve you. But I'd do anything to keep you in my life. I've never been so happy, and I'm scared that one day, I'll wake up and fuck it up. My biggest fear is losing you."

She rests her hand on my cheek and gives me the sweetest kiss. When she pulls back, she rests her forehead on mine and whispers, "You'll never lose me. My heart is yours. You can do whatever you'd like to it, but it can't be returned. It will only ever belong to you."

My eyes are still closed from the kiss and I let her words wrap around me like the most comfortable blanket.

"I promise I'll protect it," I whisper back.

"I believe you."

My hands blindly find her waist and I tug her to me as I set my mouth to hers. She shifts her body so that she's straddling me, her hands tangle in my hair to keep us impossibly close. My hands run down her back to cup her ass. She rolls her hips against the hard on that I'm now sporting and we both let out synchronized groans.

I've never wanted to be inside of somebody this badly. If I don't get more I might die, but if she's not ready that's fine, I'll happily sleep in my grave. I'd rather suffer than make her uncomfortable.

She pulls back by a fraction and my lips follow hers, but before they can attach, she moves her lips to trail kisses down my neck. Then back up again to bite my earlobe. "I love you so much."

I move my face to meet hers and raise a hand to cup the back of her neck and put my mouth to hers. This is my new favorite kiss. It's full of passion and both of us are out of breath as we try to show each other how in love we are. I bite down on her bottom lip and am immediately rewarded access. I'm filled with warmth as my tongue explores the inside of her mouth.

We get to the point where if we don't pull back, we'll pass out due to lack of air. My forehead rests on hers. "You were right. I do love your cooties," she says as I dip my head to the crook of her neck. I breathe in her lavender scent before I start pressing sloppy kisses that trail down to her collarbone. My hands have a mind of their own, because they are now finding their way under Rydell's shirt, caressing the bare skin over her ribs right below her breasts.

When my mouth finds the sweet spot under Rydell's ear, she lets out a breathy moan and tugs on my hair a little harder. I suck down hard on it as she rolls her hips. "Fuck Rydell," I mumble against her skin.

My head comes out of her neck and she lightly grabs my chin, forcing me to make eye contact with her. "I think now's a good time for you to take me to your bed."

"Rydell, if we move this to my bed, I don't know if I'll be able to stop," my breathing is heavy.

She slowly presses her lips to mine and between her soft kisses' mumbles, "I don't want you to stop."

"I don't want to make you uncomfortable. I know you wanted to take it slow," I tell her as my hands find her waist under her shirt and I rest my forehead against hers.

"Prescott Bridges I want you. All of you. I'm more than ready to take the next step with you," she bumps her nose against mine. "I trust you," she whispers.

I move to settle my hands on the backs of her thighs that are still straddling me and stand up, keeping eye contact with her the whole time I walk to my bedroom.

When we get there, I lock the door and gently settle her so that she is laying completely on the bed. Before joining her, I take my shirt off only slight breaking eye contact when I have to. She sits up and looks so pretty watching me and as I slide my pants off, her eyes leave mine to travel around my almost naked body.

Now that I'm left in only my boxers, I make my way onto the bed in front of her. I grab at the hem of her shirt, "Can I take this off?" I don't think I've ever been this nervous to sleep with a girl before. I sure as hell was never hesitant to do something as simple as taking off their shirts. But I can't fuck this up.

"Yes," she nods. I lift it over her head and move to the button on her corduroy pants.

"And these?"

"Mhmm," she hums. I unbutton and unzip her pants as slow as I can, in case she changes her mind. When I know that this is what she wants, I tap the sides of her hips, signaling her to lift them and peel her pants all the way off, throwing them to the floor.

I crawl over her so that she pushes her back to the bed and place my lips on hers. One of my hands is smoothing up and down the side of her bare stomach while the other one stays propped close to her head so that I don't crush her with my weight.

As my lips move to find her neck. My hand strategically reaches to unclip her bra as her back arches and I discard it to the ground. I pull back and take her in. Her cheeks flush red. "It's impossible for someone to be this perfect."

I go back to kiss her neck slowing down and lingering at the point of her pulse, feeling her heartbeat against my lips to remind myself that this isn't just a dream.

My mouth moves lower to work on her collarbone while my hand travels to under her panties. I groan at the feeling of her wetness on my fingers as I tease her folds with my fingers, "You're soaked baby. You weren't lying when you said you love my cooties," I smirk at her as I bring my face down to kiss her.

Before I can insert my fingers, she grabs my wrist, "I want you inside of me."

Holy shit that was hot. Those words alone almost make me cum. Thankfully I can somewhat restrain myself.

"Are you sure?" I ask as I start pulling the last bit of clothing off her.

"Yes," she replies as her underwear hit the floor.

I look down at her fully naked body before pressing my mouth to hers and mumbling, "So fucking perfect."

I pull back and quickly take my boxer's off, watching as her eyes widen at the sight of my extremely hard dick.

"Condoms?" I question.

"Table," she points to the one sitting right next to her bed.

I grab one, tear the side of it with my teeth and roll it on, then hover over Rydell.

"I haven't done this is awhile, and you're probably more experienced so if I'm bad then-"

I cut her rambling off with my lips. "We don't have to," I set my forehead against hers.

"I want to. But you're also a lot larger than the other guys I've been with and-" I laugh at that. "Hey, don't laugh at me, I'm serious."

"I'm sorry," I give her a soft kiss. "I'm not laughing at you. You'll forget about every guy to ever exist when I'm inside you."

"Just go slow," she cups the back of my neck and pulls me to meet her awaiting mouth. This kiss is slow and not as rushed as the other ones. And I know she's calm during this kiss, so I line myself up to her entrance and slowly edge my tip into her. I pull back so I can watch her eyes for any sign of discomfort. When I see none, I bury myself deeper inside of her at a painfully slow rate. When I'm all the way in we let out matching sighs.

"Are you ok?" I look at her as she squeezes her eyes shut.

"Mhmm. Just give me a second," her voice is choppy.

I lean my head down and press feather kisses all over her face: on her cheeks, forehead, lips, hoping that it will somehow soothe any pain she might be feeling.

She lifts her hips, and a throaty groan makes its way out of me as I feel myself throb against her walls. "Fuck," I breathe out.

"Ok I'm ready," with that I slowly move, gliding an inch in and out. "You can go faster," her voice is filled with lust as she wraps her legs around me, pulling my deeper inside her.

My head dives to rest in the crook of her neck as I continue my slow pace, "Fuck Rydell, if I go any faster, I'll lose it and I want this to last a while," my words fall on her shoulder.

I can tell that she needs more, but I seriously won't last long if I speed up, so I bring my hand between us to slowly rub circles around her clit.

Her head presses down deeper into the pillow as she lets out a moan that almost sets me over the edge.

I move my head out of her neck to feel the sounds she's making against my lips and increase my speed, pulling further out of her before thrusting back in.

"So good," I can barely get my words out, "You feel so fucking good."

I find a steady pace that seems to be perfect for both of us and lift myself up on one hand to look down at her as she takes me.

Her breast bounce in rhythm with each trust and I raise my other hand up to massage one of them, "Holy shit Scott."

It's painful to look at her while trying to draw this out for as long as possible. To take it a step further, I flip us around and sit up so that my back is to the headboard and she's sat on my dick.

My hands find her ass as I guide her up and down. She swivels her hips around my cock and my head falls down and I lightly bite her shoulder to keep myself from exploding. Her head tilts up towards the ceiling and she continues to ride me. I move my hands up to her waist to press her deeper onto me and stuff my face in her neck to muffle my groans.

Her breathing is heavy as I start sucking on her neck, "I'm almost there," she grips her hands down onto my shoulder, and I lift my face to watch her as I feel her walls start to clench around my throbbing dick.

She makes the sound she did before the last time I made her cum and sure enough I feel her start to drip down me as her head falls to rest against my forehead. I thrust myself up once more before I let myself go. She stays sitting on me, unmoving as we both come down from our highs.

Our breath mixes into one as we take a second to gather ourselves. She moves her forehead to my shoulder, and I rub my fingertips up and down her back.

She places a sweet kiss to my bare shoulder before shifting herself off me and plopping on the bed next to me. I stay rooted in my place and extend my head back to look at the ceiling and catch my breath.

Out of the corner of my eyes I see Rydell crawl under the covers and I move to join her, pulling her up to rest her head on my chest.

I lift the blanket up so that it reaches up to cover her shoulders completely when I notice the goosebumps marking her arms. I start rubbing up and down her arm with the hand I have wrapped around her to keep her warm.

"How are you feeling?" I mumble against her forehead as I kiss it.

She looks up at me with those pretty hazel eyes, "I'm feeling like we should've done that sooner."

I chuckle against her forehead as I kiss it again, "I didn't hurt you at all or take it too fast did I? It was good for you right?"

She props herself up and rests her hand on my chest, "Scott, it was perfect," she shakes her head and breaks eye contact. "I've had only bad experiences with sex. If I'm being honest, I think ever since the," she clears her throat. "Ever since the first time I was sexually assaulted I've been terrified of anything sex related." Her eyes are starting to water a bit, I bring my hand to give her back scratches to try and soothe her a bit.

She looks back up at me, "I didn't think I'd ever have a good experience with it. Like maybe I was destined to never get there with anyone, especially after the Trey situation. I thought that my grandpa touching me broke me to an unfixable point and that it was my fault that I'm this way. With you, I'm starting to feel not so broken."

She presses her lips to mine in a long, slow kiss. "I'm really in love with you Scott. And I feel extremely comfortable with you," she rests her forehead on mine and brushes her nose against mine. "You're fixing pieces of me that I thought were beyond saving."

CHAPTER 65: *RYDELL*

Once I fully regained composure of myself, I slipped Scott's shirt over my head and went to the bathroom.

I can't seem to wipe the stupid smile off my face. I really did not think I ever would have good sex. Like it was just something that I'd have to suck up and bare in a relationship, but sex with Scott is so good.

I wash my hands and make my way back to the bed. As soon as my footsteps out of the bathroom Sex on Fire by Kings of Leon starts playing on full blast.

I look over at Scott who starts singing the lyrics and pointing at me, causing me to hide my face in my hands to smother my laugh.

He jumps off the bed and pulls me to him by my waist and that's how I find myself yelling the lyrics and dancing around the room with Scott. I'm in his shirt. He's in his boxers. And I don't think I have ever been this happy.

He's twirling me around and I'm laughing like I'm drunk. And just when I think this moment can't get any better, he dips me while pressing his lips to mine and I think my heart might explode.

When he snaps me back up, our lips stay connected and I throw my arms around his neck. "That's how a dip is supposed to be done," he says against my lip with a smile on his face.

I pull back by a fraction, "Hey, don't act like you didn't like my attempt at a dip at that party."

He wraps his arms tightly around my waist and walks us back to his bed, laying down on his back with me on top of him. "Oh, I definitely liked it. You couldn't stop staring at my lips through that whole thing."

"Yeah. I definitely would've kissed you if we weren't interrupted."

He rolls his eyes, "Don't remind me."

"Ok, let me try again!" I exclaim as I climb off him and the bed.

"Try dipping me?"

"No. Try dipping myself. Of course, try dipping you," I grab his hands and pull him off the bed. "On your feet Scotty."

He complies and stands up. "Just so you know, I'm not going to try not to fall. You're going to have to use those muscles of yours Ry," he gives my bicep a squeeze.

I muster as much concentration as I can grab his waist and go for the dip. But it's really no fair because he's 6'5 and I'm 5'7 and I really never stood a chance at doing this correctly.

Sure, enough I drop him, and he pulls me down with him so that I land right on his chest. "You know Books, I'm starting to think that you just wanted to get me in this position again."

"Ah. Looks like you caught me. Now I can show you what I would've done last time if things went differently."

I lean down and give him a kiss. It was supposed to be a short one, but he brings his hand to the back of my hand, keeping my lips to his. He flips us over so that he hovers over me, "My sneaky little girlfriend," he mumbles against my lips. He pulls back and brushes the hair out of my face. "If you ever want to be on top of me, all you need to do is ask," he smirks down at me.

I slap his chest and wiggle my way out from under him. I move to sit on the bed, him following after me. "Are you tired?" he asks as I flop back onto the bed and yawn.

"Just a bit," I look over at the clock and see that it's already 1 in the morning. I sigh, "I should probably get home. I have an early shift tomorrow."

I go to stand up, but Scott wraps his arms around my waist and pulls me to lay down with him.

"Scotttt," I groan as he sets me on my back and lays right on top of me. I try to wiggle out, but he isn't haven't it. "You're going to suffocate me," I push at him to get off.

"Shhhh. Go to sleep Books," he stuffs his head into the crook of my neck and gives me a soft kiss.

"How am I supposed to sleep when you're on top of me. You weight like a million pounds!"

"Rude," he shifts so that our legs are tangled and he's still on top of me, but his weight is more on the bed.

"I need to get going. Get off so I can call an Uber," I push again.

He props up on his elbow to look down at me and I take the opportunity to roll out from under him, "Aha, you can't beat my ninja moves," I stay sitting on the bed across from Scott.

"You seriously need to get the word Uber out of your vocabulary. I'm not letting you get into a stranger's car when I'm perfectly capable of driving you."

"Good, get dressed then," I take his shirt off and throw it at him as I stand up to find my bra.

His eyes shoot to my chest and he pokes the inside of his poke with his tongue, "If I knew you'd take the shirt off, I would've agreed a long time ago."

"Don't get too excited," I tell him as I clip my bra back on. He groans and throws his head back onto the bed.

"I swear you're going to be the death of me."

He jumps off the bed and reaches for my waist again, "Haha sneak attack. You're no match for *my* ninja skills," Scott exclaims as he keeps me pinned to his chest.

"I don't want to be tired at work tomorrow," I explain.

"Sleep here. Problem solved."

"I have nothing to wear and I don't want to get up extra early to drive back home to get ready."

"This really wouldn't be an issue if you just moved some of your clothes into my room. I'll clear out a drawer for you."

My eyes widen, "Don't freak out Books, I'm not asking you to move in. Just keep an overnight bag here so that you can stay the night," he pauses. "However, we most certainly can live together if you'd like. There haven't been many nights where we aren't sleeping in the same bed since we've started dating."

"We can put overnight bags in each other's place. Butttt, I don't have an overnight bag right now. Therefore, I do need to go home."

"Just wear one of my shirts tomorrow," his bottom lip juts out.

"Stop pouting and let me go."

He cups the back of my neck and brings my lips down to meet his. Then pulls back by a fraction and mumbles, "I don't pout."

I laugh against his lips, "Oh yes you do. You totally pout."

"I wouldn't pout if my girlfriend stayed the night. You're so mean."

"Oh my gosh you are such a drama queen."

"It's your fault."

"How is it my fault?"

"I don't know. I think you drugged me or something. I'm addicted to you. I always have to have a fix," I hum and he adds, "Do you really want to leave me?"

"Of course not, but I have to be responsible."

He flips us over and starts leaving slow kisses on my neck, "Just for tonight. I promise I'll get you to work on time," he says between kisses. How in the world am I supposed to say no when he's gets me all flustered like this?

"Just for tonight," I cave. "And we are going straight to bed."

He unstuffs his face from my neck and gives me a salute with the dopiest grin on his face, "Yes ma'am." He pecks my lips, "I just want to wake up next to you." My heart melts.

~

"I can make them really fast. You should

really eat something before your shift Ry," my alarm went off a couple minutes ago and we're laying in bed until I absolutely need to get up.

And Scott is already trying to convince me to stay longer. "I'll be late. Speaking off, I do need to get ready. Will you find me your smallest shirt? I don't want to wear my dirty one."

I try to get up, but he wraps his arms around my waist to keep me to his chest, "5 more minutes."

I wiggle out and stand up, "I can't be late, and I have to make myself look presentable and not like I just got sexed last night."

Scott gives me a smirk, "But you totally got sexed… by me."

"Yes, and it was great. And as much as I want to stay for those pancakes, I hate not being one time. Plus, you have practice in a couple hours."

"I guess," he grumbles. "What time's your lunch break?"

"2. But I only have an hour, so I'll probably just stay there for it."

"What will you eat then? You have no lunch packed and I don't have much to give you from here."

"I'm sure I'll figure something out," he hands me his shirt and I strip off the one I have on to replace it with the clean one.

"You don't have to worry about it. I'll bring you something."

"That's during your gym time," I have his entire schedule memorized.

"I'll just switch my gym time to later tonight. Can't have my girl being hungry, now can I?" I pull my pants up my legs. He grabs the loop of them and pulls me to him.

"Any requests?" he asks as he looks down to zip and button them for me before settling his hands on my hips.

Naturally, I wrap my arms around his neck, "You don't have to do that."

He leans down and kisses me, then pulls back and rests his forehead against mine. "I know I don't have to, but I want to."

I rise to my toes to press my lips to his, "Burritos would be good," I pull back and start moving around the room to pack up my things.

CHAPTER 66: SCOTT

"The Bruins want to set up a meeting of sorts with you. The manager of the team personally wants to give you a tour of their stadium. And the coach is inviting you to a private practice with the team," Coach Michaels explains to me after practice.

"Didn't I tell you that I want to play for the Sharks?" I haven't really even thought about the Bruins since Rydell became my girlfriend.

"Yes," he pauses as he scratches his beard. "I know you want to stay close to Rydell. And I'm glad you have her, she's good for you. But, from what it sounds like, the Bruins want you. This isn't really a test to see if you're a good fit, this is them trying to convince you to play for them."

"But I don't want to play for them," I say firmly.

"It doesn't hurt to go. It's not like you're committing to them by going to a practice. Maybe it's good to have them as a back-up of sorts."

"What? You don't think the Sharks will recruit me? Trust me coach," I clap his shoulder, "they'll pick me up when they realize that I want to play for them."

"Well then, I still want you to go for the

experience. You can get a feel for what it's like to play for a professional team, and you can pick up some tricks from them that you can bring back to the team. Who knows, maybe seeing how they work will be beneficial when you play against them with the Sharks."

"The practice is after the Oregon game?"

"Yes, I've already arranged everything with them. Ruddy is also going, they're in need of a new goalie."

"Alright. But I'm only going to get tips for the team. Not because I'm going to play for them."

I make my way through the locker rooms to find Ruddy. "Bruins are recruiting a new goalie this year," I remark as I find him.

"So I've heard. They're also looking are a center."

"So I've heard," I mimic his previous words.

"And you're not going to take it?"

"Nah. I figured I'd get a change of scenery."

"Sure that's the reason?" he smirks at me.

"Oh, that's definitely not the reason. The reason is much prettier and goes by the name Rydell," I don't care how whipped I sound. "Speaking of girls, what's up with you and Sam. The two of you have been looking pretty cozy lately."

"I mean, we've hooked up a few times, but that's all it is. I don't want to jump into a long-term relationship after Serena and Sam is the not the relationship type anyways."

"Yeah, well I wasn't the relationship type and look at me now. The most important thing in my life is my relationship with Books."

"It's different."

"Why?"

"Because it doesn't matter if she wants a relationship or not because I don't. Not after Serena. You know she texted me the other day and said that she missed me and wanted to catch up."

"Please tell me you're not considering it man," Serena broke Max's heart in the worst possible way and I don't want to see him get himself into a toxic situation.

"And if I was? I mean, fuck Scott, I was with her for almost 4 years. I was looking at rings because I was prepared to propose. Those feelings don't just go away."

"Well, they did for her. She fucking cheated on you. Multiple times. With multiple guys. She was never faithful in that relationship."

"It doesn't matter, I still fell in love with her."

"But was she ever really in love with you? Look dude. I love Rydell. With everything I have. Now that I'm with her, and even before I was even with her, I didn't spare another girl a second glance. It would never even cross my mind to," Max looks down and I clap his shoulder. "Listen man, if she loved you, she wouldn't have even thought about cheating. I mean, when you were with her, did you ever think about another girl in a less then friendly way?"

"Of course not."

"See. I don't want to be a dick, but Serena didn't care about you Max. I really don't think that's something you should go back to. Not when I think you could have something good with Sam."

"There's nothing between Sam and I."

"Ok. Fine. Regardless, you should completely burn Serena out of the picture."

He absentmindedly nods his head. "Yeah. Maybe you're right."

"Of course I'm right, I always am. Now," I grab my stuff from my locker, "I have a hungry girlfriend waiting for a burrito. Catch ya later Rudds."

~

I wipe the beans off the corner of Rydell's mouth, almost getting my finger bit off as she goes in for another bite. "Oi, stick to eating the burrito, not my fingers Ry."

She tries to get out a snarky reply, but it all comes out in gibberish since she has food in her mouth. "Alright, try that sentence again. This time, less burrito and more words."

She swallows her food, "I said, you're the one who decided to wipe my mouth while I'm eating. If I had taken one of your fingers off, it would've been your fault."

I roll my eyes. "Next time I'll let you sit there with beans all over your face."

She sticks her tongue out at me before taking another bite. "Did you eat the protein bar I packed for you?" by the pace she's eating at I have a feeling she didn't.

Her nose scrunches up with something of disgust, "I'm sorry, but I almost vomited after one bite. I hate white chocolate, you know that."

"I do, but you can barely even taste it! The almonds cancel it out."

"Oh, I definitely tasted it. It was all I could taste, so I spit it out and threw the rest away."

"Hasn't anyone ever told you that spitters are for quitters Ry?" I wiggle my eyebrows at her.

She slaps my arm, "You have the dirtiest

mind."

Rydell and I are sitting at the picnic table in the backyard of the orphanage. Most of the girls aren't back from school yet, and the ones that are, are doing activity with the other employees inside.

I wrap my arm around Rydell's shoulder loosely and lean my head down to bite her earlobe and whisper to her, "I could tell you just how dirty my mind is Rydell. After all, you're involved in all the dirty things I think about."

I draw back to see the red flush that spots her cheeks and smile at her reaction.

"Keep it in your pants Prescott. There are children near."

I chuckle and move to finish my burrito.

"Yeah yeah. I'll save it for later," I tell her suggestively as I drop a kiss to the nape of her neck. "You'll never guess what Ruddy told me earlier."

"What did Max tell you earlier?"

"That Serena texted him saying that she missed him and that they should catch up," I've filled Rydell in on the whole Max and Serena situation. She even gave him advice over it. Really good advice that helped him a lot, considering she also went through a rough breakup.

"Shut that front door. He's not considering it is he?" she asks as her takes the last bite of her burrito and lets her head fall to rest on my shoulder.

"I think he is. I tried my best to help him realize that it's a bad idea, but at the end of the day, he's the one who has to make that decision."

"I guess. Fuck. I wonder if Sam knows."

"Is she still in denial about her feelings for him?"

"No," she gazes up at me with those pretty

hazel eyes. "This goes to the grave with you and I will deprive you of sex for a month if you tell anyone I told you this."

"We both know you wouldn't be able to last that long," I give her a short kiss to the lip. "You know I won't tell anyone so go on with it."

"Sam likes him. A lot. Like wants a full-on relationship with him. She said she doesn't think it was ever just a hook up. That as soon as she first met him at that party, her hookup streak was over. You know she hasn't had sex with anyone other than him since the field trip?"

"Ya, you told me. Honestly that doesn't surprise me. Now Rudds needs to get his head out of his ass and realize that he likes Sam back."

"Mmhmm," she agrees. "We really can't talk though. It took us a while to get our shit together. We were both stupidly oblivious to the other's feelings."

"Yeah, we were. But I never doubted or tried to hide how I felt about you," I grab her chin to bring her face closer to mine. "I don't think I really believed in love at first sight, but when I think back, I can't really remember a moment of knowing you when I wasn't in love. I probably should've just flat out told you when I realized what I was feeling."

"Yeah, I probably should've done the same. But I guess the only thing that matters is we got there, eventually right? Might've been weird for us to confess our love for each other within a month of meeting."

"Mmm," I hum as I connect our lips. She pulls back suddenly, "Oh! I forgot to tell you, Savannah's water broke, she should be delivering baby Olivia anytime now!" she exclaims.

"That's great! Scale of 1-10 how badly is Chris freaking out?" last time I talked to Chris on Facetime with Rydell, he was a mess about the situation. As a paramedic, he's seen pregnancies go very wrong and he's worried of anything happening to Savannah or the baby.

"He's losing his mind, but I think he's also really excited. I can't wait to see her over Christmas break. We can babysit her so that they can take a break!" She talks about me in terms of her future and my heart flips with happiness.

"You want me to go back with you for Christmas break?"

"Of course, I do. I thought that was a given. Mom's already told me she got you a stocking with your name on it."

Holy shit. "Really?" it comes out as close to a whisper.

"Really. You're practically a member of the Rivens family now. I hope you're ok with that because I don't think any of them are going to let you leave willingly. Myself included."

I have never been so happy in my entire life. I'm a part of a family. A family who wants to spend Christmas with me. A family who teaches me to surf and gets me a stocking with my name on it. A real family. Rydell's family. "I am more than ok with it," I frame her face with my hand and connect our lips. She's the best thing that has ever happened to me. Just as I go to progress the kiss, the alarm on her phone goes off.

"Duty calls," she gets up from the bench ignoring my silent protest. "Come on Scotty, you'll be late for class."

"Not like I'd miss much. We learn

practically the same exact thing in every upper div business class. It's fucking boring," we walk back inside and to the front door.

"Maybe. But unfortunately for you, attendance is a part of your grade," she walks me to my car.

"Alright smarty pants girlfriend of mine at least give me a kiss goodbye," I tug the hem of her jacket to pull her to me. She immediately wraps her arms around my neck and stands on her tippy toes, pulling me down for a sweet kiss. Her lips feel slightly cold against mine and I hope my kiss is warming her up a bit. I put my mittened hands on her waist, keeping her flush against me as I relish in the feeling of her lips against mine. She tastes like burrito and strawberry. Never thought I would love the tastes of such a weird food combination. When we pull back for air, I move to bite her earlobe, "I love you," I tell her softly.

She looks up at me with a dimpled smile, "I love you too."

CHAPTER 67: *RYDELL*

"He's going to grab fucking coffee with her," Sam throws herself onto my bed.

"Excuse me?" I say as I look up from my book.

"Max. He's going to get coffee with his ex. He said he's not getting back together with her; he just needs closure. But she seems like a manipulative bitch," she turns her head to look at me so that her cheek is resting against my comforter. "What if she convinces him to get back together with her?"

"Then he really needs to see a therapist because that sounds like a highly sadistic thing of him to do."

"Ughhh," she groans as she looks back up to the ceiling and covers her face with her hands. "I was about to ask him to be my date for the gala. I was going to ask him to come to New York with us. I'm so fucking stupid."

"You're not stupid. But you are crushing very hard. Trust me. Tell him your feelings sooner rather than later. I speak from experience."

She breathes deeply, "Yeah. I will after I see what he does with this situation."

"Fair enough."

"Have you asked Scott to be your date to the gala yet?"

"Not yet. But he might come over later. I'll ask him then," my phone starts to ring, and I grab for it as Sam leaves the room.

It's Chris on Facetime. I answer right away, and the screen fills with the face of the most precious baby. My eyes start to water instantly. "Oh my gosh," I gasp. "She's so beautiful."

"Auntie Ryles, meet Olivia Del Rivens."

I don't bother to wipe the tears that are streaming down my face, "Her middle name is Del?" I choke out.

"Mhmm. After her aunt and hopefully godmother. What do you say Ryles, you up for the task?"

"You want me to be her godmother?" I am ugly crying so hard right now.

"There's no one I'd trust more with my daughter. And once you marry Scott, he can be godfather. You have to marry him first though," he says.

"Of course, I'll be her godmother. Don't tell Scott about godfather yet though, wouldn't want to scare him away," I wipe my face. "Let me talk to Savannah."

I'm met with a very tired looking sister-in-law. "Hey mamas. How ya feeling?"

"Tired. Like I just shoved a watermelon out of my cooter. Little sucker took her time coming out."

"Stubborn, just like her mama," I say. We always joke around at the fact that Savannah rejected Chris's advances like 5 times before she said yes.

She laughs softly. I can see the tiredness laced on her face. "Well, I'm excited for her godmother to meet her in person. Christmas break is just in a couple weeks right?"

"Mhmm, I come out practically right when I get back from New York. I'm gonna spoil the shit out of that baby."

"Mmm, she's gonna love you Ryles."

"I promise, I'll be the best godmother. Well, I won't bother you guys any longer. Go enjoy some alone family time and get some rest."

The phone pans back to Chris with Olivia snuggled in his arms, "We love you Rydell. See you in a couple weeks."

"I love you guys too. Send me pictures so I can show Scott!"

I hang up the phone and wipe away the remaining tears from my eyes. My eyes shoot up to the door as I hear it open. Scott crosses the room with Olympic speed when he sees my tear-stained face.

He stands at the edge of the bed and cups my cheeks in his large hands, tilting my face up, "What's the matter gorgeous? Who made you cry because I'll give them a piece of my fucking mind?"

"Well unless you feel like threatening Chris, Savannah and their new baby that really isn't necessary. Olivia was born. Her middle name is Del and I'm her godmother."

His worried expression is replaced with a bright grin. "That's great Books. So happy tears then?"

"Yes, very happy tears," he leans down for a kiss as I say it. When he tries to further it, I push at his chest. "You're not getting on my bed. You just got back from the gym and are gross and sweaty."

"Oh ya. It was actually a part of my master plan."

"Your master plan?"

"Mhmm," he grabs my hands and lifts me off my bed, wrapping his arms around my waist. "I would go to the gym, come straight here, with an overnight bag, and convince you to shower with me."

I tilt my head back on laugh, then bring my eyes back to his, "And what makes you think I want to shower with you?" I question.

His hands move down to squeeze my ass as his head moves to my neck to press wet kisses there, between them he says, "We both know you want to shower with me Books."

I definitely want to shower with him, "Well, I do feel a little dirty," he lifts his head out of my neck and smirks down at me.

"Oh, you're super dirty. It's ok though, I'll help clean you up," he grabs the hem of my shirt and lifts it over my head as he pushes me back towards my bathroom.

When we make it in, he locks the door behind us and moves to turn the water on. Once he does, he immediately makes his way back towards me, taking his shirt off in the process.

"Pants?" I question.

"Pants," he responds. As if we are on the same wavelength, we both rush to get out of the pants that we have on so that we are left in our underwear. Only my pants get stuck on my ankle and I start going down.

Before I can totally face plant, Scott grabs my upper bicep and to keep me up right.

"So much for being sexy," I groan.

"Oh, I thought it was so sexy," I can feel the smile on Scott's face as he kisses me. "Everything about you turns me on Ry, even when you almost eat it," he says against my lips.

He unclips my bra strategically and moves his fingers to slowly pull the straps down my shoulders until it hits the floor.

He puts his knuckles under my chin to tilt my face up, "This is ok right? If you want to stop, we can."

I move my hands to the band of his boxers and push them down. When they hit the floor, he steps out of them and I take my hand and start stroking up and down his length. A throaty groan comes out of him as he drops his head to my shoulder.

"I definitely don't want to stop."

He moves his head up to bite my earlobe and whispers, "So dirty," into my ear as he pulls down my panties and grabs my waist to back us into the shower.

Closing the shower curtain behind us, he positions me right under the showerhead and I am instantly meet with the warmth of the water. The water falling down my shoulders, mixed with the feeling of Scott in my hand and his lips on my neck is overwhelming. I feel myself start to get wet, and not because of the water that's currently running down on me.

"Scott, I need you inside of me," I wrap my arms around his neck and push myself further against him so that my core is pressed against his hard on. I mean it really didn't take much for me to get him there. A few strokes with my hand and he was ready to go.

"You're sure?" he asks me once again.

"Positive," I respond as I smash my lips into his. He responds immediately and walks me so that my back hits the tile of the shower walls. I flinch slightly at the cold sensation.

Scott's hands are all over me. They slide over my shoulders, trace over my collarbone, massage my breasts, soothe over my stomach, rest on my hips and finally reach to cup the back on my thighs, "Jump," he mumbles against my lips.

I do as he says and wrap my legs around his waist as he pushes me further into the wall. He starts kissing down my neck and moves one hand down to line himself up. Before he enters, he pulls back slightly, "Fuck. Let me go grab a condom."

"I'm on birth control. I trust that you'll pull out though before, ya know."

"Are you sure?"

I hum a yes against his lips as I kiss them, then reach my hand down to stroke his cock a couple times before lining it back up. "As long as you're ok with it," I tell him between kisses.

Without another word he buries himself all the way in and we both gasp at the feeling. His long fingers dig into the flesh under my thighs as his head falls into the crook of my neck.

He sets a slow, tormenting pace coming practically all the way out before thrusting all the way back in. My head drops to the side as he kisses the tender skin right under my ear. One hand stays gripped to my thigh as the other travels up my stomach and ribs before landing right under my breast to cup the underside of it.

I let out an unvoluntary moan and at the

sound, his speed starts to pick up and I about lose my mind when his thumb moves to press down against my nipple. "Fuck," I breathe out.

As if my word caught his attention, he lifts his head up and smashes his lips into mine and are mouths slide against one another in a wet, passionate kiss.

My back arches so that my body is less on the shower wall, and Scott and I are chest to chest as he rhythmically moves inside me. "I love the way I fit inside of you," he whispers in my ear. I can barely hear him say it over the sound of the water falling, but I hear it, and it nearly drives me over the edge.

He lowers me so that one of my legs in on the shower floor but keeps the other one hitched up with the support of his hand under my thigh. "I love the way you fit inside me too," I whisper back.

His head leans back down and he licks and nips at my jaw, neck, and collarbone as he whispers sweet nothings that make my heart explode.

Ever since I started dating Scott, my heart has felt so full. Like it finally isn't broken, and somehow he helped me pick up the pieces and fix it.

As I feel him start to pulse inside me, I think back to the time when I thought I'd never be at this point. When anything related to sex scared me. When I thought it was my fault that I couldn't find pleasure in being intimate with a person.

With Scott, I'm starting to learn that it wasn't my fault. That I just needed the right person to come into my life. That I just needed Scott.

My walls clench around his throbbing dick and I drop my head against the cool tiles as I feel my release. Not soon after, Scott pulls out and strokes himself a couple more times before releasing himself.

He braces one hand on the shower wall with his head hung down. I walk the short distance and duck under his arm so that I stand in front of him. As soon as he looks up, I give his lips a quick peck. His lips follow after mine as soon as I pull back and he connects us back together for a slow kiss.

You would think that Scott would be fast and rough when it comes to sex, but he's so gentle. His kisses are soft and heartwarming. And he takes things slow, like he doesn't want it to ever end.

When he pulls back, he stays close, pressing his eyebrows against mine. Wordlessly, he tugs on my hand and places me under the water. The goosebumps that were spotting my body start to fade away as the warmth cascades down my shoulders. I close my eyes and tilt my head up, feeling in a state of complete relaxation.

My eyes open when Scott pulls me slightly out of the water and starts massaging shampoo into my hair. "So, this is why you always smell so good. I thought it was a perfume or something, but it's your shampoo."

I can barely hum out a response because the feeling of his fingers working their way around my scalp puts me into a trance.

When his hands leave my hair, I sigh at the feeling of lost contact, which causes him to chuckle a bit. "Close your eyes," he tells me as he puts me back under the water to rise.

Now that the shampoo is out of my hair, he grabs my hand, pours shampoo in it, and leans his head down, prompting me to wash is hair for him.

I smile at his actions and raise my hands to massage his scalp with the shampoo. I have to slightly rise to my toes because he towers over me. As I wash his hair for him, he sets his hands on my hips and pulls me closer to him.

"You're gonna smell like me," I tell him.

"I sure hope so," he says back while placing a small kiss to the nape of my neck.

"Ok, rinse," I swap spots with him so he's under the water and move to put conditioner in my hair, tying my hair into a low bun when I'm done to let it sit while I was my body.

"Wait, no. That's my job," Scott takes the loofa out of my hands and starts washing my body for me. He glides the soap over my shoulders, my arms, down my stomach and back. He gets cheeky and lifts my arms up to wash my armpits which makes me laugh.

And then he kneels in front of me and I almost pass out when he starts cleaning my legs. We keep eye contact when kisses the inside of my calf and lifts himself back up. He places a quick kiss to my lips as he starts washing his own body.

"Do you want conditioner?" I ask him.

"Did you use it?"

"Yes," I laugh.

"Then yes I want some too," he says, and I pour some on my hands and spread it through his hair.

Once the conditioner is out of both our hair and we are sufficiently clean, I shut the water off and move to grab towels from under the sink.

When I feel dry enough, I wrap my towel around my body and look back at Scott, who's been standing there watching me. His towel is wrapped low on his waist and his v line looks so fucking sexy.

Seriously, man's is built. God clearly has his

favorites, and Prescott Bridges is one of them.

"Wipe the drool Books," Scott smirks at me.

"Prescott. You're my boyfriend. I'm allowed to shamelessly check you out."

He puts his hands up in surrender, "Maybe you should take a picture. Save it for your spank bank."

"Good idea! Stay right there," I run to my room to grab my Polaroid and come back to Scott in the same position.

I catch him off guard and snap a pic of him when he smiles at me running back in the bathroom. "No fair! I would've flexed a bit more," he whines.

"Candid is so much better," I shake the polaroid a bit and watch it develop. I probably look like a crazy person staring down at it with a gigantic smile of my face.

"Take one of us together," Scott says as he comes to stand beside me.

I smile up at him and he leans down to kiss my dimple.

Turning around, I position myself so that my back is rested against Scott's chest, and he doesn't hesitate to wrap his arms around me from behind. My towel is a real one for staying up so well.

I raise the Polaroid and tilt my head up in a border line Facebook mom way and smile. Before I snap the shot, Scott leans in to kiss my cheek. He's so sweet.

I look down at the Polaroid now that it's fully developed and smile at how cute it is. I hand it to Scott so he can see. "Can I keep it?" he asks as he looks up at me.

"Yes. But we have to take another one so that I can have one."

"Deal. I'll take it this time," he grabs the polaroid out of my hand and lifts it to snap the shot.

I wrap my arms around his neck and press my lips to his cheek this time as he smiles at the camera.

CHAPTER 68: SCOTT

I twirl a strand of Rydell's hair between my fingers as her head rests on my chest. After changing into our pjs, well sort of pjs. Rydell's in my shirt and I'm in my boxers. We went to bed and Rydell wanted me to listen to a new artist she found, so she shuffled their songs.

"They're good right?" she lifts her head to look up at me.

"Ya. I think I like Only to Live in Your Memories best," I tell her as I drop a kiss to her forehead.

She grins at me, "That one's my favorite too. I'm gonna play it again!" she goes to grab her phone from the side of her and sits up criss cross. I lay there and watch her.

"Hey," she looks away from her phone and at me, prompting me to continue. "I love you."

She smiles that dimpled smile that melts my heart and throws herself on top of me, squishing both of my cheeks together and peppering kisses all over me face. My arms wrap around her waist to keep her flush against me.

She bites my earlobe, "I love you too." That's our thing now. We have a thing. Biting the other one's earlobe is like a silent way to say I love you. We probably look like weirdos because I've found that we do it everywhere, all the time. In the grocery store, when we hang out with friends, literally everywhere.

She sets her hands on my chest and drops her chin to them, gazing up at me with those pretty hazel eyes. "So. For the gala next week, they said we could bring a date with no expense. You don't have to come if you don't want to, but there's no one I'd rather have by my side. Plus, we get a couple of days before and after to explore New York when we aren't in meetings. It might be fun to do that together."

Fuck. I want to give Rydell everything she wants. I never want to say no because I always want to make her happy. But I'll be in Oregon for hockey. And as much as I want to skip the game to be there with her, I can't. Especially since the Sharks will be scouting at this game.

"Rydell, you know I'd be there in a heartbeat. But I'll be in Oregon for hockey for most of that week. But the gala's on Saturday? Are games on Friday, so maybe I can try to convince the coaches to let me leave on my own a little early-"

She cuts me off with a peck to the lips, "It's ok Scotty. I knew it was a long shot asking considering your schedule, but I thought I'd ask anyways."

"Rydell," I start.

She looks at me with a smile. There's a dimple, so I know it's a real one. "Scott. I promise you it's not a big deal at all. I will however expect you to answer my Facetime calls so that I can show you all the cool things I see."

"I really want to be there with you," I raise my hand to cup her cheek.

"I know you do. But, this might be for the best because Sam doesn't have a date either and she might have felt left out if you came."

"I guess," I mumble. "This will be the longest we've gone without seeing each other since we started dating."

Her cheek moves to rest against my chest so that her ear is right over the point where my heart beats. My hands move under the shirt she's wearing to give her back scratches.

"Yeah," she sighs. "But after that, we get to go to California together for Christmas break and that will be fun."

My parents found out that I'd be in California for break and invited me and Rydell to their cabin in Mammoth to ski for a couple of days. They said my grandparents also want to meet her and that they are planning a dinner. This is the first time that they've actually wanted to do something for the holidays since I've moved out and I don't know how to feel about it.

On one hand I'm thinking it might be nice to see them and try to form a better connection with them. Plus, I'd get to see Penelope. On the other hand, I don't want them to do anything to make Rydell nervous and I think the main reason I got this invite was so that they can try to convince me to be with someone else.

Not that I'm worried about them pulling Rydell and I apart, because there's absolutely nothing that can take me away from Rydell. That girl is permanently etched in my heart. There's no getting rid of her.

"I'm excited to see how the Rivens celebrate Christmas. And I'm even more excited to be a part of it," I pause. "How would you feel about meeting my family?"

Her head shoots up and she braces her hands on both sides of my head, hovering over me. "Your family?"

"My parents, grandparents, and Pen will be in Mammoth during the time we'll be out and want us to come up for a couple of days to go skiing."

There's a little worry in her face, "I don't know how to ski. I only know how to snowboard," she says.

I laugh a little to ease the tension, "Rydell, you're allowed to snowboard. You don't have to ski."

"Won't it be weird if I'm the only one snowboarding?"

"No. But if you want, I'll buy a snowboard and ditch the skis."

"But you don't know how to snowboard."

"You can teach me. However, you're a horrible teacher. You'd just laugh at me the whole time."

"Probably," I love that she doesn't even deny it.

"You don't have to buy a snowboard, but I refuse to put skis on. I hope your parents are ok with that."

She put her head back down on my chest. "Should I bring anything else besides my snowboard. Oh my gosh. What should I wear? Should I buy new clothes? Do you think they'll like me?"

"Of course they'll like you. Anyone who

doesn't like you should be put into a mental hospital. And if they don't like you, it really doesn't fucking matter. Because I love you and that's the only thing that's important. I know for a fact that Pen already loves you though from what I've told her about you."

"You told your sister about me?" I can feel her smile on my chest.

"Yeah. She thinks you're perfect for me."

"Well, I'm glad I'll at least have one person rooting for me," she shifts her body so that she's on the bed but stays curled into my side.

"If they say one bad thing about you, we'll leave right away. I won't sit there and let them make you feel uncomfortable."

"I don't want to be the reason why you miss out on family time."

"I get all the family time I need when I'm with you and the rest of the Rivens. Pen's the only one I want to see and if it comes to it, I'll just set up a different time to catch up with her."

"You don't have to leave just because I feel uncomfortable. Plus, Penelope is more than welcome to come over to my family's house if you want to see her more."

"I'll keep that in mind. But I promise, whatever my family thinks of you doesn't reflect my feelings, nor will it change my feelings at all," I reassure her. "I just want them to at least meet you. And for once, they seem interested in my life and like they might be excited to meet you."

"Of course I want to meet your family Scott. Just tell me the days and I'll be there," she fiddles with the best friend's necklace that is wrapped around my neck.

CHAPTER 69: *RYDELL*

"Please call me when you land so I know you got there ok," Scott says as he sets my backpack down next to me.

"I'm going to go the bathroom before we go through security," Sam announces as she gives Scott and I some space to say goodbye.

"I will," I raise to my toes and wrap my arms around his neck using one hand to brush the hair at the base of his head.

He wraps his arms around my waist and pulls me as close as possible, stuffing his face in my neck. He takes a big whiff like the perv he is before placing a sweet kiss and lifting his head up to set his forehead to mine.

"I don't want you to leave," he whispers.

"You act like we'll be apart for months. It's only 4 days Scotty," I nudge my nose to his.

"4 days too many," he groans. "I don't know how I'm going to fall asleep without you next to me. I mean Tuesday was torture and that was only one night."

Scott and I have been fluctuating between staying nights at the other's place. There have only been a couple nights when we didn't share a bed and each time Scott makes sure I know he's upset about it.

"Just grab a pillow and pretend it's me," I tease him.

"It's not the sameeee," he pouts.

"So dramatic," I mumble against his lips as I lift myself to kiss him.

"You're acting so calm about this. Aren't you gonna miss me?" he whines.

"Of course I'm going to miss you. But it's not like we won't be in contact with each other. I'm going to call you every day, probably more than once. And, again, it's only 4 days."

"You better call me, and text me, and snapchat me, and send me all the videos that you like on Tiktok," he leans down to press his mouth to mine in a long, sweet kiss. Then starts peppering kisses all over my face, neck, and collarbone causing me to giggle a little.

He bites my earlobe like I knew he would and whispers, "I love you so fucking much Books."

From over Scott's shoulder, I can see Sam walking back over. I divert my attention back to my clingy boyfriend, "I love you too. So much," pressing one final kiss to his lips, I detach myself from him and grab my backpack.

"Ready?" Sam asks. When I nod my head yes, she says bye to Scott and starts entering security.

"See you in 4 days," I tell Scott and start walking to follow Sam.

Before I can get much further, Scott grabs my wrist, turns me around, placing a hand on my cheek and the other on my waist and smashes our lips together.

"I needed one more," I smile up at him and he kisses my dimple. "I'll let you go now. But just so you know, I really want to throw you over my shoulder and hold you captive in my room."

"There's my little stalker. Alright, love you," I give him on last peck.

"Love you too."

~

This trip is turning into a mess. Two days in and we were late to our first meeting because our taxi driver took the wrong turn, I was pooped on by a pigeon, we missed the ferry and weren't able to see the Statue of Liberty and I really miss Scott.

I mean, we have been talking to each other consistently, but I feel so stressed with everything right now and I just want him here to calm me down. He also does a good job at that. Even over the phone, I find some relief in hearing his voice.

Not to mention, I can barely sleep. Scott seems to be having the same problem. No matter how many pillows I surround myself in, it's not the same as having him right next to me. I'm too cold to sleep and he always keeps me warm.

Tonight, we have the gala and as I sit here getting ready for it, I can't help but feel nervous. We are competing against a couple other people for sponsors and if we don't get enough, our video game might not launch how we want it to.

Tomorrow we finalize our contract, meet with our sponsors and go over a timeline of how things will work. The good thing about Ubisoft is that they are a big company. They have offices everywhere, including one in San Francisco which is only about an hour drive from Santa Cruz.

And the only time we need to be in an office

is when they want to check in on progress and when we start to put the video game out there. Otherwise, we are allowed to just work on it at home since we've decided we don't really need a team to help.

Once the game is on the market, Ubisoft has invited us to work in the office full time, if we want. They said they could use people with 'our talents'. I would work in the coding section, Sam in the graphic design section.

And while that's a great backup, I want to work for Microsoft eventually, so we'll see.

"Did you bring eyeliner?" Sam walks into the bathroom as I curl my hair.

"Yes. It should be in my bag," I point to the makeup bag on the counter.

"I'm not the only one who's nervous, am I?" she asks as she starts applying the eyeliner.

"No. I'm freaking out. I'm sure it'll be fine though. The worst that happens is we don't get the number of sponsors that we want, and the game takes a little longer to get developed."

"I guess. I just want people to like it."

"People already like it. I'm sure the sponsors will too."

She hums in agreement, "If Scott saw you in that dress, he'd lose his mind."

The gala is black and white themed so I when with a long, silk, black dress. "Probably. I wish he was here to see it."

"Have you heard anything about how the game went earlier?"

"Ya they won 2-1. Apparently, Max played really well if that's what you're wondering. Scott said he's been a little out of it with the whole meeting up with his ex-thing, but I assume he pushed it aside for the game. Have you talked to him about that at all?"

"No. And I don't particularly want to. I've been avoiding him."

That makes me frown, "Why?"

"Because," she sighs. "I don't want to sit there when he inevitable tells me that he's in love with her. The further away from him I stay, the quicker me feelings will go away."

"That doesn't seem healthy Sam."

"Maybe. But I can assure you that there will be less heartache this way."

"Somethings are worth the possibility of hurt. Think about how terrified I was that I'd end up unfixable if Scott rejected me. But he felt the same and I've never been happier than I am now that he's my boyfriend."

"Your situation is different though. Scott doesn't have an ex that he still has feelings for."

"Yeah. I guess. But you'll always have a what if with this if you ignore it. At least stop avoiding him. It might be good for the two of you to talk."

"I'll think about it," she responds as she leaves to get dressed.

~

An hour into the event and we already have enough sponsors. I tried to call Scott a couple of times tonight, but he hasn't answered which makes me a little nervous but he's probably out celebrating his win.

The gala still has about 2 hours left and we are meant to stay at it for the entirety, but I'm ready to leave.

My social battery has just about run out. I

charmed the shit out of the sponsors, the alcohol probably helped, and now I'm tired of socializing. But it seems like everyone and their mother wants to talk to me, so here I am, plastering a fake smile on my face and listening to old rich people tell me about their vacation houses in LA.

Whenever I tell people I'm from California, they have something to say about it. "But Malibu is definitely the best beach, don't you agree Rydell?"

I'm pushed out of my thoughts as one of the sponsors catches my attention. "Malibu is very pretty, but Santa Cruz beaches will always be my favorite. I grew up surfing there," I reply with a polite smile.

"Oh, my son Charles always used to beg me for a surfboard when he was younger, isn't that right Charlie?" he nods to his son who is standing next to him. "But I didn't want it to affect his grades. Might have slipped in with the wrong crowd," pretentious asshole.

"And what crowd might that be?" I fire back.

His eyes widen like he realized his mistake, "Ms. Rivens, I didn't mean to insinuate that you're the wrong crowd. If he spent all of his time surfing, he wouldn't have had time to study, and wouldn't have gotten into an Ivy league."

"I surfed practically every day, graduated top of my class, got into one of the best universities in the US for computer science, and know I'm standing in front of you because the video game I'm co-creator of is getting developed."

He's left speechless and red faced. One of his colleagues laughs a little, "She got you there Dave. Ms. Rivens I like your spirit. I think I just decided who we should sponsor. Richard Grant," he sticks his hand out and I shake it. "I work with Dave here as CEO of Golf n' Stuff."

Never in my life would I have thought Golf n' Stuff would sponsor my video game. "Rydell Rivens. Although, I assume you knew that already."

"Yes, your game has been a hot commodity tonight. Targeting children with behavior disabilities is genius."

"Thank you," I look over at Sam who's talking to another group of sponsors with a look like she'd rather be anywhere else.

The conversation goes on as they brag about the success of their company and I smile and nod not really being a huge part of the conversation. When I find an out, I excuse myself to get a drink.

"I've never seen my dad at a loss for words," I turn my head and see Charles walk into step with me to the bar.

"Glad I could put that image into your head," I say and order my drink.

"Charles Mason. But most people call me Charlie," I shake his hand.

"Rydell Rivens. But most people call me Del."

He scoots closer to me and I take a step back. "I don't bite Del."

"I'd sure hope not, you're a 20 something year old, it would be ridiculous if you did."

"Smart and funny," he smirks at me and I internally vomit.

"Smart, funny, and very much taken."

"I don't see a boyfriend around."

"Look again," I hear a familiar voice from behind me.

And there he is. My favorite person on this floating rock we call Earth. And he looks so fucking good. He's wearing a nice suit and his hair is nicely combed back. He has a hard expression on his face when he looks at Charlie, but his eyes soften as he looks down at me.

"Prescott Bridges, how the hell are you here right now?" I cross the distance between us and throw my arms around his neck.

I breathe in deeply to smell is woodsy scent. His arms wrap around my waist to push my closer to him and he stuffs his head in my neck taking a deep breath in through his nose.

He pulls back to rest his forward against mine, squeezing my hips with his hands slightly as he moves them to rest there. He leans down to press his lips to mine, going slow like he wants the moment to last for as long as possible. When we disconnect, his lips linger before he moves back to let his eyes travel up and down my body.

"You look so fucking stunning Books," he looks towards the dance floor then back at me. "Dance with me?"

I smile and nod my head. This is probably the first time tonight that I've smiled because I'm happy and not because it was expected of me. Before we move to dance, he leans down to kiss my dimple and then moves up to bite my earlobe in a silent 'I love you'.

He grabs my hand, pulling me to the dance floor, tugging me into him when we get there. One of his hands in on my waist, one of my hands is on his shoulder and our free hands are connected as he starts to sway us back and forth.

"Wanna try dipping me?" he asks with a

smirk on his face.

My head tilts back as I laugh, "In any other circumstance you know I would."

A squeal passes my lips as he moves his hand down to my thigh and the other to the small of my back, dipping me in surprise. Still in this position he says, "Guess we'll just have to leave it up to me." He snaps me back up into place and slants his lips over mine. Then peppers kisses all over my face.

"I missed you so much Ry."

I wrap both arms around his neck as his move to around my waist and we start swaying again. I don't know if this even qualifies as a dance because we're more focused on wrapping ourselves in each other.

"I missed you too. I was going crazy without you," I look up at him and it's like no one else is in the room with us.

"Glad I'm not the only one. And there you were saying 4 days isn't a long time. It's only been 3 and you're lost without me," he grins.

"Yeah, yeah. Don't let it go to your head," I brush my fingers through the hair on the back of his neck. "Seriously though, how are you here?"

"You sounded stressed after the first day of being here, so I booked a flight for right after my game. With the three-hour difference and having a game in the morning, I was able to play and then leave for the airport with enough time to get here. Sorry I'm a little late, I didn't have time to get ready before leaving."

"You're unbelievable. Did you book a hotel somewhere?"

"Sam stole your extra room key and left it

under a towel in front of your door. I wanted to keep it a surprise."

"Best surprise ever," I mumble against his lips as I kiss him.

"How are you feeling pretty girl? Was that guy over there bothering you, because I'll go talk to him if I need to?"

"I'm feeling better now that you're here. He wasn't bothering me, I'm just tired of talking to so many strangers. They all talk to me like they're better than me, it's exhausting," I stifle a yawn letting the stress of the past three days catch up with my body. I rest my head on his chest letting my eyes rest for a second.

"I can imagine. Did anyone say anything to make you upset. Point them out and I'll sort it out."

"No one said anything mean. I just have a different mindset then most the people here I guess."

"How is it going in terms of sponsors."

I lift my head back up and give him a genuine smile, "We already have more than enough."

"That's my girl," he presses a quick peck to my lips. "See. I told you you had nothing to worry about."

"You did," I look around the room and sigh. "I still have like an hour until I'm allowed to leave, if you get bored you don't have to stay."

Scott shakes his head, "I'm never bored when I'm with you," god, he is so perfect.

CHAPTER 70: SCOTT

Rydell is finally allowed to leave the gala and I'm taking my girl straight to bed. She was 2 seconds away from drooling on my jacket as we sat and watched everything around us with her head on my shoulder.

She looks exhausted. I think the exhaustion of socially interacting in a high stress environment is catching up to her. Rydell is not a shy person by any means, but after a while she needs some time to recharge her battery. And her battery has long been run out.

As she moves to open the door to her room, I stand behind her with my hands on her hips, brushing the hair off her shoulder and placing a kiss to her bare skin.

When we get in, Rydell plops onto the bed so that her face is squished into the pillow. I move to the bathroom and find her makeup wipes before moving to join her.

"Roll over," she does as I tell her to and looks at me with a confused expression as I start wiping at her face.

"What are you doing?" she questions.

"Helping you get ready for bed," I say it like

it's the most obvious thing.

"I feel bad that you came all this way just to go to a boring gala and sleep. I'm not that tired Scotty," she sits up and climbs over to kiss me. I can tell that she's trying to make it as passionate as she can, but I can feel the tiredness in it.

I hold onto her shoulders and pull back, taking in the bags under her eyes now that I've wiped some of her makeup off. "Baby, you're tired. And you really shouldn't feel bad. I'm just happy to be near you again."

She scoots closer to me and cups my jaw with her cold hands, "I just don't want you to get bored with me. Really, I can stay up for a couple more hours," she moves her fingers to start unbuttoning my shirt. I already took me jacket off when we first came in.

I grab her wrists, "I hate that you think I'd ever get bored off the girl I'm in love with. I hate that you were hurt in the past to think that you have to have sex with me to keep me around," she sits back on her knees and looks down. I immediately put my knuckles under her chin to force her to look at me.

Moving so that I'm more on the bed I set my brow to hers. "We are going to go to sleep, and when I wake up in the morning, I'm still going to want to be with you. I'm always going to want to be with you Books."

"I know. And I'm sorry. I'm really trying, it's just hard for me because of-"

"You don't need to apologize. I know you're trying. I'll never be mad at you for being worried Rydell, I know where it comes from. As long as you don't leave me, we won't have a problem."

"I'd never leave you," I press my lips to hers in a soft kiss at the comfort of her words.

"Good. Now let's get some sleep. You're not the only one who's tired."

I pick up the wipe and continue cleaning her face. She closes her eyes and lets me. When I think it's good enough, I scoop under her legs and place her so that her feet dangle off the side of the bed. I kneel down and start to unclip her heels, feeling the smoothness of her legs.

When both heels hit the floor, I press a kiss to the inside of her calf before standing up and grabbing her hands to have her stand with me.

I intertwine our fingers and walk us to the bathroom finding our toothbrushes and getting them ready. Ever since our first time brushing our teeth together, it's become the same routine. Rydell stands in front of me, her back and head resting against my chest, my arm wrapped around her middle to keep her close to me, watching each other brush our teeth through the mirror.

Rydell shifts her free hand arm to link with mine that's wrapped around her, slowly drawing circles to the top of my hand with her thumb.

When she's done rinsing her mouth, she moves out of the room as I rush to rinse mine.

Walking into the room, I sit on the edge of the bed, uncuffing my sleeves as I watch Rydell grab my shirt out of her bag. My shirt that was in the overnight bag at her apartment. Sneaky little thing. "Nice shirt," I tell her as she walks towards me, shirt in hand.

"Yours are more comfortable than mine," she turns around and looks over her shoulder, "will you unzip me?"

Rolling my sleeves up a bit, I stand to tower over her raising my hand to the top of her zipper, letting it unravel slowly as I brush my fingers against her bare skin. With the zipper all the way down, I move my hands back up and shift the straps of her dress down her shoulders.

As her dress pools at her feet, I wrap my arms around her from behind and take in the softness of her skin. She wasn't wearing a bra, leaving me blessed with a view of her perfect body.

"I said unzip my dress, not take it off you little perv," she tries to pull away, clutching my shirt to her chest. I keep my grip tight around her, not letting go.

Kissing the nape of her neck I mumble in her skin, "You're so fucking perfect Ry."

I look up to take in her side profile before she shifts her face towards mine with a dimpled smile. I kiss the dimple because I can't help it.

Turing her around him my arms, I take the shirt and pull it over her head, helping her puts her arms through the holes.

"Looks better on you anyways," I tell her.

She starts slowly unbuttoning my shirt, eyes fixated on my abs. And she calls me the perv. Pulling the shirt all the way off, she stands on her tippy toes and places a kiss on the right side of my chest, in the spot where you'd expect my heart to be.

I take my pants off, leaving myself in my boxer before Rydell and I get in the bed to get the sleep that I think we both desperately need.

Once settled under the covers I grab her thigh to wrap around my hip, trailing my hand up and down, as she scoots in to let her head fall of my chest. I feel her rub circles on the bare side of my torso where her arm is wrapped, and I finally feel like I can get some solid tonight.

"Will you tell me about your game before we fall asleep?" I have found that Rydell finds comfort in hearing me talk about my day. Most times before we fall asleep, she asks me to tell her all the details, claiming that she likes the sound of my voice.

So, I lay there with her recollecting the play by play of the game to her. When I've finished up with the last bit, I brush her hair back to see her almost completely asleep face. She always tries to stay up for the entirety no matter how tired she is and the fact that she cares that much about something as simple as my day makes my heart dance a little.

"Go to sleep baby," I mumble against her forehead as I press my lips there.

CHAPTER 71: RYDELL

Christmas break has finally commenced and that's how I find myself in the freezing ocean water with Andy.

"When does Scott come out again?" Andy asks as she lays back on her board soaking in the sun.

"Tomorrow. He wanted to get a flight for directly after his game today, but I told him he should rest for a bit."

She shifts her head to look at me, "How are you feeling about meeting his family?"

"Really fucking nervous. I mean, up until me, he was planning on letting his parents choose a girl for him to marry. He was going to marry someone he didn't love and run a company that would make him miserable to please them. I guess I'm scared that they blame me for his sudden change."

"Well, you kind of are to blame," I go to protest but she adds, "Not that it's a bad thing. I think you've saved him. Superhero Rydell."

"Or villain Rydell, in their eyes," I mumble.

"Oh yeah, that's so much better. Villain Rydell: stealing the hearts of popular hockey boys."

I laugh a little before getting serious again, "I just want them to like me."

"If they don't, you know that doesn't reflect you, right Ryles?"

"I guess. It's just… he grew up with a strain in familial relationships. He never had it like us. A good support system, family game nights, eating meals together. And now, they seem like they genuinely want to see him and know about his life. I don't want to be the one to mess that up."

"And if they're showing interest to try and break you up? To get him back on his path before you?"

"Well, I'm not going to sit there and be ok with that and neither will Scott. I'm not worried about losing him. I'm worried about him missing the chance to get close to his family."

"That's not a pressure you should be putting on yourself Ryles. Whether or not that family strengthens is up to his parents, not you."

"You're right," I sigh.

"I always am," she smirks at me.

"Alright, enough about my love life. What's going on with you and David."

"Who says David is my love life?" I give her a knowing look.

"I used to be the same way with Scott. I tried so hard to convince myself that we were just friends. Now look at me, I've never been happier."

Andy lets out a breath, "What if I tell him how I feel and I ruin everything? I'm not willing to lose him."

"But what if he has that same mindset? Think about it Andy. He's never dated anyone, he asks you to all the school dances, he gets upset when you talk about other guys. He clearly feels the same way."

"It's so awkward though. What am I supposed to do, go up to him and kiss him? Tell him straight up that I'm in love with him?"

"Yes," I deadpan. "I was the one to kiss Scott first. I got tired of dancing around my feelings, sat on his lap and planted one on him," I think about how his shock freaked me out and how scared I was. But it all turned out well in the end.

"I'm not that bold Ryles," she says with widened eyes.

"You think I'm that bold?" I laugh. "I'm definitely not that bold, but some things are worth it," Scott is worth it.

"I go up against the best wrestlers in the nation, in the world. But nothing scares me as much as messing things up with David."

"I think that your friendship is strong enough to endure it if it doesn't work out how you want it to. But I think it will work out in your favor."

"This is what you should do. Ok. Christmas is coming up soon and his family always comes over for Christmas Eve," I explain.

"Righhhttt, and?"

"And pull him away at some point in the night, hang some mistletoe up in your doorway or something, and kiss him," dang, I'm so good at making plans.

"That's actually not a bad idea. Because if he doesn't respond to it, I'll just say that I did it because it's tradition and if he does respond, then I'll know he likes me back," she sits up on her board thinking the idea over.

"I'm expecting you to name your first born after me," I grin at her as she tries to psh me off my board.

~

"She's so precious," I smile down at my goddaughter/ niece.

"She loves you Ryles, I could barely get her to calm down all day," Savannah says from beside me.

"Of course she loves me. She's already such a smarty pants," I stroke her cheek with my index finger. "Take a picture of us!" I exclaim gesturing towards my phone on the arm of the couch.

Smiling at the camera, I tilt Olivia up a bit so that her cute little face is in the frame.

I look towards Chris. "I'm moving back to Santa Cruz when I graduate."

His eyes widen. "What about your deal with Ubisoft?"

"They have a headquarters in San Fran that I can work from. Plus, most of the coding I do on my own time so I won't even really have to be there."

"Well, I guess it makes sense. You always wanted to work for Microsoft anyways. And what about Scott?"

I exhale loudly, "That's a barrier I'll cross when the time comes. He already knows I'm moving though and fully supports it. But he wants to play for the Bruins, so I'll guess we'll try long distance."

"And you think that'll work?" he asks with brotherly concern.

"Oh, I know it will work. I love him too much to let him go that easily. It just might suck sometimes."

Olivia starts squirming in my arms and I pass her to Savannah, "Think she might be hungry," I comment.

Now with free hands, I grab my phone and look down at the picture, immediately sending it to Scott.

me to stalker: *photo attached: I want one.*

I set my phone down only to pick it back up when it dings. Not surprisingly, Scott messaged right back.

stalker to me: *be ready tomorrow, I'll give you one ;)*

I laugh lightly and shake my head. I swear that man has the dirtiest mind. Not that I care.

me to stalker: *I'm sure you'd love that… at least the making process, not sure if we're ready for the actual creation.*

stalker to me: *I'm ready whenever you are. Say the word and I'll wife you up and give you a baby. I can't wait for little Scott's or Ry's running around (if that's what you want of course)*

Scott and I haven't really had the kid talk yet. But I think we both know where the other one stands. I know he wants kids, and I've always wanted a family of my own. Knowing that we want the same thing is definitely comforting.

me to stalker: *I could get behind some mini-Scott's running around, not until the far future though, I'm not ready to be a mom quite yet*

stalker to me: *just wife for now then? Got it, I'm already picking out the ring ☺*

My eyes widen. I'm sure he's joking but as much as I want to marry Scott, we have not been dating long enough for that.

me to stalker: *wife eventually. Not for a while though…*

stalker to me: *what are we thinking? A couple months?*

me to stalker: *more like a couple years!*

stalker to me: *I'll wait as long as you want me to baby, say the word and there will be a ring on your finger <3*

I dial his number. He picks up on the first ring. "That was quick. But I'll propose, if you insist. A Christmas engagement sounds pretty good to me."

"That's not why I called. I better not be

getting a ring for Christmas Prescott Bridges, I'll reject it," I deadpan.

"Ouch-"

I cut him off before he can say more. "You know I love you Scott. And I'll only ever love you. But I want to fully experience this relationship with you. Every step of it. I don't want to jump into things, I've waited too long for this," I sigh, "Plus, it's not like there's any rush. We're only in our early 20s, we have practically our whole lives ahead of us."

"I know gorgeous, I'm just messing with you. But I am serious that if you say the word, I'll make it happen."

"I know you are. Are you nervous for the game at all?" he's in Washington for today's game.

"Nope. But there are scouts here. I talked to them in Oregon and they liked what they saw, so they came to this game as well."

I get a little sad thinking that in a few months he'll be playing pro for the Bruins in Massachusetts and I'll be in California.

"That's great Scott. You liked the stadium when you went to visit with Max right? I thought they already told you to expect your name called at the draft."

"I'm not talking about scouts for the Bruins."

My mind goes into a whirl, "I don't understand what that's supposed to mean. The Bruins are the team you want to play for, they're the only scouts that matter."

"They used to be. Before I fell in love with a girl who will be living in California."

What the fuck is happening. I don't even

know how to comprehend what he is illuding to right now. Ever since I met him, the Bruins have been his dream. He's going to play for the Bruins, that's what he's always wanted. I made my peace with that.

"You still there Books?"

"Yeah. Scott that's not fair. You can't joke around like that."

"What are you talking about gorgeous?"

"What am *I* talking about?" my voice raises a little bit. "What are *you* talking about?"

"I'm talking about playing for the San Jose Sharks who just so happen to want to draft me so that I can stay close to you. Because I love you and always want to be near you."

I don't even have words. I guess I'm quiet for too long, "Come on Ry. Say something."

"I think this is probably a conversation we shouldn't be having over the phone," I need him to tell me this in person. I won't let him give up his dream for me.

"Ok. But I'm telling you right now that my mind is made up. If the Sharks draft me, I'm playing for them. So don't go hurting that pretty head of yours by overthinking," I distinctly hear someone yelling at him to wrap it up.

"We're on the ice in 30, I gotta go Books. But I'll see you bright and early tomorrow and I'll call you after the game ok?"

"Okay. I love you. Good luck," I don't want my worry to sike his game.

"I love you too," with that he hangs up and I have an existential crisis.

CHAPTER 72: SCOTT

I'm pretty sure I freaked Rydell out big time. I knew it was too soon to tell her that I'm going to play for the Sharks if the opportunity presented itself, but I couldn't keep it in anymore.

I know she's overthinking so much right now. That pretty little mind of her's is in overdrive and I need to get to her to stop it from combusting.

All night and this whole plane ride I've been thinking of every scenario. There's the easy case where she is happy that I'm moving with her and there are no problems. In a utopistic world that might be true, but I know my girlfriend too well.

It will probably play out with her being selfless as usually. Telling me that she doesn't want me to give up my dream for her. But she's my dream. A dream I never want to wake up from.

As I go to baggage claim I start figuring out how to calm Rydell down when we have this inevitable conversation. Rydell has it wrapped around her mind that she has to sacrifice her happiness for the happiness of everyone else around her. I love her for her saint-like attitude. But it sometimes makes it difficult for me.

She's scared of being hurt. And I really don't

blame her. With all the bad shit that she's been through, I understand her completely. But I need to make sure that I really think about this conversation so I can say exactly what she needs to hear.

I need her to know that I will be way happier in California then I will be in Massachusetts.

Walking out of the airport, I spot the blue Subaru that I recognize to be Rydell's family car. I rush up to said car as I watch the most gorgeous girl walk out of it lightly jogging to meet me in the middle.

I set my bag down and open my arms, catching her when she jumps into them. I cup her thighs that are wrapped around my waist as she throws her arms around my neck. Taking a big sniff of her hair I feel instant comfort from her lavender scent.

"Are you smelling my hair?" she askes as she brings her face out of my neck to look at me.

"Yep," I pop the p not even trying to deny it.

"Perv," she mumbles with a shake of the head.

"I missed your pet names," I bring my lips to hers, feeling the curve of her smiling lips against mine.

She drops her feet back to the floor, but keeps our mouths attached. I pull back, taking her bottom lip between my teeth before fully letting go.

"My gorgeous girl," I say looking down at her pretty face.

She picks up my bag from the floor, carrying it to the car for me. I try to grab it from her, but she pulls it closer to her in a death grip.

"How was your flight?" her free hand grabs

mine and she starts swinging our arms back and forth.

"Not great, the girl next to me was so fucking annoying. She wouldn't shut up."

"She was probably trying to hit on you," Rydell says matter of factly.

"Does that make you jealous," I side I eye with a smirk.

"Nope."

"It doesn't," I raise an eyebrow at her.

"I have no reason to be jealous. I know you wouldn't do anything to reciprocate her flirtiness."

I raise our connected hands to my lips and place a kiss to her knuckles, "You're damn right I wouldn't."

Placing my bags in the trunk and settling in the car, Rydell shifts in her seat to face me, "Hungry?"

"I could eat," I respond.

"Burritos?"

"Whatever you want Books."

~

It's 9am and we're eating burritos. Can't say I'm surprised. Ry hates breakfast foods and love burritos, so it really does make sense. My little weirdo.

"Next time we go for breakfast, we're getting pancakes," I take a bite out of my burrito.

"You said I could pick, if you wanted pancakes, we would've gone to Harbor Café," she stuffs her burrito in her face, getting beans on the corner of her lips as consequence.

Reaching over the booth, I take my thumb and clean it off, putting my thumb to my mouth to rid the beans.

Her cheeks flush pink, "I missed that blush of yours," I tell her which only makes her cheeks more vibrant.

She rolls her eyes at me and continues chomping down her food. Finishing mine off, I watch as her every move.

Hyper fixated on her mouth, I wet my bottom lip with my tongue and cross my arms on my chest, leaning back. I want her mouth on me so badly. On my lips, neck, collarbone, around my-

And my pants are tight. Feeling myself get turned on, I clear my throat and take a sip of my water. "So, how do you feel about San Jose? It's only a 40-minute drive from Santa Cruz. 50 minutes from Ubisoft. Silicon Valley is right there. I mean, you'd have the most high-tech companies at your disposal."

She looks at me with conflicted eyes. Her voice is serious when she speaks, "The Bruins have been your dream the minute you stepped on the ice. They want to recruit you. That's not an opportunity I want you to pass up."

"Priorities change Rydell," I tell her in a low voice.

"Something this big isn't easily changed Scott," she says back firmly.

"But it was easy Ry. As soon as I committed to you, all my decisions have been easy because I make them with the intent of being with you."

"I don't want you to regret it," she looks down.

I stand up and sit down next to her on her side of the booth. Guiding her face to mine with my hand I force her to make eye contact with me. "You really think I would regret something that keeps me close to you? You should know by now that I'd give up anything to always be near you."

She tilts her head and sighs, "I don't want you giving up something so big because of me. I know you care about me, and I know you love me. I also know that you'd sacrifice your own happiness for my benefit, and that's the last thing I want."

"You're my happiness Ry. Playing with the Bruins isn't something that would make me happy anymore. Playing hockey makes me happy. It doesn't matter where I'm playing it. Not having you by me physically would be torture. I'd endure it for you, obviously. But if I don't have to be away from you, I won't."

She lifts her hand up to play with my 'best friends' necklace while chewing the inside of her cheek. "Well, San Jose is very close to Silicon Valley. And Microsoft does have a location there."

I smile down at her, gripping her chin in my hand and planting a kiss to her lips. "I'm thinking a house in a neighborhood. Apartments our nice, but I want to get a yard so we can have a dog."

"Ok," she pats my chest, "let's not get ahead of ourselves."

"You're right… we start out with a cat since you like them better. Plus, they're probably easier to take care of. Then we get a dog. They'll be best friends. What are we thinking for names?"

She laughs, rewarding me with her dimpled smile. "If we get a cat, I think we should name it Fred. And we can call him Freddie," she plays along. I love talking about our future together.

Wrapping my arm around her shoulder, I press a kiss to her temple. "We could get twin cats and call them Fred and George."

She does a little happy wiggle that melts my heart, "And if we get a dog, we can name him Sirius!" she says it like it's the most genius idea.

"Deal. You know I've already started looking at houses."

"You have?" she looks up at me.

I brush her cheek with my index finger, "I have. There's a couple of places I could see us settling down in. I mean, we still have like 4 months until then, but will you move in with me once we graduate?"

"You're sure the Sharks is what you want? You won't miss the Bruins and Mass?"

"You are what I want Rydell Rivens."

"You already have me Prescott Bridges."

I lean down and nip her earlobe, "You didn't answer my question Books?"

"I don't think there's anything that would make me happier than moving in with you when we graduate."

CHAPTER 73: RYDELL

"You've got your board, gloves, beanie, hand warmers, thermal socks-" my mom lists off all the things I'll need for the slopes.

"I've got it all mom. Double checked and everything," I reassure her.

She sticks out a tote bag, "I made sandwiches and packed snacks for the drive. Scott, you have chains for the tires in case the roads are icy?"

"Yes ma'am," he says politely.

"Ok. I'll stop pestering the two of you. I'll see you both back on Christmas Eve, right? Scott, sweety, if you want to be with your family for longer don't hesitate to do so. Or if they'd like to come down here, they are more than welcome to."

"I'll keep that in mind Victoria. But we definitely will not be missing Christmas Eve here. I need to prove to Liam that I can beat him in corn hole."

I swear, as soon as Liam mentioned Scott entering our annual corn hole competition, the two of them have been fixated on the topic, both claiming that they are the best.

"In your dreams Scotty Boy," Liam yells out

as he jogs down the stairs to say bye.

"You're both wrong. Everyone knows Ryles always wins. She's got the best hand-eye coordination," Andy chimes in.

"Thank you Andy," I pull her in throwing my arm over her shoulder.

"It's because she cheats. She knocks the other person's off the board," Liam complains.

"Yeah, with my mad skills," last year, my winning point happened because my bag hit Liam's off.

"It's just luck," he mumbles to himself.

"Whatever helps you sleep at night Liam."

"Alright. You guys should get going so you don't have to drive in the dark," mom claims as she goes to hug Scott. "Don't let Rydell get into any trouble Scotty."

"Don't worry Victoria, I'll take care of her."

"I know you will," she pats his cheek in a motherly way, and I watch his eyes soften.

Saying our final goodbyes to everyone we load up into the car, Scott in the driver's seat and me in the passengers. We've got like a 6-hour drive ahead of us so I'm sure we'll switch at some point.

"Ready gorgeous girl?" Scott checks to make sure my seat belt is secure.

At my nod we pull out of the driveway bidding a due to my family. We'll only be in Mammoth for 2 nights, but with all the driving it'll be like we were gone for 3 days.

Flipping through my Spotify, I find my playlist called Scydell Winter '21 and hit play. Scott and I have started to make a shared playlist for every season where we add songs that we like for that time.

The first song to come on is Sexy Back, which Scott claimed will be on every playlist. We both let out twin laughs and I think back to the party when I tried to dip him.

"Seems like a long time ago doesn't it?" Scott asks as he moves his hand to grip the inside of my thigh. I set my hand on top of his and play with his fingers.

I hum in agreement, "Surprised I didn't scare you off that night," after having a panic attack in front of him for the first time, I really thought that was the end of it. I'm really glad it wasn't.

Taking his eyes off the road for a split second and then returning them to the road he says, "You can't scare me away that easily Ry. Who else would deal with my clinginess," he squeezes his hand.

"Literally any girl in the existence of this Earth. And any aliens that may exist outside of Earth. And probably half the guys as well. Don't act like you're not a hot commodity," I claim.

"Oh, I'm definitely a hot commodity baby, there's no denying that," he raises his hand higher. "You know you're the only person I've ever been touchy with. Before you I hated the mere idea of a handshake. Now, there's nothing that sounds better to me than having my hands on you. Only you," I snatch his hand that is continuing its upward journey.

"We are in a moving vehicle Prescott," I set our intertwined hands near my knee.

"Am I turning you on Books? I do have that sort of effect on people," he raises our hands and places a kiss to the back of mine.

"I'm surprised you could fit in the car with

that big head of yours," I bite back.

"You can't be feisty while I'm driving Rydell, it's distracting."

"Is it now," I say with a smirk. He's not the only one who can get the other hot and bothered.

I untangle or fingers and move my hand to rub up and down his thigh. He squirms in his seat. He makes it so easy. "Rydell," he says in a warning tone. "We're in a moving vehicle," he mimics me with a tight voice.

I look down at his lap and see a tent forming, so I raise my hand up higher so that it's at the spot where is hip and thigh meet. He doesn't make a move to stop me, so I go to his waistband and unbutton his pants. His knuckles are white as he grips the steering wheel harder.

I stick my hand down his pants and palm down on his hard on over his boxers. He lets out a loud groan. "Rydell you're going to cause an accident," I take my hand out and button his pants back up.

"Looks like you're not the only one who has a certain type of affect," I say with a triumphant grin as I sit back in my seat.

He shakes his head as he looks at me, "You're an evil little thing. I'll remember this for later Del," he says threateningly.

~

About halfway into the drive, I look up from my book as Scott pulls into an empty parking lot. We're basically in the middle of nowhere, as we start to make our way up the mountain.

Expecting for Scott to want to switch seats, I unbuckle myself and move to open the door. Scott grabs my upper arm, causing me to stop my actions,

"Not so fast. I've been waiting the past 3 hours to find an empty lot, all the while thinking about your hand around my dick."

My eyes widen. He's been turned on this whole time. "Yes, I've been turned on this whole time and I need a minute to get it under control," it's like he can read my mind.

I love that he's not asking for me to do anything to him. That he wants to take care of it himself so that I don't feel uncomfortable. But I'm not gonna lie, thinking about him turned on, turns me on so I have no complaints about helping him 'get it under control.'

I set my book aside and climb over the center console to straddle his thighs. His hand finds my waist immediately as mine cup his neck. "I never said you had to help."

"My hearing works just fine," I smash my lips into his rolling my hips the tiniest bit. His tongue parts my lips immediately and fills my mouth with warmth.

As our tongues take off in a lapping battle for dominance, his hands drive under my shirt, one rests on my ribs, the other cups my breast over my bra. My fingers thread into his hair and tug a bit pulling our mouths apart for air.

I lean in and start leaving open mouth kisses all over his neck, making sure I don't suck hard enough to leave marks but enough to get a response out of him. I don't want his parents upset that their son came home with hickeys.

He starts massaging my breast and I can feel my abdomen flutter with anticipation. Moving down, his hands grip my waist and press me further down onto him. The friction causes me to sigh as I let my head lift back up to kiss him again.

"Back seat?" he questions against my lips.

I nod my head yes and he lifts my hips up to help my maneuver my way back.

I clumsily fall back onto the seats and position myself into a lying position. The seatbelt buckle is digging into my lower back. When Scott gets back with me, he crawls on top to hover over me and places his hand on my lower back, slightly lifting me off the seat. His other hand stuffs the pillow that was in the front seat with me under so that the buckle isn't hurting me anymore.

He kisses my dimple as I smile at him then lowers to start kissing my neck. My hands work at getting his pants undone as his start dragging my sweatpants down. I was not about to wear actual pants on a 6-hour drive.

"I've never had sex in a car before, should I be worried," I ask him as he continues exploring my neck.

"I wouldn't know. This is a first for me too," his confession has me pausing my movements. He unstuffs his face to look down at me.

"Are you serious?" I ask with a raised eyebrow.

"I had so many stupid, meaningless hookups before you. I could always wait until there was a bed because it didn't matter. I want you in a way I've never wanted anyone. Sometimes I want- no, need- you so badly that it hurts," he places a soft kiss to my lips. When he pulls back, he stays close enough so that we share the same air. "If I could have you every second of everyday I would, doesn't matter where it is, I always want to be this close to you."

I lift my head to reconnect our lips and continuing pulling his pants down to below his hips. I move his underwear to the same place as he pushes my sweats and panties down and off in one motion.

I take him in my hand and stroke up and down a couple of times. His head falls to my shoulder to compose himself before he grabs his wallet and takes out a condom.

Rolling it on, he looks me in the eye, "Are you sure you want to do this pretty girl?" he always asks me before we do the deed and it always makes me want him so much more.

"Yes, are you sure?" I ask him back just in case.

"Fuck yes," he adjusts himself and starts to slowly ease himself into me until he's buried in as far as he can go.

"Holy shit," I let out a shaky breath as I indulge in the feeling of him.

"Best." He slides himself almost all the way out. "Feeling." He thrust back in deeply. "Ever." He repeats the process of going essentially almost all the way out and all the way back in a couple of times and I press my head further into the seat as I try to focus on not making too much noise.

"Tell me how you feel baby," he grazes his nose up the length on my neck and starts to increase his speed.

"So good," I choke out. "I feel so fucking good Scotty," he presses his lips down against mine with force to match his thrusts.

"If it's too much, tell me to stop," at my hum of agreement he starts to pound into me at Olympic speed and I let out a moan and wrap my legs around the back of his thighs to prompt him to hit it deeper.

He does, and with the speed he's gained, I feel like any minute the car's going to give out with the pent-up desire Scott is releasing. He wasn't lying when he said he was turned on. Not that I have any problems with it.

Slowing down slightly, he grips my sides and slams into me hard with his eyes shut tight and his bottom lip between his teeth. Opening his eyes, he looks down at me with dark eyes.

He brings his head down to rest on my shoulder as he rolls his body in a motion that hits all the right spots. At my noises of pleasure, he repeats the motion until I start to feel myself release. "Fuck Scott," I grip the back of his neck as I feel myself drip down his pulsing dick.

My walls clench around him as I feel his high hit, slowly coming to a stop. He stays inside my while we compose ourselves and places a kiss on my shoulder before pulling out and taking the condom off.

I lift myself up as Scott adjusts his pants and pull my sweats and undies back on, struggling a bit with the limited space.

When we are fully dressed, Scott opens the door and sticks his hand down to help me up.

Tugging me to an upright position, he places a sweet kiss to my lips and settles his hands under my shirt to rest on my waist.

Brow to brow, he looks at me with eyes still full of passion, "Was that ok?"

I nod against his forehead, "I think we should have car sex more often," I tell him.

"Don't tempt me. If we didn't have to be

there by dinner, I'd keep you trapped in this parking lot to go for round 2 and 3," he kisses me again. "You want to stop by somewhere to pee?" he knows that not only do I have a tiny bladder, but I also always pee after sexy time.

"Yes please, I can drive if you want."

"No. You should rest gorgeous, I'm practically keeping you on your feet here," he tightens his hold on my waist.

"It's not my fault that you destroy my insides," I pout up at him.

"I didn't hurt you, did I?" he asks with concern.

"No, you didn't hurt me. You made me feel really good, I'm just a little sore."

He places three consecutive kisses to my cheek, "Super-sized dick," he gloats, and I push at his chest.

CHAPTER 74: SCOTT

Pulling up to the driveway of my grandparent's vacation home I look over at a sleeping Rydell in the passenger seat.

I reach my hand over and brush her hair out of her face in a soothing matter. I'm so nervous right now. I have no idea what my parents' motive for this visit is. As much as I want to see it as a way of them trying to reconnect, I know it's probably more of an interrogation towards Rydell.

I don't want Rydell to think that she's the reason I'm not trying to have a relationship with that, but if they say one bad thing about her, I'm leaving.

It's extremely hard not to like Rydell so I'm being optimistic. When she starts to stir, I cup her cheek and stroke it with my thumb, "Time to wake up gorgeous," I tell her softly.

She opens her eyes a takes a deep breath in, "We're here already?" her voice is sleepy.

"Yep. How are you feeling? You still have time to back out of this."

She sits up fully in her seat and unbuckles, "No turning back now Scotty. I'm excited to meet everyone," her eyes widen when she looks at the house in front of us.

"Holy shit. This is just one of your houses?"

"Well, it's one of my grandparent's houses. My parents prefer Big Bear," I tell her casually.

"I'd hate to know what you think about my family house," she mumbles.

"I think your family's house is probably the best place I've ever stayed in," she gives me an 'are you serious?' type look. "I'm being honest. I love it there. And when we move in together, I don't want a house anything like the ones I grew up in. I want it one just like yours."

"You always know exactly what to say," she sighs.

"You know I say it because it's true, not because I think it's what you want to hear?"

"I know," she reaches over the center console and gives me a quick kiss that leaves me wanting more. "I'm ready when you are."

We both climb out and grab our bags from the back, walking up to ring the front door.

"You're late, the food is getting cold," my mom states as she opens the door.

"Hello to you to mother," I tell her, walking in as she moves aside.

"Hello Prescott," she doesn't make a move to give me a hug and hasn't even acknowledge Rydell.

"Mom, this is my girlfriend Rydell. Rydell, this is my mom,"

"It's really nice to meet you Mrs. Bridges. I would shake your hand, but my arms are very full," she says with a polite smile.

"I can see that. You brought a snowboard?" Rydell's face turns a little pink and I stiffen at the idea of her feeling uncomfortable.

"Yes. I hope that's ok, I figured I'd take this up to slopes instead of having to rent skis. My family loves snowboarding, I grew up looking forward to snow season," she's slightly rambling.

"Charming," my mother says in a slightly cold voice. "Prescott, I assume you still know your way around. You can find your room and show Rydell to one of the guest rooms."

"Mom, we're grown adults, I don't see any problem in us sharing a room," I state.

Rydell elbows me in the ribs, "The two of you aren't married. Of course there's a problem with it. We invited you here Prescott, you'll follow our rules. Unless Rydell here has something to say about it?" she looks over at Rydell who's having trouble maintaining eye contact with my mom.

"Of course we'll take separate rooms. I have no problem with it at all Mrs. Bridges."

"Good. Now hurry along, you've already kept our guest waiting for too long."

"Guest?" I question. "I thought it was just you, Dad, and Penelope for dinner tonight?"

"We invited a work partner who and his family who happened to be in town for the holidays," she walks off with any further explanation.

"I'm sorry Ry, I didn't know anyone else was coming. And I'm sorry about my mom, she's like that with most people," I set my bag down and rub the tension out of the back of her neck.

"She's very intimidating," Rydell claims and looks over at my shoulder, lifting her hand to wave it.

Turning around, I see my big sister speed

walking towards us. We embrace in a hug. I didn't realize how much I missed her.

"I missed ya Scotty," she exclaims as she pulls back. "Hi Rydell, it's nice to finally meet you in person," she hugs Rydell. Rydell tries to reciprocate but her hands are full so she's kind of just standing there.

I smile at the sight of them. Penelope is the only person in this family that I give a shit about. And Rydell's the person I care the most about, so it's good to see them getting along.

But as much as I love Pen, if she ended up disliking Rydell in any way, like if my parents convinced her to, I'd have no problem cutting her out too. It would be hard, and it would hurt a lot, but it would be way worse to let go of Rydell.

"It's nice to meet you too. Scott's showed me pictures of you, but oh my gosh, you are so much prettier in person!" Rydell exclaims with a dimpled smile as they pull back. Ok dimpled smile is a good sign.

"Says you. You are definitely out of Scott's league," I don't even try to protest it because she totally is. "How was the not so welcome party? She didn't scare you too much did she Rydell?"

"Not gonna lie I was about to piss myself," Pen laughs and Rydell looks at me. "But I'm not sure there's anything scary enough to make me leave Scott," she looks back at Pen with a smile.

I'm so fucking in love with her. "Good," Pen says with a nod. "I'm really glad he has someone like you Rydell."

"Please, call me Del, all my friends do."

"Well, Del, you can call me Pen," my chest feels a lot less heavy seeing the two of them interact.

"Let's get your bags upstairs before mom starts breathing fire. Just so the two of you know, the family joining us has a daughter your age. You know how these dinners go Scotty. Del, don't let it go to your head, my parents are assholes."

"How do these dinners go exactly," Rydell asks as she trudges upstairs.

"Mom and dad interrogate the girl to see if they're a good fit for golden boy Scotty," Pen says apprehensively.

Rydell stops in place causing me to slightly bump into her back, "Like as in marriage?"

"If you have to put a label on it, I assume marriage is the term. If you ask me it's more like a trap," Pen grumbles.

"Books, you have nothing to worry about," I don't elaborate because the other day we literally had a conversation essentially agreeing that she tells me when and I'll propose. I've already picked out the ring.

When I was I Washington, I came across an antique shop that had a ring in the display window and as soon as I saw it, I bought it. Rydell told me that she doesn't really want a tradition or flashy engagement ring. The one in display had a band with imprinted flowers and an oval shaped opal. I'm just waiting for it to be sized.

"I know. But your parents haven't even met me and they're already trying to get rid of me," she makes her way to the top of the stairs. When I join her, I set my bags down and grab hers, opening a guest room to set her things down.

She follows, sitting on the edge of the bed, looking around the room with a sad look. "I'll give you two some privacy. I'll tell them you're freshening up before eating," Pen shuts the door behind her.

I kneel in front of her and rub my hands up and down the sides of her thighs. "I just want them to like me," she says softly as she looks down at her lap, fidgeting with her fingers.

I sigh, "My parents are the type of people to judge on status, not on human decency. You, Rydell Rivens, are as perfect as a person can be. What they think of you doesn't matter, because it doesn't change the fact that you are the love of my life. I know you want everyone to like you and feel bad if they don't, but some people will dislike you without giving you a well-deserved chance. I'm going to be honest with you, my parents and grandparents are probably going to reflect that," I don't want to sugarcoat it because my parents really are dicks.

"I don't want you to feel like you can't reconnect with them because they don't accept me," she looks down at me. Her selflessness is heartbreaking.

"Ry, if they can't accept you, then they can't accept me. Hate to break it to you, but we're a package deal now."

She gives me a smile before cupping my cheeks and placing a soft kiss to my lips. Then presses a swift kiss to my cheek, "Package deal," she nods in agreement.

~

Heading downstairs feels like we are walking into a lion's den. My hand is intertwined with Rydell's as I lead her to the dining room silently hoping that this doesn't end poorly.

When we enter, both Rydell and I stop in our tracks when we see the daughter of the work partner's family. Fucking Lindsay. And there's no two seats open next to each other. One's next to Lindsay and the other is across from Lindsay.

"You'll have to excuse our son's lateness. He's been away for too long to remember his manners it seems," my dad says. I haven't talked to the man in close to a year and that's the welcome I get.

"We had a long drive. Close to 6 hours, it's hard to be on time in those circumstances," I give Rydell's hand a reassuring squeeze.

"No worries," the man who I assume to be Lindsay's dad stands up and goes to shake my hand. "Richard Conover. I own a transportation company that works with your parent's company," I shake his hand. "Lindsay told me that the two or you go to school together."

"We do. This is my girlfriend Rydell, she's a computer science major at Daxton," I pull her out from behind me.

"Girlfriend?" he looks at my dad with confusion. "Well, Lindsay why don't you sit next to mom over here so they can sit next to each other."

At least someone has sense. "Thank you, sir."

Lindsay gets up from her seat with disappointment. Fucking bitch probably knew who I was before I even introduced myself. Her parents probably told her to get close to me.

Pulling out one of the seats for Rydell, I make sure she's settled in before taking a seat. "Computer science. That's ambitious, Daxton's known for their comp sci program, comparable to MIT, isn't that right?" Mr. Conover makes conversation as the food starts to be served.

Rydell thanks the server as they set food in front of her before responding, "Yeah. The professors there are great. Most of them have worked for high tech companies so they use applied teaching from their previous experience. It's very enlightening," she says with confidence. There's my girl.

"I bet. Is there something you want to do with a that degree?"

She nods with a slightly giddy smile, "My area of interest is coding. I want to work with Microsoft. They have a coding team that helps improve the quality of healthcare in terms of technology. Landing a job doing that is ideal. But, we'll see, it's a very competitive field."

"Rydell's being modest," I place my hand on her inner thigh as I jump into the conversation. "She's top of her class and has a partnership with Ubisoft to develop a video game."

"Video games, that's what's wrong with our youth these days. They're rotting our children's brains," my mom cuts in.

"Video game development is completely different from health care, why would you waste your time on that?" my dad attacks.

Rydell replies before I can open my mouth, "The video game I'm developing is targeted to enhance normal daily functioning in kids with developmental disabilities. It's scientifically proven, that if done right, video games can help with mental issues in not just the younger generation but the older as well."

I look at her side profile as I'm filled with the pride of her standing up for herself.

"Why bother with the video game in the

first place if healthcare is the route you want to go into?" Lindsay's mom inserts herself into the conversation.

"My roommate and I got the idea for it freshman year and ran with it. After coding the first couple sequences and taking some psychology courses, I realized that it's something that could help people and wanted to go through with it. If at least one person benefits from it, all the work will be worth it. Plus, I have so much time and coding can essentially be done in any area. I figure I'd try a bunch of different jobs with it. Maybe have a contract with the healthcare line of Microsoft before switching to their division that works with Nasa. The opportunities there are endless."

"So, what you're saying is that you won't be settled with a stable job?" my dad takes it out of proportion.

"Quite the opposite. I'll be earning 6 figures working with Microsoft. I already have a pretty hefty deal signed with Ubisoft that should keep me set for most of my life."

My dad puffs out a breath knowing he's been bested. "Seems like a weird job to me, being behind a screen all day," my mom tries.

"I think it's fucking awesome," Pen grins at Rydell.

"Penelope, watch your mouth," my mom chastises.

"Rydell, it seems like you have a good head on your shoulders. I'm sure you'll be very successful in the future," Mr. Conover is a blessing.

"She doesn't need the future. She's already a huge success. Her video game surpassed the number of sponsors needed by a landslide over the other games up for development."

"Speaking of success, Lindsay is president of Alpha Delta Pi this year. She managed to get the most number of recruitments this year, breaking the record for all previous years," her mom brags. Her success is not even a grain of salt compared to Rydell's.

"Alpha Delta Pi also had a major scandal this year. They used charity money for alcohol if I remember correctly," I remember that being all over the school not too long ago.

"Is that true Linds?" her dad turns to look at her.

"Yes, but I handled the situation. The secretary was fired immediately."

"From her position, she's still a member of the sorority," I point out.

"She made one mistake; I wasn't going to completely humiliate her for it."

"Because her parents are major donors?" I fire back.

I leave Lindsay speechless. Pen coughs to cover up a laugh.

"Is that how the two of you know each other then? Through the sorority, I heard they help sponsor the hockey team," her dad asks.

"Yes, Scott and I became really close freshman year through the sorority," Lindsay recovers.

"I'm glad the two of you are friends. It's good to have connections early on, especially in this line of work," my dad claims.

"Lindsay and I aren't friends," I don't even try to pretend.

"Prescott where are your manners tonight,"

my mom is pissed.

"May I ask why the two of you aren't friends? Lindsay always has good things to say about you. She said you guys had a relationship on and off throughout the years," her dad looks confused.

"We might've been acquittances, but I stopped being anything with Lindsay the moment she locked my girlfriend in a closet out of jealously."

Rydell looks down at her lap and scoots down a bit in her chair like she's trying to make herself unnoticeable.

"You locked her in a closet?" now even her mom seems to display disappointment.

"It was just for fun, it was joke," Lindsay sputters out.

"I didn't find it funny and I don't think Rydell did either," I challenge.

"Rydell, I'm sorry for my daughter's actions. If I had any idea of her mistakes, I would've straightened her out immediately. Tonight, seems to be very enlightening in some respects," Mr. Conover gives Lindsay a stern look.

"Everyone makes mistakes Richard; kids need to get some things out of their system once they flock the nest. I'm sure she meant no harm. Our Scott seems to be taking the same path of rebellion," my mom argues.

"I wouldn't say locking someone in a closet is easily excusable," Penelope bites back.

My mom shoots daggers at her in warning. "Let's move on to lighter topics," my dad suggests. "Scott is about to graduate with his bachelor's in business."

"Ah yes. Are you excited to get into the

family business Scott?" Mr. Conover asks.

"I won't be going into the family business. I've gotten a couple offers to play pro hockey. The San Jose Sharks actually just asked me to come in for a tour of their stadium to convince me to play for them. Seems like I'll be moving to California this summer."

"The Sharks offered you a spot?" Rydell asks with shock.

"I was going to tell you on Christmas but, surprise," I look over at her.

"That's great Scotty! Congratulations," she sits up a little in her seat to wrap her arms around my neck. Letting go, she places a kiss to my cheek before settling down.

"You're playing for a couple years then retiring to take over the business?" Mr. Conover asks with confusion.

"Nope. I'll play for as long as I can. When I retire, I figure coaching would be the next step," my voice is tight.

"That's still up for discussion," my mom tries to reassure.

"Except it's not. I told you guys to start training Penelope for the job," Pen straightens up in her seat.

Mr. Conover chokes on his wine. "Penelope? That's certainly an interesting direction."

"Because I'm a girl?" Pen asks with aggression.

"Well quite frankly, yes. Not many big companies see a female running it. I hate to sound sexist, but they just don't get as much respect. It really is a societal problem, but it's true."

"I have my MBA, and a master's in

communication. I've worked hard to be where I am right now, and I'll work harder to climb the ladder until I'm at the top. Regardless of the company," Pen gives my parent's a challenging look.

"Well, I wish you the best of luck then," Mr. Conover puts an end to that conversation.

The rest of the dinner talk turns to the parent's bragging about the success of their business and I drown it out as Rydell and I have a subtle conversation with Penelope who is sitting across from us.

The Conover's are getting ready to leave and Ricard approaches Rydell and I, "I'm sorry about tonight, I know that in these types of families we get cornered into dinners that seem rather old fashion. I had no idea that you had a girlfriend. Rydell you seem like a lovely girl," he looks back at me. "I wouldn't let that one goes if I were you."

I shake his hand, "I don't plan on it, sir," we watch them leave the house.

When their headlights are lighting up the road, I turn to look at my parents, "You brought a girl for me to meet at dinner when you knew my girlfriend was going to be here?" I spit out.

"Watch your tone young man. I know you've been gone away but that doesn't mean that you should lose your sense of respect," my dad warns.

"Respect goes both ways," I say without hesitation. "If you can't respect my relationship with Rydell then you need to tell me right now so we can save the trouble of staying here for two nights."

"There's no need for dramatics Prescott. We won't say anything about this phase," my mom adds.

"Phase," I laugh without humor. "I'm only going to say this once. If you can't wrap it around your heads, then that's your own problem. I'm in love with Rydell Rivens. I'm going to marry her one day with or without your blessing. I'm going to play pro hockey and I won't run your company. So, you guys need to start thinking how you will adjust to these changes. We're going to bed," I grab Rydell's hand. "If you're still acting like assholes in the morning, we're leaving. But I would really enjoy hitting the slopes as a family tomorrow, so please consider acting like decent human beings for once," I tug Rydell's hand to prompt her to follow.

CHAPTER 75: RYDELL

I'm stirred awake by a dip in the bed and arms wrapping around my middle, pulling my back into a warm chest. To be honest, I was only partly asleep, I can't stop thinking about how poorly the night went.

I feel comfort in the arms I know to be Scott's and let myself adjust to his cuddle. Then my eyes shoot open, remembering where we are. I don't need another reason for his parents to hate me.

I sit up, but he keeps a tight grip on me, stuffing his head into my stomach. "Prescott Bridges, you can't be in here. Your parents already don't like me."

"I can't sleep without you Books," Scott whines. "Especially when I know you're two doors down from me. Plus, I knew that pretty little head of yours would be running still."

Before I forced Scott to go back to his room the first time, we had a reassuring talk about the dinner. I know where Scott stands with me, so I'm really not worried about our relationship and he knows that. He was just trying to cheer me up because he knew I was sad that his parents seemed to dislike me so much.

"I was almost asleep before you woke me up," I claim.

"Well, you can be fully asleep now. Lie back down gorgeous," he coaxes me.

I lie down so that we are facing each other, brow to brow. His eyes are closed. "Your mom doesn't want us to sleep in the same room," I remind him.

"My mom can choke on a dick. I really don't give a fuck what she wants."

"But I do. As much as I want you in here with me, I'm scared that she'll get mad."

"I'll leave before anyone wakes up. I promise. Just sleep for a bit Ry," he opens his eyes and raises his hand to brush his fingers through my hair.

"Ok. But you better be gone in the morning," I demand.

"Yes ma'am," he presses a kiss to my lips and wraps his arm around my shoulder, laying on his back to bring my head to his chest.

~

Scott stayed true to his word and left the room at close to 5 this morning with a kiss to my lips.

Walking up to my alarm set for 8, I start move around the room to get ready for the day. We're supposed to eat a small breakfast before making our way to the slopes. His grandparents are coming later this evening for an early dinner.

I slide into some thermal leggings before putting on my black snow pants and hoodie. I put my hair in two low buns and secure a beanie over my ears for extra warmth. You would think living in Massachusetts for so long would make me used to the cold, but it unfortunately has not.

I grab my jacket and snowboarding boots with the intent to put them on before we leave and head back downstairs.

Scott's family is spread out in the living room, "Good morning everyone," I say with the most charming smile I can muster.

Scott gestures me to sit next to him on the couch, placing a kiss to my cheek when I sit down.

"Good morning Rydell. There's pastries and fruit in the kitchen if you're hungry," Scott's dad says in a civil tone.

I smile at change in attitude, "Thank you. I'll grab some before we head out."

"How'd you sleep Rydell? I see you're all ready for the day," his mom asks.

I guess Scott's talk really worked. "I slept well, thanks for asking. And yep, I'm excited to get up there. It's been too long since I've snowboarded."

"Have you ever considered skiing before?" his mom asks.

"I tried it once when I was little, but I feel much more comfortable on a board. Probably the surfer in me," I tell her.

She lets out a puff of air, "She surfs too, why am I not surprised. You really do take after your father."

"Mom," Scotts warns.

"You know who my dad is?" I knew that my dad knew Scott's family, but I didn't think they realized that I was a Rivens connected to my grandpa considering that I was raised away from all of it.

"As soon as Scott said your last name was Rivens we put the pieces together. We went to school with Connell and watched him make certain decisions. It was a big topic of discussion. I suppose it still is with the passing of his father."

I wince at the mention of my grandpa and wrap my hand around my wrist. Scott stands up and grabs my hands to take me with him. "Rydell and I are going to grab some food while you consider your next words carefully."

Once we get into the kitchen, I let out a breath I didn't realize I was holding in. "Jesus Ry, I'm sorry. I didn't even think about them mentioning him. I shouldn't have brought you here, maybe we should just leave. I can make up some sort of excuse."

"I love that you'd do that. But it's fine Scott. Really. I just remember that he's in a place where he can't hurt me again and I get past it."

"Are you sure Books?" he frames my face with his hands and tilts it up.

"Positive. Plus, I really do want to get some good runs in, I have missed snowboarding," I tell him with an easy smile.

"Ok," he gives me a kiss. "Say the word, and we leave."

~

"You're handling yourself really well you know?" Pen says from beside me on the chairlift. Since getting to the ski resort, everything's been pretty fun. The snow is good and there have been no more argument.

Scott seems fairly content skiing with his family. His mom only did a couple runs before heading back to the house for work, but Scott convinced his dad to stay and hang out with us.

I think I'm growing on Scott's dad. He

hasn't said anything bad about me since last night. In fact, we had a pretty good conversation about technology in the business industry and I think I convinced him that my line of work is important.

"I don't think I've ever tried so hard to impress people. Your parents are tough nuts to crack," I tell her.

"They are. And I'm going to be honest with you, they might never fully accept you," what she's saying doesn't necessarily upset me. I've come to terms with the fact that Scott's parents won't change their views because of me. "But you've won me over and I'm the only one that really matters," she links her arm through mine.

"I'm glad I have your blessing," I laugh.

She looks back at the chairlift behind us that seats her dad and Scott, waves and looks back at me. She pulls a travel shot of fireball out of her coat and hands it to me, "Don't let dad see," she tells me as she opens her own.

I look at her with amusement, "Are you trying to get me in trouble?"

"I'll take the fall," she winks. "Bottoms up Del," she clicks her shot to mine, and we down them. I forgot how much I hate fireball; I don't think I've had it since freshman year.

Reaching our destination, Pen and I make our way to the benches. I strap in my boot as we wait for Scott and his dad.

"You guys really aren't that sneaky," Scott skis up next to us.

"Kind of rude of you not to share," Mr. Bridges add.

Penelope's eyes widen, "You want to take a shot with us?!" she exclaims as if she has entered a dimensional universe.

"As long as you don't tell your mother," he says with a grin.

Penelope pulls out more shots. Good god, where is she storing all of these. "By all means," she hands one to each of them.

"This is me trying," he looks at Scott with a new look.

Scott raises his shot in a cheers before both of them throw it back.

~

Snowboarding with the Bridges turned out to be so much more fun than I anticipated. After the tension of disapproval faded and Scott's dad actually started getting to know me as something other than the girl that tainted his son, everything's been easy.

We took a couple breaks to grab beer at the ski resort restaurant. Scott, Pen and I convinced Mr. Bridges that we shouldn't go to the fancy private longue and that the outside seating was significantly better and sure enough he seemed to have a good time.

~

"No, do not ask Rydell to teach you something! She'll just laugh at you, it happened when she tried to teach me to surf," Scott exclaims as we climb out of the car.

"I only laughed because you claimed that you'd be a natural and waist deep in, a wave took you out," everyone's laughing as we walk through the door.

"I would love to see Scott wipeout," Pen nudges Scott's shoulder.

"Ditto," Connor chimes in. That's right, I'm

on first name basis with Scott's dad. One down, one to go.

"I'm glad that the four of you are having a good time. You've left your parents waiting for an hour Connor," Scott's mom comes into view with an angry expression.

"We lost track of time. You really should've stayed Melissa; it was a nice break away from work."

"Someone had to entertain your parents while you were out acting like a hooligan," she gets close to him and takes a sniff. "Have you been drinking?"

"We had a couple of drinks at the bar in between runs," he replies.

"I leave for a couple hours and you go completely off the rails. I'm guessing drinking was Rydell's idea," ouch.

"Actually, it was mine. And from the looks of it, you're in desperate need of one," Penelope crosses her arms.

"We're all adults Melissa, we are allowed to have a couple drinks," Connor indicates.

"There you are. Is this how you welcome your parents in their own home Connor? I didn't think I'd have to keep you straight in terms of manners. We might have to have a chat about that," the sound of the voice makes my stomach drop.

Please be someone else. Please be someone else. Please be someone else.

I slowly look towards the door and am met with eyes I could never forget. My breath intakes and my heart feels like it's one beat from jumping out of my chest.

Oh my god I'm going to vomit. My knees

buckle and I hunch over placing my hands on my knees trying to control my breathing.

Scott puts his hand on my lower back and looks at me with a concerned look, "Are you ok Books?" he asks.

"She probably drank too much. See Prescott, I told you she was no good for you," I gulp at the air as I feel my throat start to close.

I can't breathe. "Shut up mom," Scott looks rubs my back and straightens me up. "What's the matter pretty girl," he asks lowly.

"I can't breathe," I choke out, putting my hands on my ears. Hands. I feel his hands on me and I flinch. Scott removes his hand, probably thinking that he's the problem.

"Rydell you're having a panic attack, come sit down with me," he maneuvers me to the couch.

"What's going on, is she ok?" I faintly hear Pen ask.

I hear Scott tell her to grab my airpods and for someone else to get water but I'm not really paying attention to it.

I make the mistake of looking up and seeing Scott's grandpa staring at me with a tilted head. "I don't want to be here. I don't want to be here. I don't want to be here," I sound like a broken record as I repeat it.

I distinctly hear Scott's mom say something about me wanting attention to make them seem like the bad guys. I hear Connor start to argue with her. I hear Pen freaking out. I hear Scott's grandpa's voice. I hear his voice and I'm transported to a dark closet.

"Everyone shut the fuck up!" Scott yells at his family.

"Rydell, look at me," I shake my head and

press my hands further into my ears.

He grips my chin in his hand, "Come on Books. Count with me," he looks deeply in my eyes. I shake my head back and forth. How am I supposed to tell him that his grandpa sexually assaulted me?

"Baby please, you're breathing too fast, you'll pass out," he tries again.

Just let me pass out, I think that would be better than dealing with all this fucked up shit.

He sticks his finger up, "1," he continues counting. When he realizes it's not working, he cups my cheeks in his hands and starts wiping away my tears.

"I don't want to be here," I say again, with a shakey voice.

"Tell me why Del," I don't want to hurt him, but this isn't really something I should keep to myself.

I feel a huge lump in my throat. With tears rolling down my face I look up at Scott, "He's the other one," it's barely over a whisper.

Scott looks at me with confusion before I watch his face fall with recognition. "I'm going to fucking kill him."

Scott leaves my side, running a hand through his hair before he storms towards his grandpa. Rubbing at his knuckles a bit, he swings at his grandpa's cheek, with enough force to knock him down.

I mean, Scott's grandpa is probably in his 70s, so it's not that hard to do, but he's a very large man.

Everyone starts yelling, Scott follows his grandpa to the floor and starts pounding at his face. I squeeze my eyes shut trying to stop my hyperventilating.

When I open my eyes, Scott is barely being contained by his dad and Penelope. Connor is just as tall as Scott and with the help of Pen they can somewhat keep him back, but they are struggling big time as he tries to get out of their grip.

"Let me go," he grunts out.

"What the hell do you think you're doing? You'll kill him Scott," his dad's face is red from the strain of holding Scott back.

"That's the point. This mother fucker sexually assaulted my girlfriend when she was 8 fucking years old."

There's a scatter of gasps around the room. I think it's Scott's grandma who speaks next, "Watch your mouth young man. Why would you spread a lie like that?"

"Do you see the fucker denying it," Scott jerks against his dad and sister.

Scott's grandpa lifts his bloodied face off the floor. I'm pretty sure his nose is broken, and he might be missing a tooth. He looks me dead in the eye and says, "I knew you looked familiar. You really filled out Rydell, I'll think about that the next time I pleasure myself," he smirks at me with a demonic look.

Scott easily rips out of the hold they have on him, dropping to the floor and knocking consecutive punches to his grandfather's already broken face. I'm pretty sure I'm about to pass out. My vision starts to blur as I watch his dad and Penelope regain control of him.

The last thing I remember is Scott's mom calling the police before I pass out.

CHAPTER 76: SCOTT

I cradle Rydell in my arms, trying to ignore the blood that I have all over my hands.

She doesn't stay out for more than a couples minutes as she regains consciousness in my arms. "I'm sorry. I'm so sorry Rydell," I can feel tears streaming down my face as I apologize to her.

She scans the room, "My dad took him outside, the police are picking him up right now. I promise I won't let him get near you. Fuck Rydell. I'm so sorry," I lean down to press my forehead to her's needing to feel her skin on mine.

"It's not your fault," she says in a whisper.

"It is. If I didn't bring you here in the first place none of this would've happened."

I don't know how she's ever supposed to look at me the same anymore. Not when I came from that shitbag of a person.

Rydell picks up my bloody knuckle and sits up. Her eyes are red and puffy, but her breathing is back to normal. I think passing out reset it or something.

"You're hurt," she examines my hand.

"I'm fine," I say as she tries to stand up, but wobbles a bit as she does so. I grip her calves for support and move to stand with her.

She tugs on my unharmed hand and walks me to the bathroom. Looking under the sink, she pulls out what looks like a first aid kit. She turns on the sink, gestures for me to stick my hands under and then turns it off. "Sit," she points to the toilet.

She just had a major panic attack, was confronted with the man who sexually assaulted her, passed out and she's still trying to take care of me.

I move to sit on the toilet lid trying to soak up the last moments I have with the girl I thought I'd spend the rest of my life with.

I watch her every move as she lets out a shaky breath, grabbing the rubbing alcohol and gauze.

With a cotton pad she distributes the rubbing alcohol and stands between my legs raising my injured knuckle to her eye level. I wince at the feeling on the cotton pad rubbing against my hand and set my head on her stomach. I take a deep breath of her lavender scent and start to cry again.

The room is filled with the noise of my sobs and the distant sound of the water dripping from the facet.

As she finishes wrapping my hand, she sets a hand on my shaking back and starts lightly scratching it.

I wrap my arms around her waist, pulling her as close as possible and I press my face further into her stomach.

"Scott, it's not your fault," her voice is wobbly like she might also start to cry. I need to get my shit together. I'm the one who should be comforting her. Not the other way around. I need to collect myself so that I can take her pain away. Every time she looks at me, she'll see him. I told myself that there was nothing in this world that could take me away from her. But I was wrong, because I won't torture her by trying to keep this relationship together.

I pull back and stand up, placing my hands on her hips. I take a deep breath and do the hardest thing I've ever done. "I'll have someone drive you home. Penelope will pack your things, and I'll make sure you get back safely."

Rydell's eyes fill with more tears and she starts shaking her head back and forth. "Rydell, I'm not going to sit in front of you and stand as a constant reminder of my shitty grandfather. I won't do it. You deserve more than that," my voice is tight, and I feel like I'm about to pass out. "You deserve more than me," I whisper with a nod.

"No," she doesn't try to stop the tears from falling. "No. You promised. You promised you'd protect my heart. If you leave me, you'll break it," she tries to convince me.

"No, I am protecting it. I'll make you miserable if I stick around."

"You won't," she shakes her head aggressively and grips my hands that are set on her hips to keep them there. "Scott, I love you. You know I love you. Please don't do this."

"You won't forget. I'll just keep reminding you. Every time you look at me, you'll be reminded of what they did to you. I can't do that to you. I won't do that to you," I say with finality as I place a kiss to her forehead, letting it linger there as I think about how I've lost everything today.

I remove her hands, release contact and walk out of the door, barely being able to walk away at the sound of her calling my name. I go to find Penelope to beg her to drive Rydell home.

"You can't just leave her like this Scott. You're doing more damage."

"You don't know shit about our relationship Penelope. I've watched her have multiple panic attacks over this. Panic attacks so bad that she almost passes out. This time she did pass out. No matter how selfish I want to be, she's better off without me."

"Scott, I really think-"

"Please Penelope," I say with desperation. "Please, I'll never ask you for anything ever again. I'll give you anything you want. I'll do anything you want. Just, please drive her home. I don't want a stranger driving her and I trust you. You can fly back once she's home safe."

"Ok. But you need to think long and hard about what you're doing to her. She loves you. You love her. I don't think you leaving is good for either of you," with that she goes to pack Rydell's things and drive her home.

I lock myself in my room, sitting on the edge of my bed with my head in my hands. And I feel every part of myself break. Whenever I thought about losing Rydell I understood that, if it happened, I'd be broken beyond saving. Now that it's happened, I don't even think I'm entirely alive.

Like a part of me died and is never coming back. Everything hurts so badly, and I don't know how I'm supposed to ever recover from this feeling.

When I hear the front door shut and a car drive off, I unlock the door and go downstairs to find a drink.

Discarding a glass, I pick up the bottle of Jack Daniels, unscrew the top, raise the bottle and tilt my head as I start chugging.

"I think you should slow down son," my dad walks in the living room.

"I think you should mind your own fucking business," I bring the bottle back to my lips taking another long swig.

"This isn't how you should deal with your problems Scott," he tries to remain calm.

"Yeah?" I raise my voice. "And how am I supposed to deal with losing the only person who made me feel anything good? Huh, what am I supposed to do now that I've lost the girl that I'm in love with? The girl I told myself I would marry and have kids with. I've just lost everything. She was everything, and I've lost it. So please, enlighten me dad, how do you suggest I deal with this, when I feel like I'm dying," I don't hide the tears as they fall.

My dad always told me crying was for the weak. The first time I remember him saying it is when I broke my arm falling off my bike. He told me to suck up my tears and to man up.

"I don't think you should have let her walk out of this door without you for one," he tells me.

I laugh, "You would know all about the right time to walk out right?" I down some more of the alcohol letting myself suffer in the burning feeling down my throat.

"This isn't about me," he reasons.

"No, it's not, so leave me the fuck alone," I'm starting to feel the effects of the bottle I've finished close to half of.

"Scott," he tries again.

I slam the bottle down and watch it shatter on the floor. Gripping my hair in my eyes I start breathing heavy, "Stop fucking talking," it comes at as a strangled plead. "I can't live without her, but I can't live knowing how much it'd hurt her to stay with her. I'd rather fucking die," I try to take in air but it's getting more difficult.

"Scott, sit down," I listen to him because if I don't sit, I might pass out. I think I'm having a panic attack. I've watched Rydell have them and this is what I think it would feel like.

The idea of her feeling this way just makes everything hurt so much more.

"You need to let Rydell make up her own mind. When she walked out of here tonight, she looked more broken then when she laid eyes on your grandfather."

"She'll get over it eventually. No one needs me," I whisper letting the alcohol take control of my words.

"I really don't think that's true. Especially not with her. I've watched the two or you these last couple of days. I wanted to hate her. I really did. I thought she was taking you away from the life I thought was best for you. But then I got to know her, and I got to know you with her, and I've never seen two people more in love. I've never seen two people so meant for each other. And maybe that's because I grew up watching arranged marriages, but you two are connected by some supernatural force. You can't let her go; it'll destroy both of you."

"What if she can't look past it? What if I end up hurting her more and she hates me for it?"

"I think that's a risk you should be willing

to take," he claps my shoulder and leaves it to rest there.

"I've fucked up so badly. I just fucking broke her heart, there's no way she'll even want to see me," I lean back on the couch wishing I had more alcohol to help me forget.

"Tomorrow I'll take you and help you get your girl back," he stands up. "For now, you need to rest and think about how you're going to apologize for acting like an idiot."

CHAPTER 75: RYDELL

This is what I'd imagine hell to feel like. Penelope dropped me off with the promise to knock some sense into her idiot brother and I haven't left my room since.

That was about 20 hours ago. I can't eat, I can't sleep, I can barely move. All my siblings and parents have tried to comfort me, but all I want is Scott.

I'm not even mad at him. I know he's doing it because he thinks it's protecting me, but I need to tell him that him leaving does nothing but make me want to crawl in a hole and stay there for the rest of my pathetic existence.

My cheeks haven't felt dry since he left me and I'm not sure how I have tears left in my system, but they seem to be in everlasting supply.

"Rydell, you need to eat something," my dad comes into my room. "Olivia, Chris and Savannah just got here, why don't you come down with me to say hi?"

"I'm not hungry," I whisper trying to ignore the lump in my throat.

"Look at the bright side; the fucker who hurt you is going to be locked up probably for the rest of his shit life," Chris tries as he walks up behind dad.

"There's no bright side to this if I've lost Scott," my bottom lip starts to wobble. "I can't do this without him," I can barely get my words out.

"I know. He'll come around; I think he thought he was doing the right thing. You have to understand his side too Rydell. He just found out that the girl he loves was sexually assaulted by his own grandpa. That's the thing about the two of you. You sacrifice your happiness for the others. Remember when you freaked out because he said he was going to play for the Sharks? It's not the same, but you were close to giving up everything to make sure that he would play for the Bruins because you thought that would make him the happiest," Chris sits down on my bed.

When I don't respond, he continues, "You need to feel what you need to feel, then gather the strength I know you have and get your boy back."

"I just want him to be here with me," I turn my head into my pillow.

"I know you do Ryles, but until he gets here, you have all of us. Even Liam is sticking around, and you know how he always likes to go with his friends when he's back for the holidays," he jokes.

I laugh a little, "He really does abandon us every time," I bring my head back out. When my face turns back serious, my dad jumps in.

"Rydell Rivens. You are probably my most independent child. If there's one thing I'm glad you learned from me it's that you need to walk through life and get what you want with or without the help of others. I've watched you do that through being top of your class, signing with a company to create a video game, moving halfway across the country by yourself to go to a good college. There's nothing you can't do Ryles. And that includes being happy," he pauses. "Happiness is a construct Rydell, you shape it into what you want. If that's in the form of Scott, go and get him. If it's not, then let him go."

I hear a lot of noise start to come from downstairs, like everyone is speaking at once.

I hear multiple feet walking up the stairs, "I need to see her Andy," I sit up in bed thinking that I'm in some sort of hallucination.

"You better fix this or I swear to god, I'll feed you your balls," I hear from outside my voice.

There's no way he's actually here, right? Chris opens my door and I jump out of my bed, running up to Scott and throwing my arms around his neck.

I faintly notice my dad, Chris, and Andy shutting the bedroom door to leave us alone. I take in his woodsy scent and am instantly filled with comfort.

Pulling back, I frame his face in my hands and scan him, still thinking that he's not really here. He's the mirror image of me: red, puffy eyes, major bags probably from lack of sleep, disheveled hair like he hasn't bothered to take care of himself in our short time apart.

"Rydell, I don't know what I'm supposed to do," his voice is raspy and dry like he's been just as bad as me.

"Whatever you do, please don't leave me again," my voice cracks in desperation.

"How are you supposed to get over this? I left you when you needed me because I thought that's what would help. I'm not good for you. I don't know how to deal with these types of situations," he rests his forehead on mine.

"If you really don't want to be with me anymore, you need to look me in the eye and say it to my face. I don't know if it's because you think I'll resent you for the actions of your grandpa, which I never would. I don't know if it's because you can't be with me because I'm tainted by him in some sort of way-"

"That's not it Rydell," he pulls his face back, but grips onto my waist to keep contact. "I love you so fucking much to the point where I don't want to live if I don't have you. But I'd rather die than be a reminder of all the bad shit that's hurt you in the past."

"How could you think that I would ever see your grandpa in you? Scott, when I look at you, I see the man I'm in love with," I stroke his cheek with my thumb when he looks at his feet, tears falling down his eyes. "I see my happiness. I see my future. I see everything I've ever wanted. Nothing changes that."

He lifts his head and looks at me like he's trying to grasp onto the entirety of my words. "You make me forget about all the loneliness I've ever felt. Rydell, I don't want to lose you, but I don't want to hurt you," his grip on me tightens.

"You'd hurt me if you left me again," I play out my next words carefully to convince him to stay.

"I told myself that if love ever found me, I would take it with apprehension and I wouldn't let myself fall out of balance because of it. That I wouldn't lose sight of my priorities and that I'd put myself and my goals first. And I know that sounds selfish, but I couldn't risk letting everything I've worked so hard for fall apart. I almost did that with

Trey. I thought that maybe he was worth more than I deserved so I applied to schools near him even though they didn't match what I really wanted. And I guess I dodged a bullet with that one because we both know how that turned out."

"I'm not-"

"Let me finish," I tell him. "I was so mad at myself for even thinking about it and made an internal promise to never do that again. But Scott, I've been off balance since the moment you came up to me in Spanish class. And I thought that would be a bad thing, but I like being off balance with you," I wrap my arms around his neck. "I don't want either of us giving up things to stay together. I want to find a new balance. And I want to find it with you. Because I really don't know how to go on after you. If you really want to break up with me, then that's your decision. But don't do it because you think it's for my benefit, because it's not."

"Rydell, if I've ever done anything right in my life, it was giving you my heart," he connects our brows. "You're permanently etched there. And I'm sorry for being an idiot, the last thing I want is for us to break up."

I let out a breath that makes me feel about 10 pounds lighter, "Good. If you pull any shit like that again, I swear I'll sick Andy on you."

The sound of his laugh is like the sweetest sound to my ears. He gets serious again, "How do I make it up to you Books?"

"You don't need to make it up to me. You're allowed to make mistakes. I really do understand where you're coming from. If roles were reversed, I would've tried to do the same thing," I admit.

"Can I kiss you now?" he says as we intake

the same air.

"Please do," I respond, not waiting long for him to surge his mouth on mine. And just like that, my world is put together. With one kiss, everything falls back into place.

"I booked a hotel room just in case your family wouldn't let me it, do you want to go away with me for the night?" he asks against my lips.

~

Walking into the hotel room, we gravitate right to each other. Grabbing at each other's clothes, we start to strip until we're left in nothing but our underwear. I think we're so desperate to show each other how in love we are and to let out all are pain without wasting any time.

Scott guides me to the bed, not taking his mouth off me the entire time. He's placing wet kisses on my collarbone as the back on my knees hit the bed and I scoot myself back so that I lay in the center.

Scott follows me with every step, moving to hover over me. He gets slower and slower with every kiss he's trailing down my neck, like he wants to take his time exploring it. He's the slowest when he finds my pulse, the spot on my neck where he can my feel my heart beating.

You'd expect it to be skyrocketed at this point, but I'm always so calm when I'm around him.

I breath heavy when I feel his hand slide under my panties, pressing down lightly on my clit. "Do you want me to stop?" he asks between kisses.

"Absolutely not," I tug his hips down to my pelvis, feeling his hard on against my core.

We let out twin sighs like we always do at the feeling of intense contact. He continues marking my neck while his hand starts to increase the speed on the circles he's rubbing.

I stick my hand in his underwear and take him in my grip, match his speed. "You drive me so fucking crazy Rydell," he groans in my ear, biting my earlobe as he does so. "I love you so much," he whispers.

"I love you too," hooking my legs around his thighs, I pull him closer than humanly possible. "Did you bring a condom?"

He contemplates getting up before quickly striding across the room and pulling a condom out of the pocket of his pants. Taking his boxer's off before getting back on the bed, I reach around and unclip my bra.

His eyes darken at my actions as he hurries back to crawl on top on me, pressing his now wrapped up dick right on my still covered pleasure point.

"This ok?" he asks as he pulls my panties down slowly as if I'd ever stop him.

"Yes," I give him the reassurance he needs before he lets them fall to the floor. Without any more warning, he pushes himself fully into me, letting his head fall to my shoulder as he starts a painfully slow rhythm.

I lift my hips to meet his pace, silently telling him to speed up. "You fit me so perfectly Rydell," he places another open-mouthed kiss to my neck, to my collarbone, to center of my chest. "So fucking perfectly," he mumbles. While his pace is slow, his thrusts are deep and my body tingles in delight at the feeling.

"I want to feel every inch of you," he rolls his hips, grinding down on me in a way that almost sets me over the edge. He keeps this rhythm for what feels like forever before he switches directions, "What do you want gorgeous," he lifts his head to make eye contact.

"I want you to go faster," I say with a heavy voice.

Without further question, he starts increasing his speed until the whole bed is shaking in our pleasure. He continues to go faster until I feel my eyes start to squeeze shut, "You feel so good Scott," I moan wrapping my legs around his waist to get him to go deeper.

He takes the hint and slows down a bit to bury himself as far as possible. I feel myself lose control as my walls start to clench around his pulsating dick. "Let go baby, I'm right there with you."

At his words I release, him following right after me. He stays still inside of me, pressing soft kisses all over my face. When he rolls off me and discards the condom, I try to catch my breath, watching as he grabs his shirt from off the ground.

Before I can question what he's doing, he sets it down next to me, "For when you want to pee," I smile up at him, loving him for knowing me so well.

CHAPTER 76: SCOTT

She picks up my shirt and makes her way to the bathroom like I knew she would, grabbing her underwear from the floor on her way there.

I slide my boxer's on as I get up to throw the condom away. Settling onto the bed as I wait for her with my back against the headboard.

God, I am the world's biggest idiot. I can't believe I almost let her go like that. I just thank my lucky stars that she took me back. I left her when she needed me, I shouldn't have been given a second chance.

"Don't think so hard, you'll hurt yourself," my head shoots up as I look at Rydell sitting on the middle of the bed. "What's on your mind?"

I look at her, taking in her perfect face, "Do I have something on my face?" she questions as she starts wiping at her cheek.

"No. I'm just thinking about how lucky I am. I royally fucked up yesterday Rydell."

She crawls over towards me and sits on my lap, wrapping her arms around my neck. "You were put in a difficult situation," she tries.

"It doesn't matter," I set my head on her shoulder. "I should've known how to handle it for you. Instead, I made it worse."

"Maybe, but you fixed it. Do you think I'm mad at you or something? Because I'm not," she says softly, brushing my hair with her fingers.

"No. I don't think you're mad at me. I'm just mad at myself," I wrap my arms around her waist, pulling her closer to me.

"Well, don't be. Relationships aren't meant to be perfect Scott. There's going to be difficult moments, but I know that we'll always be able to get through them and that's all that really matters," she pulls back and grips my chin. "As long as you're willing to stick by me when things get rough, then there's nothing to worry about," she places a firm kiss to my lips.

"Trust me, I'm never leaving your side. I'll be here for as long as you'll have me."

"You better be, because I'm not planning on letting you ever get away from me," she scoots off my lap and lays flat on her back.

I shift down and lay my head on her chest as my body weight presses down on her, legs tangled. One of her hands is in my hair, running her fingers through it in a soothing way.

"And here we thought the hardest part of the weekend was getting your parents to like me," Rydell says lightly.

"Well, my dad likes you. He was the one who helped me get here. He sobered me up, got a private jet to take me here, and told me to go get the girl."

"I won Connor over the moment we raced down the mountain and won. Does your mom still hate me?" she questions. I don't miss the disappointment lace her voice as she asks it.

"I'm convinced that my mom is a robot whose sole purpose in life is to work until death. Even my dad was pissed at her. I don't think I've seen them get so mad at each other."

"Because of me?" she asks with concern.

I prop up on my elbow and look down at her, "No. Of course not. Because of work," I sigh. "Do you want to have this conversation now. I know we have to have it at some point but if it's too soon we can change subjects," I assure her.

She sits up in a criss cross position, facing me as I lean against the headboard. "No, we should talk about it. What happened when the police got there?"

"When the police took him, we were in the bathroom, but my dad told them the extent of it. He's out but will be put up for trail. You'll have to testify, your dad will probably have to testify to confirm that he was at the house that day, I'll testify to tell them the reaction you had to seeing him. My grandpa has powerful connections, so it might take a while, but I swear I'll do everything in my power to get the fucker locked up. My dad already said that he'll provide the best lawyer he can find and apparently there have been rumors in the company that, before he retired, my grandpa was inappropriate to some of the female employees, so they are going to see if there's anything there."

She nods slowly, "What will happen with the company? Isn't this a scandal that could hurt it? I don't want your family to suffer because of me," she's so fucking selflessness.

"Don't worry about the company. I'd rather see it burn to the ground then let my grandpa off the hook," I sigh. "That's why my parents were arguing.

My mom wanted to discuss how they were going to cover this up and my dad lost it. He wants people to know what a shitty person my grandpa is and doesn't care if it puts a strain on the company, as long as you get justice."

"How big of a strain would it put on the company?"

"Honestly, it would probably blow over pretty quickly. It might be a hot topic for a month, but powerful people only care about money in the end."

She chips at her nail polish as she looks down, "Do you think they'll believe me?" her voice is just above a whisper.

"I have no idea," I don't want to sugarcoat it, or give her false hope. "But I do know that a lot of people are going to do everything in their power to get him put away for good. Myself included."

"And you'll be with me for all of it?" I hate that she even has to question it.

"Every step of the way Books," I grab her waist and move us into a laying position with her head resting on my chest.

~

I'm woken up in the morning to a cold hand on my cheek, warm lips on mine, and a lavender scent that I love so much.

"Go back to sleep Books," I mumble as a grab her waist and flip us over so that I'm lying on top of her with my cheek to her chest.

"We have to go back home, it's Christmas Eve," she says home. Not my house, home, and it brings a smile to my face. I still need to see the stocking they hung up for me.

But I'm selfish and I want to relish in the

feeling of her in bed with me for a little longer, so I make no point to move, "10 more minutes won't hurt anyone," I turn my head and place a kiss right to the center of her chest.

She's squirming under me and if I didn't have morning wood before, I definitely do now. "If you keep wiggling around like that, I'll never let you leave this bed," I mumble against her skin.

"I have to help Andy prepare for her big confession tonight," I remember Rydell telling me about the plan she came up with to help Andy and David finally get together, it involves mistletoe. "Plus, baby Olivia will be there, and you haven't properly met her yet," she groans as she puts her hands on my sides and tries lifting me off her, failing miserably.

I lift my head to look at the clock, and sure enough, it's already close to 11:30. I don't think either of us slept when we were apart, so it makes sense.

I prop up on my elbow and look down at the pretty girl under me, taking in her messy hair and dimpled smile. I lean down to kiss said dimple, ignoring the scrunch of her face when she complains about morning breath.

"Alright stalker, enough staring," she rolls out from under me and I grab the back of her shirt to hold her steady right before she falls off the bed. "I was testing your reflexes," she plays it off as she gets off the bed and starts rummaging around the room.

CHAPTER 77: RYDELL

Watching Scott hold Olivia is giving me major baby fever that I absolutely do not need. I mean seriously, how am I not supposed to melt at the sight?

She looks so much smaller in his arms since he's practically a giant. He was so nervous to hold her because he was scared he'd hurt her, and now he's slightly rocking her like she's the most fragile thing he's ever held.

His facial expression is soft, and he has a small smile on his face and I want to steal him away and smother him in kisses because of how good he looks right now.

"Don't get any ideas," my dad sits down next to me. "I like Scott, but you two do not need a baby right now."

"No, we do not," I agree. "I think he's my form of happiness," I take my eyes off Scott and look at my dad. "When you were talking about me shaping my happiness, it feels a little bit stupid to put it into a person, but he makes me really happy dad," I look back towards my not-so-little stalker to see him looking at me with a smile. I mirror his face.

"I don't think it's stupid to find happiness in

people. I did that with your mom. If I didn't have her, I would be a very miserable man."

I keep the smile on my face thinking about how lucky I am to have such a good example of a healthy relationship. My dad gets up suddenly and starts to head to the kitchen where my mom is at the same time, Scott starts walking over to me.

Olivia is now in Savannah's arms, probably about to get fed. "I want one," Scott sits down next to me, putting his arm around my shoulder, and tucking me into his side.

We sit back on the couch comfortably, "That'll take a couple years buddy," I pat his chest.

He places a kiss to my temple, "I can wait," he replies. "Our babies are going to be so fucking cute. I hope they get that dimpled smile of yours. And your eyes. And your intelligence, your kindness, your patience. Actually, I hope everything about them embodies you."

"Not everything. I want them to have your hair," I lean up and run my fingers through his dark, thick hair. "And your strength, physically and mentally," I clarify. "Your determination and charisma. I want them to be a good mix of both of us," I saw with certainty.

"So, you're saying you want to have a family with me," he gives me a lopsided grin.

"Eventually," I lean back down to rest my head on his chest. "I think we'd make pretty good parents."

He opens his mouth to speak, but before he can everyone looks towards a running Andy, "Andy will you give me a second to respond? God, this is why we never get anywhere, you always run away when things don't go exactly how you play them out to be in your head," David chases after her.

Oh shit. "Can we not do this here?" Andy whisper yells at him.

"No. No, I think we should do this right here," David responds immediately. Andy gives him a warning look. Damn, I wish I had popcorn. "Everyone, I'd like to make an announcement. Andromeda kissed me. Right on the lips. She kissed me and without a word, she ran away."

Andy's face is bright red and I move to get up to consult her, but Scott moves his arm to rest around my hip and pins me into place. He's probably right, they need to sort this out on their own.

David continues, "Instead of letting me even try to respond, she decided to blow everything out of proportion when I slightly pulled back because I was confused," I would also run away if the guy I was scared to kiss pulled back.

"So," David spreads his arms out like he's talking to a crowd, "let me tell everyone exactly what I would've told Andy is she let me." He takes a deep breath and sets his arms back down to his side. "Andy, you're my best friend," uh oh. "You're my best friend, and I never wanted to ruin what we had because I don't want a life if you're not in it. That's why I haven't told you that I'm in love with you even though every single time I'm near you I want to blurt it out over and over again until I know you believe me. I've wanted to tell you at every wrestling practice, every time we go to the boardwalk together, whenever we're surfing. I wanted to tell you when you won state for the first time and when you lost that match at nationals. Every time you take a fucking breath, I want to tell you that I love you," he walks to stand in front of her.

"I hate that you would think for one second that I don't," he speaks softly and frames her face in his hands. Andy's face is still flushed, and her eyes are watery. "Andromeda Violet Rivens, I am in love with you, as much more than a friend."

"I probably should've have ran away," David laughs as soon as she says it.

"Now, I'm going to kiss you in front of our families, so no tongue," David jokes. And sure enough, he plants an innocent kiss to her lips, and everyone breaks out in cheers and mutters of 'finally' and 'it's about time'.

I sit up and face Scott, "My plan worked!"

"Good job Books," he kisses my cheek.

Andy and David walk somewhere more private to talk about what just happened and light chatter goes on around us. "We thought our oblivion was bad, there's was so much worse," I state. "That's like 12 years of walking around their feelings."

"Ryles and Scott, come help decorate cookies," my mom yells from the kitchen.

"Duty calls," I stand up reaching my hands down for Scott's to haul him up.

Except he doesn't make it easy for me. No matter how hard I tug on his hands, he doesn't budge. "Come on Ry, use those muscles," he teases me.

"This wouldn't be so hard if you weren't like a freaking tree," I grunt, grasping his wrists in hopes that it will give me some leverage. After a couple more seconds of my struggle, he gives in and essentially stands up on his own.

"Good effort Books," he leans down and kisses the pout on my lips before grabbing my hips from behind to guide me to the kitchen. He leans down to bite my earlobe on our way there and I try to suppress the stupid blush creeping up my neck.

"I love it when you blush pretty girl," he drops a kiss to the top of my head.

~

Christmas Eve comes to an end and my family and I spread out as we watch The Grinch who Stole Christmas. Scott's sitting on my toes to warm them up because they are freezing cold. One of his hands is running up and down the length of my calf and it is nearly putting me to sleep.

My mind is in a whirl of the events that happened today. I think the best part was watching Scott's face light up when he saw his stocking. He was so excited that he prompted me to take a picture of us in front of them and immediately posted it to his Instagram page.

Decorating cookies, he was upset that mine looked so much better than his and whined about it like the child he is. So inside of decorating, he helped my mom make peppermint hot chocolate. The sight of them laughing and interacting made my heart so full, I thought it would burst.

He's slowly becoming one of Olivia's favorites because she never seems to cry in his arms and smiled up at him on multiple occasions. I claim it to be gas, but Scott's convinced it's because she likes him.

We had a pullup contest on the bar on Andy's door and he won by a landslide. Liam and Chris claimed he was on steroids, they're just sore losers. My man is fit as fuck. Not going to lie, watching his muscles tense with every pull up got me all hot and bothered and I did not hear the end of it from everyone.

"What's got you thinking so hard gorgeous," I'm prompted out of my thoughts by the sound of Scott's voice and realize that the end credits are rolling.

Everyone is shuffling around the living room probably getting ready for bed. I remove my feet from under his butt and crawl over until I'm cuddled right into him. "Just about how much I enjoyed today. Especially with you here," I yawn.

He puts his arms under the backs of my knees and lifts me to his lap, the blanket that was wrapped around me falling slightly off my shoulders. My arms wrap around his neck like it's a reflex. "I'm glad I got to be a part of it. I almost messed that one up," I hate that he is still hung up on that.

"You wouldn't have lasted long with out me. Dad was giving me a pep talk to get you back right before you walked into the room. I would've hunted you down and dragged you here if I had to."

That puts a smile on his face, and I'm glad for it. "Tired?" he questions.

I nod slightly and he lifts us off the couch, setting me to my feet so that we can say goodnight to everyone.

Making our way to the room, we get straight under the covers. We had already gotten ready for bed before the movie started in case I fell asleep during it.

On instinct, our legs tangle, my head falls to his chest, and his arm wraps securely around me in a comfortable position.

"Thanks for coming back to me," I whisper when we're fully settled.

"I'll always come back to you Books," he strokes my hair. "And I promise, I'll never leave again."

"I believe you," I sit up to take a look at his handsome face. The lights are off so I can only faintly see it. "I really love you. And I'm excited for our future."

"I'm in your forever future?" he asks for confirmation.

I lean down and place a sweet kiss to his lips, pulling back slightly, "You're permanently etched there."

EPILOUGE 1: *SCOTT*

I place my hand over her knee that is bouncing up and down repeatedly. Her hand is so tightly wrapped around her wrist that her knuckles are turning white. I don't think I've ever seen her this nervous, and I don't blame her.

After a long five months in and out of the court, we will finally get an answer on if the fucker I used to call my grandpa gets locked up.

Rydell has been so strong throughout the entire thing. I think going back to see a therapist has really helped her, they directed her to an outreach program that connected her with other survivors and having that support system is exactly what she needed.

Rydell leans over and puts her face in her hands to try to slow her breathing. I raise my hand and rub up and down her back in silent comfort.

"Alright, the jury has come to a decision," the sound of the judges voice has Rydell straightening up in her seat. "Henry Bridges is found guilty on the accounts of rape on former employees of Bridges and Co, Emily White and Christen Harper. Henry Bridges is also found guilty for the sexual assault of a minor, Rydell Rivens at age 8. The guilty will be sentenced 20 years in federal prison," with a clank of his gavel, the wait has finally ended.

Rydell has tears in her eyes and I don't waste any time in wrapping her up in a hug. I feel her tears leak through the sleeve of my shirt and brush my hand through her hair to soothe her.

Pulling back, I wipe her tears away and give her a kiss on the cheek, "I'm glad this is finally over," she says as she composes herself.

"Me too," I trail after her as she goes to consult the other victims.

My dad comes up to us, giving Rydell a hug. "How are you feeling sweetheart?" he asks when pulling back.

"Like a huge weight has been lifting off my shoulders," she claims. "Connor, I don't know how I'm supposed to thank you. Without your help I don't know-"

"Rydell you don't need to worry about that. I'm glad I got to help. That fucker deserves what he got."

"Well, we're having dinner at our house later this evening. Nothing special, probably just some pizza and we'd love it if you could come," I smile when she says 'our house'.

Rydell and I just recently graduated this month, and before we did, I bought us a house. Rydell and I had taken a look at a couple during spring break and there was one that we both instantly were drawn to.

It's a simple one story with a nice backyard where we can have family/friend get togethers, a porch for Rydell to read on, and a good kitchen for making pancakes. I bought it as soon as we got back to Massachusetts without telling Rydell because I knew she'd make a fuss about us splitting the cost. Which is completely unnecessary since I got a massive signing bonus from the Sharks.

Rydell was mad about it for a week, but I promised that I'd let her buy the furniture and other accommodations to please her. I mean, she's making 6 figures as a coder for Microsoft, so she can afford it.

A lot happens in 5 months. Rydell and Sam's video game was a huge success as soon as it hit the shelves 2 months ago and Microsoft didn't have to think twice about hiring her.

"I have to catch a flight to New York, but next time I would love to come for dinner," my dad's voice snaps me out of my thoughts.

"Definitely let us know next time you're in town, we'll set something up," Rydell goes to hug my dad goodbye, then turns to me, "I'm gonna go talk to my parents."

I kiss her cheek and turn to my dad. I give him a smile, "Thank you dad," we embrace in a hug. Last year, if you told me I'd be hugging my dad, I would've laughed in your face. I don't think I've ever hugged my dad before the night I almost lost Rydell, but now it's normal and it felt weird at first, but now it's like I finally have a real parent.

"Send me a schedule of your games when you get it, preseason included. I want to buy season passes," I nod at his words. "Look Scott, I know I've been a shitty parent. I can't believe something like this situation had to make me realize it," he sighs. "I should've spent more time with you growing up, and I should've made time for your games, and if I could go back in time and have a redo, I would. But

I'm going to be here from now on. You need me, just say the word and I'm there, ok?"

"I know you will be dad. You've really been a big part in this trial, and I don't know what we would've done without your help. I'm not going to sit here and praise your parenting styles, because, quite frankly, they sucked. There were a lot of parts of my childhood that I wish you were around for and it took a long time for me to feel anything other than lonely. I think as soon as I met Rydell she fixed that broken part of me. But I want to try at a relationship with you, I want us to be a family. Who knows, maybe mom with eventually come around."

"Don't hold your breath on that one son," he claps my shoulder. "But you can be sure that I'll put in the effort. I love you Scott," I'm pretty sure that's the first time he's ever told me he loves me. My eyes feel a little watery.

"I love you too dad," I say in just above a whisper.

"Alright kid, I'll see you soon," with that he walks away.

As soon as I walk up to Rydell, she takes in my face, which probably looks on the verge of tears, "You alright?" she grabs me hand and gives in a squeeze.

"I'm perfect," I reassure her.

~

Walking into our new house, I hang my keys up, while Rydell speed walks to the couch. I know exactly where she's going.

Along with buying the house, I bought an orange tabby kitten that we named Fred. I figured if I got the cat, not too long after we'd get a dog that we can name Sirius.

That one might take a couple more months, but Rydell is obsessed with that kitten, sometimes I think she loves him more than she loves me.

Sure enough, Rydell is sat on the couch with Freddie curled up in her lap. When I sit down next to her, Fred walks onto my lap, stretches out, and lays down. "No fair," she pouts. "Why does he like you so much?"

I chuckle and raise my hand to pet the top of his head. I've never really been the biggest cat person, but Freddie is cute as fuck. He's still only about 5 months old. I mean, my hand is bigger than him. Ignoring her complaints, I say something that I know will put a dimpled smile on that pretty face of hers. "I love our little family," there it is. I lean down to kiss her dimple. When I pull back, she sets her head on my shoulder and starts petting Fred.

"Me too," she agrees. She takes a deep breath, "I'm glad that we don't have to deal with that trial anymore. It took a lot out of me."

"I know it did pretty girl. But I'm so proud of how strong you were throughout the whole thing. Seriously Rydell, you handled all of it so well."

"It helped having you to help me," she claims as she wraps her arms around my torso, further snuggling herself into me.

I wrap my arm around her shoulders to tuck her closer, dropping a kiss to the top of her head while I think about how lucky I am.

EPILOUGE 2: RYDELL

The first game of Scott's second season with the Sharks was a success. I'm glad it was a home game because Scott wanted to celebrate their win, just the two of us, and that's how I find myself with nothing but sheets to cover me.

Laying in our bedroom, in our house that I love so much I look over at Scott, smiling when he hands me his shirt before I retreat to the bathroom.

Coming back in record speed, Scott doesn't waste anytime in pulling me back on the bed and stuffing his head in the crook of my neck, inhaling deeply. I raise my hand up to run my fingers through his hair and hear him sigh with content.

His hand goes under his shirt and runs up and down my bare side. Pausing his movements, he sits up and lifts the hem of his shirt to reveal the tattoo on the right side of my stomach.

Sophomore year of college I had my siblings and parents draw a flower and had them all tattooed in a line that follows the curve of my right side. "I want one," he says as he traces the flowers, staring at it intensely.

"A flower tattoo?" I question.

"No, I want you to get a tattoo of a flower I

draw," he leans down and trails soft kisses across the length of the tattoo.

I let out a snort, "You'll have to marry me first," I claim. When I first got the tattoo, I had the idea that when I had a husband and kids of my own, their flowers would be tattooed on my left side.

"Ok, marry me," he says in the most serious tone he can muster.

"You don't mean that," I say.

Without another word, Scott gets off the bed and crosses the room to rummage through his sock drawer.

He walks back with a small box that most definitely carries a ring in it, standing in front of me as I move to sit on the edge of the bed. "I've had this since my game in Washington senior year of college. We had just finished talking on the phone and I told you that as soon as you gave me the ok, I'd propose. I mean, we had only been dating for like a month or two, but I knew you were the only person I'd ever want to spend my life with. After that call, I was walking past an antique store and I swear it was like the universe telling me that we were meant to be together, because in the display window, there was a ring that made me think of you instantly," he opens the box and my eyes widen at quite possibly the prettiest ring I've ever seen.

He kneels on one knee, rubbing his free hand up and down my calf that is dangling off the bed. "Rydell, my whole life I thought I was destined to be alone. My parents didn't want me. My sister was there but had more important things to prioritize. I had so many people who wanted to call themselves my friend, and was always surround by a crowd, but no matter how many people were around, I always felt lonely. Until you. You didn't treat me like I was an object to promote your social status or like I was just someone you wanted to brag about sleeping with. You continue to fix parts of me that I thought would always be broken and I love you so so much. I love how smart you are. I love your ability to make people feel like they belong. I love how sweet you are. I love your dimpled smile, your pretty hazel eyes, your squeezable ass," that makes me laugh.

My eyes are starting to fill with tears as he continues, "I want to have kids with you. I want to go surfing with you and to the boardwalk when you feel like you need a breather. I want to see you in the crowd at my games and I want to stay up late watching you be a superstar coder. I want to grow old with you and give you everything you've ever wanted and all the love you deserve," I'm full-on sobbing now.

"Rydell Rivens I want you to be my wife. Will you marry me?" his eyes feel with something like nervousness.

That look doesn't last long because I surge forward grabs his cheeks in my hands and smash my mouth to his. "Yes," I mumble against his lips. "Yes, I'll marry you," wrapping my arms around his neck in the tightest hug I can muster. He stands up spinning me around.

He sets me on my feet and peppers kisses all over my face, lingering on my lips. He slips the ring onto my finger and I wipe off the tears that stain his cheeks as he does the same for me as we stand there smiling at each other. "I love you so much," he leans down for a slow kiss.

We slightly jump apart at the sound of

scratching at the door. I look up at Scott with pleading eyes, "Fine. Fucking cock blocking dog," he mumbles as he opens the door.

As soon as he does our black lab, Sirius, jumps on to the bed and runs around in circles waiting for attention. I don't know why he complains so much, he's the one who wanted the dog in the first place.

"Look at our sweet boy," I move over to the bed, Siruis immediately places his head in my lap as I sit down. "He wants to be the ring bearer!" I exclaim as Sirius nudges at my ring finger.

Not too long after, Freddie moseys his way into the room, walking in between Scott's legs. "Here's my favorite child," he picks up Freddie and moves to sit down next to me.

I cover Sirius's ear, "Scott, that is so mean. He doesn't mean that Sirius. We love you both equally," I pat his head.

Scott rolls his eyes, "Sirius always interrupts at the worse times," he groans.

"Watch out Scotty, you're starting to sound like you're jealous of a dog," I tease him.

"Ok that's enough pets, time for Sirius to go outside for a bit," he shoos the animals out, opening the backyard door for Sirius to play outside.

Coming back into our room, he shuts the door and crawls onto the bed, pushing my back to the mattress so that he hovers over me. One of his hands moves to under my shirt, rubbing circles on my bare skin, "I can't wait to spend the rest of my life with you," he leans down and giving me, the sweetest kiss and I think about how lucky I am.

EPIOLOUGE 3: SCOTT

I am pleasantly woken up by the feeling of kisses on my neck and jaw. Sensing my wakefulness, Rydell bites my earlobe. "Happing wedding day," she pulls back to look at me, hovering over me with hands on either side of my head.

I wrap my arms around her waist and flip us over so that I'm the one above her. "Happy wedding day," I tell her as I press my lips to hers. I look over at the clock to see that it's 5:30 in the morning. One of Rydell's only requests for the wedding was that the morning of, we'd go for a family sunrise surf. Of course, I agreed because I'd give that girl anything she wants.

Neither of us wanted anything big, and besides our family and few friends, there weren't many people we wanted to invite. That's why we decided to go for a backyard wedding at her parents' house. They have a large backyard and with a little bit of work, the whole wedding planning process really has not been stressful at all.

I'm not going to lie, Rydell and I do pretty well for ourselves. We are both earning a heafty living and could easily afford whatever wedding we want. But neither of us are very flashy so a backyard wedding seemed like the way to go.

We hired wedding planner people to organize the setup and take down of the ceremony and reception, an In-N-Out truck to cater, an open bar service, DJ, and photographer and called it good.

"How are you feeling, soon to be Mrs. Bridges?" I ask her as we both get up and start putting our swimsuits on.

"Excited. Happy. Ready to take the next step with you," she stands in front of my, turning around to prompt me to tie her top.

I let my hand slowly graze the smooth skin on her back, taking my time to help her with her top. When it's securely tied, I drop a kiss to her shoulder and wrap my arms around her waist from behind, slightly swaying us back and forth.

"I love you so much," I whisper in her ear.

She turns around in my arms, interlinking her hands behind my neck, "I love you too. So much." She has the biggest grin on her face and starts slightly jumping up and down. "We're getting married today!" she exclaims like it's the best news in the world.

I match her excitement, grab under her thighs mid jump to wrap her legs around my torso and spin her widely around our hotel room.

The space is filled with the sounds of her laughter. I think I'd give anything to make this moment last forever.

Settling down, I toss her onto the bed, quick to follow and hover over her. I leave kisses all over her face, neck and collarbone while she hums in contentment. I pull back to look at my pretty soon-to-be wife, going back down to kiss her dimple when I see it.

~

Meeting up with her family, we didn't waste any time to run into the water. It's springtime, so the water is finally starting to warm up again.

Now that I've been with Rydell for about 2 and half years, my surfing skills have finally developed to the point where I'm not of the verge of drowning.

I look over at Rydell who's laughing with her sister as I paddle over to them.

"What are you two giggling about?"

"Just girl stuff," Rydell smiles at me.

"As much as I hate to break up sister time, can I steal the almost Mrs. Bridges away?" I look towards both of them. When Rydell scoots towards me I add, "Andy can you watch her board?"

"Watch my board?" Rydell says out of confusion.

"Yeah, come catch a wave with me," I have been practicing my surf game a lot lately so that I can have enough balance to share a wave with Rydell.

"Are you about to pull a Lilo and Stich?" she questions. When I watched that movie with her about a year ago, she gushed about how cute David and Nani, especially when they surf together.

"Hell yeah I am," she hands her board off to Andy and swims over to my board, easily lifting herself to sit criss cross on the tip of my board.

I position myself in the paddling position, placing a kiss to the center of her back and she sits in front of me.

After a couple minutes of waiting, a set came in and we took off. Rydell was laughing and shoot her arm out to the side to let her fingers run through the water.

Just when I got the confidence to try to squat down and kiss her, I ate it. Dammit.

Rydell managed to stay planted on the board and when I came up for air, she could barely paddle over to me with the amount of laughing she was doing.

"Don't laugh," I pout as I set my forearms on the board, keeping most of my body in the water.

"You totally ate it," she keeps laughing.

"I was trying to be romantic," I whine. "I've been practicing for so long."

She leans down and places a salty kiss on my lips, "You're so cute," she says between kisses.

And right when she doesn't expect it, I put my hands under the board and flip it over so that she falls right in with me. Now it's my turn to laugh.

When she comes back up, her hair is attached to the side of her face and she launches herself at me to shove my head under water.

I wrap my arms around her waist as I come up for air and tread the water to keep us above the surface.

"That was so mean," she wraps her arms around my neck.

"Yeah. I'm the meanest," I admit as I give her a sweet kiss.

"Alright lovebirds break it up and save it for later, we have a wedding to get ready for," Rydell's mom says as her family paddles by.

~

Before Rydell even started walking down the aisle, my eyes started tearing up. But then she came out looking like the angel that she is, and I absolutely lost it.

She has her mom and dad on either side of her and is walking to Slipping Through my Fingers and I can't stop crying happy tears.

God this is the best day of my life. Her dad shakes my hand and her mom gives me a hug as they pass her over to me.

My hands are shaking as I take hers into them. Before I can set them down in front of us, she lifts her hands to frame my face and wipe my tears.

"Hey handsome," she whispers.

"Hey pretty girl," my voice is wobbly. "You look so fucking stunning Books," I say as I take in the sight of her. "I really want to kiss you right now," I admit.

That makes her laugh quietly, "Have some restraint Scotty," she smiles at me with that fucking dimpled smile.

I lean down and peck it quickly because I simply can't help myself.

Finally getting myself under control, the priest starts the ceremony.

But as soon as it's time to exchange vows, I'm back to square one, "Scott you're up first."

I take a deep breathe and grab the wedding vows I have written out of my pocket. "Rydell Catherine Rivens, I'm so in love with you. Falling in love with is hands down the best thing I've done in my entire life," I start to feel a lump in my throat as I try to continue.

I take a second before clearing my throat and continuing. "I grew up so lonely. I thought that was how it was supposed to be and I came to terms with it. I was miserable most of the time, but I never had to worry about getting hurt by people because I never got close enough to them. But then you came into my life and showed me how it felt to be loved and taught me how to express my own love, and now I feel like I am finally complete as a person. You're love fills me in so many ways and you healed a lot of part of me that I thought would be empty and broken forever. I can't wait to start a family with you," my tears start to fall again.

I put my notes down and look her straight in the eyes. "I can't wait to cheer you on in all your success and stay up late with you when you're too focused to sleep," she raises her hands to stroke my cheek. "I promise I'll always keep you safe and love you with everything I have. You and me against the world Books," I finish my vows and take the ring from Max, my best man, to slip it on her finger. There isn't a dry eye in the audience. But they just keep going as Rydell starts hers.

"Scott, I've never loved anyone the way I love you," she's been doing so well but the tears are going to start falling any second now.

"Nothing in my life has been easy. I've been hurt so many times that I came to a point where I thought maybe I was destined to always feel like I deserved all the bad things that happened to me. As soon as you came along, that feeling instantly went away. You make me a better version of myself. You give me happiness that I never thought I'd have, and you've filled a hole in my heart that I thought would be open forever. I love how protected you make me feel. I love that you validate our feelings equally and always compromise with me. I love laughing at you when you eat it on a surfboard, and I love when you flip my board for making fun of you. Prescott Connor Bridges, I'm so lucky that I have you and I've never been more excited about something than I am about being your wife." She finishes slips my ring on my finger as I wipe the tears she let fall. I set my forehead down on hers as soon as she's done.

Fuck I want to kiss her so badly.

The priest wraps it up and ends with, "Scott, you may now kiss your bride."

I don't wait any longer as I mumble, "Finally," and connect my lips to my wife's, dipping her in the process.

We pull apart to the cheering of our families and friends and I scoop her up in the warmest hug I can muster spinning her around a couple times before I grab her hand and walk her back down the aisle to Home by Edward Sharpe and The Magnetic Zeros.

Stealing her away somewhere private, we walk through the sliding doors of the backyard and standing in her parent's kitchen.

I look down at my beautiful bride, "Hey wifey," I have the biggest smile on my face.

"Hey handsome husband of mine," I chuckle lowly and press my mouth to hers for a slow, sweet kiss.

Moving away from the kiss I nip her earlobe and whisper, "I love you so much."

"I love you too," she wraps her arms around my waist. "So much."

I take in the warmth of her hug and think about how lucky I am.

EPILOUGE 4: RYDELL

Fuck. This wasn't supposed to happen yet. I mean, we've only been married for like a year, Scott is about halfway through his third pro hockey season and still has years to be in his prime playing years.

I was just asked to be on a coding team for a groundbreaking piece of technology for healthcare. It was way too soon for us to have a baby.

But here I am sitting on the toilet staring at three positive pregnancy tests on the verge of a mental breakdown.

Not too long-ago Scott and I both agreed that we should wait at least two years before we start trying. I know he won't be, but I can't help to be scared that this news will stress him out.

God, how am I supposed to even approach him with this?

I guess I was too engrossed in my thoughts to realize that Scott was back home from practice until I heard the bathroom door open.

"There you are. I called your name like three times," I scramble to hide the tests behind my back. "What's wrong gorgeous?" Dammit, I can't hide anything from him. "What's behind your back?"

"Nothing and nothing," I get up and tuck the tests into the waistband of my leggings.

"Books, I saw you hide something behind your back. Let me see," he lunges towards me and I strategically duck under his arm with my ninja skills.

Scott glares at me for a bit and then starts smirking, leaning his hip against the counter. "Were you about to release so tension," he wiggles his eyebrows at me suggestively. Oh my god, he thinks I was about to masturbate. That little perv. "No need for whatever's behind your back baby, I can help you."

He takes slow steps towards me, giving me major sex eyes. Oh no he doesn't, this is the reason we're in this situation right now. I stick my hand up to push his chest away as soon as his hands reach my waist.

Before I can get out of his reach, he brings my closer to him leaning down to kiss me. He moves up to bite my earlobe and then places a kiss to behind my ear before whispering, "Tell me what you want Ry and I'll make it happen."

Great, now I'm turned on. I'm blaming it on the baby hormones.

I go to respond, but as I do Scott reaches my waistband and snatches the pregnancy tests.

Shit.

I jump on him trying to grab them from his hands, but he's a giant and even with my legs wrapped around his middle and my arm in the air, he easily keeps it from my reach. Scott's laughing and trying to steady his arm to get a good look at what's in his hand.

"Scott, give me that back," I extend my arm

further.

The laughing dies down and I assume Scott has come to a realization as the bathroom gets deadly silently.

I slowly slide my body down and off his, planting my feet to the floor and taking a step back.

I don't get far as Scott uses his free hand to grab my hip and pin me in place. I look at the floor.

"Is this real?" he questions quietly.

"Surprise," I look up and peer at him through my eyelashes. "Look I know we said we wanted to wait and I don't know what I'm supposed to-"

I'm cut off by his lips attaching to mine, kissing me with so much passion that I feel lightheaded.

When he pulls back, he rests his forehead to mine, "We're going to have a baby?" he whispers, tears running down his cheeks and a soft smile on his face.

I nod my head against his, "If it's ok with you, then yeah."

"Are you kidding me? Of course, it's ok with me. I mean as long as it's what you want too. Rydell I don't think there's anything that makes me happier than the idea of having kids with you."

"I know it's early then expected but, I'm so excited for us to be parents." I'm not going to lie. I was freaking out when I first found out. Of course, I've always wanted kids but with the fear of Scott freaking out, I was scared. Seeing his face when he found out took away every single worry I had in my head.

Scott kneels down in front of me and lifts up the hem of my shirt. "What are you doing?" I laugh lightly.

"Shhh Books, I'm having a chat with my kid here," he smiles up at me as he places a kiss to my flat stomach.

I run my fingers through his hair as I look down at him with the biggest grin. "Hi baby," he brings both hands up and rubs my nonexistent baby bump. "I promise I'll be the best daddy ever. I'm going to spoil the shit out of you. But you need to be nice to mommy while you cook in there. Because I love your mama so much and I don't want anything hurting her, ok," he lightly pokes my stomach.

And the tears start to flow on my end. "I promise, there will not be one day where you feel unloved. Because your mommy and I are going to make sure you know how much we love you all the freaking time. I love you so much all ready and you're probably the size of a little rice grain. Good talk baby, now we need to get mommy to the hospital to have everything checked out," he presses consecutive kisses to my stomach mumbling 'I love you' between all of them.

~

I swear to god I'm going to kill him. Max, Oliver, and Asher came into town and they went for drinks after Scott's practice.

I was totally all for it and encouraged him to go out with his friends because I knew how much he missed them. But now it's 3:32 in the morning, he's not home, no one is answering their phones, and I'm freaking out because he said he'd be home by midnight.

Not to mention that like Ella is treating my uterus like her own little drum set, my back is killing me, and my feet are swollen and achy.

I faintly hear Sirius start to bark and not long after the sound of Scott's voice, "Shh, Sirius, you'll wake up mommy," he whispers yells. I hear his friends laughing at Scott calling me mommy and get up to grab pillows and blankets for them.

"Already awake," I say with irritation as I make my way out into the living room.

I shoot daggers at Scott and, turning to his friends with a smile. I did miss all of them. "Here you guys go. If you guys can civilly work it out against yourselves, one of you can sleep in the guest room."

Max grabs the sleeping supplies out of my hands, "You really shouldn't be carrying all of this," he complains with a slur. They are all very out of it. "Sorry that we woke you up."

"Don't worry about it. I'll grab some waters and Advil for the morning," making my way to the kitchen, I start to take down the cups as two hands snake around my waist.

I wiggle in Scott's grip, but he refuses to let me go, "I'm sorry gorgeous. My phone died and I lost track of time. And then Webbs started talking about the teacher he's crushing on and accidently sent a drunk text message and we were trying to fix that, which is difficult when there's alcohol in your system," he stuffs his face in my neck and kisses it lightly.

I rub my hand over my face in exhaustion, "I just wish you texted me or called me from one of their phones. Scott, I thought you were in a ditch somewhere and that you were going to leave me a widow with a baby on the way," I sniffle.

He takes in a sharp breath of air. When he turns me around in his arms, he has a guilty expression on his face. He reaches his hands up to wipe my tears. "Stupid hormones," I mumble.

He chuckles softly before getting serious. "I'm sorry Books, I should've called. I wasn't thinking because I'm an idiot," he rests his forehead on mine and brings his hands up to rub my baby bump. "I would never leave you or El." The nickname he already has for our daughter melts my heart and makes me forget why I was ever mad at him. "I love both of you so much."

He places a kiss to my forehead, "Go back to bed gorgeous. I'll grab their water and Advil and be in soon, ok?"

I give him a nod and make my way back to our bedroom, pausing to check on the boys in the living room. They are already passed out with Fred curled up on Max's stomach and Sirius sandwiched between Asher and Oliver. I smile and shake my head at the sight of them before returning to the comfort of my bed.

My eyes finally start to drift close as the security of Scott's safety starts to sink in. Not long after I feel the mattress dip and warm arms pulling me back to an even warmer chest.

Scott's hand runs up and down my stomach, staying in place when I turn to face him.

Ella delivers a swift kick to Scott's hand. "Hey! What do you think you're doing up this late ya little bugger?"

"She's been rowdy all night," I yawn.

"She must've missed me," he smiles as he rubs my belly like a genie bottle. "Just because you missed me, does not mean you can kick mommy. Now calm down and let mama sleep Bug."

"Does it hurt baby?" he reverts his attention

up to me.

"No as much as my back," I reply with a sleepy voice.

His hands don't hesitate to rub up and down my back in a soothing matter that makes me drift off to sleep thinking about how lucky I am.

EPILOUGE 5: *SCOTT*

"Scott it hurts so badly," my heart aches as I watch sweat collect on her forehead.

"What do you need pretty girl?" I question as I sit in the visitor's seat next to the hospital bed and brush Rydell's hair out of her face. The doctor said it could still take a couple hours before baby number two even starts to make his way out.

"Just try to distract me. How is Ella? Was she scared at all when you took her to the waiting room with mom?"

Ella, at just two years old has become the center of our lives. Well, her and now little Jude who is about to come out soon.

"You know Bug, she is as empathetic as they get. I think she's just worried about you. She kept asking if you were hurt. Then she said she'd attack the person who hurt you," my little spitfire girl.

That causes Rydell to let out a breathy laugh, "She said she'd beat them up?"

"Oh yeah. She asked for a Spiderman costume so that she could be 'mommy's hero'," Ella has a fascination for all things superhero's, especially Spidey. "Then your mom told her that they could go get a sundae from the McDonald's next door. On their way out I heard her exclaim that July 13th was National French Fry Day, so I'm sure she convinced your mom to buy her some."

That gets a proper laugh out of her and she looks a little less in pain which eases my worries a bit. "Like mother like daughter, huh?" I tease her.

"Yeah. She does love her national holidays, doesn't she?" she closes her eyes and takes a deep breath.

"She just likes them because if it's good food, she knows you'll buy her it if she asks," I chuckle.

"You're one to talk," she chastises me. "Last National Ice Cream Day you brought back like 10 flavors from the grocery store."

"She couldn't pick one because 'all flavors are her favorite'! How was I supposed to say no when she asked for all of them," I pout. I'd give the little girl an entire ice cream store if she asked for it. "You're lucky I didn't come back with every flavor in the whole damn store. And I didn't see you complaining when you were chowing down on it."

She lifts her arm and fails at trying to punch it, "Don't hurt yourself Books," I set her arm back to her side.

She groans, "I can't even lift my arm to punch you," there's a frown on her face.

I grab her arm and lift it again, "Make a fist," I tell her. She does as I say and I guide her knuckles to punch my bicep.

"Thanks," she gives me a tired, dimpled smile.

"No problem Ry. Feeling better?"

"Yes, can you get me more ice chips?"

I don't deny her request as I stand up and

go to fill up her cup.

Coming back into the room, I rush to her side as she starts to scream with the doctor setting up shop to deliver our baby.

Mother fucker. I leave for a minute and the little brat decides then is a good time to make his entrance into the world.

Not hesitating for a second, I rush to sit next to Rydell reciting words of encouragement as she pushes out our son.

"You're doing so good baby. They hardest parts over," I kiss her temple as the head and shoulders slip out.

"Just a couple more pushes Rydell," the doctor starts as she guides our baby out.

I let Rydell squeeze my hand as she presses her head to the pillow and pushes a couple more times like a champ.

"Congratulations Mrs. and Mr. Bridges. It's a boy," the doctor confirms.

I'm tearing up and Rydell's exhausted but a layer of relief floods through the room.

I guide Rydell's chin with my hand and plant a kiss to her lips as a silent thank you before I get up to check on our boy.

Cutting his umbilical cord and watching him get cleaned up, I his little form. Dang he's got a big little ding dong. That's my boy.

I watch the nurse hand him over to Rydell as I settle back down next to her. Rydell runs her index finger over the swell of his tiny cheek. "Little Jude," she whispers as she looks down at him with adoration. She is the best mom.

The door to the room opens and Rydell's parents step in with Ella in Connell's arms. As soon as he sets her down, she waddles her way over to me and I scoop her up in my arms. "Hey little bugger," I kiss her cheek. "Do you want to meet your baby brother?" I ask her as she stares down at her mom with wide eyes.

"Hat's too big," she looks at the oversized beanie type hat on his head.

"It's to help keep him nice and warm," I tell her gently and she stands up on my legs and leans over to get a closer look at Jude. I tug the back of her shirt to keep her from falling off the chair.

"Come here lovey," Rydell opens her free arm that isn't cradling Jude and I set Ella down on the bed. She curls up to her mom's side and looks down at her brother.

"He's so tiny," she squeals as if she isn't a baby herself. I smile down at my family and warmth fills my whole body.

"Yep and we have to be very very careful with baby brother so that we don't hurt him ok? Like how we have to be gentle with Freddie," Rydell reminds our excited girl.

Ella softly sets her hand on Jude's head and pets him like he's a cat. She's so slow and patient as she meets her brother and I'm proud of her for being a good listener.

"Alright, let's give daddy a chance to properly say hi," Rydell shifts Jude in her hands and sets him into mine.

I make sure to give his head enough support and look down and his tiny body. I try to keep my tears at bay, but my eyes quickly get watery.

I had a bad childhood. I never even thought about being a parent before Rydell because I was scared that my bad experience would reflect my parenting. When Ella came along, I was terrified the first couple months because I thought I'd fuck up somehow.

But my babies are my greatest gift. Other than Rydell of course.

And I sure as hell am nothing like my parents. My dad has turned around now that we're older, which I'm grateful for. My mom hasn't. But I'm nothing like them. I make sure my kids know how much I love them. I make sure that they never feel lonely and can always come to me when they need help.

"I'm gonna be the best dad buddy," I promise Jude.

"He is the best dad Jude!" Ella exclaims. "And mama is the best too," she adds as she wraps her little arms around Rydell's neck.

Rydell and I mirror each other's smile and I revel in the love of my perfect family.

~

"You guys better be the best listener for mama," I squat down and look at 4-year-old Ella. She's in a jersey with my number on it. It looks a little big on her, but she looks so freaking cute. "Be a big girl and help mommy out with Jude and Tommy ok?" I brush the hair out of her face.

"I will daddy! Don't get hurt," she pokes my chest with attitude to match her mom's.

"I won't Bug," I promise her.

Rydell's parents and my dad walk up with Tommy and Jude. "Good luck daddy!" Jude hugs my leg before I take him in my arms and smoother his face in kisses. Handing him over to Connell, I turn to Victoria and take my 4-month-old out of her arms.

"Hey little man," Tommy places a slobbery kiss to my cheek and tugs at my hair like it's a toy. Little stinker. My dad opens his arms, prompting me to hand him over.

When I do Victoria says, "We'll take them to the seats so you two can have a little moment to yourselves," as she grabs Ella's hand.

I turn to my beautiful wife and mother of my children and pull her close to me as I place my hands on her hips. "Good luck kiss?" I ask as I lean down, knowing she won't deny me.

Rydell wraps her arms around my neck and gives me a sweet kiss. "Go get 'em number 15," she pulls back placing her forehead to mine.

8 years later and the girl still drives me crazy. I swear, one kiss from her and I want to forget all our responsibilities and carry her away to some place private If there's one thing I've never doubted, it's my love for Rydell (and our children).

"No wandering to the parking lot without me. Wait on the bleachers please," I am very protective over my family.

"Yeah, yeah," she pulls back and slaps my ass. "Good luck handsome."

I make my way to the ice, looking over my shoulder to see her watching me, giving me a little wave before turning around and finding her seat.

I step on the ice and win the game, all the while thinking about how lucky I am.

Acknowledgements

To all of those who came from Wattpad, I would not be here without every one of you. I started writing *Permanently Etched* at a time in my life where I was struggling with a lot of things. With anxiety, with figuring myself out, with being happy. Being able to sit down and be creative let me take my mind off all the shit happening in my life. And then I had this story with these developed characters and I said 'fuck it' and published the first chapter. When people started reading it and commenting that they enjoyed reading my book, I swear I felt this happiness that made me feel so good about myself.

My whole life, I never really have had friends. Then I started writing, and then I started uploading chapters to Wattpad, and all of a sudden, I had this huge support system that seems to get me through so many things.

So thank you, from the bottom of my heart, for reading my story and (if you ever left a comment) for the nice words. It's helped me more than you know.

And thank you to my amazing little sister. My best friend forever. Without you, I would have never continued writing the book. I would have never uploaded a chapter on Wattpad. And I certainly never would have published it on Amazon. Your support and presence in my life is one thing I am most grateful for, and I love you so much.

To those of you who have faced any of the issues mentioned in this book (or anything that makes you upset at all), I feel for you, I support you, and you can always reach out to me if you need someone.

Printed in Great Britain
by Amazon

79379231R00315